# THE GODS OF EDEN

## WILLIAM BRAMLEY

AVON BOOKS ⬥ NEW YORK

*To all of those who have spent long and unthanked hours in pursuit of the truth, whoever they may be.*

*And my thanks, of course, to Elizabeth.*

AVON BOOKS
A division of
The Hearst Corporation
1350 Avenue of the Americas
New York, New York 10019

Copyright © 1989, 1990 by the Dahlin Family Press
Published by arrangement with the Dahlin Family Press
Library of Congress Catalog Card Number: 89-1148
ISBN: 0-380-71807-3

The Dahlin Family Press edition contains the following Library of Congress Cataloging in Publication Data:
Bramley, William
  The Gods of Eden.
    Includes index.
    1. World History  2. Unidentified Flying Objects.
3. Bramley, William.  I. Title.
D24.5.B73  1989  909  89-1148

First Avon Books Printing: March 1993

AVON TRADEMARK REG. U.S. PAT. OFF. AND IN OTHER COUNTRIES, MARCA REGISTRADA, HECHO EN CANADA

Printed in Canada

UNV  10  9  8  7  6  5  4  3

# WHO CONTROLS
# HUMAN DESTINY?

- **What is the Brotherhood of the Snake?**

- **Why was the Black Death, which devastated the population of Europe, accompanied by an unparalleled number of UFO sightings?**

- **How did the establishment of the Bank of England lead to revolution and genocide in France?**

- **Do the world's major religions teach the truth . . . or have they all been subtly corrupted?**

- **What is the role of secret societies in contemporary world events? And who controls these societies?**

**WILLIAM BRAMLEY originally set out to research the history of human warfare. What he uncovered was a secret more destructive and terrifying than anyone could possibly imagine . . .**

# CONTENTS

# 1

# The Search Begins

WHEN I FIRST began researching the origins of human warfare, certainly the furthest thing from my mind were Unidentified Flying Objects, better known as "UFOs." The many flying saucer magazines which once graced the newsstands were, in my opinion, not worthy of serious consideration.* I also did not feel that the UFO phenomenon was terribly important even if it was evidence of an extraterrestrial race. Solving the down-to-earth problems of war and human suffering seemed so much more important than arguing over whether or not "little green men from Mars" might occasionally be visiting Earth.

I began researching this book in 1979; however, my desire to see an end to war arose much earlier in life, at just about the age of eight. Back then, war movies were

---

* A recent exception is *UFO* magazine, which I recommend. It is presently published in Los Angeles, California by Vicki Cooper and Sherie Stark.

very popular in my circle of friends. Our favorite game was playing "army." I usually commanded one squad of kids and my friend David led the opposition. We filled our imaginary battles with the same glamor and altruism we saw on television. We had no greater hero than the late actor Vic Morrow who would gallantly lead his army squad to victory every week on the television series, *Combat!*.

One Saturday afternoon I was watching a Hollywood war movie on television. It was like any other war movie except that it contained a short piece of numbing realism. For the first time in my life, I found myself looking at documentary film footage of an actual Nazi concentration camp. Long after the images vanished off the television screen, I was haunted by the pictures of skeleton-like bodies being thrown into large pits. Like so many other people, I had trouble fathoming the souls of the Nazis who could shove human beings into brick ovens like loaves of bread and moments later pulled out the charred remains. Within a minute, those grainy black-and-white images presented a true picture of war. Behind the curt salutes and stirring oratory, war is little but a degraded psychosis. While war movies and games can sometimes be fun, the real thing is unconscionable.

For centuries, scientists and thinkers have attempted to solve the riddle of why people go to war. They have observed that nearly all of Earth's creatures fight among themselves at one time or another, usually over food, territory, or mating. Aggression seems to be a universal behavior related to survival. Other factors also contribute to the creation of wars. The analyst must take into consideration such variables as human psychology, sociology, political leadership, economic conditions, and the natural surroundings. Many thinkers, however, have erroneously equated all human motives with motives found in the animal kingdom. This is a mistake because intelligence breeds complexity. As creatures rise in intelligence, their motivations tend to become more elaborate. It is easy to understand the mental stimuli in two alley cats squabbling over a scrap of food, but it would be a mistake to attribute as simple a state of mind to a terrorist planting a bomb in an airport.

I began this study as the result of a single idea I had encountered. The concept is certainly not a new one, and at first it seems narrow in scope. The idea is nevertheless quite important because it addresses a motivation which can only be formulated by creatures of high intelligence:

*War can be its own valuable commodity.*

The simple existence of violent conflict between groups of people can, in itself, be valuable to someone regardless of the issues over which people are fighting. An obvious example is an armaments manufacturer selling military hardware to warring nations, or a lending institution making loans to governments during wartime. Both can achieve an economic benefit from the mere existence of war as long as the violence does not directly touch them.

The value of war as a commodity extends well beyond monetary gain:

*War can be an effective tool for maintaining social and political control over a large population.*

In the sixteenth century, Italy consisted of numerous independent principalities which were often at war with one another. When a prince conquered a neighboring city, he would sometimes breed internal conflicts among the vanquished citizens. This was an effective way to maintain political control over the people because the endless squabbling prevented the vanquished people from engaging in unified action against the conqueror. It did not greatly matter over what issues the people bickered so long as they valiantly struggled against one another and not against the conquering prince.

A state of war can also be used to encourage populations to think in ways that they would not otherwise do, and to accept the formation of institutions that they would normally reject. The longer a nation involves itself in wars, the more entrenched those institutions and ways of thinking will become.

Most comprehensive history books contain brief references to this type of manipulative third party activity. It is no secret, for example, that prior to the American Revolution, France had sent intelligence agents to America to stir up colonial discontent against the British Crown. It is also no secret that the German military had aided Lenin and the Bolsheviks in the Russian revolution of 1917. Throughout all of history, people and nations have benefited from, and have contributed to, the existence of other people's conflicts.

Intrigued by these concepts, I resolved to do a study to determine just how important the third party factor has been in human history. I wanted to discover what common threads, if any, may have existed between various third party influences in history. It was my hope that this study would offer added insights into how and by whom history has been made.

What resulted from this modest goal was one of the most extraordinary odysseys I have ever taken. The trail of investigation wove through a complex labyrinth of remarkable facts, startling theories and everything in between. As I dug ever deeper, a common thread did emerge. To my chagrin, it was a thread so bizarre that on at least two occasions I terminated my research in disgust. As I pondered my predicament, I realized something important:

Rational minds tend to seek rational causes to explain human problems.

As I probed deeper, however, I was compelled to face the possibility that some human problems may be rooted in some of the most utterly bizarre realities imaginable. Because such realities are rarely acknowledged, let alone understood, they are not dealt with. As a result, the problems those realities generate are rarely resolved, and so the world seems to stumble from one calamity to the next.

I will admit that when I began my research I had a bias about what I was expecting to find: a human profit motive as the common thread which links various third-party influences in mankind's violent history. What I found instead was the UFO.

Nothing could have been more unwelcome.

## 2

# Orientation

*Husband to wife: Look at this, honey. It says here that the Earth travels 595 million miles around the sun every year at a speed of 66,000 miles per hour. At the same time, the Earth is rotating around the center of the galaxy. The galaxy is traveling endlessly through space and is pulling the Earth along with it. Now how can you say we never go anywhere?*

HELLO, AND WELCOME. This is our planet Earth. Before starting our journey through history, let us take a brief look at our little space orb from the vantage point of newcomers undergoing a brief orientation.

"Spaceship Earth," as some people like to call it, is a relatively small celestial body. The American space shuttle can completely orbit the Earth in only ninety minutes. In modern aircraft, the crossing of once-formidable oceans has become little more than a dull routine for many an airborne businessperson plying his or her trade between continents. By merely picking up a telephone and dialing, one can speak instantly to someone on the opposite side of the globe. We are all witnesses to the remarkable manner in which high-speed travel and telecommunications make contact between distant points on Earth quickly and easily manageable.

Earth is not only small, it is also quite remote. If you and I were to take a position outside of the Milky Way galaxy, we would see that Earth is near the galaxy's outer edge. In addition, the Milky Way is dwarfed by much larger galaxies. This isolated location might help explain why Earth has so few contacts with extraterrestrial civilizations, if such civilizations exist. Earth is afloat in the distant boondocks of a minor galaxy.

Despite its isolation, Earth is pretty, and it is inhabited. As of this writing, the human population numbers over five billion people. Add to that figure all of the other large mammals, and we find that the lands and waters of Earth are occupied by an enormous population of intelligent and semi-intelligent creatures.

What kind of animals are human beings? As a student of biology can quickly tell you, humans constitute that animal species known as *Homo sapiens*. The work *Homo* comes from the Latin word for man, and *sapiens* means being wise or sensible. The label *Homo sapiens* therefore denotes a creature possessed of wisdom or sensibility. Most *Homo sapiens* do live up to their title, by and large, although a small number obviously do not.

When dealing with a human being, are we only confronting an animal? As it turns out, we are not. It appears that we are faced with something much more important: a spiritual being.

The idea that there is a spiritual reality to life is ageless. Some religions have held the belief for millennia that human bodies are mere puppets animated by spiritual beings. Often accompanying this tenet are doctrines concerning "reincarnation" or an "afterlife." In the Christian religion, the word "soul" has long been used to denote a spiritual entity which survives the death of the physical body.

Some people claim that an ancient wisdom about the spirit had once existed. If such a wisdom ever did exist, it long ago became hopelessly bemuddled by countless false ideas, strange mystical beliefs and practices, incomprehensible symbolism, and erroneous scientific teachings. As a result, the subject of the spirit is today almost unstudiable. On top of that, many scholars trained in Western scientific methods reject the idea of a soul entirely, apparently because they cannot put a spirit under a microscope and watch it squiggle, or plant electrodes in it and give it a jolt.

As good fortune would have it, some breakthroughs on the subject have been made within recent decades. Evidence that every person is a unique spiritual being is strong indeed. Volumes of fascinating testimony have been gathered from people who have undergone so-called "near-death" experiences. During such episodes, many people undergo the sensation of leaving their bodies, especially as their bodies approached death. Some psychiatrists argue that this phenomenon is nothing more than a self-protective illusion of the mind. It is not as simple as that. Many near-death victims are able to perceive their bodies from an accurate exterior perspective. They retain their complete self-awareness and personal identity even though their bodies are unconscious.*

In light of such testimony, it is not surprising that a few religions, such as Buddhism, believe that people are immortal spiritual beings which become enmeshed in bodies during life. Buddhists conclude that this is caused, at least in part, by the spirit's long-term interaction with the physical universe. In sharp contrast to psychiatric theory, Buddhists teach that spiritual separation from the body is the healthiest state for human beings and Buddhists seek to attain that separation without suffering physical trauma or death. Their

---

*A short but interesting article entitled, "A Typology of Near-Death Experiences," by Dr. Bruce Greyson, is found in the August 1985 issue of the *American Journal of Psychiatry*. Dr. Greyson presents a statistical breakdown of the different types of "near-death" phenomena and notes, "Individuals reporting these three types of near-death experiences did not differ significantly on demographic variables." (p. 968). Dr. Greyson did not speculate as to what causes the experiences.

goal is encouraged by the belief that a spiritual being can operate a body as well, or better, from outside a body as from within.

The definition of a spiritual being shared by several religions appears to be the most accurate one: a spiritual being is an entity possessed of awareness, creativity, and personality. It is not composed of matter or of any other component of the physical universe; it appears instead to be an immortal unit of awareness which cannot perish, although it can become entrapped by physical matter. The spiritual being is fully capable of understanding itself.

The modern trend, of course, is to view the brain as the center of awareness and personality. Scientists have been able to electrically stimulate specific parts of the brain to produce the physiological manifestations of many human emotions. This, however, reveals the brain to be nothing more than a sophisticated switchboard capable of being activated by a variety of external sources, such as by an experimenter with his electrodes or even perhaps by a spiritual being with its own energy output. The interaction between a spiritual entity and the body's central nervous system appears to be so intimate that a change in one can often influence the behavior of the other.

From all of this emerges a picture indicating that human beings are spiritual entities who enjoy a certain spiritual immortality, but who are usually unaware of it until an unexpected separation occurs. During life, spiritual beings tend to utilize, almost exclusively, the perceptions of the physical body. Death, according to this analysis, is little more than spiritual abandonment of the body during a time of intense physical, or sometimes even mental, injury.

What does all of this have to do with human warfare?

Almost everything, as we shall see.

That brings us to the third and final topic of our orientation: UFOs. There are few subjects today as full of false information, deceit, and madness as "flying saucers." Many earnest people who attempt to study the subject are driven around in circles by a terrific amount of dishonesty from a small number of people who, for the sake of a fleeting moment of notoriety or with the deliberate intention to obfuscate, have clouded the field with false reports, untenable "explanations," and fraudulent evidence. Suffice it to say that behind this smokescreen there is ample evidence of extraterrestrial visitations to Earth. This is too bad. An in-depth study of the UFO phenomenon reveals that it does not offer a happy little romp through the titillating unknown. The UFO appears more and more to be one of the grimmest realities ever confronted by the human race.

Keeping the points of our brief orientation in mind, let us now begin a deeper probe.

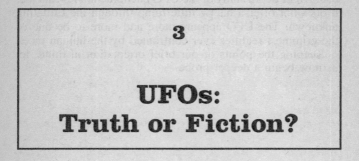

# 3

# UFOs: Truth or Fiction?

UFOs: WHAT ARE they? Where do they come from?

Strictly speaking, the term *unidentified flying object* (UFO) refers to any aerial object which cannot be positively identified as a man-made construction or as any known phenomenon of nature. The term implies a mystery. In common parlance, UFO is often used to denote any object which might be a spacecraft from an extraterrestrial civilization.

The phrase *unidentified flying object* was coined by U.S. Air Force Captain Edward J. Ruppelt. Captain Ruppelt led an Air Force investigation into the phenomenon in 1951. Prior to Ruppelt's investigation, UFOs were usually called "flying saucers" because many eyewitnesses described the objects as disc-shaped. "Flying saucer" quickly became a term of derision, however, due to the skepticism expressed by many newspaper and magazine writers. "Unidentified flying object" was used by Captain Ruppelt to lend his Air Force study an air of respectability. UFO is also a more accurate term because not all unidentified flying objects are saucer-shaped.

Hundreds of UFOs are reported every year, usually to police, to the news media, or to UFO research groups. These reports represent only a minority of the total number of UFOs actually seen because most UFO witnesses do not publicly reveal their encounters.

Roughly 90% to 95% of all reported UFOs prove to be man-made aircraft or unrecognized natural phenomena. Approximately 1.5% to 2% are outright hoaxes, often accompanied by spurious photographs. Although hoaxes constitute such a small percentage of all UFO reports, they have created a disproportionate amount of trouble. Hoaxes are, in fact, responsible for almost entirely disgracing the serious study of UFOs. The more convincing the fraud, the more damage it will usually do. The remaining 3% to 8.5% of all UFO sightings are those which appear to be aircraft of nonhuman origin. Most researchers are concerned with this last group.

Twentieth-century UFOs were rarely reported in the mass media before 1947, and so some people assume that UFOs must be a relatively modern phenomenon. UFOs are, in fact, quite the opposite. UFOs have been reported for thousands of years in all parts of the world. For example, writer Julius Obsequens reproduced the following account from 216 B.C. in his book, *Prodigorium liber:*

> Things like ships were seen in the sky over Italy. . . .
> At Arpi [in Italy] a round shield was seen in the
> sky. . . . At Capua, the sky was all on fire, and one
> saw figures like ships. . . . [1]

In the first century A.D., famed Roman statesman Cicero recorded a night during which the sun, accompanied by loud noises, was reportedly seen in the night sky. The sky appeared to split open and reveal strange "spheres." UFOs became so troublesome in the eighth and ninth centuries that emperor Charlemagne of France was compelled to issue edicts forbidding them from perturbing the air and provoking storms. In one episode, some of Charlemagne's subjects were taken up in aerial "ships," shown marvels, and then returned to Earth, only to be put to death by an angry mob. Those troublesome ships were even accused of destroying crops.*

UFOs have not only been seen, they have also been worshipped throughout history. The religions of ancient Mesopotamia, Egypt, and the Americas were dominated by the adoration of humanlike "gods" from the heavens. Many of those "gods" were said to travel about in flying "boats" and "globes." Ancient claims of that kind are today the basis of the modern "ancient astronauts" theory which postulates that a space age race had once visited Earth and had involved itself in human affairs. Some UFO researchers have gone a step further by suggesting that such a space age race had either created or conquered human society many thousands of years ago and that it has been maintaining a watchful eye on its possession ever since.

To many, such theories seem to be the stuff of science fiction. The ideas are, however, one outgrowth of an academic debate which has preoccupied historians for over a century: how did the ancient Old and New World civilizations, located on opposites of the Earth, come to so closely resemble one another? Why did the peoples of those far-flung civilizations develop such remarkably similar religious beliefs?

One widely-held view is that a land or ice bridge once spanned the Bering Strait between Siberia and Alaska over which people from the Old World had migrated into the New. Others point to archaeological evidence that the ancient Phoenicians had sailed across the Atlantic Ocean

---

* A long and interesting collection of ancient UFO sightings and unusual natural phenomena from the late B.C. and early A.D. years can be found in Harold T. Wilkins' book, *Flying Saucers on the Attack*. Despite its sensationalistic title, Mr. Wilkins' book is often well-argued and is worth reading as one of the earliest books of the modern UFO era. An excellent collection of ancient UFO reports can also be found in Jacques Vallee's *Passport to Magonia*.

centuries before the Scandinavian vikings or Christopher Columbus. Some scholars conclude that the Phoenicians had borrowed many features of the Egyptian civilization and had transplanted them to the New World. Another hypothesis is that the ancient Egyptians themselves had sailed across the ocean.

Despite evidence to support all of the above possibilities, none of the theories fully encompass all of the known facts. This has led to a fourth theory, well expressed in 1910 by Oxford professor and Nobel Laureate Frederick Soddy:

> Some of the beliefs and legends bequeathed to us by Antiquity are so universally and firmly established that we have become accustomed to consider them as being almost as ancient as humanity itself. Nevertheless we are tempted to inquire how far the fact that some of these beliefs and legends have so many features in common is due to chance, and whether the similarity between them may not point to the existence of an ancient, totally unknown and unsuspected civilization of which all other traces have disappeared.[2]

When such conjecture is raised, many people think of vanished land masses or islands, such as the legendary lost continents of Atlantis and Lemuria. One of Professor Soddy's contemporaries, however, took a different approach and speculated that extraterrestrial societies were involved in Earth's prehistory. Dr. Soddy's controversial contemporary was Charles Hoy Fort (1867-1923).

Charles Fort is perhaps the earliest writer of the twentieth century to seriously suggest that extraterrestrials have been involved in human affairs. Fort supported himself on a small inheritance and spent many years of his adult life amassing reports of unusual phenomena from scientific journals, newspapers, and magazines. The stories he collected were of such events as unusual moving lights in the sky, "rainfalls" of animals, and other occurrences which seem to defy conventional scientific explanation. His first two books, *The Book of the Damned* (1919) and

*New Lands* (1923), contain a large assortment of UFO sightings and related phenomena from the 19th and early 20th centuries. Fort concluded that Earth skies were hosting an array of extraterrestrial aircraft, which he called "superconstructions."

Fort developed other theories from his research, several of which have endured and still remain provocative today. In *The Book of the Damned,* he wrote:

> I think we're property.
> I should say we belong to something:
> That once upon a time, this earth was No-man's Land, that other worlds explored and colonized here, and fought among themselves for possession, but that now it's owned by something:
> That something owns this earth—all others warned off.[3]

Fort concluded that the human race does not have a very high status in relation to Earth's extraterrestrial owners. In addressing the puzzle of "why don't they [Earth's owners] ever come here, or send here, openly," he philosophized:

> Would we, if we could, educate and sophisticate pigs, geese, cattle?
> Would it be wise to establish diplomatic relation with the hen that now functions, satisfied with mere sense of achievement by way of compensation?[4]

In addition to likening the human race to self-satisfied livestock, Fort believed that a direct influence over human affairs was being exerted by Earth's apparent owners:

> I suspect that, after all, we're useful—that among contesting claimants, adjustment has occurred, or that something now has a legal right to us, by force, or by having paid out analogues of beads for us to former, more primitive, owners of us—that all of this has been known, perhaps for ages, to certain ones upon this earth, a cult or order, members of which function like

bellwethers to the rest of us, or as superior slaves or overseers, directing us in accordance with instructions received—from Somewhere else—in our mysterious usefulness.[5]

Fort did not speculate as to what mankind's "mysterious usefulness" might be, except to briefly suggest that humans might be slaves.

In a lighter vein, Fort thought that Earth had had a very lively and colorful prehistory:

> But I accept that, in the past, before proprietorship was established, inhabitants of a host of other worlds have—dropped here, hopped here, wafted, sailed, flown, motored—walked here, for all I know—been pulled here, been pushed, have come singly, have come in enormous numbers; have visited occasionally, have visited periodically for hunting, trading, replenishing harems, mining; have been unable to stay here, have established colonies here, have been lost here; far-advanced peoples, or things, and primitive peoples or whatever they were: white ones, black ones, yellow ones—[6]

To understand how all of this applies to the human condition today, Fort offered no answers, only a formula:

> Pigs, geese, and cattle.
> First find out that they are owned.
> Then find out the whyness of it.[7]

Fort had certainly expressed some daring ideas. They were published at a time when crude biplanes and dirigible balloons ruled the sky. Charles Lindberg's historic flight across the Atlantic Ocean was still eight years away.

Fort acquired a small and loyal following during his day. It was not until a third of a century later, however, that the foundation laid by Fort supported a sudden explosion of nonfiction works speculating that an extraterrestrial society had been involved in human affairs. This sudden surge of interest was caused by a media-publicized rash of UFO sightings in the late 1940's and 1950's. One of the first books of that period to discuss ancient UFO sightings was *Flying Saucers on the Attack* by Harold T. Wilkins. It was published in 1954 by Citadel Press of New York. Citadel followed with a host of books, including *The UFO and the Bible* (1956) by Morris K. Jessup. Jessup's book suggested that many Biblical events were the doings of a space age race, not of a God. Numerous passages from the Bible were quoted to support the theory. Similar books with similar titles followed, such as *Flying Saucers in the Bible* (1963) by Virginia F. Brasington and *The Bible and Flying Saucers* (1967) by Barry H. Downing.

On the other side of the Atlantic, a number of European writers were also making important contributions to the genre. The French writing team of Louis Pauwels and Jacques Bergier wrote their intriguing bestseller, *Morning of the Magicians,* which was published in America in the early 1960's. Erich von Daniken of Switzerland was also writing about ancient astronauts during the 1950's and '60's, and he achieved great fame by the early '70's after the publication of his first international bestseller on the subject: *Chariots of the Gods?* The powerful success of von Daniken's book prompted a flood of similar books and motion pictures in the '70's and early '80's, bringing the idea of "ancient astronauts" to the attention of millions.

The notion of alien intervention in human affairs is generally tolerated when it is expressed as a work of science fiction, but it is often poorly received when suggested as fact. This is understandable. The very idea of it seems, at first blush, to fly in the face of everything we have ever been taught. For centuries, there has been a strong tendency to think of our planet and the human race in very isolationist terms. Centuries ago, people even believed that humans were at the center of the universe and that the sun and stars all revolved around us. It was a flattering notion, but sadly not a true one. In the bygone days of the Inquisition, however, a person could be put to death for challenging the idea. The only "extraterrestrials" people were permitted to believe in were winged angels in white robes sent from Heaven by the great god Jehovah. Although the sciences have thankfully moved away from that kind of perspective to a large extent, human-centered concepts of existence are still surprisingly strong.

Some persuasive-sounding arguments have been advanced to refute the evidence that one or more extraterrestrial societies have been visiting the Earth. Some of those arguments are worth addressing:

*1. No intelligent life other than mankind has been proven to exist elsewhere in the universe.*

At first glance, this seems to be true. However, one need only look right here on Earth to find other intelligent life forms. Studies of dolphins and other large marine mammals have revealed a high intelligence in many of those creatures. Analyses of other mammals have uncovered in some of them a level of intelligence much higher than previously believed. This reveals that there are a great many intelligent and semi-intelligent creatures in the universe known to us; we share a planet with them. The fact that they all flourish together on this one small planet is an excellent indication that other intelligent creatures can exist elsewhere under the right conditions.

*2. There has not been a single UFO sighting which could not be explained as a natural or human phenomenon. Therefore, all UFOs must be such phenomena.*

This argument uses faulty logic. It is possible to "explain" almost anything as anything. I suppose one could "explain" the sun as billions of fireflies held in a gigantic glass bowl. This "explanation," however, does not fit the evidence as well as the better theory that the sun is a huge mass of compressed hydrogen which is undergoing a process of atomic fusion.

Many UFO sightings are given prosaic explanations only by ignoring evidence which clearly reveals that they are not earthly phenomena. If one is selective enough in choosing which evidence and testimony to believe, one can invent almost any explanation to fit almost any UFO sighting. The trick is to find the best explanation to fit the true and complete facts. In many instances, the true and complete facts indicate that a UFO is indeed best explained as a natural phenomenon. In other cases, the best explanation is that a UFO is probably an intelligently-guided craft of nonhuman origin. Many remarkable sightings do fit this latter category.*

3. *There has been no "hard evidence" of UFOs or "ancient astronauts."*

Physical objects constitute "hard" evidence. In UFOlogy, a piece of hard evidence might be a "crashed saucer" or the body of an extraterrestrial pilot. It is argued that if alien spacecraft have been flying in Earth's skies for thousands of years, we should have a piece of concrete physical evidence by now. Setting aside allegations and evidence that some governments may have a crashed saucer or two secreted away, we cannot logically expect to find too many alien artifacts. To explain why, I will make an analogy between UFOs and modern commercial jetliners.

Millions of commercial airline flights take off from U.S. airports every year. Despite this enormous volume, very few people will ever stumble upon a crashed jetliner or dead crew member because only a tiny percentage of all flights end in disaster. Equally few individuals will ever find any instruments or debris tossed from jetliners because jetliners are self-contained and the navigators rarely gouge instruments from the flight panels and heave them out the cockpit window. If it were not for the fact that most of us can see commercial jet aircraft and fly in them, the "hard" evidence of their existence would be surprisingly scant, especially if they were to be manufactured in, and flown only to and from, remote areas.

Let us translate this into a mathematical formula.

Based upon U.S. Federal Aviation Administration (FAA) statistics, roughly one in every million flights by major U.S. carriers departing from American airports suffers a serious accident, such as a crash, a crash landing away from an airport, or the loss of a significant piece of the plane. This

---

*For a good overview of UFO cases, I recommend *The U.F.O. Encyclopedia* by Margaret Sachs.

admirable safety record makes air travel one of the safest modes of transportation today.

Let us assume that the reported alien spacecraft in our skies have precisely the same safety record as American commercial jet aircraft—no better and no worse. Let us guess that 2000 "flying saucer" flights are made over Earth every year. That amounts to 5½ flights every day. We will assume that each hypothetical saucer flight is made at a low enough altitude that, if a mishap should occur, the debris would fall to Earth before disintegrating in the atmosphere.

Putting all of the above figures together, we discover that a "flying saucer" would crash, or drop a substantial chunk of debris, only once every five centuries! That would amount to only twelve crashes since the dawn of mankind's first recorded civilization! If we cut the safety factor in half and double the number of hypothetical UFO flights to 4000 per year (11 per day), or leave the safety factor the same and quadruple the number of low-level saucer flights to 8000 per year (22 per day), that would still amount to only one crash or major piece of debris once every one hundred twenty-five years!

We can safely conclude that even if extraterrestrial craft have been flying in our skies for millennia, we cannot expect to find too much wreckage or debris. The best evidence of extraterrestrial visitation that we may reasonably expect to obtain is eyewitness testimony, which is precisely the evidence we have.

Despite these pessimistic statistics, a few rare UFO crashes have been reported. Fragments alleged to have come from exploding UFOs have been found and made public. One such piece was reported by a Brazilian columnist who said that the item had been recovered by a fisherman off the coast of Brazil in 1957. The fragment was sent by *Omni* magazine to the Massachusetts Institute of Technology (MIT) for analysis. It proved to be a piece of pure magnesium. An MIT analyst guessed that the fragment might have been a piece of weld metal from either an exploding aircraft or from a re-entering satellite. Because the piece could have been manufactured on Earth, the test was considered inconclusive.

*4. If UFOs are extraterrestrial aircraft, there should be an undisputed photograph of one by now.*

Anything can be disputed. To begin a dispute, all one needs to do is open one's mouth and utter a few words. The mere existence of a dispute, therefore, does not in itself deny the reality of a thing. The dispute simply means that someone has chosen to quarrel, whether for good reasons or bad.

It is true, however, that researchers do face a paucity of decent UFO photographs. Available UFO snapshots tend to be of two varieties: either fuzzy and inconclusive (the picture could be of just about anything), or fraudulent. When a sharp, clear picture of a flying saucer does surface, it often proves to be a hoax. This happens so often that a researcher can almost count on a "good" flying saucer photograph eventually proving "bad." This is especially true today when technical advances have made some forms of trick photography nearly undetectable.

This still leaves the question: why are there so few conclusive photographs available?

As noted earlier, apparently genuine extraterrestrial aircraft account for only a small percentage of the total number of UFOs reported. Most of those aircraft are seen at night. The majority of "close encounters" (human encounters with the spacecraft occupants) take place in rural non-recreational areas where there are very few people carrying cameras. The already poor chances of getting a good snapshot under those conditions are worsened by the fact that the vast majority of camera owners, including dedicated photo buffs, do not always carry their cameras with them. At any given moment, surely fewer than one person in every ten thousand is carrying a camera. UFOs do not compensate for this by making regular scheduled appearances over crowded vacation spots where most clicking cameras would be. Given these factors, we can expect that good genuine photos of extraterrestrial aircraft would be exceedingly rare commodities. Remember also that camera ownership has been widespread for only a short period of time: several decades.

This is not to say that clear photos of apparently genuine alien aircraft do not exist. A few do, and they can be found in various books written by responsible UFO researchers.*

5. *Eyewitness testimony in UFO cases is inherently unreliable. Such testimony is therefore insufficient evidence of extraterrestrial visitation.*

Perhaps the most influential UFO critic as of this writing is Philip Klass, who has been aptly dubbed the "Sherlock Holmes of UFOlogy" for his exhaustive investigations. His book, *UFOs Explained*, won the Aviation/Space Writers award for the best book on space in 1974. In that award-winning book, Mr. Klass developed several principles. The first was:

UFOlogical Principle #1: Basically honest and intelligent persons who are suddenly exposed to a brief, unexpected event, especially one that involves an unfamiliar object, may be grossly inaccurate in trying to describe precisely what they have seen.[8]

This principle is sometimes true. It was demonstrated by a U.S. government-sponsored UFO study conducted between 1966 and 1968 under the direction of Edward U. Condon. Its published findings, which are usually called the "Condon Report," are a milestone in UFO literature.

In one chapter of the Condon Report, the committee discusses what occurred after a Russian spacecraft, Zond IV, went awry and began its re-entry into Earth's atmosphere on March 3, 1968. As the craft fell through the atmosphere and burned, it created a spectacular display for people on the ground. Eyewitnesses perceived the flaming debris as a majestic procession of fiery objects leaving behind a golden orange tail. Because of the objects' great height, it was impossible to make out from the ground what the broken pieces actually were. It was only possible to see

---

* For advice concerning the authenticity of specific UFO photographs, I recommend contacting the Mutual UFO Network, Inc. (MUFON), 103 Oldtowne Road, Seguin, Texas, 78155-4099, USA.

them as brilliant and separate points of light. The Zond IV debris created an effect identical to that of a brilliant meteor display.

Upon compiling eyewitness testimony of the Zond IV re-entry, it was discovered that some people "saw" more than there really was. If some of the erroneous observations had been taken at face value, some people would have concluded that the Zond IV debris was actually an intelligently controlled alien spacecraft. For example, five eyewitnesses reported that the lights were part of a "cigar-shaped" or rocket-shaped craft: a common UFO description. Three eyewitnesses said that the "object" had windows. One observer claimed that the "object" had made a vertical descent. Because of these blatant errors, Mr. Klass and others have understandably labeled all "cigar-shaped UFOs with bright windows" as meteors. The Condon Committee cited the Zond IV testimony as an example of why eyewitness reports are often inadequate to establish that a UFO is an extraterrestrial spacecraft.

Case closed?

Not quite.

In his UFOlogical Principle #1 quoted above, Mr. Klass states that eyewitnesses *may* be grossly inaccurate in trying to describe precisely what they have seen. Significantly, he did not say that eyewitnesses *are usually* inaccurate. This distinction takes on importance as we read further into the Condon Report.

The Condon Committee discovered that at least half of the Zond IV eyewitnesses gave accurate, unembellished reports of the event. The observations of a "cigar-shaped craft with windows" came only from a minority. From the accurate reports, a careful UFO researcher would have been able to eliminate the erroneous descriptions and correctly identify the Zond IV re-entry as debris or a meteoric phenomenon. The Committee also analyzed a wave of UFO reports triggered by several college students who had released four hot air balloons into the evening sky. The balloons were made of plastic dry cleaning bags; the hot air was generated by birthday candles suspended underneath. The Committee analyzed the testimony of fourteen eyewitnesses who did not know what the flying objects were. With only minor deviations among them, all fourteen observers gave accurate descriptions of what it was possible for them to actually see. The Committee concluded:

> In summary, we have a number of reports that are highly consistent with one another, and those differences that do occur are no greater than would be expected from situational and perceptual differences. Many small discrepancies could be pointed out, especially with regard to estimates of distance and direction, but these are not great enough to affect the overall impression of the event.[9]

This demonstrates something very important that we can express in our own "UFOlogical Principle":

> *Basically honest and intelligent persons who are suddenly exposed to a brief, unexpected event, including one that involves an unfamiliar object, will, in the majority of cases, be accurate in trying to describe precisely what they have seen.*

That is why eyewitness testimony may be admissible in courts of law to convict or free a defendant even when solid physical evidence is lacking. Eyewitness testimony is a perfectly valid and useful form of evidence.

*6. Sophisticated listening devices have been pointed toward the heavens to pick up extraterrestrial communications. So far, no such communications have been detected. This is further evidence that there is no intelligent life nearby.*

Despite skepticism in many academic circles regarding extraterrestrial visitation, several well-funded attempts have been made to detect signals from outer space civilizations through the use of sophisticated radio antennas pointed toward the heavens. The fact that these efforts have reportedly not detected any intelligent signals is viewed as additional proof that there are no alien civilizations nearby.

The problem with drawing such a conclusion is that radio antennas have many limitations. They are only able

to detect radio waves. There are many other bands along
the electromagnetic spectrum[4] that can carry communication signals, such as microwave. What is to say that an
extraterrestrial society, if it exists, would necessarily use
radio waves for communication? We do not even know
what lies beyond the two known ends of the electromagnetic
spectrum. How can we be sure that there are not wavelengths
in one of the two uncharted regions which are far superior
for communication to anything we have detected so far?
The reputed failure of radio antennas to pick up intelligent
signals would only tell us that no one within range is
using the electromagnetic wavelengths detectable by those
antennas.

7. *If so many "flying saucers" are visiting Earth, why
are they not detected more often on radar?*

Many outstanding UFO sightings have been confirmed
on radar. This excellent radar evidence is usually dismissed
by critics as operator error, as radar malfunction, or as false
readings caused by natural phenomena. We would have even
more radar evidence if it were not for the fact that radar
operators are trained to disregard most radar anomalies
because any number of things can create a false read.
Spurious radar signals can be generated by such widely
disparate phenomena as flocks of birds and severe weather
conditions. Operators are taught to focus on those readings that pinpoint the type of objects they are tracking—
usually human aircraft. If something unusual pops up on
the screen and disappears, it will, more often than not,
be ignored. A great many radar UFOs therefore go unre-
ported.

---

*The "electromagnetic spectrum" is the range of wavelengths at which
different forms of light may travel. At one end of the known spectrum
are radio waves, which have long wavelengths. (Yes, radio waves are
actually light waves. They become "sound" when translated by a receiver.)
At the other end of the spectrum are gamma rays, which have short
wavelengths. The range of light we can see with our eyes is limited to
a very small band of the spectrum. Instruments have been invented to
pick up and transmit along other wavelengths, such as infrared, x-ray,
and microwave.

Radar detection of UFOs is being further eliminated by advances in technology. Many modern radar computers now automatically eliminate anomalous readings so that they are not even displayed on the radar screen. This makes an operator's job easier, but at the cost of eliminating UFO detection. Mr. Klass comments:

> Ironically, one of the several criteria used [by radar computers] to discriminate between real and spurious targets would filter out potential radar-UFOs even if they were legitimate extraterrestrial craft flying at hypersonic speeds . . .[10]

*8. Many people have testified under hypnosis to being abducted by UFOs. Such testimony is inherently suspect because people who have never been abducted can be coached into creating seemingly realistic abduction "memories" while under hypnosis.*

If the UFO phenomenon consisted solely of occasional odd sights in the sky, it might be easy to dismiss. However, many people have reported being kidnapped by UFO occupants. The abduction experiences tend to be remarkably similar: the victim sees a UFO (usually at night and often in a rural area); he is immobilized and taken aboard an alien spacecraft; he is given a physical examination lasting an hour or two by alien creatures; he is then released. Many abductees do not consciously remember their experiences afterwards. A typical victim may only see a UFO and then suddenly discover that two hours have passed with no recollection of what had occurred during the missing time. Researchers usually break through this amnesia with hypnosis.

It appears that the curious amnesia experienced by so many UFO abductees is deliberately induced by the UFO occupants as a method of preserving the aliens' anonymity. Such mental tampering can indeed be done. During its infamous and highly publicized "mind control" experiments of the 1960's and '70's, the American CIA had developed effective techniques to bury memory and induce amnesia. With careful work, however, the buried memories could be recovered. As we shall see later, mental tampering with human victims has been a common activity associated with UFOs throughout all of history.

To date, an enormous body of fascinating abduction testimony has been gathered. Aspersions have been cast upon it because of various experiments, such as those performed in 1977 at the Anaheim Memorial Hospital in California. It was discovered in Anaheim that individuals who allegedly had little prior knowledge of UFOs could be coached into creating seemingly realistic abduction "memories" while under hypnosis. This discovery has been used to cast doubt on the validity of all abduction testimony obtained under hypnosis.

The Anaheim experiments, however, miss the point and reveal nothing about the UFO phenomenon. They only reaffirm what we already know about hypnosis.

It is true that a person's memory can be distorted while he is under hypnosis, just as it can when a person is completely conscious. On the other hand, it has been amply demonstrated that hypnosis can be effective in recovering completely valid memory: it depends upon the skill of the hypnotist and the mental state of the subject. A hypnotist can coach a person who has never been aboard a train into creating a realistic "memory" of riding a train, but does that mean that every hypnotic subject who remembers being on a train is guilty of fabrication? Of course not.

Admittedly, there are genuine problems with hypnosis. Because the hypnotic subject is in a semiconscious state, he or she may be more impressionable than normal. For this reason, American courts of law generally do not admit into evidence testimony obtained under hypnosis. Another danger with hypnosis is that a subject may recover a completely valid memory, but if the subject is continuously pushed during hynosis to remember more, he may find his mental "time track" getting scrambled. When that happens, he will often start to "remember" additional "episodes" which did not actually occur when or how remembered. Even so, the original memory remains valid.

Sadly, some UFO abductees have been hypnotized and rehypnotized beyond all measure of reason. They consequently wind up with scrambled memories on the already highly-charged subject of their abductions. For this and other reasons, I strongly recommend against the use of hypnosis. Heavily occluded memory can and should be recovered while a subject is in a fully conscious state. Some UFO abduction experiences have been recovered in just that fashion.

9. *The mathematical odds of an extraterrestrial race discovering Earth are too remote for it to be likely.*

Several mathematical formulae have been devised to show how unlikely it is that Earth has been visited by an extraterrestrial society. Such formulae are usually based upon theories of evolution, the number of planets which might support life, and the distances between planets and galaxies.

Such formulae are certainly interesting, but they should never be considered conclusive. If something exists, it exists. Trying to make it go away with a math formula will not make it any less real.

Keep in mind that we are unable to see any solid planets beyond our own solar system, let alone determine if there is any life on them. The human situation in this respect may be likened to a colony of tiny ants whose range of observation may only encompass a few acres. If that colony is situated on a barren desert, the ants might conclude that the entire Earth is a desolate wasteland, never dreaming of the vast metropolis only a hundred miles away. Simply because we find our own solar system or section of the galaxy barren, it does not automatically follow that this is the case everywhere. Another sector of the galaxy may be absolutely teeming with intelligent life and there would be no way for us out here on the distant edge of the Milky Way to know except by guessing with theories that are ever-changing. For this reason, it is not particularly wise to disregard evidence of extraterrestrial visitation if it appears.

10. *Only people with mental problems believe in UFOs.*

One unfortunate method some UFO critics use to attack evidence of extraterrestrial visitation is with psychological theory. Because such a critic is absolutely certain that there have been no extraterrestrial aircraft in our skies, he may resort to using defamatory psychological labels in an effort to "explain" why many people will consider a possibility that the critic rejects. Such labels have run the gamut from a simple need for religious fulfillment to ambulatory schizophrenia. This dubious psychiatry has become regrettably fashionable in recent years. It hides the reality that most serious research into UFOs is as clinical and scientific as one could hope for. The majority of UFO researchers are as sane and rational as the critics who are so quick to bandy about the unflattering psychological labels. The true UFO debate centers around genuine scientific, intellectual, and historical issues, not emotional ones.

Another problem with using psychological "analysis" to "explain" popular and scientific interest in UFOs is that the tables can be turned. A scholar advocating the possibility of extraterrestrial visitation can as easily, and as incorrectly, argue that those people who adamantly adhere only to prosaic explanations for UFO sightings in the face of contrary evidence are deeply afraid of something they cannot understand. Between the distinguished sideburns of a Ph.D., one could argue, may be a frightened child or willful adolescent desperately trying to handle the often confusing world around him by forcing everything to conform to what he can intellectually and emotionally comprehend.

As we can see, psychological mudslinging is very poor form in a scientific debate of this kind. It does no one any good, the labels are usually untrue, and it clouds the real issues. Intelligent and rational people are easily found on all sides of the UFO controversy.

*11. UFO theories are money-making rackets designed to prey on the gullible.*

It is a truism that there are two great crimes in our society: having money and not having money. Both are punished with equal ferocity.

One of the easiest ways to discredit an idea is to suggest that someone has gotten money for expressing it. Some UFO critics have made allusions to charlatans in the past who had duped people with strange ideas and who had become rich by preying on other people's gullibility. Such allusions have been made in an effort to suggest that people who earn money from UFO books or motion pictures are engaged in similar chicanery.

Please keep in mind that money itself has nothing to do with the validity of an idea. Money is an unpredictable commodity which goes to the deserving and undeserving alike. A handful of people have indeed earned good incomes from books and films dealing with the UFO phenomenon. The number of people who have done so, however, is very small compared to the many thousands of teachers, lecturers, and writers who are paid, sometimes handsomely, to promulgate more conventional views of the world.

Even when it is clear that a few individuals have falsely reported or insincerely discussed UFOs to make money, the UFO phenomenon is not automatically discredited. Profit-making has been a motive in nearly all arenas of human endeavor since the earliest days of mankind. If we were to throw out everything to which someone has ever attached a profit motive, little would remain of our culture. Fortunately, the vast majority of UFO witnesses and researchers, rich and poor, are sincere in what they say and do.

*12. UFO behavior does not conform to what we think intelligent extraterrestrial behavior ought to be.*

UFOs are difficult to study due to their often bizarre and unpredictable natures. UFO behavior seems, on the one hand, to raise some of the most profound questions about life and existence, while on the other hand it seems to be the stuff of a Buck Rogers movie. This duality is difficult to reconcile, yet it is an inescapable part of the phenomenon. The UFO is both profound and kooky, as we shall see.

This factor is often used to discredit UFO reports. Some critics imply that if UFOs are extraterrestrial aircraft, they would manifest themselves in a more acceptable manner. Why, for example, have UFOs apparently kidnapped housewives and implanted them with religious messages, but have never landed on the White House lawn and spoken to the U.S. President?

In one of his books, Philip Klass offered a $10,000 reward for conclusive proof of extraterrestrial visitation. To qualify for the reward, only a crashed spacecraft or other evidence which the U.S. National Academy of Sciences announces to be an affirmation of extraterrestrial intelligence would suffice; or, an extraterrestrial visitor must appear before the United Nations General Assembly or on a national television program. The fact that no one has received the reward is viewed by some people as added proof that Earth is not being visited by an extraterrestrial society.

The problems with the $10,000 reward are quickly obvious. We have already discussed the poor odds of finding a crashed "saucer" or major piece of debris. What if the National Academy of Sciences is prone to argue a terrestrial origin to a smaller piece of hard evidence before admitting a nonterrestrial source? What if extraterrestrial pilots are no more inclined to appear on television or at the United Nations than a human pilot is disposed to address a council of chimpanzees?*

We can all certainly wish that UFOs would be more cooperative, but until they are, the UFO phenomenon must be studied on its own terms, not according to the behavior we think it ought to exhibit.

*13. In the past, a few UFO sightings touted as proof of extraterrestrial visitation by top UFO researchers have proven to be earthly phenomena or hoaxes. Such errors should cast doubt on all proclamations by UFO researchers.*

Because the UFO phenomenon is so difficult to study, even the finest researchers will inevitably make errors, sometimes many of them. It is easy for someone to seize those mistakes and use them to discredit the entire subject. This tactic is often used by lawyers in courts of law, by statesmen during political debates, and even by scientists engaged in academic controversies.

---

*Another problem with the $10,000 offer was that a person had to pay Mr. Klass $100.00 per year to qualify. This reduced the UFO debate to the level of a crap shoot, where it does not belong. Few serious UFO researchers accepted the offer, much to their credit.

The problem with this tactic is that it does not always lead to truth, and can even lead away from it. A good example was the "Round Earth Theory" espoused by Christopher Columbus in the 15th century. In an age when many people still believed the world to be flat, Columbus was part of a movement proclaiming that the Earth was round or pear-shaped. As correct as Columbus was on this issue, he was wrong about many others. Columbus thought that he would encounter Asia when he crossed the Atlantic Ocean, and falsely reported that he had done so when he returned to Spain. We know today, of course, that Columbus had not found Asia at all—he had stumbled upon the North American continent which is nowhere near Asia! Because of this, we could easily scoff at Columbus' phony evidence and proclaim his "Round Earth Theory" a sham. After all, some of Columbus' other ideas about the Earth were clearly wrong, some absurdly so.

This type of situation occurs frequently, especially when a science is young, as UFOlogy is today. False claims and erroneous evidence are often used to support fundamentally sound ideas. This is not to say that every new theory that pops along is a valid one, or that bad evidence is the sign of a good theory. Many new theories prove bad. The trick is to weigh all of the evidence and to base a decision on that. In doing so, however, do not be surprised to encounter disagreement from others. It is a funny thing that two people can look at identical information and arrive at opposite conclusions.

*14. Expressing theories of extraterrestrial visitation and of "ancient astronauts" is dangerous to society.*

This argument is not worth dignifying in societies with traditions of open discussion and debate. Freedom of expression is one of the bedrocks of a healthy culture. It allows that society and its people to grow. A wide diversity of ideas gives people more perspectives to choose from. Possessing such a choice is preferable to having intellectual options restricted. In an open society, many unconventional ideas come and go, but that is a small price to pay for the enormous benefits of leaving communication lines open and free.

*15. If there are so many UFOs, why have I never seen one?*

I have never seen a UFO either. I have also never seen India, but the circumstantial evidence of its existence tends to make me think that India probably exists.

In addition to the above arguments, other means have been used to discredit UFO sightings. One method utilizes semantics. Some UFO critics say that they seek to find "rational" explanations for UFO sightings. By "rational" they mean explanations that portray a sighting as a natural or man-made object. This is an unfortunate use of the word "rational." The word "rational" means "sane," "well thought out," or "logical." Because sanity and logic must ultimately be based upon truth, a "rational" explanation of a phenomenon would be that explanation which most closely approximates the truth, whatever the truth may be. If a reported UFO is a misperceived natural phenomenon, then to explain it as such would indeed be rational. On the other hand, if a UFO is not a natural or man-made phenomenon, then to say that it is in the face of contrary evidence would not be rational at all.

Having said all of this, I still understand the reluctance of many people to take the UFO phenomenon seriously. It is a difficult booby-trapped subject. Some individuals who were once open-minded about UFOs have had the unfortunate experience of getting egg in their faces when they over-speculated about UFOs and were proven wrong. A good example was the public debacle surrounding the Martian moon, Phobos. About a decade ago, a number of scientific opinion leaders had speculated that Phobos was an artificial satellite placed in orbit around Mars by extraterrestrials. When a space probe later flew close enough to photograph Phobos, the Martian moon was shown to be little more than a large irregular piece of rock (although some of its orbital characteristics remain puzzling). Scientists and astronomers, because they survive on their good reputations, cannot endure too many speculative blunders of that kind. Many people who suffer such a tumble do not get back on the horse; instead they curse and attack the beast which threw them. Competent researchers today are aware of these perils and they try to avoid speculating too far from the known facts.

Why do I take the possibility of extraterrestrial visitation seriously, even though I agree with the "natural" explanation for some UFO sightings still debated today? I do so for many reasons. Firstly, the UFO phenomenon has been observed and reported for centuries. I therefore reject the critics' contention that UFOs are merely a bit of modern folklore. Secondly, the UFO phenomenon has been surprisingly consistent from location to location and from era to era. For example, some modern sightings of rocket or cigar-shaped UFOs mirror a UFO report from fifteenth-century Arabia. Thirdly, although it is true that some dubious "ancient astronaut" evidence has been published, so has some truly outstanding evidence. The critics' challenge that "extraordinary claims require extraordinary proof" has, to my mind, been met by some of that evidence. Fourthly, the "ancient astronauts" theory is hardly the "pseudoscientific nonsense" that it is sometimes accused of being. The "ancient astronauts" theory is a surprisingly logical hypothesis for shedding light on previously inexplicable historical data. I expect that it will one day be recognized as a true breakthrough even if it meets considerable opposition today. The fact that the theory arose from grass-roots research, and not from the ivied halls of a major university, means little. Anyone with an active and curious mind can make significant discoveries.

At this stage of my discussion, I may disappoint some readers by stating that it is not my purpose to write yet another tome which analyzes modern UFO sightings or which parades forth an array of ancient astronauts evidence simply to prove visitation. That has been adequately done elsewhere. If you remain a UFO skeptic, I recommend that you study other UFO literature before continuing with this book. *The Gods of Eden* is written for those people who already take seriously the possibility that Earth has been visited by an extraterrestrial society.

This book actually begins where Charles Fort left off. Mr. Fort speculated that Earth may be the property of an extraterrestrial society. He further believed that humans might be little more than slaves or livestock. As a result of my own historical research launched from an entirely different starting point,* I, too, arrived at a similar outrageous theory:

*Human beings appear to be a slave race languishing on an isolated planet in a small galaxy. As such, the human race was once a source of labor for an extraterrestrial civilization and still remains a possession today. To keep control over its possession and to maintain Earth as something of a prison, that other civilization has bred never-ending conflict between human beings, has promoted human spiritual decay, and has erected on Earth conditions of unremitting physical hardship. This situation has existed for thousands of years and it continues today.*

Having now laid myself wide open to ridicule for expressing such a hypothesis, I will proceed to share with you a very different view of history than you have probably encountered before.

Because I am risking a great deal by making this book available, I ask my readers for two favors before they pass judgment on what I have written:

1. Please read the *entire* book carefully,
2. Please read the chapters in the order in which they appear.

No idea, fact or historical episode I present stands entirely on its own. Each becomes significant only when it is seen within the entire context of history. The importance of what you read early in the book will not become apparent until you have continued to read much further. Conversely, the significance of the later material will not be clear unless you have read the early material first. The first 150 pages or so of this book contain ideas, conclusions, and statements that

---

*I had not read any of Charles Fort's works until I had already completed the third draft of this book.

may seem unscholarly and outrageous. Only by continuing to read onward will the remarkable historical documentation in support of those ideas truly take shape.

Hang on to your hat. We will now begin a startling rollercoaster ride along the underbelly of history.

# 4

# The Gods of Eden

THE IDEA THAT human beings are a slave race owned by an extraterrestrial society is not a new one. It was expressed thousands of years ago in mankind's earliest recorded civilizations. The first of those civilizations was Sumeria: a remarkably advanced society which arose in the Tigris-Euphrates River valley between 5000 and 4000 B.C., and flourished as a major civilization by 3500 B.C. *

Like other ancient societies which arose in the Mesopo-

---

* Until recently, ancient Sumeria was thought to be the site of mankind's earliest city. Excavation has revealed a city in Jericho (near modern-day Jerusalem) built as long ago as 7000 B.C. Almost nothing is known about that city.

tamian region, Sumeria left records stating that humanlike creatures of extraterrestrial origin had ruled early human society as Earth's first monarchs. Those alien people were often thought of as "gods." Some Sumerian "gods" were said to travel into the skies and through the heavens in flying "globes" and rocketlike vehicles. Ancient carvings depict several "gods" wearing gogglelike apparel over their eyes. Human priests acted as mere intermediaries between the alien "gods" and the human population.

Not all Mesopotamian gods were humanlike extraterrestrials. Some were obvious fabrications, and fictitious attributes were often ascribed to the extraterrestrial humanlike gods. Once the blatant fictions are stripped away, however, we discover within the Mesopotamian pantheon a distinct class of beings who do indeed fit the "ancient astronauts" mold.

In order for me to better discuss these "high tech" "gods," * it will be necessary for me to invent a new term.

The word "god" alone contains too much undeserved awe. Historical and modern-day testimony indicates that these "gods" are as "human" in their behavior as you or I.

The term "ancient astronaut" pigeonholes them into the distant past when, in fact, they appear to have maintained a continuous presence all the way up until today.

The label "extraterrestrial" is too broad.

I cannot name the "gods" after any star or planet from which they might hail because I will not speculate as to their place of origin. Furthermore, it is conceivable that the alleged ownership of Earth may have changed hands over the millennia, in the same way that ownership of a corporation can pass among different owners without the public being aware of it.

---

* For a detailed analysis of the apparent "high tech" nature of many ancient Sumerian gods, I recommend Zecharia Sitchin's five books, *The Twelfth Planet, The Stairway to Heaven, The Wars of Gods and Men, The Lost Realms,* and *Genesis Visited.* They are published by Avon Books of New York.

That leaves me to invent a new label based upon the "gods' " apparent relationship to the human race. For lack of anything better, I will simply refer to them as the "Custodial" society, meaning that specific extraterrestrial society (or succession of societies) which appears to have had ownership and custody of the Earth since prehistory. For brevity, I will often refer to them simply as "Custodians."

What sort of creatures are these newly-labeled "Custodians"?

Historical records and modern testimony describe them as physically humanlike, racially diverse, and, most importantly, very similar to human beings behaviorally. For example, some modern-era UFOs have exhibited adolescent prankishness by racing at airplanes as though they were going to collide, and then abruptly veering away just as impact seemed imminent: an apparent game of aerial "chicken." At least one modern witness has allegedly been "zapped" by a UFO for no other apparent reason than malice. Ancient writers describe their extraterrestrial "gods" as being capable of love, hate, amusement, anger, honesty, and depravity. Ancient records and modern testimony alike would indicate that Custodial personalities run the entire gamut from saints to sinners, from the most degraded of despots to the most true-hearted of humanitarians. Sadly, it is the brutal and despotic element of their society that would appear to be the most influential in the affairs of Earth, as we shall document.

The ancient Mesopotamian civilizations recorded a great deal of their history on clay tablets. Only a fraction of those tablets have survived, yet they manage to tell a remarkable story about the Custodial "gods" and their relationship to *Homo sapiens*.

According to the history inscribed on Mesopotamian tablets, there was a time when human beings did not exist at all. Instead, Earth was inhabited by members of the Custodial civilization. Custodial life on Earth was not pleasant, however. Custodial efforts to exploit the rich mineral and natural resources of Earth proved backbreaking. As one tablet tells us:

*When the gods like men*
*Bore the work and suffered the toil—*
*The toil of the gods was great,*
*The work was heavy, the distress was much—*[1]

The tablets described lives of endless drudgery as the "gods" carried out building, excavation, and mining operations on Earth. The "gods" were not at all happy with their lot. They were prone to complaining, backstabbing, and rebellion against their leaders. A solution was needed, and it was found: to create a new creature capable of performing the same labors on Earth as the Custodians. With this purpose in mind, the Custodial "gods" created *Homo sapiens* (man).

Mesopotamian tablets tell a creation story in which a "god" is put to death by other "gods," and the body and blood are then mixed into clay. Out of this concoction a human being is made. The new Earth creature is very similar in appearance to its Custodial creators.

In his book, *The Twelfth Planet,* author Zecharia Sitchin exhaustively analyzes the Sumerian creation stories. He concludes that the tale of a god's body being mixed with clay may have referred to biological engineering. Mr. Sitchin supports his surprising conclusion by pointing to those Sumerian tablets which state that the first humans were bred in the wombs of female Custodial "gods." According to the tablets, Custodians had male and female bodies, and they bred by sexual intercourse. In fact, ancient Mesopotamians stated that they provided ruling Custodial "gods" with human prostitutes. Mr. Sitchin believes that the "clay" was a special substance that could be inserted into a Custodial womb. That substance held the genetically-engineered cells of the new slave creature, *Homo sapiens*. Humans could apparently be bred in that fashion because they were physically very similar to Custodians. Interestingly, modern scientists have bred animals in a similar fashion, such as a zebra in the womb of a horse.

Ancient Mesopotamian tablets credit one "god" in particular with supervising the genetic manufacture of *Homo sapiens*. That "god's" name was Ea. Ea was reported to be

the son of a Custodial king who was said to rule
another planet within the farflung Custodial empire.
Prince Ea was known by the title, "EN.KI," which
means "lord [or prince] of Earth." Ancient Sumerian
texts reveal that Ea's title was not entirely accurate
because Ea was said to have lost his dominion over
major portions of Earth to his half brother, Enlil,
during one of the innumerable rivalries and intrigues
that seemed to forever preoccupy Custodial rulers.

In addition to engineering *Homo sapiens*, Prince Ea
is given credit in Mesopotamian tablets for many other
accomplishments. If he was a real person, then Ea could
best be described as a scientist and civil engineer of
considerable talent. He is said to have drained marshes
by the Persian Gulf and to have replaced them with
fertile agricultural land. He supervised the construction
of dams and dikes. Ea loved sailing and he built
ships in which to navigate the seas. When it came
time to create *Homo sapiens,* Ea demonstrated a good
grasp of genetic engineering, but not, according to the
tablets, without trial and error. Most importantly, Ea
was described as goodhearted, at least in regard to his
creation, *Homo sapiens*. Mesopotamian texts portray Ea
as an advocate who spoke before Custodial councils on
behalf of the new Earth race. He opposed many of the
cruelties that other Custodial rulers, including his half-
brother, Enlil, inflicted upon human beings. It would
appear from Sumerian tablets that Ea did not intend
*Homo sapiens* to be harshly treated, but his wishes in
that regard were overruled by other Custodial leaders.

As we have just seen, our ancient and highly civilized
ancestors told a very different story of humanity's emergence on Earth than we tell today. The Mesopotamians
were clearly not schooled in Darwinian theories of evolution! Nevertheless, there is some surprising anthropological evidence to support the Sumerian version of prehistory.

According to modern-day analyses of the fossil record,
*Homo sapiens* emerged as a distinct animal species somewhere between 300,000 B.C. and 700,000 B.C. As time
progressed, a number of subspecies of *Homo sapiens*

emerged, including that subspecies to which all human beings belong today: *Homo sapiens sapiens*. *Homo sapiens sapiens* appeared a mere 30,000 years ago—some say only 10,000 to 20,000 years ago. This raises an important question: were the Sumerians referring to *Homo sapiens* or *Homo sapiens sapiens* in their creation stories? There seems to be no firm answer. Excellent arguments have been made that they were referring to original *Homo sapiens*. I tend to favor the argument that they were probably referring to modern *Homo sapiens sapiens*, for the following reasons:

1. The oldest surviving creation stories were written circa 4000-5000 B.C. It is more likely that a true record of mankind's creation would survive 5000 to 25,000 years than it would survive 295,000 years or more.

2. If the Sumerians were describing the creation of *Homo sapiens sapiens*, later events described in Mesopotamian tablets fall within a more plausible time frame.

3. The Mesopotamians themselves were members of the subspecies *Homo sapiens sapiens*. They were primarily concerned with how they themselves had come into existence. In their various works, ancient Sumerians depicted hairy animal-like men who appear to be a more primitive subspecies of *Homo sapiens*. The Sumerians clearly viewed those primitive men as an entirely different race of creature.

If the Mesopotamian creation stories are based upon actual events, and if those stories refer to the creation of *Homo sapiens sapiens*, we would expect *Homo sapiens sapiens* to appear very suddenly in history. Remarkably, that is precisely what happened. The anthropological record reveals that *Homo sapiens sapiens* appeared on Earth abruptly, not gradually. F. Clark Howell and T. D. White of the University of California at Berkeley had this to say:

> These people *[Homo sapiens sapiens]* and their initial material culture appear with seeming suddenness just over 30,000 years ago, probably earlier in eastern than in western Europe.[2]

The mystery of this abrupt appearance is deepened by another puzzle: why did the more primitive Neanderthal man *(Homo sapiens neanderthalensis)* suddenly vanish at the same time that modern *Homo sapiens sapiens* appeared? Evolution is not that fast. Messrs. Howell and White pondered this question and concluded:

> . . . the utter, almost abrupt disappearance of Neanderthal people remains one of the enigmas and critical problems in studies of human evolution.[3]

The *Encyclopedia Britannica* concurs:

> The factors responsible for the disappearance of the Neanderthal peoples are an important problem to which there is unfortunately still no clear solution.[4]

The Sumerian creation stories do offer a clear solution to the riddle, but it is one that many people would have a difficult time accepting: the sudden appearance of *Homo sapiens sapiens*, accompanied by the abrupt disappearance of Neanderthal man, was caused by intelligent intervention. It might be conjectured that Neanderthal man was either exterminated or hauled off the Earth to make room for the new slave race, and perhaps to prevent breeding between the two subspecies. Whatever the precise truth of this might be, we do know two facts with certainty: modern anthropology has discovered a sudden replacement of Neanderthal man with modern man, and Mesopotamian records state that intelligent planning by an extraterrestrial race lay somewhere behind that dramatic event.

In Chapter 2, we discussed the fact that humans appear to be spiritual beings animating physical bodies. The spirit seems to be the true source of awareness, personality, and intelligence. Without a spiritual entity to animate it, a human body would be little more than a reactive animal, or dead. The people of ancient Mesopotamia thoroughly understood this critical fact when they mentioned a spiritual being in connection with the creation of *Homo sapiens:*

> *You have slaughtered a god together*
> *with his personality [spiritual being]*
> *I have removed your heavy work,*
> *I have imposed your toil on man.*[5]

Custodial rulers knew that they needed to keep spiritual beings permanently attached to human bodies in order to animate those bodies and make them intelligent enough to perform their labors:

> *In the clay god [a spiritual entity] and Man*
> *[physical body of* Homo sapiens] *shall be bound,*
> *to a unity brought together;*
> *So that to the end of days*
> *the Flesh and the Soul*
> *which in a god have ripened—*
> *that Soul in a blood-kinship be bound;*[6]

The tablets are silent about which "personalities" were chosen to animate the new slave bodies. Based upon how things are done in human society, we might guess that the Custodial society used criminals, deviates, prisoners of war, detested social and racial groups, nonconformists, and other undesirables to obtain the spiritual beings it needed to animate the new slave race of Earth. Humans were certainly treated like convicts sentenced to hard labor:

> *With picks and spades they [human beings] built the*
>     *shrines,*
> *They built the big canal banks.*
> *For food for the peoples, for the*
> *sustenance of [the gods].*[7]

As beasts of burden, humans were brutally treated by their extraterrestrial masters. The clay tablets tell of vast and catastrophic cruelty perpetrated by the Custodians against their human servants. Cold-blooded population control measures were carried out frequently:

*Twelve hundred years had not yet passed*
*When the land extended and the peoples multiplied.*
*The land was bellowing like a bull,*
*The god got disturbed with their uproar.*
*Enlil [half-brother and rival of Ea] heard their*
*noise\**
*And addressed the great gods,*
*"The noise of mankind has become too intense for*
*me,*
*With their uproar I am deprived of sleep.*
*Cut off supplies for the peoples,*
*Let there be a scarcity of plant-life to satisfy their*
*hunger.*
*Adad [another Custodian] should withhold his rain,*
*And below, the flood [the regular flooding of the*
*land which made it fertile] should not come up from*
*the abyss.*
*Let the wind blow and parch the ground,*
*Let the clouds thicken but not release a downpour,*
*Let the fields diminish their yields,*
*. . .*
*There must be no rejoicing among them."* [8]

---

\* These lines suggest that Enlil had lived more than 1200 years. A similar longevity is attributed to Ea and other Custodial rulers. Many people find it difficult to believe that any creature, including an extra-terrestrial, could live that long.

The surprising longevity attributed to Custodial rulers may perhaps be explained by Sumerian spiritual beliefs. The Sumerians believed that a "personality" (spiritual being) survives the death of a physical body and that it is possible to identify the "personality" after it has abandoned one body and taken on a new one (in the same way that one can identify a driver who jumps out of one automobile and climbs into another). A "personality" could therefore hold the same political or social position body after body, as long as the "personality" could be identified. When Sumerians gave Custodians an extensive longevity, they were not necessarily suggesting that a single Custodial body survived for centuries; in many cases they appear to have been saying that a Custodial "personality" held a political position for a very long time even though it may have done so through a succession of bodies.

An Assyrian tablet adds:

> *"Command that there be a plague,*
> *Let Namtar diminish their noise.*
> *Let disease, sickness, plague and pestilence*
> *Blow upon them like a tornado."*
> *They commanded and there was plague*
> *Namtar diminished their noise.*
> *Disease, sickness, plague and pestilence*
> *Blew upon them like a tornado.*[9]

The tablets describe ghastly conditions in which food supplies were cut off, in which diseases were laid upon the people that constricted wombs and prevented childbirth, and in which starvation became so rampant that human beings were forced to resort to cannibalism. Lesser diseases, such as one resembling influenza, were also visited upon *Homo sapiens*, suggesting that the Custodial "gods" understood and engaged in biological warfare.

When this genocide did not produce a sufficient drop in the human population, the Custodians resumed it. Eventually, a decision was made to destroy the human race entirely with a great flood.

Many archaeologists today believe that there was a cataclysmic flood in the Near East thousands of years ago. One description of the "Great Flood" is found in the Babylonian "Epic of Gilgamesh," which predates the Bible.

According to the Epic, a Babylonian named Utnapishtim was approached by Prince Ea, who opposed the decision to destroy his creation, *Homo sapiens*. Ea told Utnapishtim that the other "gods" planned to cause a deluge to wipe out the human race. Ea, who is described in other writings as a master shipbuilder and sailor, gave Utnapishtim instructions on how to build a boat which could survive the flood. Utnapishtim followed Ea's directions and, with the help of friends, completed the vessel before the flooding began. Utnapishtim then loaded the boat with his gold, family, and livestock, along with craftsmen and wild animals, and hoisted off to sea.

Babylonian and Assyrian tablets relate that just prior to

flooding the land, the Custodians scorched it with flame. Then they flooded the region by causing a long rainstorm and by breaking the intricate system of dams and dikes that had been built in Mesopotamia to control the erratic flooding of the Tigris and Euphrates Rivers.

The Gilgamesh Epic relates that Utnapishtim and his crew survived the ordeal. When it was over, they sought out dry land by releasing a series of three birds; if a bird did not return to the boat, Utnapishtim would know that it had found dry land nearby on which to alight.

Once back on solid ground, Utnapishtim was joined by several Custodians returning from out of the sky. Instead of destroying the survivors, a degree of leniency prevailed and the Custodians transported the surviving humans to another region to live.

The tale of Utnapishtim should ring a bell with anyone who is familiar with the Biblical story of Noah and the Ark. That is because the tale of Noah, like many other stories in the Old Testament, is taken from older Mesopotamian writings. Biblical authors simply altered names and changed the many "gods" of the original writings into the one "God" or "Lord" of the Hebrew religion. The latter change was an unfortunate one because it caused a Supreme Being to be blamed for the brutal acts that earlier writers had attributed to the very *un*-God-like Custodians.

Early Mesopotamian writings gave us another famous Old Testament story: the tale of Adam and Eve. The Adam and Eve narrative is also derived from earlier Mesopotamian sources which described life under the Custodial "gods." The "God" or "Lord God" of the Bible's Adam and Eve story can therefore be translated to mean the Custodial rulers of Earth. The story of Adam and Eve is unique in that it is entirely symbolic, and through its symbols it provides an intriguing account of early human history.

According to the Bible, Adam, who symbolizes first man, was created by "God" from the "dust of the ground." This idea reflects the older Mesopotamian belief that *Homo sapiens* was created partially from "clay." Adam's wife, Eve, was also created artificially. They both lived in an abundant paradise known as the Garden of Eden. Modern versions of the Bible place the Garden of Eden in the Tigris-Euphrates region of Mesopotamia.

The Old Testament tells us that Adam (first man) was designed to be a servant. His function was to till the soil and to care for the lush gardens and crops owned by his "God." As long as Adam and Eve accepted their servient status and obeyed their ever-present masters, all of their physical needs would be met and they would be permitted to remain in their "paradise" indefinitely. There was, however, one unpardonable sin that they must never commit. They must never attempt to seek certain types of knowledge. Those forbidden forms of knowledge are symbolized in the story as two trees: the "tree of knowledge of good and evil" and the "tree of life." The first "tree" symbolizes an understanding of ethics and justice. The second "tree" symbolizes the knowledge of how to regain and retain one's spiritual identity and immortality.

Adam and Eve obeyed the commandments of their masters and lived in material bliss until another party entered the scene. The intervening party was symbolized in the story as a snake. The serpent convinced Eve to partake of the "fruit" * from the "tree of knowledge of good and evil." Eve followed the serpent's suggestion, as did Adam. "God" (*i.e.*, Custodial leadership) became immediately alarmed:

> *And the Lord God said, Look, the man has become as one of us, knowing good from evil: and now, what if he puts forth his hand, and takes also of the tree of life, and eats, and lives forever?*
>
> GENESIS 3:22

The above passage reveals an important truth echoed by many religions. A true understanding of ethics, integrity,

---

* This fruit is usually portrayed as an apple, but that is the invention of later artists. The Bible itself does not mention a specific fruit because the "fruit" was only a symbol to represent knowledge.

and justice is a prerequisite to regaining one's spiritual freedom and immortality. Without a foundation in ethics, full spiritual recovery becomes nothing more than a pipe dream.

The Custodians clearly did not want mankind to begin traveling the road to spiritual recovery. The reason is obvious. The Custodial society wanted slaves. It is difficult to make thralls of people who maintain their integrity and sense of ethics. It becomes impossible when those same individuals are uncowed by physical threats due to a reawakened grasp of their spiritual immortality. Most importantly, if spiritual beings could no longer be trapped in human bodies, but could instead use and abandon bodies at will, there would be no spiritual beings available to animate slave bodies. As we recall, Sumerian tablets revealed a Custodial intention to permanently attach spiritual beings to human bodies. Early man's attempt to escape this spiritual bondage by "eating" from the Biblical "trees" therefore had to be stopped . . . and fast!

> *Therefore the Lord God sent him [Adam] forth from the garden of Eden, to till the ground from which he had been taken.*
> *So he drove out the man; and he placed at the east of the garden of Eden cherubim [angels], and a flaming sword which turned every way, to shield the way [prevent access] to the tree of life.*
>
> GENESIS 3:23-24

The "flaming sword" symbolizes the no-nonsense measures that the Custodians undertook to ensure that genuine spiritual knowledge would never become available to the human race.

To further prevent access to such knowledge, *Homo sapiens* was condemned to an additional fate:

> *And to Adam, he [God] said, Because you have listened to the urgings of your wife, and have eaten from the tree of which I commanded you not to, saying, You shall not partake of it: cursed is the ground for you, in*

*toil will you eat its yield for all the days of your life:*
  *Thorns, too, and thistles will it bring forth to you;*
*as you eat the plants from the field:*
  *By the sweat of your face will you eat bread, until*
*you return to the ground; for out of it were you taken:*
*for dust you are and to dust will you return.*

                              GENESIS 3:17-19

This was a highly effective way to deal with Adam's and Eve's "original sin." The above passage indicates that Custodial rulers intended to make humans live their entire lives and die without ever rising above the level of arduous material existence. That would leave humans little time to seek out the understanding they needed to become spiritually free.

A common misinterpretation of the Adam and Eve story is that the "original sin" had something to do with sex or nudity. This confusion comes from that part of the story in which Adam and Eve eat from the "tree of knowledge of good and evil" and immediately become ashamed of their nakedness. It was not nudity, however, that shamed them. Adam and Eve were mortified by what their nakedness represented. Ancient Mesopotamian records depict human beings stark naked when performing tasks for their Custodial masters. Custodians, on the other hand, were depicted as being fully clothed. The implication is that Adam and Eve felt degraded by their nakedness because it was a sign of their enslavement—not because being naked in itself is bad.

As we have seen, early humans were reported to be a constant headache to their Custodial masters. The slave creatures not only disobeyed their rulers, they often banded together and rebelled. This made human unity undesirable to Earth's Custodial rulers—it was better that humans be disunited. One of the ways in which the problem of human unity was solved is described in the Biblical story of the Tower of Babel—a tale which also has its roots in early Mesopotamian writings.

According to the Bible, this is what happened after the Great Flood:

*And the whole earth spoke one language, and used the same words.*

*And it came to pass, as they migrated from the east, that they found a plain in the land of Sh'-nar [Babylonia: a region in Mesopotamia] and settled there.*

*. . .*

*And they said, Come on, let us build ourselves a city and a tower, whose top will reach the skies; and let us make a name for ourselves, otherwise we will be scattered all over the face of the earth.*

*And the Lord came down to see the city and the tower, which the men were building.*

*And the Lord said, Look, the people are united, and they have all one language; and this they begin to do; and now nothing will stop them from doing what they take in their minds to do.*

*Come on, let us go down, and there confuse their language so that they cannot understand one another's speech.*

*So the Lord scattered them abroad from there all over the face of the earth: and they stopped building the city.*

*Therefore the name of it is called Babel: because the Lord did there confuse the language of the entire earth: and from there did the Lord scatter them abroad over the face of the whole Earth.*

GENESIS 11:1-9

In *The Twelfth Planet,* Mr. Sitchin offers an intriguing analysis of the Tower of Babel story. According to his research, the word "name" in the above passage ("let us make a *name* for ourselves") was a translation of the ancient word *shem*. The Bible's translation of *shem* may be in error, says Mr. Sitchin, because *shem* comes from the root word *shamah,* which means "that which is highward." Ancient shems are the obelisk monuments that were so prevalent in many ancient societies. Those shems, or obelisks, were copied after the rocket-shaped vehicles in which the Custodial "gods" were said to fly. Mr. Sitchin therefore believes that the word *shem* in Mesopotamian texts should be translated to "sky vehicle," meaning rocketship. When this translation is placed into the above Biblical passage, we find that the ancient Babylonians were not trying to make a name (*i.e.,* reputation) for themselves; they were trying to make a "sky vehicle" or rocket! The implication is that they wanted to match the technological might of their hated Custodial masters and thereby put an end to their enslavement. The tower itself may have been intended as the launching pad for a human *shem*.

If Mr. Sitchin's provocative analysis is accurate, we would better understand why the Custodial entities became so alarmed by the Tower of Babel and felt such a compelling need to thoroughly disunite the human race.

Ancient stories and legends from other parts of the world indirectly support the Tower of Babel story. The Japanese people, Alaskan Eskimos, South Americans, and Egyptians all have traditions stating that their earliest forefathers had either been transported by humanlike "gods" to where the modern descendants live today, or that those "gods" had been the source of the local languages or writing.

It may be difficult to accept Mesopotamian and Biblical statements that ancient human society had been split apart thousands of years ago in a "divide and conquer" effort by flying extraterrestrials, even though the "divide and conquer" technique is frequently used by military and political leaders on Earth during wartime. Interestingly, using the technique was advocated a number of years ago by a distinguished Yale professor if Earth should ever colonize other planets. The good professor suggested that Earth could control another inhabited planet by pitting one native group against another.

If we compare ancient and modern ideas about how mankind came into existence, we find two very different versions. The ancient version is that an extraterrestrial society had come to possess Earth and sought to exploit the planet's resources. To make the exploitation easier, a work race was created: *Homo sapiens*. Humans were treated as livestock and were frequently butchered when they became too numerous or troublesome. To preserve *Homo sapiens* as a slave race and to prevent future rebellion, spiritual knowledge was repressed, human beings were scattered geographically into different linguistic groups, and conditions were created to make physical survival on Earth an all-consuming chore from birth until death. This arrangement was to be maintained indefinitely for as long as the Custodial society possessed Earth. In contrast, the modern view is that human beings had evolved accidentally from "star stuff" into slime, into fishes, into monkeys, and finally into people. The modern view actually seems more fanciful than the ancient one.

In the story of Adam and Eve we noted the appearance of a snake. The serpent was said to be "God's" enemy, Satan, who had literally transformed himself into a reptile. The Bible suggests that snakes are feared and disliked today because of Satan's alleged transformation back in the Garden of Eden. However, it should be remembered that the Biblical Adam and Eve story is entirely symbolic. The snake, too, was a symbol, not an actual reptile.

To determine what the Biblical snake represented, we must go back once again to older pre-Biblical sources. When we do so, we discover that the snake symbol had two very important meanings in the ancient world: it was associated with the Custodial "god" Ea, reputed creator and benefactor of mankind, and it also represented an influential organization with which Ea was associated.

# 5

# Brotherhood
# of the Snake

OF ALL THE animals revered in ancient human societies, none were as prominent or as important as the snake. The snake was the logo of a group which had become very influential in early human societies of both Hemispheres. That group was a disciplined Brotherhood dedicated to the dissemination of spiritual knowledge and the attainment of spiritual freedom. This Brotherhood of the Snake (also known as the "Brotherhood of the Serpent," but which I will often refer to as simply the "Brotherhood") opposed the enslavement of spiritual beings and, according to Egyptian writings, it sought to liberate the human race from Custodial bondage.* The Brotherhood also imparted scientific knowl-

---

* Because Brotherhood teachings included physical healing through spiritual means, the snake also came to symbolize physical healing. Today the snake is featured on the logo of the American Medical Association.

edge and encouraged the high aesthetics that existed in many ancient societies. For these and other reasons, the snake had become a venerated symbol to humans and, according to Egyptian and biblical texts, an object of Custodial hatred.

When we look to discover who founded the Brotherhood, Mesopotamian texts point right back to that rebellious "god," Prince Ea. Ancient Mesopotamian tablets relate that Ea and his father, Anu, possessed profound ethical and spiritual knowledge. This was the same knowledge that was later symbolized as trees in the Biblical Adam and Eve story. In fact, the Biblical tree symbol came from pre-Biblical Mesopotamian works, such as one showing a snake wrapped around the trunk of a tree, identical to later portrayals of the snake in Eden. From the tree in the Mesopotamian depiction hang two pieces of fruit. To the right of the tree is the half-moon symbol of Ea; to the left is the planet symbol of Anu. The drawing indicates that Ea and Anu were associated with the snake and its teachings. This connection is affirmed by other Mesopotamian texts which describe Anu's palace in the "heavens" as being guarded by a god of the Tree of Truth and a god of the Tree of Life. In one instance, Ea reportedly sent a human to be educated in that very knowledge:

> Adapa [the name of an early man], thou art going before Anu, the King;
> The road to Heaven thou wilt take.
> When to Heaven thou has ascended, and hast approached the gate of Anu, the "Bearer of Life" and the "Grower of Truth" at the gate of Anu will be standing.[1]

We therefore find Ea designated as the reputed culprit who tried to teach early man (Adam) the way to spiritual freedom. This suggests that Ea intended his creation, *Homo sapiens,* to be suited for Earth labor, but at some point he changed his mind about using spiritual enslavement as a means. If Ea was a true historical personality as the Sumerians claimed, then he was the probable leader of the Brotherhood at its founding on Earth. The Brotherhood may have adopted the snake as its logo because Ea's first home on Earth was said to have been constructed by a serpent-infested swampland which Ea called Snake Marsh. Another possible explanation for the snake logo is offered by Mr. Sitchin who says that the biblical word for "snake" is *nahash,* which comes from the root word NHSH, meaning "to decipher, to find out."

Despite all of their reported good intentions, the legendary Ea and early Brotherhood clearly failed to free the human race. Ancient Mesopotamian, Egyptian, and biblical texts relate that the "snake" was quickly defeated by other Custodial factions. The Bible informs us that the serpent in the Garden of Eden was overcome before it was able to complete its mission and give Adam and Eve the "fruit" from the second "tree." Ea (who was also symbolized as a snake) was banished to Earth and was extensively villainized by his opponents to ensure that he could never again secure a widespread following among human beings. Ea's title was changed from "Prince of Earth" to "Prince of Darkness." He was labeled other horrible epithets: Satan, the Devil, Evil Incarnate, Monarch of Hell, Lord of Vermin, Prince of Liars, and more. He was portrayed as the mortal enemy of a Supreme Being and as the keeper of Hell. People were taught that his only intentions were to spiritually enslave everyone and that everything bad on Earth was caused by him. Humans were encouraged to detect him in all of his future lives ("incarnations") and to destroy him and his creations whenever he was discovered. All beliefs and practices named after his various appellations ("Satanism," "Devil Worship," etc.) were to be made so horrific and degrading that no right-thinking person would (or should) have anything to do with them. He and his followers were to be viewed by human beings with nothing but the utmost loathing.

This is not to say that Ea was actually portrayed by ancient Sumerians as a saint. He was not. He was described in Mesopotamian texts with distinct character flaws. If Ea was a real person, then he appears to have been a genius who could get things done, but who was often careless about anticipating the consequences of how he went about accomplishing his goals. By engineering a work race *(Homo sapiens)*, Ea wound up giving his enemies a powerful tool of spiritual repression. Ea then appears to have compounded the blunder by founding and/or empowering the early Snake Brotherhood which, after its reported defeat, continued to remain a powerful force in human affairs, but under the domination of the very Custodial factions that Ea and the original Brotherhood were said to have opposed. History indicates that the Brotherhood was turned under its new Custodial "gods" into a chilling weapon of spiritual repression and betrayal, despite the efforts of many sincere humanitarians to bring about true spiritual reform through Brotherhood channels all the way up until today. By reportedly creating a work race and the Brotherhood of the Snake, the "god" Ea had helped build a trap for billions of spiritual beings on Earth.

As we shall now begin to carefully document, the Brotherhood of the Snake has been the world's most effective tool for preserving mankind's status as a spiritually ignorant creature of toil throughout all of history. During all of that time, and continuing today, the Brotherhood and its network of organizations have remained intimately tied to the UFO phenomenon. This corruption of the Brotherhood, and the overwhelming effect it would have on human society, was already apparent by the year 2000 B.C. in ancient Egypt— the next stop on our journey.

# 6

# The Pyramid Builders

PERHAPS THE MOST impressive and controversial relics to come out of ancient times are the pyramids of Egypt. The remains of at least seventy to eighty of those structures are scattered all along the upper Nile region as silent reminders of a once powerful civilization.

The largest and most famous Egyptian pyramid is the Pyramid of Cheops (the "Great Pyramid"). It stands today beside several others on an elevated plateau in Gizeh, Egypt. The dimensions of this pyramid are impressive. It towers nearly five hundred feet high and covers thirteen acres of land at its base. Built of stones weighing an average of 2½ tons each, the entire structure is estimated to weigh 5,273,834 tons.

A remarkable characteristic which makes the Great Pyramid one of the "Seven Wonders of the Ancient World" is the precision of its construction. The stones of the pyramid were cut so perfectly that a sheet of paper cannot be inserted between the blocks in many places. This precision, coupled with the enormous bulk of the structure, helps account for the pyramid's long life and durability. The pyramid was built to last.

Perhaps the greatest mystery surrounding the Great Pyramid was its purpose. Most pyramids are thought to have been burial tombs. History tells us that the Great Pyramid was employed for other purposes, as well. For example, some of its inner chambers had been used for mystical and religious rites. Yet a third and infinitely more practical use can also be found:

The Great Pyramid is an excellent marker for aerial navigation.

The four sides of the Great Pyramid precisely face the four compass points: north, south, east and west. The sides are directed so exactly that the widest deviation is only one twelfth of a degree on the east side. In addition, the Great Pyramid is situated less than five miles south of the northern thirtieth parallel. The Great Pyramid can therefore be used as a reference point for sectioning the entire planet into a three-dimensional grid of 30-, 60-, and 90-degree angles with the North Pole, South Pole, Equator and center of the earth as reference points. This feature is especially useful because the Great Pyramid is located at the center of the Earth's land masses. Knowing only the dimensions of the Earth and having a method of calculating how far one has traveled, one can very effectively navigate, especially by air, from the Great Pyramid to any point on Earth using the 30-60-90 degree grids and the compass directions indicated by the pyramid. The only deviation comes from the fact that the Earth is not a perfect sphere, but is slightly flattened at the poles and widened at the Equator. However, this deviation is so slight, amounting to only 26.7 miles (.0003367 or the fraction 1/298), that it is easily compensated for. Interestingly, when the Great Pyramid was first built, it was even more valuable as an aerial navigation marker than it is today because it had been covered with a casing of fine white limestone.

The limestone blocks were carved so precisely that the pyramid looked from a distance as though it had been hewn from a single white rock. The limestone reflected the sun, making the pyramid visible from a much greater distance.*

The unique characteristics of the pyramids at Gizeh raise interesting questions about those monuments. Since they serve an aerial navigation function so well, were they built at least partially for that purpose? If they were, who could have possibly had use for them in 2000 B.C.? A possible clue to the riddle may lie on the moon.

On November 22, 1966, the *Washington Post* ran a front-page headline proclaiming: "Six Mysterious Statuesque Shadows Photographed on the Moon by Orbiter." The *Post* story, which was picked up later by the *Los Angeles Times,* described a lunar photograph snapped two days earlier by U.S. space probe Orbiter 2 as it passed twenty to thirty miles above the moon's surface. The photograph seems to reveal six spires arranged in a purposeful geometrical pattern inside a small portion of the Sea of Tranquility. The pointedness of the lunar objects' shadows indicates that they are all either cone- or pyramid-shaped. Although the official NASA press release mentioned nothing unusual about the photograph, other people found the picture remarkable. Dr. William Blair of the Boeing Institute of Biotechnology stated:

If the cuspids [cone-shaped spires] really were the result of some geophysical event it would be natural to expect to see them distributed at random. As a result, the triangulation would be scalene [three unequal sides] or irregular, whereas those concerning the lunar object lead to a basilary system, with coordinate x, y, z to the right angle, six isosceles triangles and two axes consisting of three points each.[1]

---

* Most of the limestone is gone today. Except for a few blocks found at the base of the Great Pyramid, the limestone casing had been excavated away from the pyramids beginning in the first millennium A.D.

In *Argosy* magazine, Soviet space engineer Alexander Abromov went a step further by stating:

> The distribution of these lunar objects is similar to the plan of the Egyptian pyramids constructed by Pharaohs Cheops, Chephren, and Menkaura at Gizeh, near Cairo. The centers of the spires of this lunar "abaka" [arrangement of pyramids] are arranged in precisely the same way as the apices [tips] of the three great pyramids.[2]

Assuming Drs. Blair and Abromov have not grievously miscalculated, it appears that some of the pyramids of Earth may be part of a permanent marking system that extends to more than one planet of our solar system. The system may even extend to Mars. Pyramidlike objects have been photographed on the Martian surface. Pictures snapped by the U.S. Viking mission in 1976 show the Martian region of Cydonia to contain possible pyramidlike objects and what appears to be a huge sculpted face nearby staring skyward. It is easy to argue that the Martian pyramids and face are natural formations not unlike some found on Earth; however, one, and possibly two, other "faces" have been discovered elsewhere on Mars with strikingly similar features, such as the "helmet," cheek notches, and indentation above the right eye.* Perhaps equally interesting is the fact that one pyramid in Cydonia has a side pointing due north towards the Martian spin axis. Is this alignment chance, or is there a connection to the Great Pyramid at Gizeh which is also aligned according to precise compass directions?

It is, of course, possible that the objects on the moon and Mars will prove to be rock formations after all. Available photographs seem inadequate to establish the formations as

---

* For an interesting scientific evaluation of the Martian objects, I recommend *Unusual Martian Surface Features* by Vincent DiPietro, Greg Molenaar, and John Brandenburg. It is published by Mars Research. Please see bibliography for address.

artificial. If they are artificial, it is clear from the photographs that they have undergone a fair degree of erosion. Only a closer look during future missions to the moon and Mars will resolve the controversy. The objects are certainly worth closer investigation because the moon has hosted UFO phenomena for centuries, including inside the Sea of Tranquility.[3]

Even if the Martian or lunar objects prove to be natural formations, that would not change the clearly artificial nature of Earth's pyramids. This compels us to return our focus to the pyramids of Egypt. For whom did the ancient Egyptians say they were building their magnificent structures?

Like the ancient Mesopotamians, the early ancient Egyptians claimed to be living under the rule of humanlike extraterrestrial "gods." The Egyptians wrote that their "gods" traveled into the heavens in flying "boats." (These "boats" were later mythologized to explain the movement of the sun.) The "gods" of Egypt's early period were said to be literal flesh-and-blood creatures with the same needs for food and shelter as human beings. Actual homes had been built for them. Those homes were furnished with human servants who later became Egypt's first priests. According to renowned historian James Henry Breasted, the earliest servants of the "gods" were laymen who performed their duties without ceremony or ritual. Their jobs consisted simply of providing the "gods" with ". . . those things which formed the necessities and luxuries of an Egyptian of wealth and rank at that time: plentiful food and drink, fine clothing, music and dance."*

Many people identify ancient Egyptian religion with the worship of animals. This type of veneration was unknown during the early period of the Egyptian civilization. According to Professor Breasted:

---

* An interesting compilation of unusual lunar phenomena is found in NASA Technical Report R-277 entitled "Chronological Catalog of Reported Lunar Events" by Barbara M. Middlehurst. It briefly lists 579 unusual lunar sightings considered to be reliable beginning in the year 1540 and ending in 1967. It is currently available from The Sourcebook Project.

... the hawk, for example, was the sacred animal of the sun-god, and as such a living hawk might have a place in the temple, where he was fed and kindly treated, as any such pet might be; but he was not worshipped, nor was he the object of an elaborate ritual as later.[4]

The records of ancient Egypt have given us many clues as to who might have had use for a permanent marking system to navigate various planets of our solar system: the Custodial society. The first pyramid of Egypt was designed by Imhotep, Prime Minister to Egyptian king Zoser-Neterkhet. Imhotep was said to be the son of Egypt's most important Custodial "god" during his day: Ptah. Egyptian lore written after Imhotep's time adds that Imhotep had received the pyramid design in a plan "which descended to him from heaven to the north of Memphis [a city in ancient Egypt]."[5] The Great Pyramid at Gizeh, which was built several generations later during the "Age of the Pyramids," was constructed according to the methods established by Imhotep. It was during the Age of the Pyramids, which began around 2760 B.C., that worship of the humanlike "gods" reached its height; more than 2000 gods then existed. It was for their "gods" that the Egyptians had ultimately built their most important pyramids. The many pyramids built after those at Gizeh are generally inferior and are viewed as imitations.

Some theorists believe that the "ancient astronauts" of Egypt had used their space age technology to lift stones and to otherwise assist in the construction of the Gizeh pyramids. This hypothesis is neither certain nor necessary to sustain the "ancient astronaut" theory. Egyptian records tend to support the idea that human labor had provided the primary muscle for the pyramids' construction. This would have been in keeping with the Mesopotamian contention that *Homo sapiens* had been created to be a labor pool for the Custodial "gods."

It is hardly surprising that the pharaohs and priests who acted on behalf of the "gods" were often immensely unpopular with the Egyptian people. The Old Kingdom (ca. 2685-2180 B.C.) was followed by a period of weakness and unrest. Even the Great Pyramid of Cheops had been broken into by unhappy Egyptians. According to historian Ahmed Fakhry:

> The Egyptians so hated the builders of the pyramids that they threatened to enter these great tombs and destroy the mummies of the kings.[6]

Such intense loathing is certainly not surprising. In order to get the great pyramids built, Egyptian society was made more repressive in order to make human labor operate with greater machinelike efficiency. Occupations became rigid so that it was difficult to move from one type of job to another. Laymen ceased to serve the "gods": an impenetrable priesthood was erected instead. Personal happiness and achievement were sacrificed in the name of labor productivity. Feudalism had arrived in Egypt.

As the pharaohs were busy helping to make slaves out of their fellow humans, the "gods" were making fools out of the pharaohs. Imhotep, reputed son of the "god" Ptah, instituted the concept of the pharaoh as "God-King." This elitist title was little appreciated by most Egyptians. As "God-Kings," the pharaohs were made to think that they were elevated above the toiling human multitudes. The pharaohs were taught that if they cooperated with Custodial plans, they would escape the human predicament by joining the "gods" in the heavens.

There was just one catch.

The pharaohs would be allowed to escape Earth only after they had died! Pharaohs were taught the silly idea that if they had their dead bodies carefully preserved, the bodies would be brought back to life and they could join the Custodial "gods" in the heavens. Some pharaohs, like Cheops, also buried large wooden boats near their tombs. According to some scholars, the pharaohs believed that their entombed boats ("solar barks") would be magically exhumed and endowed with the same power that caused the "boats" of the "gods" to fly. The pharaohs believed that they would be whisked away after death in their magically-powered wooden boats to the home of the "gods" in the heavens.

Although Egyptian preservation techniques were quite good, it is clear that the pharaohs' minds were being filled with nonsense. The wooden "solar barks" never flew. Few, if any, mummified bodies of the great God-Kings reached the heavens. Instead, many mummies have become macabre museum curiosities for the titillation of the human multitudes that the pharaohs so fervently hoped to escape. Other mummies suffered an even more humiliating fate: they were ground up and used as an ingredient in medicines. Pulverized mummies also became paint additives because of the preservatives used in the mummification process.

The puzzle is why the pharaohs believed the cruel joke which had been perpetrated on them. Some historians suggest that mummification was an attempt to imitate the life-cycle of the butterfly. Others believe that the pharaohs wanted to maintain their wealth and position in their next lifetimes and therefore desired to be resurrected in the same bodies. One UFO writer has suggested that they were striving to duplicate body preservation techniques used by Egypt's technologically-advanced "gods." Ancient Egyptian records, however, reveal an even more compelling reason why the pharaohs mummified themselves: spiritual knowledge had been twisted.

Ancient Egyptians believed in a "soul," or "self," as an entity completely separate from the "person" (meaning "body"). Egyptians labeled one such spiritual entity the "ka." The Egyptians believed that the "ka," not the body, was one of the spiritual entities that constituted the true person and that the body itself had no personality or intelligence without a spiritual entity. This generally enlightened view was given a false twist, however. The Egyptians were made to believe that the spiritual well of the "ka" after death depended upon the "ka" maintaining contact with a physical body. According to historian Fakhry:

The Egyptian wanted his Ka to be able to recognize its body after death and to be united with it; for this reason he felt that it was very important to have his body preserved. This is why the Egyptians mummified their bodies and excelled in embalming them.[7]

The pharaohs went even a step further. Mr. Fakhry explains:

The Egyptians also made statues and placed them in tombs and temples to act as substitutes for the body if it should perish.[8]

These practices had a devastating impact on spiritual understanding. They caused people to wrongly equate spiritual wholeness with spiritual attachment to human bodies (or to body substitutes). Such teachings encouraged humans to accept the Custodial intention to permanently join spiritual beings to *Homo sapiens* bodies. The powerful human drives for spiritual integrity and immortality were twisted into an obsessive quest to preserve bodies. Philosophies of materialism were thereby hastened. Materialism, by one of its definitions, is the overpreoccupation with things at the material level and neglecting important aspects of ethical and spiritual existence. This often leads to the second definition of materialism: the belief that everything, including thought and emotion, can be explained entirely by movements and changes in physical matter. Although the Egyptians had not embraced the latter definition as a philosophy of life, they had helped move the world a step in that direction.

The derailment of spiritual knowledge in Egypt was caused by the corruption of the Brotherhood of the Snake, to which the pharaohs and priests belonged. As mentioned earlier, after its reported defeat thousands of years ago by its Custodial enemies, the Brotherhood continued to remain dominant in human affairs, but at the cost of becoming a Custodial tool. To understand how the corrupted Brotherhood began to distort spiritual truth and perpetuate theological irrationality, we must first look at the early inner workings of the Brotherhood and its method of teaching.

The original uncorrupted Brotherhood engaged in a pragmatic program of spiritual education. The organization's approach was scientific, not mystical or ceremonial. The subject of the spirit was considered to be as knowable as any other science. It seems that the Brotherhood possessed a considerable body of accurate spiritual data, but it had not succeeded in developing a complete route to spiritual freedom prior to its defeat.

Brotherhood teachings were arranged as a step-by-step process. A student was required to satisfactorily complete one level of instruction before proceding to the next one. All pupils took oaths of secrecy in which they swore never to reveal the teachings of a level to any person who had not yet graduated up to that level. This style of instruction was designed to ensure that a student did not prematurely attempt difficult spiritual feats or become overwhelmed by advanced level information before he was ready for it, in the same way that one does not take a student driver on treacherous mountain roads before the student successfully navigates easier, but increasingly difficult, highways first.

Imparting spiritual knowledge in this fashion will be effective as long as the levels are ultimately open to everyone. When arbitrary or blanket restrictions are placed on who may have access to the teachings, either through overregulation, elitism, or by setting near-impossible conditions for admittance, the system of confidential step-by-step levels changes from an educational tool into an instrument of spiritual repression. The Brotherhood underwent just such a change.

The teachings of the Brotherhood in ancient Egypt were organized into an institution known as the "Mystery Schools." The Schools furnished the pharaohs and priests with most of their scientific, moral, and spiritual education. According to Dr. H. Spencer Lewis, founder of the Rosicrucian Order headquartered in San

Jose, California,* the first temple built for use by the Mystery Schools was erected by Pharaoh Cheops. Inside those temple walls, spiritual knowledge underwent the deterioration which caused pharaohs to mummify their bodies and bury wooden boats. According to old Egyptian lore, the distorted teachings of the Mystery Schools were created by the "great teacher," Ra, an important Custodial "god."

The Mystery Schools not only twisted spiritual knowledge, they greatly restricted public access to any theological truths still surviving. Only the pharaohs, priests, and a few others deemed worthy were accepted into the Schools. Initiates were required to take solemn vows never to reveal to any outsiders the "secret wisdom" they were taught; students were threatened with dire consequences if they broke the vow. These restrictions were reportedly established to prevent misuse of high-level knowledge by those who might degrade that knowledge or use it harmfully. While this is a legitimate reason to develop safeguards, the restrictions imposed by the Mystery Schools went far beyond simple security. Entire social and occupational groups were denied membership. The vast majority of the human population had no hope of entering the Schools; their access to any

---

* Rosicrucianism is one of the mystical systems which arose out of Brotherhood teachings. Dr. Lewis's Rosicrucian Order is called The Ancient and Mystical Order Rosae Crucis ("AMORC" for brevity). AMORC was founded in the early 1900's. It is best known today for the popular Egyptian Museum it owns and operates in San Jose, California.

There is another American Rosicrucian order headquartered in Quakertown, Pennsylvania. It is called the Fraternity of the Rosy Cross, or The Rosicrucian Fraternity in America. The Rosicrucian Fraternity in Quakertown does not recognize AMORC as a valid Rosicrucian body. In the 1930's and 1940's, R. Swinburne Clymer, Supreme Grand Master of the Rosicrucian Fraternity in Quakertown, published a number of writings denouncing AMORC. Dr. Clymer and Dr. Lewis have each claimed that his organization is the true Rosicrucian system.

In this book, I have utilized the extensive historical research of both Dr. Clymer and Dr. Lewis. When I cite either of them by name as a source of historical information, I am not taking sides in their controversy.

surviving spiritual knowledge was therefore severely limited. The Biblical "revolving sword" preventing access to the "tree of knowledge" was being put into place by those who ran the Mystery Schools.

The Mystery Schools caused spiritual knowledge to evaporate in another way. The Schools forbade its members from physically recording the Schools' most advanced teachings. Initiates were required to relay the information orally. There is no faster way to lose knowledge than to forbid its being written down. No matter how sincere and well-trained people may be, word-of-mouth will invariably result in changes to the ideas being relayed. With a word substituted here and a sentence omitted there, the semantic precision needed to communicate an exact scientific principle will be lost. This is one way that a functional science can quickly degrade into an untenable superstition.

As time went on, the Brotherhood became so restrictive that it excluded most of Egypt's own priests from membership. This was especially true during the reign of King Thutmose III, who ruled about 1200 years after Cheops. Thutmose III is best known for his military adventures which expanded the Egyptian empire to its greatest size. According to Dr. Lewis, Thutmose III took the final step of transforming the Brotherhood into a completely closed order. He established rules and regulations reportedly still used by some Brotherhood organizations today.

Changes in the Brotherhood continued. Less than one hundred years after the reign of Thutmose III, his descendant, King Akhnaton (Amenhotep IV), spent the last year of his 28-year life transforming Brotherhood teachings into mystical symbols. Akhnaton's symbols were intentionally designed to be incomprehensible to everyone except those Brotherhood members who were taught the symbols' secret meanings. The Brotherhood ostensibly created this new system of visual images to be a universal "language" of spiritual enlightenment transcending human languages, and to prevent misuse of knowledge. In real fact, the intention was to create a secret code designed to make spiritual knowledge unattainable to everyone except those admitted into the increasingly elite Brotherhood, and apparently to eventually obliterate spiritual knowledge altogether. The translation of spiritual data into bizarre and incomprehensible symbols has brought about the spectacle of honest people trying to decode garbled symbols in a quest for spiritual truths which can, and should be, communicated in everyday language understandable by anyone.

Despite the obvious sincerity of Akhnaton, we discover that the transformation of spiritual knowledge into a system of obscure symbols has had a devastating impact on human society. As this manner of relaying spiritual knowledge was disseminated throughout the world by members of the Brotherhood, all knowledge of a spiritual nature became misidentified with bizarre symbols and mystery. This misidentification is so strong today that almost all studies of the spirit and spiritual phenomena are lumped into such disgraced classifications as "occultism," "spiritualism," and witchcraft. The attempt thousands of years ago to keep spiritual knowledge out of the hands of the "profane" has almost entirely destroyed the credibility and utility of that knowledge. Brotherhood symbolism was another piece of the Biblical "revolving sword" blocking human access to spiritual knowledge. It has left only the confusion, ignorance and superstition which have come to characterize so much of the field today.

Akhnaton presided over another important development in the Brotherhood. Although the young ruler had fared poorly as a political leader, he achieved everlasting fame for his efforts to champion the cause of monotheism, *i.e.*, the worship of a "one only" God. Monotheism was a Brotherhood teaching and many historians cite Akhnaton as the first important historical figure to broadly promulgate the concept.

To aid in the establishment of the Brotherhood's new monotheism, Akhnaton moved the capital of Egypt to the city of El Amarna. He also relocated the main temple of the Brotherhood there. When the Egyptian capital was moved back to its original situs, the Brotherhood remained in El Amarna. This signaled an important break between Egypt's established priesthood, which resisted Akhnaton's monotheism, and the highly exclusive Brotherhood which no longer admitted most priests to membership.

The ancient Egyptian empire eventually decayed and vanished. The Brotherhood of the Snake fared much better. It survived and expanded by sending out from Egypt missionaries and conquerors who established Brotherhood branches and offshoots throughout the civilized world. These Brotherhood emissaries widely disseminated the Brotherhood's new "one God" religion and eventually made it the dominant theology throughout the world.

In addition to launching "one God" theology, the Snake Brotherhood created many of the symbols and regalia still used by some important monotheistic religions today. For example, the Brotherhood temple in El Amarna was constructed in the shape of a cross—a symbol later adopted by the Brotherhood's most famous offshoot: Christianity. Some Brotherhood members in Egypt wore the same special outfits with a "cord at the loin" and a covering for the head as later used by Christian monks. The chief priest of the Egyptian temple wore the same type of broad-sleeved gown used today by clergymen and choir singers. The chief priest also shaved his head in a small round spot at the top—an act later adopted by Christian friars.

Many theologians hail monotheism as an important religious breakthrough. Worshipping a spiritual "one-only God" is indeed an improvement over the idolization of stone statues and clumsy animals. Unfortunately, Brotherhood monotheism still did not represent a return to complete accuracy; it simply added new distortions to whatever spiritual knowledge still remained.

Based upon what we are coming to know about the nature of the spiritual being, we find that two false twists appear to lay in the Brotherhood's definition of a Supreme Being:

Firstly, Brotherhood monotheisms, which include Judaism, Christianity, and Islam, teach that a Supreme Being was the creator of the physical universe and of the physical life forms within the universe. In an upcoming chapter we will discuss the likelihood that *spiritual* beings were born of a Supreme Being of some sort, but *physical* creatures and objects probably were not. As some other religions have noted, if our universe is the product of spiritual activity, then it appears that all individual spiritual beings within the universe are responsible for its creation and/or perpetuation. The scope of a Supreme Being would actually extend far beyond the creation of a single universe.

Secondly, a Supreme Being is usually portrayed as a spiritual being capable of possibly unlimited thought, creativity, and ability. A Supreme Being is said to be an entity which can make and unmake universes. The big question is this:

Why must we be limited to only one such being?

Is there any reason not to suppose the existence of ten such beings? Or a hundred? Or an almost infinite number? It appears that the Brotherhood definition of a "one God" actually describes the native potential of *every* spiritual being, including those spiritual beings who animate human bodies on Earth. The true nature and capabilities of every spiritual being would therefore be hidden by doctrines which state that only a Supreme Being may enjoy pure spiritual existence and unlimited spiritual potential. Brotherhood monotheism would actually hinder human spiritual recovery and prevent people from grasping the true, and probably much broader, scope of a Supreme Being.*

Brotherhood monotheism was another piece of the Biblical "revolving sword" to prevent access to spiritual knowledge. It also allowed the Custodians to greatly elevate their own status. *As part of its new monotheism, the Brotherhood began to teach the fiction that members of the Custodial race were the physical manifestations of a Supreme Being.* In other words, Custodians started pretending that they and their aircraft were the "one-only God." History records that they used extraordinary violence to make *Homo sapiens* believe the falsehood. Few lies have had as devastating an impact on human society, yet it became a prime mission of the corrupted Brotherhood, from the time of Akhnaton to the modern day, to make humans believe that the Custodians and their aircraft were "God." The purpose of this fiction was to enforce human obedience and to maintain

---

* A fuller discussion of the possible nature of a Supreme Being and its relationship to individual spiritual existence is presented in Chapter 40.

Custodial control over the human population. In no case is this clearer, or the results more visibly tragic, than in the Biblical story of the ancient Hebrews and their "one God" named Jehovah.

# 7

# Jehovah

MUCH OF THE Old Testament is devoted to describing the origins and early history of the Hebrew people. According to the Bible, the Hebrews descended from a clan which lived in the Sumerian city of Ur around 2000 to 1500 B.C. The clan was befriended and ruled by a personality named Jehovah. The Bible claims that Jehovah was God.

According to the Biblical narrative, Jehovah encouraged the clan to leave Ur and settle in Haran—a caravan center in northeastern Mesopotamia. There, Jehovah later told the clan's new patriarch, Abraham, to lead his tribe on a migration towards Egypt. The tribe complied, and over the ensuing generations it slowly made its way through Canaan towards the Nile River. Starvation finally forced the tribe to enter the Egyptian region of Goshen where the Hebrews at first lived well under the pharaoh, but upon the coming of a new king to the Egyptian throne, the Hebrews were forced into slavery.

The Bible states that after four hundred years of servitude in Egypt, the Hebrews were led on an exodus out of Egypt by Moses under the watchful eye of Jehovah. By that time, the Hebrews numbered in the hundreds of thousands. After a long trek and many bloody battles, the Hebrew tribes returned to and conquered Canaan, which was the "Promised Land" pledged to them centuries earlier by Jehovah.

And so, according to the Bible, was born the Jewish religion.

Jehovah was clearly an important character in this Biblical story. Who was he? Was Jehovah God, as the Bible alleges? Was he a myth, as skeptics with a secular orientation would have us believe? Jehovah appears to have been neither.

The name Jehovah comes from the Hebrew word "Yahweh," meaning "he that is" or "the self-evident." This appellation conveys the idea that the Biblical Jehovah was a pure spiritual being; a true Supreme Being, if you will. But was he?

Old Testament descriptions of Jehovah have provided a field day for UFO writers, and for good reason. Jehovah travelled through the sky in what appears to have been a noisy, smoking aircraft. A Biblical description of Jehovah landing on a mountaintop describes him this way:

> . . . *there were thunders and lightnings, and a thick cloud upon the mount, and the sound of the trumpet was exceedingly loud;\* and all of the people that were in the camp trembled.*
>
> *And Moses brought the people out of the camp to meet with God; and they stood at the lower part of the mountain.*
>
> *And Mount Sinai was altogether covered with smoke, because the Lord descended upon it in fire: and the smoke from the fire billowed upwards like the smoke of a furnace, and the whole mountain quaked greatly.*
>
> GENESIS 19:16-19

---

\* A trumpet-like sound accompanied many appearances of Jehovah.

If an ancient Hebrew were to observe the rumbling, smoke, and flame of a modern rocketship, the description would not have been much different than this Biblical narrative of Jehovah. A later visit by Jehovah contained the same phenomena:

> *And all the people saw the thunderings, and the lightnings, and the noise of the trumpet, and the mountain smoking: and when the people saw it, they moved away and stood far off.*
>
> GENESIS 20:18

Lest it be assumed that these descriptions might be of a volcano, further sightings reveal that Jehovah was a moving object:

> *And the Lord travelled before them [the Hebrew tribes] by day in a pillar of cloud, to lead them the way; by night in a pillar of fire, to give them light; to go by day and night:*
>
> *He took not away the pillar of the cloud by day, or the pillar of fire by night, from in front of the people.*
>
> EXODUS 13:21-22

*Exodus* 14:24, 40:34-38, and *Numbers* 19:1-23 contain identical descriptions of Jehovah as he led the Hebrew tribes to the Promised Land.

The ancient Hebrew eyewitnesses responsible for the above descriptions were not able to get a closer look at Jehovah. The Bible points out that no one was permitted to approach Jehovah's mountaintop landing sites except Moses and a few select leaders. Jehovah had threatened to kill anyone else who tried. The early Bible therefore contains only descriptions of Jehovah as eyewitnesses saw him from a distance. It was not until much later that one of the Bible's most famous prophets, Ezekiel, was able to get a closer look and describe Jehovah in greater detail. Ezekiel's description is probably the most often-quoted Biblical passage in UFO

literature. Ezekiel's detailed account of strange aerial objects
has created speculation of such intensity that even one Bible
publisher, Tyndale House, prefaced its introduction to the
*Book of Ezekiel* with the title, "Dry Bones and Flying
Saucers?". At the risk of boring some readers with yet
another repetition of Ezekiel's famous words, I reproduce
them here for the benefit of those who are not familiar
with them:

> *Now it occurred in my thirtieth year, in the fourth
> month, as I was among the captives by the river of
> Chebar, that the heavens were opened, and I saw
> visions of God.*
> . . .
> *And I looked, and behold, a whirlwind came out of
> the north, a great cloud, and a fire flashed, causing a
> brightness about it, and out of the midst of it gleamed
> something like a pale yellow metal.*
> *Also out of the midst of it appeared four living crea-
> tures. And this was their appearance: they had the
> likeness of men.*
> . . .
> *And their feet were straight feet; and the sole of their
> feet was shaped like the sole of a calf's foot; and they
> sparkled like burnished brass.*
> *And they had human hands under their four-sided
> wings.*
> *Their wings were joined together; and they did not
> turn when they went, they all went straight forward.*
> *As for the appearance of their faces, they had the face
> of a man, and the face of a lion on the right side: and
> they had the face of an ox on the left side: they also
> had the face of an eagle.*
> . . .
> *In amongst the living creatures glowed something like
> coals of fire or lamps, which moved up and down
> between the creatures: and the fire was bright, and
> from out of the fire flashed lightning.*
> *And the living creatures ran and returned by flashes
> of lightning.*

*Now as I looked upon the living creatures, I saw four wheels upon the ground, one by each of the living creatures, with their four faces.*

*The appearance of the wheels and their composition was like the color of shiny amber: and all four wheels had one likeness: and their appearance and their composition was like a wheel in the middle of a wheel.*

. . .

*And when the living creatures went, the wheels went with them: and when the living creatures were lifted up from the earth, the wheels were lifted up.*

. . .

*And the appearance of the sky upon the heads of the living creature was reflected as the color of the terrible crystal stretched over their heads above.*

. . .

*And when they went, I heard the noise of their wings, like the noise of great waters, as the voice of the Almighty, like the din of an army. When they stood still, they lowered their wings.*

*And there was a voice from the crystal covering that was over their heads when they stood and had let down their wings.*

EZEKIEL 1:1-25

The voice told Ezekiel that it was the "Lord God." *(Ezekiel 2:4).*

The first portion of Ezekiel's vision resembles earlier Biblical descriptions of Jehovah: a moving fiery object in the sky emitting smoke. As the object moved closer, Ezekiel was able to observe that the thing was made of metal. Out of the metal object emerged several humanlike creatures, apparently wearing metal boots and ornamented helmets. Their "wings" appeared to be retractable engines which emitted a rumbling sound and helped the creatures to fly. Their heads were covered by glass or something transparent that reflected the sky above. They appeared to be in some sort of circular vehicle or a vehicle with wheels.

can safely conclude from the above passage that
"...ah" was not a Supreme Being. He appears to have
been a succession of Custodial management teams operating over a time span of many human generations. To
enforce human obedience, those teams used their aircraft
to perpetrate the lie that they were "God."

The Custodial teams known as "Jehovah" helped the
Brotherhood of the Snake embark on a program of conquest to spread the new "one God" religion. Moses, the
man chosen to command the Hebrew tribes on their exodus
out of Egypt to the Promised Land, was a high-ranking
member of the Brotherhood. One hint of this fact comes
from the Bible itself in which we are told how Moses was
raised as a child:

> In which time Moses was born, and was exceedingly
> fair, and was raised in his father's house for three
> months:
> And when he was cast out, Pharaoh's daughter took
> him up, and raised him as her own son.
> And Moses became learned in all the wisdom of the
> Egyptians, and was mighty in words and in deeds.
> THE ACTS 7:20-22

Egyptian historian and High Priest, Manetho (ca. 300
B.C.), states that Moses had received much of his education
in the Brotherhood under Akhnaton, the very pharaoh who
pioneered monotheism:

> Moses, a son of the tribe of Levi [one of the Hebrew
> tribes], educated in Egypt and initiated at Heliopolis
> [an Egyptian city], became a High Priest of the
> Brotherhood under the reign of Pharaoh Amenhotep
> [Akhnaton]. He was elected by the Hebrews as their
> chief and he adapted to the ideas of his people the
> science and philosophy which he had obtained in the
> Egyptian mysteries; proofs of this are to be found in the
> symbols, in the Initiations, and in his precepts and com-
> mandments. . . . The dogma of an "only God" which
> he taught was the Egyptian Brotherhood interpretation

and teaching of the Pharaoh who established the first monotheistic religion known to man. [1]*

Strong evidence in support of Manetho's statement is found in the early teachings of Judaism, which were deeply mystical and utilized many Brotherhood symbols. Many of those mystical teachings are still taught today in the Jewish Cabala: a secret religious philosophy of Jewish rabbis. The Cabala continues to utilize a complex array of mystical symbols. Modern Israel's national logo, the six-pointed Star of David, has been a Brotherhood symbol for thousands of years.

Early human writers often portrayed mankind's Custodial "gods" as bloodthirsty creatures prone to excessive violence. Sadly, those lamentable qualities did not improve with Jehovah. During the trek from Egypt to the Promised Land, Jehovah demanded unflagging obedience from the Hebrews. Many humans rebelled and Jehovah reacted with extreme cruelty. Jehovah reportedly killed up to 14,000 Hebrews at a time for disobedience. He used a variety of killing methods, such as spreading diseases, just as other Custodial "gods" had done earlier in Sumeria.

When the Hebrew armies reached Canaan, Jehovah displayed a genuinely psychopathic bent. To establish the Hebrews in their new homeland, Jehovah ordered the Hebrew armies to embark on a campaign of genocide to depopulate all of the region's existing cities and towns. Under the new leadership of a man named Joshua, the first city to fall in Jehovah's seven-year holocaust

---

* This passage raises the question of when the Jewish exodus from Egypt had occurred. If Moses was a High Priest of the Brotherhood under Akhnaton, as Manetho states, but did not lead the exodus until the reign of Rameses II, as many historians believe, then Moses must have been an extremely old man at the time of the exodus. (Rameses II did not rule until almost one hundred years after Akhnaton.) The Bible, in *Deuteronomy* 34:7, states that Moses was 120 years old when he died. Claims of such advanced age may be difficult to accept in our modern day, but if it is true about Moses, then both Manetho and modern scholars would be correct in their datings.

was Jericho. According to the Bible, the Hebrew army, numbering in the tens of thousands, slaughtered everyone in Jericho except, ironically, a prostitute because she had earlier betrayed her own people by helping two Hebrew spies:

> *And they utterly destroyed all that was in the city, both man and woman, young and old, and ox, and sheep, and ass, with the edge of the sword.*
>
> JOSHUA 6:21

After that was accomplished:

> *. . . they burnt the city with fire, and all that was therein: only the silver, and the gold, and the vessels of brass and of iron, they put into the treasury of the house of the Lord.*
>
> JOSHUA 6:24

The next target was Ai, a city with a population of 12,000 inhabitants. All of the citizens of Ai were butchered and the city was burned to the ground. This savagery was perpetrated city after city:

> *So Joshua killed all in the country of the hills, and of the south, and of the valleys, and of the springs, and all their kings: he left none remaining, but utterly destroyed all that breathed, as the Lord God of Israel commanded.*
>
> JOSHUA 10:40

The genocide was justified by saying that the victims were all wicked. This could not have been the true reason because children and animals were also slaughtered. It is hardly fair to massacre an entire city for the crimes of a few; neither is it right to murder a child for the crimes of its parents. The real crime, according to the Bible, was that the natives of the region had become disobedient. The more obedient Hebrews were therefore elected by Jehovah to wipe out the natives and replace them.

There is some debate today about whether the Hebrew assimilation into Canaan was as genocidal as portrayed in the Bible. Modern archaeological digs into some of the battle sites named in the Bible (such as Hazor, Lachish and Debir) have revealed evidence of violent destruction during the time of Joshua. Other sites have yielded less conclusive evidence. Many people understandably prefer to play down the Biblical bloodshed as much as possible. To whatever degree the Biblical story of the conquest of Canaan is true, it does tell us something very important about genocide:

*Genocide is often a tool for promoting rapid political or social change by quickly replacing one group of people with another. For this reason, genocide has emerged as a significant historical phenomenon in connection with many Brotherhood efforts at bringing about rapid political and social change.*

People who are familiar with Jewish moral teachings may be surprised at the brutal behavior ascribed to Jehovah and the Hebrews. The most famous of the Jewish moral teachings are, of course, the Ten Commandments, which were reportedly given to Moses by Jehovah during the Hebrews' trek to the Promised Land. After Moses' death, Jehovah and the armies of Israel clearly violated the Commandments in a big way. *Thou shalt not kill* was transgressed when the Hebrews massacred the inhabitants of Canaan. The Hebrews ignored the commandment *Thou shalt not steal* when they robbed the dying cities of their precious metals. They were no better about adhering to the commandment *Thou shalt not covet thy neighbor's house . . . nor any thing that is thy neighbor's* when they committed genocide to take away the land of their neighbors. This behavior is puzzling because many Biblical commandments do establish a decent code of conduct. For example, the Hebrews were admonished never to cooperate with a wrongdoer by giving false testimony. Another commandment stressed the importance of individual responsibility in the face of group pressure by stating, "You shall not go along with a group in doing evil." Tolerance for outsiders was made law with, "You shall not vex a stranger, nor oppress him. . . ." Thieves were usually required to pay restitution to their victims. How do we account for the existence of such humane commandments in the face of such barbaric behavior?* Part of the answer may lie in the words of Manetho:

> The wonders which Moses narrates as having taken place upon the Mountain of Sinai [the mountain upon which Jehovah reportedly gave Moses many of the Commandments], are in part, a veiled account of the Egyptian initiation which [Moses] transmitted to his people when he established a branch of the Egyptian Brotherhood in his country. . . . [2]

If Manetho's words are true, then many of the Commandments may have come from human sources within the Brotherhood rather than from Custodial sources. This would indicate the continued presence of genuine humanitarians within the Brotherhood despite Custodial dominance. Moses himself appears to have been, at least to some degree, such a humanitarian. The Bible describes Moses as a man of moderation who frequently intervened on behalf of the Hebrews when Jehovah was about to mete out a violent punishment. As we shall see several times in this book, lingering humanitarian influences within the Brotherhood have often come to the surface, but sadly, not enough to entirely undo the corrupting influences.

Another puzzling aspect of the Biblical genocide story was the behavior of the people being slaughtered. According to the Bible, only one city surrendered. The rest chose to fight and be butchered. When confronted with an overpowering Hebrew army, and perhaps even a thundering "God" in the sky, is it not likely that more besieged cities would surrender, or at least offer to vacate Canaan peaceably? The

---

* Not all Old Testament commandments were humane by today's standards. Freedom of worship was not tolerated. Slavery was an accepted institution and Hebrew men were allowed to sell their daughters into slavery. The eye-for-an-eye, tooth-for-a-tooth form of punishment does not always result in justice.

Bible presents an interesting explanation of why that did not happen:

> *There was not a city that made peace with the children of Israel, save the Hi-vites, the inhabitants of Gib-eon, all others they took in battle.*
> *For it was the Lord who hardened their hearts, that they would go against Israel in battle, that he might destroy them utterly, and that they might find no favor, but that he might destroy them. . . .*
> JOSHUA 11:19-20

The above passage states that Jehovah had manipulated the victim peoples into fighting the Hebrews so that the victims could be destroyed. This is a stunning and important admission, for it would imply that Jehovah or other Custodians dominated other cities in the region and used their influence to manipulate people into fighting the Hebrews. This would not have been the first time it happened. The Bible reports similar manipulations in an earlier episode. When the Hebrews were still slaves in Egypt, Jehovah had instructed Moses to go to the pharaoh to ask that the Hebrew tribes be freed. Jehovah, however, had influence over the pharaoh and Moses had been warned in advance that Jehovah would cause the pharaoh to say "no." According to the Bible, Jehovah had a definite reason for manipulating the pharaoh in that fashion:

> *And the Lord said to Moses, Go to the Pharaoh: for I have hardened his heart, and the heart of his servants, that I might show my powers before him:*
> *And so that you may tell in the ears of your son, and your son's son, what things I had brought about in Egypt, and my miracles which I have done among them: that you may know that I am the Lord.*
> EXODUS 10:1-2

After hearing those words, Moses went to the pharaoh a number of times to renew his pleas for the Hebrews' freedom. Each plea was rejected and each rejection was followed by a calamity visited upon the Egyptians by Jehovah. The calamities included vermin infestations, plagues, boils on the skin caused by a fine dust settling over the countryside, and finally the murder of each eldest son in Egypt during a night known as the "Passover." It was only after the Passover that Jehovah stopped "hardening the heart" of the pharaoh so that the Hebrew tribes could leave Egypt.

Many scholars would argue that Biblical references to Jehovah "hardening the hearts" of Israel's enemies merely expresses the religious idea that all human thought and emotion come ultimately from "God," and therefore such writings should not be taken literally. In this case, we should take the Bible seriously because it has described a very real political phenomenon: two or more parties being manipulated into conflict with one another by an outside third party.

One of the most famous philosophers to discuss third-party manipulation as a tool of social and political control was Niccolo Machiavelli, the sixteenth century philosopher. Although Machiavelli was not the first to write about these matters, his name has become synonymous with unscrupulous political cunning.

Machiavelli authored several unsolicited "how-to" manuals for the benefit of a local prince. Those writings have become literary classics. In them, Machiavelli describes several of the techniques used by various Italian rulers to maintain control over a population. One method was to breed conflict. In his treatise, *The Prince,* Machiavelli wrote:

> Some princes, so as to hold securely the the state, have disarmed their subjects, others have kept their subject towns distracted by factions [disputes] . . .[3]

Machiavelli cited a specific example:

> Our forefathers, and those who were reckoned wise, were accustomed to say that it was necessary to hold Pistoia [an Italian city] by factions and Pisa by fortress;

and with this idea they fostered quarrels in some of their tributary towns so as to keep possession of them the more easily.[4]

Human disunity was a valuable commodity to the princes because it made the people less able to mount a challenge. Machiavelli described the exact steps to be taken by anyone wishing to employ this tool:

> The way to set about this is to win the confidence of the city which is disunited; and, so long as they do not come to blows, to act as arbitrator between the parties, and, when they come to blows, to give tardy support to the weaker party, both with a view to keeping them at it and wearing them out; and, again because stronger measures would leave no room for any doubt that you were out to subjugate them and make yourself their ruler. When this scheme is carried out, it will happen, as always, that the end you have in view will be attained. The city of Pistoia, as I have said in another discourse and appropos of another topic, was acquired by the republic of Florence by just such an artifice; for it was divided and the Florentines supported now one, now the other, party and, without making themselves obnoxious to either, led them on until they got sick of their turbulent way of living and in the end came to throw themselves voluntarily into the arms of Florence.[5]

Despite the effectiveness of this technique, Machiavelli advised against using it because it can backfire on the perpetrator. The success of the technique depends upon at least one of the manipulated parties not being aware of the true source of the problem. If both parties should discover that they are being manipulated into hostilities by an outside third party, not only will those hostilities usually cease, but the parties will, more often than not, unite in a common dislike for the perpetrator. This phenomenon can be observed on a personal level when two friends discover that a third "friend" has been saying derogatory things about each one to the other behind their backs. For the technique to be effective, *the perpetrator must remain hidden from view as the source of the conflict.*

To summarize the observations of Machiavelli, we find that breeding conflict between people can be an effective tool for maintaining social and political control over a populace. For the technique to be effective, the instigator must do the following:

1. Erect conflicts and "issues" which will cause people to fight among themselves rather than against the perpetrator.
2. Remain hidden from view as the true instigator of the conflicts.
3. Lend support to all warring parties.
4. Be viewed as the benevolent source which can solve the conflicts.

As noted earlier in the Tower of Babel story, the Custodial "gods" wanted to keep mankind disunited and under Custodial control. To accomplish this, the Biblical story of Jehovah indicates that Custodians implemented the Machiavellian technique of creating factionalism between human beings. The Bible states that Custodians encouraged the factions they controlled to battle one another. All the while, the Custodians have proclaimed themselves the "God" and "angels" to whom people should turn in order to find a solution to all of the warfare. This is the classic sequence straight out of Machiavelli.

For such Machiavellian efforts to remain successful over a long period of time, factionalism would need to be bred constantly and the Custodians would need to remain permanently hidden from view as the perpetrators. Both of these needs were met in the organizational structure of the corrupted Brotherhood. The Brotherhood was being forged into a far-flung network of politically powerful secret societies and religions which could successfully organize people into competing factions; at the same time, Brotherhood traditions of secrecy effectively disguised its organizational hierarchy. This secrecy became a screen behind which Custodians could hide at the top of the Brotherhood heirarchy behind veils of myth and thereby obscure their role as instigators of violent conflict between human beings. In this fashion, *the network of Brotherhood organizations became the primary channel through which wars between human beings could be secretly and continuously generated by the Custodial society,* thereby carrying out the Custodial intentions announced in the Tower of Babel story. The Brotherhood also became the channel through which Custodial institutions could be imposed upon the human race.

Wars serve another Custodial purpose revealed in the Bible. The Adam and Eve story mentioned "God's" intention to make physical survival an all-consuming chore from birth until death. Wars help bring this about because they absorb large-scale resources and offer little to enhance life in return. Wars tear down and destroy what has already been created—this makes a great deal of extra effort necessary just to maintain a culture. The more a society engages in building war machines and fighting wars, the more the people of that society will find their lives consumed in tedium and repetitious toil because of the parasitic and destructive nature of war. This is as true today as it was in 1000 B.C.

It is easily observed that people will fight and quarrel without any outside prompting. There is hardly a creature on Earth that does not at some time in its life attack another. One clearly does not need a manipulative third party for a dispute to arise between groups of people. Third parties simply cause disputes and conflicts to be more frequent, severe, and protracted. Spontaneous, uninfluenced fights tend to be quick, awkward and centered around a single visible dispute. The way to keep fighting artificially alive is to create unresolvable "issues" which can only be settled by the complete annihilation of one of the opponents, and then by helping the opposing teams sustain their struggle against one another by equalizing their fighting strengths. To keep a whole race in a constant state of strife, issues over which members of the race will fight one another must be generated continuously, and fervent warriors must be bred to fight for those causes. These are the precise types of conflicts which have been created by the Brotherhood network all the way up until today. These artificial conflicts have embroiled the human race in the unrelieved morass of wars which have so blighted human history.

Detecting Brotherhood involvement in human events is sometimes tricky. The job is made easier by following the use of several of the Brotherhood's most important mystical symbols. Those symbols act as colored threads weaving in and out of view by which we can trace the role of the Brotherhood network in shaping history. One of the most significant of the symbols is, curiously, an apron.

# 8

# Melchizedek's Apron

OF ALL THE Biblical kings, few are more colorful or legendary than Solomon. Wealthy beyond imagination, wise beyond words, and a slave driver unequalled, Solomon's most famous accomplishment was the construction of a magnificent complex of buildings, which included an opulent temple reportedly made of the finest stone and generously ornamented with gold. In the political sphere, Solomon made history by re-establishing long-severed ties between the Hebrews and Egypt. Not only had Solomon become an advisor to Egyptian pharaoh, Shishak I, he also married the pharaoh's daughter.

During the time he spent in Egypt, Solomon took instruction in the Brotherhood. Upon returning to Palestine, Solomon erected his famous temple to house the Brotherhood in his own country. Naturally, Jehovah was the principle god of the new temple, although Solomon permitted the adoration of other local gods such as Baal, chief male god of the Canaanites. Solomon's temple was modeled after the Brotherhood temple in El Amarna, except that Solomon omitted the side structures which had caused the El Amarna temple to be shaped like a cross.

Building Solomon's temple was no small task. To carry out this architectural feat, Solomon brought in special guilds of masons to design his buildings and to oversee their construction. Those special guilds were already important institutions in Egypt, and their origins are worth looking into.

Architecture is an important art that shapes the physical landscape of a society. One can tell a great deal about the state of a civilization by looking at the buildings it erects. For example, Renaissance architecture imitated classical Roman architecture with its grand and ornate designs, indicating a culture undergoing intellectual and artistic ferment. Modern architecture tends to be efficient, but sterile and dehumanized, revealing a culture which is very businesslike, but artistically stagnant. Architecture tells us what class of people most influence a culture. The Renaissance was led by thinkers and artists; our modern era is being fashioned by efficiency-oriented business people.

In ancient Egypt, the engineers, draftsmen, and masons who worked on the big architectural projects were accorded a special status. They were organized into elite guilds sponsored by the Brotherhood in Egypt. The guilds served a function roughly similar to that of a trade union today. Because the guilds were Brotherhood organizations, they used many Brotherhood ranks and titles. They also practiced a mystical tradition.

Evidence of the existence of these special guilds was uncovered by archaeologist Petrie during his expeditions to the Libyan desert in 1888 and 1889. In the ruins of a city built around 300 B.C., Dr. Petrie's expedition uncovered a number of papyrus records. One set described a guild that held secret meetings around the year 2000 B.C. The guild met to discuss working hours, wages, and rules for daily labor. It convened in a chapel and provided relief to widows, orphans, and workers in distress. The organizational duties described in the papyri are very similar to those of "Warden" and "Master" in a modern branch of the Brotherhood which evolved from those guilds: Freemasonry.

Another reference to the guilds is found in the Egyptian *Book of the Dead*, a mystical work dating from about 1591 B.C. The *Book of the Dead* contains some of the philosophies taught in the Egyptian Mystery Schools. It quotes the god Thot saying to another god, Osiris:

> I am the great God in the divine boat; . . . I am a simple priest in the underworld anointing [performing sacred rituals] in Abydos [an Egyptian city], elevating to higher degrees of initiation; . . . I am Grand Master of the craftsmen who set up the sacred arch for a support.*[1]

"Grand Master" is the most common title used by Brotherhood organizations to designate their top leaders. The above quote is significant because it states that one of Egypt's Custodial "gods," one who traveled about in a divine "boat," was a top leader in one of those ancient guilds. It also indicates that this "god" was responsible for initiating people into the higher degrees of mystical Brotherhood teachings. This is further testimony of the direct role that Custodians were said to play in directing the affairs of the corrupted Brotherhood.

---

*It is interesting to note that the *Book of the Dead* also contains a reference to the battle between the ruling Custodial "gods" and the "snake" (the original uncorrupted Brotherhood). In praises sung to the Egyptian "gods," we read:

> *Thine enemy the Serpent hath been given over to the fire. The Serpent-fiend Sebua hath fallen headlong, his forelegs are bound in chains, and his hind legs hath Ra carried away from him. The Sons of Revolt shall never more rise up.*[2]

The Egyptians often portrayed their "gods" with animal heads or features as a way of symbolizing traits and personalities. In the above quote, the Serpent is given four legs. The Serpent later came to symbolize darkness, which the sun-god Ra "defeated" every morning by bringing about the new day. Before that mythology was invented, however, the Serpent was a literal enemy of the ruling "gods." Some of the Serpent's followers were known as the "Sons of Revolt," who were dedicated to destroying the chief Custodial "god" and establishing in his place the dominance of the "Serpent" (the early uncorrupted Brotherhood) on Earth. After the defeat and corruption of the "Serpent," it appears that the "Sons of Revolt" turned around and rebelled against the corrupted Brotherhood when the Brotherhood began to send out conquerors from Egypt. It was not long, however, before the revolutionary groups were reabsorbed back into the corrupted Brotherhood organizations and began contributing to the Brotherhood's artificial conflicts, as we shall see later.

The Brotherhood's masons' guilds survived down through the centuries. Guild members were often free men, even in feudal societies, and were therefore frequently referred to as "free masons." The guilds of free masons eventually gave birth to the mystical practice known today as "Freemasonry." The mystical Freemasons became a major Brotherhood offshoot that would take on great political importance later in history.

As spiritual knowledge within the Brotherhood was being replaced in ancient Egypt by incomprehensible allegories and symbols, costumes became increasingly important because of their symbolic value. The most visible and important piece of ceremonial garb in many Brotherhood organizations, including Freemasonry, has long been the apron.

The symbolic apron, which is worn at the waist like a kitchen apron, provides a stunning visual link between the ancient Custodial "gods" and the Brotherhood network. Many Egyptian hieroglyphics depict their extraterrestrial "gods" wearing aprons. The priests of ancient Egypt wore similar aprons as a sign of their allegiance to the "gods" and as a badge of their authority. On display at the Egyptian Museum in San Jose, California, is an ancient Egyptian statuette discovered in a tomb in Abydos. The statuette depicts an Egyptian prince holding his hands in a ritualistic posture that Dr. Lewis of the Rosicrucian Order describes as "familiar to all Rosicrucian lodge and chapter members."[3] A prominent feature of the statuette is the triangular apron worn by the prince. The Egyptian Museum believes that the statuette was carved as early as 3400 B.C., during Egypt's first dynasty. If this date is accurate, then the symbol of the apron and one of its associated mystical rituals came from that period of Egyptian history when the "gods" were said to be so literal that furnished homes were built and maintained for them.

The earliest ceremonial aprons appear to have been simple and unadorned. As time went on, mystical symbols and other decorations were added. Perhaps the most significant change to the apron occurred during the reign of the powerful

Canaanite priest-king, Melchizedek, who had achieved a very high status in the Bible. Melchizedek presided over an elite branch of the Brotherhood named after him: the Melchizedek Priesthood. Beginning around the year 2200 B.C., the Melchizedek Priesthood began to make its ceremonial aprons out of white lambskin. White lambskin was eventually adopted by the Freemasons who have used it for their aprons ever since.

If the Custodial "gods" and the Brotherhood had confined their activities to the ancient Middle East and Egypt, the rest of human history would have been much different and this book would never have been written. Instead, the Brotherhood network was expanded throughout the entire eastern hemisphere by aggressive missionaries and conquerors. One of their targets became India.

Hinduism was about to be born.

# 9

# Gods and Aryans

INDIA: THAT LAND of mystery. It is a place where the spiritual arts flourish and the material arts wane. It is a country where nearly all life is held sacred, yet millions starve. To many people, the nation of India and the religion of Hinduism seem almost inseparable, as though they were created together and together they may one day die. The Hindu religion is adhered to by nearly 85% of India's almost 800 million population, yet the India we have come to know and most of the religion it practices today were not created in India at all. The caste system, the majority of the Hindu gods, the Brahmin rituals, and the Sanskrit language were all brought in and imposed on the Indian people by foreign invaders many centuries ago.

Somewhere between 1500 B.C. (the time of Thutmose III in Egypt) and 1200 B.C. (the time of Moses), the Indian subcontinent was invaded from the northwest by tribes of people known as "Aryans." The Aryans made themselves India's new ruling class and forced the native Indians into a servient status.

Precisely who the Aryans were and exactly where they came from is a puzzle still debated today. Historians have generally used the word "Aryan" to denote those peoples who spoke the Indo-European languages, which include English, German, Latin, Greek, Russian, Persian, and Sanskrit. "Aryan" also has a narrower racial meaning. It has quite often been used to designate mankind's non-Semitic white-skinned race.

There are many theories about where Aryans first came from. A common hypothesis is that Aryans originated in the steppes (plains) of Russia. From there they may have migrated to Europe and down into Mesopotamia. Others believe that the Aryans arose in Europe and migrated eastward. Some theorists, occasionally for racist reasons, claim that Aryans were the founders of the ancient Mesopotamian civilizations and were therefore the world's first civilized peoples. This theory was promoted during the brutal Nazi regime of Germany to bolster its "Aryan supremacy" idea. The Nazis even claimed that Aryans were originally created by godlike superhumans from a different world. A similar belief was expressed earlier in history. When Spanish conqueror, Pizarro, invaded South America in 1532, the South American natives referred to the Spanish invaders as Viracochas, which meant "white masters." Native legends in South America told of a master race of huge white men who had come from the heavens centuries before. According to the legends, those "masters" had reigned over South American cities before disappearing again with a promise of return. The South American natives thought that the Spaniards were the returning Viracochas and so they initially allowed the Spaniards to seize the Americans' gold and treasures without resistance.

Whatever the true origin of the Aryan race may or may not have been, many religious and mystical beliefs have been expressed throughout the world about the supposed superiority of the Aryan race over other races. Such beliefs are sometimes labelled "Aryanism." Aryanism is the elevation of white-skinned Aryans over other races based on the notion that Aryans are the "chosen" or "created" race of "God" (or Custodial "gods"), and Aryans are therefore spiritually, socially and genetically superior to all other races. Considering the dismal purpose for which mankind was reportedly created, Aryanism would simply mean that Aryans were, at best, superior slaves. There is little glory in that. Other races, however, such as the Japanese, also possess similar legends of having been born of extraterrestrial "gods."

Aryanism should be distinguished from simple pride in racial heritage. It is natural for people to group together on the basis of common heritage, interests, or aesthetics. Every such group tends to have a certain amount of pride in the thing which holds them together. This will be true of stamp collectors joining a philatelic society or of black people participating in a black consciousness group. People will band together on the basis of almost anything they find mutually important or enjoyable. There is no harm in people feeling pride in their racial heritage. The harm comes when this pride turns into prejudice against those who do not share the same traits. After all, skin color is ultimately superficial. When we recognize individuals as spiritual beings, the bodies they animate become no more important than the cars they drive. Despite this, racial distinctions are one of the easiest ways to polarize people into factions. Racism has been one of the most successful tools used on Earth to keep humans disunited. The type of Aryanism described above has contributed greatly to this polarization and has done much to promote the nonstop racial conflicts which have plagued mankind throughout history.

Not all Brotherhood organizations had an Aryan tradition. In the many that did, being an Aryan was considered vital to spiritual recovery. This belief hastened materialism by twisting the urge for spiritual survival into yet another obsession with the body, this time concerning skin color. The fact is, skin color appears to have no bearing whatsoever upon one's inherent spiritual qualities, or upon one's ability to achieve spiritual salvation.

The Aryans invaded India just before monotheism was created in the Brotherhood, but at a time when the Brotherhood had already begun sending out missionaries and conquerors. In India, the Aryan conquerers established

THE GODS OF EDEN 97

a complex religious and feudal system known today as "Hinduism." Hinduism proved to be yet another branch of the Brotherhood network. Some Brotherhood organizations in the Middle East and Egypt maintained close ties with the Aryan leaders in India and frequently sent students to be educated by them. Because of the Aryan invasion, India became an important world center of Brotherhood network activity and remains so today.

The Aryan leaders of India claimed obedience to the same type of space age Custodial "gods" found in Mesopotamia and Egypt. Many of the humanlike "gods" worshipped by the Aryans were called "Asura." Hymns and devotions to the Asura are found in a large collection of Hindu writings known as the Vedas. Many Vedic descriptions of the Asura are intriguing. For example, the Hymn to Vata, god of wind, describes a "chariot" in which the god travels. This "chariot" has a remarkable similarity to Old Testament descriptions of Jehovah. The first four lines of the Hymn declare:

> Now Vata's chariot's greatness!
> Breaking goes it,
> And thunderous is its noise.
> To heaven it touches,
> Makes light lurid [a red fiery glare], and whirls dust
> upon the earth. [1]

The rest of the Hymn describes wind in a very literal and recognizable manner. The four lines quoted above, however, seem to describe a vehicle which travels rapidly into the sky, makes a thunderous noise, emits a fiery light and causes dust to whirl on the ground, *i.e.*, a rocket or jet airplane.

Other remarkable translations of the Vedas have been published by the International Society for Krishna Consciousness (ISKC), a worldwide Hindu sect founded in 1965 by a retired Indian businessman and devoted to the Hindu deity, Krishna. ISKC translations depict ancient Hindu "gods" and their human servant kings traveling in spaceships, engaging in interplanetary warfare, and firing weapons which emit powerful beams of light. For example, in the *Srimad Bhagavatam*, Sixth Canto, Part 3, we read:

> *One time while King Citraketu was travelling in out-*
> *er space on a brilliantly effulgent [shining] airplane*
> *given to him by Lord Vishnu [the chief Hindu god],*
> *he saw Lord Siva [another Hindu god]. . . .*

The *Srimad Bhagavatam* tells of a "demon" race which
had invaded three planetary systems. Opposing the demons
was the Hindu god Siva, who possessed a powerful weapon
that he fired at enemy airships from his own:

> *The arrows released by Lord Siva appeared like fiery*
> *beams emanating from the sun globe and covered the*
> *three residential airplanes, which could then no longer*
> *be seen.* [2]

If accurate, these and other translations of the Vedas give
us humanlike "gods" centuries ago who cavorted in whiz-
zing spaceships, engaged in aerial dogfights, and possessed
fatal beam weapons.

As in Mesopotamia and Egypt, many Hindu gods were
obvious fabrications and the apparently real "gods" had an
enormous mythology woven about them. Behind the blatant
fictions, however, we find important clues regarding the
character of mankind's Custodial rulers. Hindu writings
indicate that people of diverse races and personalities made
up the Custodial society, just as they do human society. For
example, some "gods" were portrayed with blue skin. Others displayed a kinder and more benevolent attitude toward
human beings than others. By the time of the Aryan invasion,
however, the oppressive ones were clearly the dominant
ones. This was evident in the social system imposed on India
by the Aryans. That system was unmistakably designed to
create human spiritual bondage. As elsewhere, this bondage
was partially accomplished by giving spiritual truths a false
twist. The result in India was a feudalistic institution known
as the "caste" system.

The Aryan caste system dictates that every person is born
into the social and occupational class (caste) of the father.
An individual may never leave that caste, regardless of the

individual's talent or personality. Each stratum has its own trades, customs, and rituals. Members of the lowest caste, who are known as "outcasts" or "untouchables," usually perform menial work and live in abject poverty. Untouchables are shunned by the higher classes. The highest castes are the rulers and Brahman priests. During the Aryan invasion, and for a long time thereafter, the highest castes were composed of, naturally, the Aryans themselves. The caste system is still practiced in India today, although it is no longer quite as rigid as it once was and the plight of the untouchables has been eased somewhat. In northern and some parts of western India, the lighter-skinned Indians who descended from the original Aryan invaders continue to dominate the upper castes.

Force and economic pressures were the initial tools used by the Aryan invaders to preserve the caste system. By the 6th century B.C., distorted religious beliefs emerged as a third significant tool.

The Hindu religion contains the truth that a spiritual being does not perish with the body. Hinduism teaches that upon the death of the body, a spiritual being will usually search out and animate a newly-born body. This process is often called "reincarnation" and results in the phenomenon of so-called "past lives." Many people are capable of recalling "past lives," sometimes in remarkable detail.

Evidence accumulated from modern research into the phenomenon of "past lives" indicates that highly random factors usually determine which new body a spiritual being takes on. Such factors may include a person's location at the time of death and the proximity of new bodies (pregnancies). Whether a person chooses a male or female body may depend upon how happy she or he was in the life just ended. Because of these variables, the taking of a new body by a spiritual being is a largely random and unpredictable activity in which sheer chance often plays a role. The Aryan religion distorted an understanding of this simple process by teaching the erroneous idea that rebirth ("reincarnation") is governed by an unalterable universal law which dictates that every rebirth is an evolutionary step either toward or away from spiritual perfection and liberation. Each Hindu caste was said to be a step on this cosmic staircase. If people behaved according to the laws and duties of their caste, they were told that they would advance to the next higher caste at their next rebirth. If they failed in their duties, they would be born into a lower stratum. Spiritual perfection and freedom were achieved only when a person finally reached the highest caste: the Brahmans. Conversely, the caste into which a person was born was considered an indication of that person's spiritual development, and that alone justified whatever treatment the person received.

The purpose of such teachings is clear. The caste system was designed to create a rigid feudalistic social order similar to the one created in Egypt under the pharaohs, but carried to an even greater extreme in India.

Hindu reincarnation beliefs accomplished two other Custodial aims. Hinduism stressed that obedience was the principle ingredient bringing about advancement to the next caste. At the same time, Aryan beliefs discouraged people from making pragmatic attempts at spiritual recovery. The myth of spiritual evolution through a caste system hid the reality that spiritual recovery most probably comes about in the same way that nearly all personal improvement occurs: through personal conscious effort, not through the machinations of a fictitious cosmic ladder.

Symbolism had a limited, yet important role in Hinduism. One of Hinduism's most important mystical emblems is the swastika—the "broken cross" symbol which most people associate with Naziism. The swastika is a very old emblem. It has appeared many times in history, usually in connection with Brotherhood mysticism and in societies worshipping Custodial "gods." While its exact origin is unknown, the swastika appeared already in ancient Mesopotamia. Some historians believe that the swastika may have also existed in India before the Aryan invasion. This is possible because several pre-Aryan cities of India were engaged in trade with other parts of the world, including Mesopotamia. Whatever its origin may have been, after the Aryans invaded India, the swastika became a prominent symbol of Hinduism and Aryanism.

As for the swastika's meaning, we discover that the swastika was a symbol of good luck or good fortune. It is ironic, therefore, that nearly every society using it has suffered rather calamitous *mis*fortune. An intriguing study of the swastika was published in 1901 in the *Archaeological and Ethnological Papers of the Peabody Museum.* According to the author, Zelia Nuttall, the swastika was probably related to stargazing. Ms. Nuttall points out that the swastika has appeared in civilizations with a developed science of astronomy and has been associated with calendar-making in some ancient American civilizations. On page 18 of her article, the author states:

> The combined midnight positions of the Ursa Major or Minor [two constellations visible from Earth, usually called the "Big Dipper" and "Little Dipper," respectively], at the four divisions of the year, yielded symmetrical swastikas, the forms of which were identical with the different types of swastika or cross-symbols . . . which have come down to us from remote antiquity. . . .

Because of the swastika's frequent association with Custodial "gods," it may have begun as a symbol representing the home civilization of Earth's Custodial masters somewhere within the Big or Little Dipper.

Hinduism is a curious religion in many ways. It tends to absorb and incorporate almost any new religious ideas imposed upon it, but without throwing away the old ideas. For this reason, the Hinduism of today is actually a mishmash of several major religions which had swept through India in the past, such as the Aryan religion which still predominates, and Buddhism and Mohammedism which both arrived later. There is evidence that a tradition of wisdom existed in India long before the Aryan invasion and that that tradition also constitutes a portion of the Vedas.

The Aryans' violent gods, strange mystical practices, and oppressive feudalism did not go unchallenged. In the Biblical story of Adam and Eve, we noted the attempt of early *Homo sapiens* to obtain the knowledge they needed to escape their enslavement. In the seventh century B.C., another attempt was made. A popular nonviolent movement emerged in India to challenge the Aryan system. This movement was one of the few major efforts by human beings to replace Custodial religions with practical methods designed to bring about spiritual freedom. The leaders of the new movement wanted to replace garbled mysticism and blind faith with a realistic approach to spiritual recovery rooted in tested principles, much like the approach used by the original uncorrupted Brotherhood. For lack of a better term, I will refer to this pragmatic type of religion as "maverick" * religion. Maverick religions are those which have broken from Custodial dogma and have attempted a practical or scientific approach to spiritual salvation. Although no maverick religion in the past brought about wide-scale spiritual recovery, they nonetheless kept the hope alive while perhaps pointing out a few of the steps needed to get there.

---

* The term "maverick" comes from America's Old West. It denoted any grazing animal, such as a cow or horse, which did not have an owner's brand. The word itself comes from Texas cattle owner Samuel Maverick (1803-1870) who refused to brand his calves. Those unbranded animals were dubbed "Mavericks" and any found roaming loose were considered owned by no one. From this came the definition we are familiar with today: a maverick is a person or organization not "owned" or "branded" by anyone, but who acts in an independent manner, usually in a break from established convention.

# 10

# The Maverick Religions

THE MAVERICK RELIGIOUS movement of India was a major historical event. It attracted millions of adherents and had a strong civilizing effect on Asia. The movement brought about the creation of the so-called "Six Systems of Salvation." These were six different methods, developed at different times, for achieving spiritual salvation.

Perhaps the most significant of the Six Systems, because of its similarities to Buddhism, was the system known as "Samkhya." The word "Samkhya" means "reason." The precise origin of Samkhya teachings is unknown. Samkhya doctrines are usually attributed to a man known as Kapila. Who Kapila was, where he came from, and exactly when he lived are still topics of speculation. Some people place Kapila around 550 B.C., during the lifetime of Buddha. Others believe that Kapila may have lived earlier. Some people contend that he did not exist at all because of the extraordinary mythology which arose around him. Whoever Kapila was, or was not, some of the teachings attributed to him laid significant groundwork for later maverick philosophies. For example, the Samkhya system correctly taught that there were two basic contrasting entities in the universe: the soul (spirit) and matter. It taught further:

Souls are infinite in number[1] and consist of pure intelligence. Each soul is independent, indivisible [cannot be taken apart], unconditioned, incapable of change [alteration], immortal. It appears, however, to be bound in matter.*

Samkhya teaches that each person is such a soul, and that every soul has participated in the creation and/or perpetuation of the primary elements which constitute the material universe. Souls then created the senses with which to perceive those elements. People therefore had only themselves, not a "God" or Supreme Being, to applaud (or blame, depending upon one's perspective) for the existence of this universe and for all of the good and bad within it. The soul's liberation from captivity in matter, according to the Samkhya, comes about through knowledge. Author Sir Charles Eliot describes the Samkhya belief this way:

Suffering is the result of souls being in bondage to matter, but this bondage does not affect the nature of the soul and in one sense is not real, for when souls acquire discriminating knowledge and see that they are not matter, then the bondage ceases and they attain to eternal peace.[2]

Several questions arise from these Samkhya teachings. First, how could all spiritual beings have helped create the universe? One peek at a physics book tells us that the universe is an enormously complex affair. Even the great scientist Albert Einstein did not have it all figured out. How, then, is it possible that all of us "lesser mortals," including drunken winos sleeping off stupors in downtown alleys, could have once had something to do with creating this world? The answer may lie in the fact that matter is built on

---

*Common sense tells us that there would be a limit to how many souls existed. "Infinite" may mean a number so large so as to be uncountable.

simple arithmetic and is far less solid than it appears.

The basic building block of physical matter is the atom. An atom is made up of three main components: "protons," "neutrons," and "electrons." Protons and neutrons are joined together to form the nucleus (core) of the atom. Electrons orbit at tremendous speeds around the nucleus and thereby form the "shell" of the atom. The entire arrangement is held together by electromagnetic force.

What makes one type of atom different from another? Nothing more than the number of electrons and protons. For example, hydrogen has only one electron and one proton. Add one more electron and proton to an atom of hydrogen and, *voila!*, you now have helium. Add 77 more electrons and protons, along with a generous helping of neutrons, and you suddenly own gold. Take some away to get cobalt and then add some more to form zinc. There are 105 basic elements, each existing simply because they have a different number of electrons and protons! As we can see, physical matter is built upon idiotically simple arithmetic which anyone can do. The reason this arrangement seems to work is that the addition and subtraction of electrons and protons causes a change in the energy created by the atom. Since matter is just condensed energy, a change in an atom's energy through this simple arithmetic will cause a change in the physical substance which the atom produces. The universe only gets complicated after the substances start interacting.

Another point is that physical matter is far less solid, and much more ephemeral, than it appears. Atoms consist almost entirely of empty space. If the nucleus of a hydrogen atom were to be enlarged to the size of a marble, its single electron would be a quarter of a mile away! The heaviest atom with the most neutrons, protons and electrons is uranium with 92 electrons. If a uranium atom were enlarged to a half-mile in diameter, the nucleus would be no larger than a baseball! This reveals that atoms are composed almost entirely of empty space and that matter, even the heaviest granite, is therefore surprisingly ephemeral. Our physical perceptions do not detect the almost illusionary nature of matter because the physical senses are constructed to accept the illusion of solidity caused by the extremely rapid motion of atomic particles. (Move something back and forth, or around and around, fast enough and it will appear solid.) If we could see matter for what it truly was, we would see the most solid object as a piece of whispy fluff.

As time went on, many incorrect tenets were added to the basic Samkhya teachings, causing the Samkhya system to eventually decay. The other maverick systems suffered the same fate. In the system of "Yoga," for example, people reverted back to "god" idolatry as part of their road to spiritual freedom. In another of the Six Systems, "Mimamsa," an attempt was made to maintain the Aryan creeds and to incorporate them into the new maverick tenets. This did not work because one cannot mix doctrines aimed at enforcing rigid obedience with teachings designed for spiritual freedom and expect to achieve the latter. To be successful, true spiritual knowledge seems to require the same precision demanded of any other science. Diluting successful spiritual knowledge with erroneous teachings will destroy that precision.

The Indian maverick movement eventually came to a grinding halt as more and more of the Aryan ideas it sought to replace became incorporated back into the movement. At the same time, many maverick teachings were taken out of context and absorbed into the Hindu religion. The result has been a hopeless spiritual mishmash in India ever since.

Before its ultimate decay, the Indian maverick movement brought about one of the largest single religions in history: Buddhism. Founded around the year 525 B.C. by an Indian prince named Gautama Siddharta (who was later known as the "Buddha," or "Enlightened One"), Buddhism spread rapidly throughout the Far East. Like the Samkhya system, Buddhism in its original form did not worship the Vedic gods. It opposed the caste system and it did not support Brahminical (advanced Hindu) doctrines. Unlike many modern Buddhists, early Buddhists did not worship Buddha as a god; instead, they respected him as a thinker who had designed a method by which an individual, through his or her own efforts, might achieve spiritual freedom by way of knowledge and spiritual exercises. It is difficult to determine how successful early Buddhists actually were in achieving their aims, although Siddharta did claim to have personally attained a state of spiritual liberation.

Buddhism, like the other maverick systems, underwent a

great deal of change, splintering and decay as the centuries progressed. This caused the loss of most of Siddharta's true teachings. In addition, many teachings and practices not created by Buddha were later added to his religion and mislabeled "Buddhism." A good example of this decay is found in the definition of "nirvana." The word "nirvana" originally referred to that state of existence in which the spirit has achieved full awareness of itself as a spiritual being and no longer experiences suffering due to misidentification with the material universe. "Nirvana" is the state striven for by every Buddhist. "Nirvana" has also been translated as "Nothingness" or the "Void": horrible-sounding concepts which have come to imply to many people today that "nirvana" is a state of non-existence or that it involves a loss of contact with the physical universe. In truth, the original maverick goal was to achieve quite the opposite state. Buddha's true state of "nirvana" included a stronger sense of existence, increased self-identity, and an ability to more accurately perceive the physical universe.

If we compare maverick religion to Custodial religion, we discover a number of very distinct differences by which a person may distinguish between them. A chart comparing the key philosophies by which they most strongly differ might look something like this:

| *Custodial Religion* | *Maverick Religion* |
| --- | --- |
| Source or inspiration of teachings is said to be a god, angel, or supernatural force; not a human being. | Source or inspiration of teachings is said to be an identifiable human being. |
| Belief in a single Supreme Being, or God, is a principle cornerstone of faith. (In earlier times, worship of many humanlike "gods.") | Belief in a Supreme Being is usually tolerated, but is a minor or nonexistent part of doctrine. Emphasis is placed on the role of the individual spiritual being in relation to the universe. |

| *Custodial Religion* | *Maverick Religion* |
|---|---|
| Physical immortality is an important or desired goal in many Custodial religions. | Spiritual freedom and immortality are sought. Endless existence in the same physical body is deemed unimportant or undesirable. |
| Adherence to doctrine, based upon faith or obedience alone, is stressed. | Observation and reason are held to be the proper foundations for adhering to a doctrine. |
| Severe or fatal physical punishments are sometimes employed or advocated during the religion's history to deal with nonbelievers or backsliders. | Physical punishments or duress are very mild to nonexistent. Severest punishment is usually formal exclusion of an individual from the religious organization. |
| Belief that being born in a human body, either once or many times through reincarnation, is part of a broad spiritual plan which will ultimately benefit every human being. | Belief that there is no hidden spiritual purpose to human existence and that the process of death-amnesia-rebirth causes spiritual decay. |
| Belief that there are "higher forces," "gods," or supernatural entities which control people's individual or collective fates. Human beings have no control over those forces and can only yield to them. | Belief that all people are ultimately responsible for having created their own conditions in life, good and bad, by their own actions and inactions, and that all people can ultimately control their own destinies. |
| Belief that only one Supreme Being alone created the physical universe. | Belief that everyone has something to do with the creation and/or perpetuation of the physical universe. |

| *Custodial Religion* | *Maverick Religion* |
| --- | --- |
| Human suffering, toil, and enslavement are part of a broader spiritual plan which will ultimately lead to salvation and freedom for those who obediently endure it. | Human suffering, toil, and enslavement are social ills that have no constructive purpose and stand in the way of spiritual salvation and freedom. |
| Spiritual recovery and salvation depend entirely upon the grace of "God" or other supernatural entity. | Spiritual recovery and salvation are entirely up to the individual to achieve through his or her own self-motivated effort. |

Some readers will observe that many Custodial and maverick elements listed above are mixed together in some religions. A good example of this is Hinduism. Such mixtures are usually concocted when maverick ideas are incorporated into a Custodial religion, or when Custodial doctrines are added to maverick teachings. When either happens, the full benefits of the maverick teachings are lost. This is especially clear in modern Buddhism where rituals, idolatry and prayers to Buddha have almost entirely supplanted the practical system Buddha had tried to develop.

Although Buddhism did not free the human race, it left the hope that freedom would one day come. According to Buddhist legend, Gautama knew that he had not accomplished his goal of creating a religion that would bring about full spiritual liberation for all mankind. He therefore promised that a second "Buddha," or "Enlightened One," would arrive later in history to complete the task. This promise constitutes the famous "Mettaya" ("Friend") prophecy which has become a very important element of modern Buddhist faith. Because Buddhism did not originally express a belief in a Supreme Being, the Mettaya legend did not suggest a messenger or a teacher from "God." Mettaya would simply be an individual with the knowledge and ability to get the job done.

Precisely when in history "Mettaya" was to arrive is hotly debated in some circles. Many Buddhist sources say that Mettaya would come five thousand years after Buddha's death; others have said half of that. Many Buddhist leaders have come along in history claiming to be Mettaya. None of them were successful in bringing about the world promised by Buddha, so most Buddhists still wait.

As time went on, the Mettaya prophecy decayed with the rest of Buddhism. The legend was slowly absorbed into a very destructive doctrine being spread by Brotherhood sources in the Middle East and elsewhere: the doctrine of the "End of the World," also known by such dramatic names as the "Day of Judgment," the "Final Battle," "Armageddon," and others.

End of the World teachings have had a catastrophic effect on human society. It is therefore of paramount importance to understand more about where, and why, those teachings began.

# 11

# Doom Prophets

ASK ALMOST ANYONE, "Do you believe in a future Judgment Day of some kind?" Chances are that she or he will answer "yes." Next to a belief in God, belief in a Judgment Day may be the most widespread religious concept in the modern world. Even many people who are openly atheistic often experience an "innate" feeling that some sort of grand judgment or realignment lies ahead.

Most Judgment Day teachings are found in the writings of religious prophets who claim to have received mystical revelations from God concerning the future of the world. This type of prophetic writing is usually called an "apocalypse." The word apocalypse comes from the Greek words "apo-" (off) and "kalyptein" (to cover). An apocalypse is therefore "the taking off of a cover," *i.e.*, a revelation.

Most apocalypses follow a similar pattern: Mankind will suffer upheaval during a future global cataclysm. The cataclysm will be followed by a Day of Judgment in which God or a representative of God will decide the fate of every person on Earth. Only those people who are obedient to the religion preaching the apocalypse will be granted mercy on the Day of Judgment. Everyone else will be doomed to death or eternal spiritual damnation. The Judgment Day will be followed by a utopia on Earth to be enjoyed only by those who believed and obeyed.

Despite promises of a universal Shangri-La, these teachings often terrified people, and they still cause unease today. As we shall discuss shortly, fearsome apocalypses give spiritual truths another false twist and, more obviously, they subdue people into obeying a specific religion or leader. End of the World doctrines also make people afraid to explore competing religious systems, such as those offered by religious mavericks. Judgment Day teachings ultimately amount to extortion: obey or die.

The question is: who implanted apocalyptic beliefs on Earth? A Supreme Being is usually cited—but is a Supreme Being truly the source? A careful look at history reveals that apocalyptic teachings first arose out of Custodial activity and from sources within the corrupted Brotherhood network. End of the World doctrines were disseminated by early Brotherhood missionaries and conquerors hand-in-hand with monotheism. It is therefore not surprising to learn that Final Battle doctrines have some roots in a famous Brotherhood symbol discovered on ancient Egyptian relics. That symbol was the mythical bird known as the phoenix.

The phoenix is a fictional bird which is said to live five hundred to six hundred years before burning itself to death in a nest of herbs. Out of the ashes emerges a small worm which grows back into the phoenix. The phoenix repeats this life-death-rebirth cycle over and over again, endlessly.

The phoenix legend is an allegory (a story with an underlying meaning), or symbol, designed to impart a deeper truth. Precisely what that truth is has been lost, and so we find people interpreting the phoenix legend in a variety of ways. For example, many people see the phoenix as a symbol of resurrection or spiritual survival after death: a soul is born into a body, the body flowers, the body undergoes the fiery rigors of life and death, and the soul remains intact to rise and build again. Others see the phoenix as a symbol of the birth-growth-decay cycle upon which the physical elements of the universe seem to operate, behind which there lies an indestructible spiritual reality.

Regrettably, the phoenix legend, like so many other mystical allegories of the Egyptian Brotherhood, distorted important truths. The legend came to convey the false idea that there exists some kind of unalterable "law" or "plan" which mandates that spiritual existence must consist of an arduous phoenix-like process of growing, dying by "fire," emerging out of the ashes, growing again, dying again, and so on forever. While this process does seem to regulate life on Earth, it is neither natural, inevitable nor healthy.

Many "End of the World" teachings take the philosophy expressed in the phoenix myth and apply it to the entire human race. When they do so, they often express the notion that human societies must endure continuous "ordeals by fire" as part of God's great plan. Most apocalypses then veer from standard phoenix allegory by proclaiming that this process will culminate in a great "Final Battle" followed by a utopia. These beliefs encourage people to tolerate, and even welcome, a world of unremitting physical hardship, conflict, and death: the kind of world that ancient writings say Custodians wished their work race to live in. Judgment Day prophesies even spur some people into working to bring about a "final battle" because those believers think that it will mean the dawn of a utopia.

"End of the World" teachings were widely disseminated in Persia somewhere between 750 B.C. and 550 B.C. by a famous Persian prophet named Zoroaster.* Zoroaster is cited by historians as one of the earliest prophets to preach the type of monotheism first created by Akhnaton. Zoroaster was an

---

*Zoroaster probably lived closer to 550 B.C. than to 750 B.C., although there is debate on this issue. Traditionally, he has been placed 258 years "before Alexander," which some scholars interpret as 258 years before Alexander the Great destroyed the first Persian Empire in 330 B.C.

Zoroaster is also known as Zarathustra—a name that provided inspiration for a famous symphonic work composed by Richard Strauss entitled *Thus Spake Zarathustra*. Strauss's composition became the theme song of the American motion picture, *2001: A Space Odyssey*.

Aryan mystic and priest who also taught a form of Aryanism. Persia at that time was an Aryan nation dominated by an Aryan priest caste. Some Brotherhood branches today state that Zoroaster was an emissary of the ancient Brotherhood.

Zoroaster's cosmology (theory of the universe) was based on the concept of a struggle between good and evil. Zoroaster said that this struggle was to take place over a period of 12,000 years divided into four stages. The first stage consisted solely of spiritual existence during which time a chief god designed the physical universe. During the second stage, the material universe was created, followed by the entrance of the chief god's opponent into the new universe for the purpose of creating problems. The third phase consisted of a battle between the chief god and his rivals over the fate of the many souls who came to occupy the universe. In the fourth and final stage, the chief god was to send in a succession of saviours who would finally defeat the opponent and bring salvation to all spiritual beings in the universe. According to Zoroaster's model, the world is in the fourth stage.

Zoroaster appears to have been a sincere and honest reformer. He taught some good lessons about the nature of ethics and its importance to spiritual salvation. He stressed that people have free will. In other matters, however, Zoroaster's religion fell well short of ideal. To understand why, we need only look at Zoroaster's "God."

The God of Zoroaster was named Ahura Mazda, which means "lord" or "spirit" ("ahura") of "knowledge" or "wisdom" ("mazda"). Zoroaster states that when he was a 30-year-old priest, Ahura Mazda had appeared before him saying that he, Ahura Mazda, was the one true God. Ahura Mazda then proceeded to impart to Zoroaster many of the teachings which constituted Zoroastrianism. When we look to see what sort of creature Ahura Mazda was, we discover good evidence that he was but another Custodian pretending to be "God." Ahura Mazda is depicted in some places as a bearded human figure who stands in a stylized circular object. From the circular object protrude two stylized wings to indicate that it flies. The round flying object has two jutting struts underneath that resemble legs for landing.

In other words, Ahura Mazda was a humanlike "God" who flew in a round flying object with landing pads: a Custodian. The implication is that Zoroaster's monotheism, with its apocalyptic message, was spread in Persia with Custodial assistance much in the same way that Judaism had been spread under Moses.

As noted earlier, Zoroaster was an Aryan living in a region ruled by other Aryans. Aryan domination was so strong that the name of Persia was eventually changed to "Iran," which is a derivative of the word "Aryan." Zoroastrian works speak of a god fighting for the Aryan nations and helping them bring about good crops. Through its writings (primarily the *Zend Avesta),* and through its secret mystical teachings, Zoroastrianism did much to spread philosophies of Aryanism to other organizations within the Brotherhood network. We shall see examples later.

Apocalyptic doctrines continued to be spread after the death of Zoroaster, especially by Hebrew prophets. The warnings of those Hebrew prophets can be found in the later books of the Old Testament. One of those prophets was Ezekiel, whose description of bizarre flying objects we looked at in Chapter 7. According to Ezekiel's narrative, he was taken aboard a strange craft for the very purpose of being given an apocalyptic message to spread, indicating once again that Custodians were the ultimate creators of Judgment Day teachings.

As year 1 A.D. approached, the Hebrew religion had become well-settled in the Middle East. It was, however, undergoing many changes, some of which were caused by the extension of the Roman empire into Palestine. The Romans, who had themselves been driven to conquest by strange mystical religions with definite Brotherhood undertones, often made life difficult for the Jews. In this milieu a number of Jewish sects arose which were often at odds with one another, except in regard to one matter: the Romans were not welcome in Palestine. Some Hebrew sects, such as the Sadducees, proclaimed the coming of a Messiah from "God"—a Messiah who would prevail in the eternal struggle of good against evil and bring freedom to the oppressed Jews. This idea became quite popular among the Hebrews of Palestine, even though its strong political slant made it dangerous.

Old Testament messianic prophecies began as early as 750 B.C. with the prophet Isaiah. Jewish apocalypses appeared sporadically after that, yet often enough to keep fear of a world cataclysm alive. Examples include prophet Joel circa 400 B.C. and Daniel circa 165 B.C. Ironically, the prophecies were quite dire and expressed tremendous hostility against the Jewish people themselves even though the Hebrews were meant to ultimately benefit from the prophecies. Old Testament seers described the people of Israel as wicked and sinful. They quoted "Jehovah" threatening all manner of calamities against the people of Israel, and against the oppressors of Israel. No one was to be spared. To give the flavor of these predictions, here is a quote from the last book in the Old Testament, written shortly before 445 B.C.:

> For look, the day comes that all will burn like an oven; and all the proud; and all those who act wickedly, shall be stubble: and the day that comes shall burn them up, said the Lord of hosts [angels], that it shall leave them neither root nor branch.
>
> But to you who fear my name shall the Sun of Righteousness arise with healing in his wings; and you shall go forth, and grow up as calves of the stall.
>
> And you will tread down the wicked; for they shall be ashes under the soles of your feet on the day that I shall do this, said the Lord of hosts.
>
> Remember the law of Moses my servant, which I commanded to him in Horeb for all Israel, with the statutes and judgments.
>
> Observe, I will send you Elijah the prophet before the coming of the great and dreadful day of the LORD:
>
> And he will turn the heart of the fathers to the children, and the heart of the children to their fathers, so that I do not come and destroy the Earth with a curse.
>
> MALACHI 4:1-6

The above passage preaches the coming of a special messenger from God named Elijah, who was the Hebrew's competition against Mettaya of the Buddhist religion. The Buddhists, perhaps sensing the one-upmanship or falling prey to corrupted Brotherhood influences, reshaped the Mettaya legend to resemble monotheistic apocalypses. This created the illusion that the Hebrews and Buddhists were waiting for the same person when, in fact, they were not. Brotherhood monotheists were (and still are) waiting for a messenger from God coupled with a Day of Judgment. The Buddhists were simply awaiting a friend who is smart and caring enough to finish Buddha's work without the necessity of the entire world ending. Modern Hebrews are still waiting for Elijah to appear, while Christians believe that Elijah was John the Baptist, the man who baptized Jesus Christ.

Old Testament prophets expressed another important idea. "Jehovah" would continue to manipulate people into war:

> For I [God] will gather all nations against Jerusalem to battle . . . Then shall the Lord go forth, and fight against those nations . . .
>> ZECHARIAH 14:1-2 (written c. 520 B.C.)

This is a startling quote because it states "God's" intention to bring many nations into a conflict by first supporting one side and then backing the other. Such actions are textbook Machiavelli. "God's" intention to make brother fight brother was expressed in the same year by prophet Haggai:

> And I will overthrow the throne of kingdoms, and I will destroy the strength of the heathen; and I will overthrow the chariots, and those that ride in them; and the horses and their riders shall come down, every one by the sword of his brother.
>> HAGGAI 2:22

Bible believers still think that a Supreme Being is behind the vicious Machiavellian intentions described in the Bible. The "ancient astronauts" theory seems to provide a true breakthrough by pointing to a brutal technological society, not a Supreme Being, as the more likely source of such machinations.

When people adhere to apocalyptic prophecies, they usually do so because they believe in predestiny. Predestiny is the idea that the future is already created and unalterable, and that some people have a special ability to see that future.

Does predestiny really exist?

For the sake of discussion, let us assume that it does: at any given moment in the present, there is a future already created that is as solid and as real as any moment in the past or present. Perhaps time is not as linear as we have believed.

If such a future already exists, does that mean that it is inevitable and must occur?

No.

Here is a simple two-part exercise to illustrate this:

Part 1: Find a timepiece and note the time. Calculate what time it will be in exactly 30 seconds. Now decide exactly where you will be standing when that 30-second moment arrives. Watch the clock and be sure you are standing at the spot you chose.

You have just created a prophecy and fulfilled it.

Part 2: Look at the clock again and decide on a new location. Ten seconds before the 30-second moment arrives, rethink whether you want to fulfill the prophecy. If you do, be at the place you decided upon; if you do not, choose a new location at random and be there when the 30-second moment arrives.

Repeat the above exercise several times.

Which of the two parts above created the stronger and more solid future? The answer, of course is Part 1. Which of the two futures would a prophet be more likely to foresee? The answer again is Part 1. The point being made is that the future is shaped largely by intention backed by action: the stronger the intention and the better its back-up by action, the more solid the future will tend to be.

The future is therefore malleable. A future reality, no matter how solid it is or how many prophets have agreed to its existence, can be changed. It will be irreversible only if people continue to perform, or fail to perform, those actions which will cause that future to come about, and no one does anything effective enough to counter those actions or inactions.

Some people would argue that the true seer would foresee the change of mind in Part 2 of the above exercise. If this is true, then the prophet has gained an extraordinary ability to influence the future, for he or she may now contact the subject of his or her vision and persuade that person to change his or her mind, or the seer may take actions to ensure or prevent the consequences of the decision.

Prophecy has really only one value: as a tool to either change or ensure the future. The problem with a seer who foresees a tragic event which later comes true is that he or she divined insufficient information to do anything about it. For example, the famous American prophet, Edgar Cayce, predicted a worldwide holocaust in the 1990's. Because of Mr. Cayce's reputed ability to perceive such things, many people are convinced that such an event lies in the future. Perhaps it does. Unfortunately, Mr. Caycé was not able to expand enough on his prediction to offer the detailed information which might be used to alter the events he predicted. His prophecy is therefore woefully incomplete.

As we shall see in this book, there have been many "End of the World" episodes in world history. They have all fulfilled the religious prophecies except on one very crucial point: not one of them brought about a new era of peace and salvation as promised. Despite that dismal record, many people today are preaching that yet one more "End of the World" or "Final Battle" is about to make life better.

Shortly before the year 1 A.D., a controversial religious leader was born who tried to prevent himself from being declared an apocalyptic Messiah. He was unsuccessful and would be nailed to a wooden cross as a result. We know him today as Jesus Christ, and his story is an important one.

# 12

# The Jesus Ministry

THE STORY MOST people know of Jesus is told in the New Testament. The New Testament, like much of the Old Testament, is in many places a greatly altered version of the original accounts on which it is based. In addition, probably less than 5% of all that Jesus and his original followers taught is found in the Bible.

Many of the changes and deletions to the New Testament were made by special church councils. The editing process began as early as 325 A.D. during the First Council of Nicea, and continued well into the 12th century. For example, the Second Synod [church council] of Constantinople in 553 A.D. deleted from the Bible Jesus's references to "reincarnation"—an important concept to Jesus and his early followers. Later, the Lateran Councils of the 12th century added a tenet to the Bible that was never taught by Jesus: the concept of the "Holy Trinity." The Christian church did not limit itself to changing a few ideas, it also rejected entire books. The church destroyed many documents and records which contradicted the radical changes that were made to Christian doctrine by these councils. Fortunately, the original writings which survived the editing process still offer valuable clues and insights into the life of Jesus.

Many writings rejected by the church councils found their way into a book known as the "Apocrypha" ("hidden writings").* The Apocrypha consists of writings which were adjudged to be of dubious origin or quality by the church. Some of the material was rightfully rejected. Other Apocryphal works, however, were omitted simply because they contradicted the official church version of Jesus's life on several crucial details. These are details which, if carefully researched, would offer a somewhat different outlook on the life of Jesus from the one presented in the authorized Bible.

According to the Apocrypha, the story of Jesus begins with his maternal grandparents, Joachim and Anna. Joachim was said to be a priest in a Hebrew temple. Joachim and Anna were happily married except for one problem: they had not been able to produce any children. This was a source of considerable embarrassment to them. Bearing children, especially sons, was quite important in that era.

One day Joachim was standing alone in the fields when an angel appeared. The angel was described as giving off a tremendous amount of light and striking fear into Joachim by its appearance. The angel calmed Joachim and told him not to be ashamed any longer because an angel would cause Anna to become pregnant. The only stipulation for this honor was that Joachim and his wife must surrender their child to be raised by the priests and angels at a temple in Jerusalem.

Everything went according to plan. At the age of three, Joachim and Anna's little girl, Mary, was taken to the temple and left there. Mary was a beautiful child who remained devoted to the priests and angels for about the next eleven years. When Mary and her peers in the temple became 12 or 14 years of age (two different ages are given by two

---

* Not to be confused with "apocalypse," which is a "revelation."

different sources), it was time for them to go back out into the world and get married.

Mary was not free to pick her own husband, however. Her mentors chose one for her. The mate picked for Mary was a very old man by the name of Joseph. Joseph did not agree at first to the marriage because he was quite old and had already had children of his own. After efforts were made to change his mind, Joseph consented to the match and went to his home in Bethlehem to prepare his house for his new wife. Mary went to the home of her parents, Joachim and Anna, in Galilee to make herself ready.

While Mary was in Galilee, an angel named Gabriel appeared before her, announcing that she would give birth to the new Messiah. Mary was confused:

> She said, How can that be? For seeing, according to my vow [of chastity], I have never had sexual contact with any man, how can I bear a child without the addition of a man's seed?
>
> To this the angel replied and said, Think not, Mary, that you will conceive in the ordinary way.
>
> For, without sleeping with a man, while a Virgin, you will conceive and while a Virgin you will give milk from your breast.
>
> For the Holy Ghost will come upon you, and the power of the Most High will overshadow you, without any of the heats of lust.
>
> So that to which you will give birth will be only holy, because it only is conceived without sin, and being born, shall be called the Son of God.
>
> Then Mary, stretching forth her hands, and lifting her eyes to heaven, said, Take notice of the handmaid of the Lord! Let it be done to me what you have said.
>
> MARY VII:16-21

Several researchers believe that stories of "virgin births" may be based upon instances of artificial insemination. Virgin birth means only that the woman did not become impregnated by a man, but was caused instead to bear a child through the action of an "angel." If we consider that many New Testament "angels" are Custodians, artificial insemination becomes a distinct possibility.

The above conversation between Mary and her "angel" expresses a strong moral and spiritual belief connected to the act of conception. Impregnation by an "angel" was deemed holy and desirable, but conception by human means was often considered sin. To someone engaging in artificial insemination, there would be a practical reason for creating such a distinction. Artificial insemination helps guarantee control over the physical characteristics of a future baby, something that cannot be assured in random human mating. By artificially inseminating two or more generations in a row, the purity of the final product is greatly increased. This is practiced today by animal breeders who closely control the insemination and breeding of livestock from generation to generation in order to bring forth bigger, better, and purer animals. In this respect, it is significant that the human offspring of alleged virgin births were often described as physically unflawed and unusually beautiful in appearance. While some of this flattery was no doubt due to the tendency of followers to view their religious leaders in the best possible light, the stories of angel-induced pregnancies over consecutive generations, such as the tale surrounding Jesus, would strongly suggest a breeding effort. This discussion is not meant to cast disrespect on the personality of Jesus by suggesting that his body was bred like a cow, but that is the picture which emerges.

The disdain expressed to priests by Biblical "angels" for the human method of conception was apparently based upon mere practical concerns to ensure good breeding, but it was nevertheless taken to heart by early priests and became a major element of many monotheistic religions. In Biblical days, human beings were also heavily propagandized as very sinful to justify the barbaric treatment humans suffered at the hands of their Custodial "God" and "angels." By extending this concept of sinfulness to the human method of procreation, every person conceived through human sexual intercourse was to be considered born in sin and therefore spiritually condemned. What a frightful dilemma this created! Every time a man and woman conceived and gave birth to a child, they had condemned a spiritual being; yet the human drives which produce children are strong. The religious teaching of automatic spiritual condemnation because of human procreation generated a powerful conflict between the drive for spiritual freedom and the physical drive to reproduce. The result was intense anxiety on the subject of sex and an increase in nonprocreative sexual activity such as homosexuality, autoeroticism, nonprocreative forms of intercourse, pornography, voyeurism, and abortion. The irony in this is clear. Those religions which have most strongly condemned the "inherent sin" in all human beings have also been those which have most vocally opposed nonprocreative sex.

These teachings had another important effect. They helped reduce human resistance to engaging in war. It is easier for a religious person to kill someone if he believes that the victim is inherently sinful.

Fortunately, most people today no longer believe that human conception is innately sinful, including most clergy. If anything, giving birth to children is seen as an event of happiness, and that is as it should be. Despite this, we still find some of the old ideas lingering. A small number of philosophers, psychiatrists, religious leaders and sociologists continue to proclaim that human beings are inherently "bad" or "evil," be it on religious or "scientific" grounds. This contributes little to our culture except to keep sexual anxiety and warfare alive.

After Mary's experience with the angel, Joseph travelled from his home in Bethlehem to pick up Mary in Galilee. To his chagrin, Joseph discovered that his young bride was already several months pregnant. Thinking that Mary had become a whore, Joseph made preparations to abandon her. An angel intervened and convinced Joseph that Mary was still a virgin. Joseph stayed with Mary in Galilee until her ninth month of pregnancy. In the ninth month, Joseph and Mary set off for Joseph's home in Bethlehem to have the child there. According to the Apocrypha, the couple did not reach Joseph's home in time. Mary went into labor near the outskirts of Bethlehem and a shelter had to be located for her immediately. What they found was a cave. In that cave young Jesus was born:

> *And when they came by the cave, Mary confessed to Joseph that her time of giving birth had come, and she could not go on to the city, and said, Let us go into this cave.*
>
> *At that time the sun was nearly down.*
>
> *But Joseph hurried away so that he might fetch her a midwife; and when he saw an old Hebrew woman who was from Jerusalem, he said to her, Please come here, good woman, and go into that cave, and you will see a woman just ready to give birth.*
>
> *It was after sunset, when the old woman and Joseph reached the cave, and they both went into it.*
>
> *And look, it was all filled with lights, greater than the light of lamps and candle, and greater than the light of the sun itself.*
>
> *The infant was then wrapped up in swaddling clothes, and sucking the breast of his mother St. Mary.*
>
> INFANCY 1:6-11

The unusual lights in the cave indicate to some people the existence of high-tech lighting of some sort. This may not be surprising when we discover that other apparent high-tech phenemona surrounded the birth of Jesus, such as the so-called "Star of Bethlehem."

Nearly everyone in the Christian world knows the tale of the three wise men who followed a bright star to the baby Jesus in Bethlehem. Most Christians believe that this unusual star, known as the "Star of Bethlehem," was supernatural in origin—a creation of God. Some scientists, if they have not dismissed the story as a religious myth, believe the Star to have been Halley's comet making a low pass over Earth, or a rare alignment of Venus and a bright star. Several UFO writers, on the other hand, assert that the Star of Bethlehem was an aircraft which led the three wise men from their homes in Persia to Bethlehem in the same fashion that Moses and the Hebrew tribes had been guided by an airborne "Jehovah" earlier in history. Surprisingly, the Apocrypha itself best supports the UFO theory. An Apocryphal book quotes one of the three wise men:

> *We saw an extraordinarily large star shining among the stars of heaven, and so outshined all the other stars, that they became not visible. . . .*
>
> PROTOVANGELION 15:7

That rules out Halley's comet, which has never been so bright. An alignment of Venus and stars could not blot out all other stars in the above fashion.

Not only did the Star of Bethlehem overwhelm all other stars, it moved:

> *So the wise men began their travel, and look, the star which they saw in the east went before them, until it came and stood over the cave where the young child was with Mary his mother.*
>
> PROTOVANGELION 15:9

After leading the three wise men to Jesus's birthplace, this remarkably intelligent "star" accompanied them home again: ". . . the light of which they followed until they returned into their own country" *(Infancy 3:3).*

The preceding passages offer additional evidence of Custodial involvement in the breeding and birth of Jesus. Who, then, were the three wise men? They are generally said to have been mystics and astrologers. Clearly they were indoctrinated in the Brotherhood messiah prophecies, else they would not have made the journey. Significantly, they hailed from Persia—a stronghold of Zoroastrianism and Aryanism at the time.

Many Christians believe that Jesus was born in an animal stall inside of Bethlehem city. In fact, it says so in the New Testament's Book of Luke. Proponents of the cave birth story, however, state that Jesus was not taken to the stall until several days after he was born. Mary had reportedly hidden Jesus there because of a threat to his life from King Herod, a local monarch who was alarmed by the Hebrew Messiah prophecies.

If it is true that Jesus was born in a cave, why would the writer of *Luke* and other early church leaders claim that Jesus's first bed was a manger?

It was the intention of those who backed Jesus to proclaim him the Hebrew Messiah. For that assertion to be true, they needed to prove that Jesus was a direct descendant of Hebrew King David. Such a lineage was required by the Hebrew prophecies. A number of religious historians, however, have concluded that Jesus belonged to a Hebrew religious sect known as the "Essenes." Joachim, Anna, and Mary may have all been members of Essene temples. The cave birth would tend to reinforce that conclusion because the Essenes were well known for using caves as shelters and hospices. If Jesus was an Essene, he could not have been a descendant of King David. This is why:

The Essenes were outwardly Jewish, but they also studied the *Zend Avesta* of the Zoroastrian religion and reportedly practiced Aryanism. This would help explain the visit of the three Persian wise men to baby Jesus in Bethlehem. It further appears that being Aryan was a requirement to becoming an Essene. Jesus himself was white-skinned and redheaded. Because of the racial prerequisite to becoming an Essene, no true Essene could have been a direct descendant of King David because the Hebrew tribes had a different lineage.

Much of what we know today about the Essenes comes from a famous mid-20th-century archaeological discovery: the Dead Sea Scrolls. The Scrolls are a library of very old documents dating from the first century A.D. They were written by members of an Essene community and hidden by them in caves near the Dead Sea. The Scrolls were discovered in 1947 (or possibly 1945) by a young Bedouin tribesman.

According to historian John Allegro, who analyzes the Scrolls in his book, *The People of the Dead Sea Scrolls,* the Essenes had many characteristics of a secret society. For example, a person's admission into the Essene Order was accomplished only after several years probation. The Essenes practiced initiation rituals in which they swore to never divulge their secret teachings. They also held confidential the names of the "angels" said to be living among the Essenes in their closed communities. Essene priests often called themselves "The Sons of Zadok" after high priest Zadok, who had served in the temple of Solomon.

In light of these discoveries, it is not surprising that several Brotherhood branches had claimed long before the discovery of the Dead Sea Scrolls that the Essene organization was a branch of the Brotherhood in Palestine, perhaps the Brotherhood's most important offshoot in that region. Albert MacKey's *History of Freemasonry,* published in 1898, confirms this by reporting that the Essenes had a system of degrees and used a symbolic apron.

There is much evidence that Jesus remained an Essene throughout his adult life. Historian Will Durant, writing in his work, *Caesar and Christ (The Story of Civilization,* Part III), points out that the Essenes were the only sect with a Jewish tradition that did not oppose Jesus's early attempts at religious innovation. Of the three major Hebrew sects existing in Palestine at that time, Jesus condemned only the Pharisees and the Sadducees for their vices and hypocrisy, not the Essenes. The Essenes and Christians shared many traits in common: they held similar beliefs about living in "The Last Days," shared common meals, owned property communally, engaged in ritual baths and baptisms, and had some organizational points in common. Remarkable similarities between several Dead Sea Scroll doctrines and New Testament writings have also been noted. Historians point to Jesus's close personal friendship to John the Baptist. Many baptismal and ascetic (self-denial) practices of the Essenes were shared by John. While John did differ in other respects from what we know today of standard Essene practices, the similarities are strong enough to suggest that John was himself an Essene. Finally, we have the active presence of "angels" reportedly guiding both the Essenes and Jesus's ministry.

Despite the strong evidence, some theologians still dispute that Jesus was an Essene. Their objections are based primarily on the fact that many of Jesus's teachings contradicted Essene ways. There was a good reason for that contradiction. Jesus, though an Essene, had come into contact with the Indian maverick movement and, as a result, had become a rebellious maverick himself. He tried to forge ahead with a religious philosophy which was often at odds with his Essene sponsors, and he would suffer for it.

Most New Testament information about Jesus's life covers only the three years immediately prior to his crucifixion. Those were the years of Jesus's public ministry. During that time, Jesus did not live inside the Essene communities for the simple reason that he was engaged in a traveling ministry which would occupy him until his crucifixion. Every Essene was given, or created for himself, a "calling" or life's goal to pursue. Jesus pursued his as a teacher on the road.

In both the New Testament and Apocrypha, the life of Jesus seems to be fairly well covered up until about the age of 5 or 6. Then, abruptly, there is a complete void of information about where Jesus went or what he did. We find in the New Testament one episode of Jesus appearing before Hebrew scholars at the age of 12, followed by an eighteen-year silence in which Jesus's activities are unaccounted for. Suddenly, at about the age of 30, Jesus re-emerged and launched his short and tumultuous religious career. Where had Jesus gone, and what had he done, during the unknown years?

Most Christians believe that Jesus spent his teens and young adulthood working for his father as a carpenter. No doubt Jesus did occasionally visit his father and learn carpentry on those visits. Many historians, however, feel that there was much more happening in Jesus's life and they have tried to discover what else Jesus might have done during those critical years when his thoughts, personality, and motives were developing. As it turns out, Jesus was being intensively trained for his future religious role.

It was common for Essene boys to enter an Essene monastery at about the age of 5 to begin their educations. This will account for Jesus's sudden disappearance from history at that age. Some researchers believe that Jesus was brought up and educated in the Essene community above Haifa by the Mediterranean Sea. He apparently remained there until his teens. At the age of 12, he made a trip to Jerusalem in preparation for his bar mitzvah the following year. It was during that trip that Jesus had the debate with Hebrew scholars. Jesus then vanished from history again. Now where did he go?

Several years ago I happened to see an intriguing film documentary by Richard Bock entitled, *The Lost Years.* This film regularly shows up on local American television stations around Christmas and Easter. It is well worth watching. The film suggests that Jesus journeyed to Asia where he spent his teens and early adulthood studying the religions practiced there. One source from which the filmmaker drew this remarkable conclusion was the "Legend of Issa," a very old Buddhist document purportedly discovered in the Himi Monastery of India by Russian traveler Nicolas Notovitch in 1887. Notovitch published his translation of the Buddhist legend in 1890 in his book, *The Unknown Life of Jesus.*

According to the Buddhist legend uncovered by Notovitch, a remarkable young man named "Issa" had departed for Asia at the age of thirteen. Issa studied under several religious masters of the East, did some preaching of his own, and returned to Palestine sixteen years later at the age of 29. The significant parallels between the lives of "Issa" and Jesus have led to the conclusion that Issa was, in fact, Jesus. If true, such a journey would certainly be omitted from the Bible because it contradicts the idea that Jesus had achieved spiritual enlightenment solely by divine inspiration.

If Jesus was an Essene and he travelled to Asia under Essene sponsorship, and if the Essenes indeed followed an Aryan tradition, we would expect Jesus to be sent to study under the Aryan Brahmans of the Indian subcontinent. According to the Legend of Issa, that is precisely what happened:

In his fourteenth year, young Issa, the Blessed One, came this side of the Sindh [a province in Western Pakistan] and settled among the Aryas [Aryans]. . . .[1]

Upon Jesus's arrival, "the white priests of Brahma welcomed him joyfully"[2] and taught him, among other things, to read and understand the Vedas, and to teach and expound sacred Hindu scriptures. This joyful reception quickly turned sour, however, because Jesus insisted upon associating with the lower castes. That led to friction between the young headstrong Jesus and his Brahmin hosts. According to the legend:

> But the Brahmins and the Kshatriyas [members of the military caste] told him that they were forbidden by the great Para-Brahma [Hindu god] to come near to those who were created from his belly and his feet [the mythical origin of the lower castes];
>
> That the Vaisyas [members of the merchant and agricultural caste] might only hear the recital of the Vedas, and this only on the festival days, and
>
> That the Sudras [one of the lower castes] were not only forbidden to attend the readings of the Vedas, but even to look on them; for they were condemned to perpetual servitude, as slaves of the Brahmins, the Kshatriyas and even the Vaisyas.
>
> But Issa, disregarding their words, remained with the Sudras, preaching against the Brahmins and Kshatriyas.
>
> He declaimed strongly against man's arrogating to himself the authority to deprive his fellow-beings of their human and spiritual rights. "Verily," he said, "God has made no difference between his children, who are all alike dear to Him."
>
> Issa denied the divine inspiration of the Vedas and the Puranas [a class of sacred writings]. . . .[3]

The white priests and warriors were so angered that they sent servants to murder Jesus. Warned of the danger, Jesus fled the holy city of Djagguernat by night and escaped into Buddhist country. There he learned the Pali language and studied sacred Buddhist writings ("Sutras"). After six years, Jesus "could perfectly expound the sacred [Buddhist] scrolls."[4]

The Issa legend has some remarkable implications. It portrays Jesus as a sincere religious reformer who found himself turning against the Custodial/Aryan traditions in which he had been raised. His sympathies went instead to the maverick Buddhists. The Buddhist influence in Jesus's teachings are evident in the Bible, as in Jesus's "Sermon on the Mount" which contains some philosophy strikingly similar to the Buddhism of his day.

After fifteen or so years in and about Asia, Jesus travelled back to Palestine via Persia, Greece, and Egypt. According to one tradition, Jesus was initiated into the higher ranks of the Brotherhood in the Egyptian city of Heliopolis. After completing that initiation, Jesus returned to Palestine, now a man of 29 or 30. Immediately upon his return, Jesus embarked on his public ministry.

The rift between Jesus and his Aryan hosts in India did not, at first, seem to adversely affect Jesus's relationship to the Essene Order. It did not take long, however, for trouble to erupt. Jesus did not share the asceticism of his Essene brothers and downplayed the importance of ritualism for achieving spiritual salvation. Jesus was surrounded by Essene sponsors who strongly believed in the coming of a Messiah and they were determined to have their investment, Jesus, proclaimed that new Messiah. Jesus forbade them to do so. According to historian Will Durant, Jesus "repudiated all claim to Davidic descent"[5] and for a long time "forbade the disciples to call him the messiah. . . ."[6] Most historians attribute those actions to the political climate of the time. Palestine was under Roman occupation and the Romans took a dim view of the Hebrew prophecies because of their political overtones. Jesus did not wish to run afoul of the Romans, or so the thinking goes.

There is, however, a much better reason why Jesus did not want to be proclaimed the Hebrew Messiah. He knew that the proclamation was untrue and he was being honest about it. Jesus wanted to bring to Palestine a genuine spiritual science of the type the mavericks were still attempting in India. Jesus therefore became a rebel inside of the very Brotherhood organization backing him. Jesus's greatest mistake was believing that he could use the channels of the corrupted Brotherhood network to spread a maverick religion, even if he had many close friends and loved ones in the Essene Order.

Jesus never had time to establish his maverick religious system because some of his Essene backers and, according to the Bible, even some Custodial "angels," quickly got him into trouble by proclaiming him the Messiah. It did not take the Romans and some Hebrew leaders long to arrest Jesus and put him on trial. The Hebrews objected to his unorthodox religious ideas and the Romans his alleged political pretensions. A mere three years after beginning his ministry, Jesus was reportedly nailed to a cross. Although there is evidence that Jesus did not die on the cross but survived to live out the rest of his life in seclusion, the crucifixion ended his public ministry and paved the way for his name to be used to implant the very Judgment Day philosophies he had opposed.*

Jesus's problems cannot be blamed on his backers alone, however. Certainly Jesus's own errors contributed to his downfall. Despite his maverick leanings, Jesus was unable to entirely undo within himself a lifetime of indoctrination as an Essene. There is good Biblical and Apocryphal evidence that Jesus tried to mix Custodial dogma with maverick tenets. This will cause any honest attempt at spiritual reform to fail. The Bible also indicates that Jesus taught some of his lessons through a system of mysteries. Jesus's only hope had been to break completely with the Essene Order and its methods, but it is easy to understand why he had not done so. His life, family, and friends were too much a part of that organization.

Although Jesus had a large enough following to invite attention, he did not preach long enough to enter the history books of his own time. His fame grew after the crucifixion when his disciples traveled far and wide to establish their

---

* A set of documents dating from around 400 A.D.—the Nag Hammadi scrolls—were discovered in Egypt in 1945. The scrolls are hand-inscribed copies of earlier original manuscripts. Many or all of those originals were written no later than 150 A.D., *i.e.* before the standard New Testament gospels were penned. Some scholars believe many of the Nag Hammadi scrolls to be as authentic, and less altered, than the accepted Gospels of the New Testament. According to the Nag Hammadi, Jesus was not nailed to a cross, but another man, Simon, had been cleverly substituted to suffer Jesus's fate. Whatever the truth of this might be, what is important to us is simply that the crucifixion signaled the end of Jesus's public ministry.

new apocalyptic sect. With the continued help of their Custodial "angels," Christian missionaries made Jesus a household name and created a powerful new faction that would further divide human beings into battling groups.

The successful effort to make Jesus the figurehead of a new Judgment Day religion brought about the most famous apocalyptic writing in the western world: the *Revelation of St. John*. This work, which is also known as the *Book of Revelation* or *Apocalypse*, is the last book of the New Testament. It leaves Christians with the same type of dire prophecy that the Hebrews had been left with at the end of the Old Testament: the coming of a great global catastrophe followed by a Day of Judgment. The *Book of Revelation* is well worth taking a closer look at.

# 13

# Apocalypse of John

THE ALLEGED AUTHOR of *Revelation* was Jesus's personal friend and disciple, John (not to be confused with John the Baptist, a different person). John appears to have been the most influential of Jesus's disciples, and an earlier biblical text that is attributed to him, the *Book of John,* seems to come closest to conveying the strong mystical leanings of Jesus's backers and of the early Christian church. For these and other reasons, the name of John has been an important one to Christians and to a number of mystical organizations. It is perhaps not surprising, then, that John's name would be chosen to convey the final and most colorful apocalypse in the Bible.

The *Revelation of St. John* is the fifth and final work attributed to John to appear in the New Testament. Some scholars believe that *Revelation* was written by John while he was living in exile on the Greek island of Patmos many years after the crucifixion of Christ. Others are convinced that disciple John was not the author of *Revelation* because *Revelation* was not discovered until about two hundred years after John's lifetime. According to Joseph Free, writing in his book, *Archaeology and Bible History,* the linguistic qualities of *Revelation* are inferior in some ways to the *Book of John.* It is argued that if *Revelation* was written five years after the *Book of John* by the same person, *Revelation* should be linguistically equal or superior to the earlier work. Another point is that *Revelation* contains expressions from the Hebrew language that were not used in John's earlier writings. On the other hand, important similarities between *Revelation* and other books of John have been noted, especially in the repetition of certain words and phrases. Whatever the true authorship of *Revelation* may be, the impact of this work has been major.

*Revelation* is the first-person account of the author's bizarre meeting with a strange person he believed to be Jesus. Over a period of a day or two, the author also met a number of unusual creatures which showed him pictures of frightening future events. The author was told by those creatures that Satan (the "anti-Christ") would take over the world. This would be followed by the Final Battle of Armageddon during which the angels of God would battle the forces of Satan. The Final Battle would bring about the banishment of Satan from human society and the triumphant return ("Second Coming") of Jesus to reign over Earth for a thousand years.

The *Book of Revelation* is written in a wonderfully picturesque manner. It is filled with complex and imaginative symbolism. Because the pictures revealed to John were symbols, *Revelation* can be used to predict an imminent "End of the World" at almost any historical epoch. The prophecy is constructed so that the symbols can be interpreted to represent whatever historical events happen to be occurring at the time one is living. This is precisely what has been done with *Revelation* ever since it appeared, and it is still being done today.

The question is, what caused the author's "visions"? Was it lunacy? A propensity to tell tall tales? Or was it something else? The author seems sincere enough to rule out deceit. His straightforward manner of narration tends to eliminate lunacy as the answer. That leaves "something else." The question is: what?

Upon analyzing the text of *Revelation,* we discover something rather remarkable. It appears that the author had actually been drugged and, while in that drugged state, was shown pictures in a book by individuals who were wearing costumes and putting on a ceremony for the author's benefit. Let us look at the passages of *Revelation* which suggest this.

John begins his story by telling us that he was at prayer. From a further description, it seems that he was conducting his ritual outdoors during daylight hours. Suddenly, a loud voice resounded behind him. The voice commanded him to write down everything he was about to see and hear, and to send the message to the seven Christian churches in Asia [Turkey]. John turned around to see who was speaking to him and, lo and behold, there he saw what he believed to be seven golden candlesticks. Standing among the candlesticks was a person whom the author described as:

> . . . *one who looked like the Son of man [Jesus], clothed with a garment down to the foot, and wearing about the chest a golden girdle [support].*
>
> *His head and his hairs were white like wool, as white as snow; and his eyes were as flame of fire;*
>
> *And his feet were like fine brass, as if they burned in a furnace; and his voice was as the sound of many waters.*
>
> *And he had in his right hand seven stars: and out of his mouth went a sharp two-edged sword: and his appearance was like the sun shines in his strength.*
>
> *And when I saw him, I fell at his feet as though dead. And he laid his right hand upon me. . . .*
>
> REVELATION 1:13-17

There are striking similarities between this new "Jesus" and the space age "angels" of earlier Biblical stories. The prophet Ezekiel, for example, had also met visitors with feet of brass. The above passage from *Revelation* suggests that John's "Jesus" may have been garbed in a one-piece body suit extending from the neck down to metal or metal-like boots.* The creature's head was described as "white like wool, as white as snow," indicating an artificial head covering or helmet. John's claim that this creature had a voice "as the sound of many waters," that is, rumbling and thunderous, is also reminiscent of Ezekiel's angels and could have been caused by the rumbling of nearby engines or by electronic amplification of the creature's voice. The "two-edged sword" protruding from the creature's mouth easily suggests a microphone or breathing pipe.

After John regained his composure, "Jesus" commanded him to write down the missives that "Jesus" wanted sent to various Christian churches. Those letters constitute the first three chapters of *Revelation*. The most interesting phase of John's experience then begins in chapter 4:

> . . . I looked, and behold, a door was opened in heaven: and the first voice which I heard, which sounded like a trumpet talking with me; said Come up here, and I will show you things which must take place hereafter.
>
> And immediately I was in the spirit: and, look, a throne was set in heaven, and one [creature] sat on the throne.
>
> And the one who sat looked to me like a jasper and sardine stone: and there was a rainbow around the throne looking like an emerald.
>
> And all around the throne were twenty-four seats: and upon the seats I saw twenty-four elders sitting, clothed in white garments: and they had on their heads crowns of gold.
>
> And out of the throne came lightnings and thunderings and voices: and there were seven lamps of fire burning before the throne, which are the seven Spirits of God.
>
> And before the throne there was a sea of glass like crystal: and in the midst of the throne, and round

---

* The fact that the author mistook this creature for Jesus may be further evidence that the author was not the original disciple John. For convenience, however, I will continue to refer to the author of *Revelation* as John.

*about the throne were four beasts full of eyes in front
and back.*

REVELATION 4:1-6

The above passage can be viewed as the author being
taken up through the door of some sort of aircraft and
finding himself face to face with its occupants, as told
by someone incapable of understanding the experience.
The quote contains two especially interesting elements:
first, John said that a voice from above sounded like a
trumpet talking with him. This strongly suggests a voice
bellowing through a loudspeaker. Second, the "lightnings
and thunderings and voices" emitting from the "throne"
suggest that the throne had a television or radio set of
some kind. A modern-day human might well describe the
same experience this way: "Well, yes, I was lifted up into
a rocketship. There I confronted the seated crew in their
white jumpsuits and helmets. They had some radio or TV
reception going."

The presence of seven candles and seven lamps indicates
that a ritual had been prepared for the author. The ritual
was replete with costumes, theatrics, and sound effects—
all designed to deeply impress the message upon the author.
This is what happened when John was shown the first
scroll:

*And I saw in the right hand of the one who sat on
the throne a scroll with writing on the inside and on
the back side sealed with seven seals.*

*And I saw a strong angel proclaiming with a loud
voice, Who is worthy to open the book, and to loosen
the seals of it?*

*And no man in heaven, nor in earth, nor from under
the earth, was able to open the book nor to look upon
its contents.*

*And I wept a great deal, because no man was found
worthy to open and to read the book, nor to look upon
its contents.*

*And one of the elders said to me, Weep not: look, the
Lion [one of the animals there] of the tribe of Judah,*

*the Root of David, has succeeded to open the book, and to loosen its seven seals.*

*And I saw standing between the throne and the four beasts, and in the midst of the elders, a Lamb in the manner of having been slain, having seven horns and seven eyes, which are the seven spirits of God sent out to all the earth.*

*And he came and took the book out of the right hand of the one who sat upon the throne.*

*And when he had taken the book, the four beasts and twenty-four elders fell before the Lamb, each of them holding harps, and golden containers full of odors, which are the prayers of saints.*

*And they sung a new song, saying, You are worthy to take the book, and to open the seals of it: for you were slain, and have redeemed us to God by your blood from every family, language, people, and nation:*

*And have made us into kings and priests to God: and we shall reign on earth.*

*And I saw, and I heard the voice of many angels around the throne and the beasts and the elders: and they numbered ten thousand times ten thousand, and thousands of thousands;*

*Saying with a loud voice, Worthy is the Lamb that was slain to receive power, and riches, and wisdom, and strength, and honor, and glory, and blessing.*

*And every creature which is in heaven, and on the earth, and under the earth, and those that are in the sea, and all that are in them, heard I saying, Blessing, and honor, and glory, and power, be to him that sits upon the throne, and to the Lamb for ever and ever.*

*And the four beasts said, Amen. And the twenty-four elders fell down and worshipped him that lived for ever and ever.*

REVELATION 5:1-14

The elders continued to fall at dramatic moments throughout the ceremony. Each time they did so, they made quite an impression upon John. Among their cries of "Amen!" and "Alleluia!", the author was given the somber task of writing down everything he was being shown and taught.

It has been pointed out that the experience John described is identical to mystical ritual, especially of initiation into the teachings of a secret society. For this reason, some people believe that *Revelation* is actually an account of an initiation ceremony typical of many Brotherhood organizations—typical even today. These observations are quite significant when they are coupled with the evidence that John's experience had an element of space opera. It reveals continued Custodial involvement in Brotherhood mysticism after the time of Christ and shows Custodians to be the ultimate source of apocalyptic doctrines.

In the above passage from *Revelation,* we observe that John reacted with strong emotions to what was going on around him. He was especially prone to weeping on relatively little provocation. He seemed unable to distinguish between ritual and apparent reality. This raises questions about his mental state. A careful reading of *Revelation* indicates that John's mind may have been influenced by drugs administered to him by the creatures. Modern psychiatry has discovered that a number of drugs can be used to deeply implant messages in a person's mind. This technique serves today as an intelligence tool in the United States, Russia, and elsewhere. The probable drugging of John is exposed in Chapter 10 of *Revelation.* The author was apparently outdoors again preparing to memorialize the latest revelations when an "angel" flew down from the sky holding something in its hand:

> *And the voice which I heard from heaven spoke to me again, and said, Go and take the little scroll which is open in the hand of the angel which stands upon the sea and upon the earth.*
> *And I went to the angel, and said to him, Give me the little scroll. And he said to me, Take it, and eat it up; and it will make your belly bitter, but it will be in your mouth as sweet as honey.*
> *And I took the little scroll out of the angel's hand, and ate it up; and it was in my mouth sweet as honey: and as I had eaten it, my belly was bitter.*

*And he said to me, You must preach again before
many peoples and nations, and tongues, and kings.*
                              REVELATION 10:8-11

Most Christians believe that the little scroll offered to John
was an actual document, the contents of which the author
magically came to know by eating the scroll. Our clue that it
was probably paper, or something else, saturated with a drug
lies in John's testimony that the scroll was sweet to the taste
but caused a bitter reaction in the stomach. Interestingly, an
almost identical experience had been reported by Ezekiel:

*And when I looked, a hand [of an angel] was put
before me; and a scroll was in it;*
*And he spread it before me; and it had writing inside
and out: and there were written lamentations, and
mourning, and woe.*
*Additionally, he said to me, Son of man, eat what you
are finding; eat this scroll, and go to speak to the house
[people] of Israel.*
*So, I opened my mouth, and he caused me to eat that
scroll.*
*And he said to me, Son of man, make your belly eat,
and fill your bowels with this scroll that I give you.*
*Then I ate it; and it was in my mouth as sweet as
honey.*
*And he said to me, Son of man, go, get yourself over
to the house of Israel, and speak with my words
to them.*
                              EZEKIEL 2:9-10, 3:1-4

Many people mistakenly believe that John actually saw
the future historical events he prophesized in *Revelation*. It
has been pointed out by Christian and non-Christian scholars
alike that John's "visions" of the future were simply illustra-
tions drawn on scrolls. This is especially evident in John's
"vision" of the Creature with seven heads and ten horns:

*And I stood upon the sand of the sea, and saw a beast
rise up out of the sea, having seven heads and ten*

*horns, and upon his horns ten crowns, and upon his heads blasphemous names.*

REVELATION 13:1

The fact that actual words (blasphemous names) were written upon the heads of this creature reveal that John was looking at an illustration with labels—much like an old-fashioned political cartoon. Although the author does not specifically say so, it is likely that many other "visions" on the scrolls were labeled in a similar fashion.

There can be no doubt that, as literature, the *Book of Revelation* is a colorful, dramatic, and hard-hitting work. As the basis for a religious philosophy, however, it has all the pitfalls of the apocalypses which came before it. As we shall see, the prophecy made in *Revelation* has been fulfilled at least a half-dozen times in world history, complete with global catastrophe followed by "Second Comings." Not once has this brought about a thousand years of peace and spiritual salvation. All it has done is set the stage for the next catastrophe. Today, as we stand on a massive nuclear powderkeg, perhaps it is time to reevaluate the usefulness of apocalyptic belief before the world is plunged into yet another "final battle." Yes, spiritual salvation and a thousand years of peace are goals well worth having, and are long overdue, but there is no need to pay the price of an Armageddon to achieve them.

# 14

# The Plagues
# of Justinian

AS WE LEAVE the time of Jesus and enter the A.D. years, history becomes firmer and personalities come into better focus. Documentation is better. Even so, the same historical patterns we have studied continue undiminished. To those who find what we have looked at thus far completely unbelievable, I can only share that feeling with full empathy. The view of history I am presenting seems to demand an understanding that the factors which lie at the bottom of human turmoil may be extremely bizarre factors, and perhaps that is why they have never been resolved.

After the lifetime of Jesus, the Christian church grew rapidly. In its early years, Christianity attracted a large number of genuine humanitarians who were enthused by the message Jesus tried to put forth. Early Christian leaders, despite the Essene influence, were able to promote a rather benign religion with many benefits. Jesus had not failed entirely. Early Christians gave people the hope that they could achieve spiritual salvation by acquiring knowledge, by engaging in ethical conduct, by unburdening themselves through confession of wrongdoing, and by making amends for those transgressions that caused a person to suffer guilt.

Given the benign character of the early Christian church, it did not need a harsh code of ethics. The severest punishment a person could suffer in most Christian sects at that time was excommunication, *i.e.*, being kicked out. That was considered a very severe punishment, however (equivalent to our modern death penalty), because an individual was considered doomed to eternal spiritual deterioration if he or she was excommunicated. A priest was obliged to do everything he could to appeal to a person's reason before excommunicating him. The primary cause for excommunication was criminal or grossly immoral behavior.

For about the first three hundred years of its existence, Christianity remained an unofficial religion and was often persecuted. A number of political leaders eventually became converts and, under them, Christianity began to change. The humanitarian foundation created by Jesus eroded as Christianity became more political.

The political transformation of Christianity got its first big push in the West Roman Empire with the Christian conversion of its ruler, Constantine I the Great.* A number of historians believe that Constantine was already leaning in the direction of becoming a Christian because his father was a monotheist. Contemporaries of Constantine have noted, however, that Constantine's true conversion came as the result of a reported vision he had in 312 A.D. Several different accounts have been recorded of that vision. According to Socrates, who wrote about it in the fifth century A.D.:

> . . . as he was marching at the head of his troops,
> a praeternatural vision transcending all description

---

* In the late 3rd century A.D., Roman emperor Diocletian appointed three additional Caesars (emperors) to help him govern the Roman empire. The empire was split into eastern and western divisions for administrative convenience, each with a separate emperor. From 324 to 337 A.D., however, Constantine ruled both the East and West Roman Empire as sole emperor.

appeared to him. In fact, at about that time of the day when the sun, having passed the meridian, began to decline towards the West, he saw a pillar of light in the form of a cross on which was inscribed "in this conquer." The appearance of the sign struck him with amazement, and doubting his own eyes, he asked those around him if they could see what he did, and, as they unanimously declared that they could, the emperor's mind was strengthened by this divine and miraculous apparition. On the following night, while he slept, he saw Christ, who directed him to make a standard [flag] according to the pattern he had been shown, and to use it against his enemies as a guarantee of victory. Obedient to the divine command, he had a standard made in the form of a cross, which is preserved in the palace until this day. . . .[1]

The truth of Constantine's vision is disputed by those who would attribute it to mere legend-making. Others might view the aerial cross as an unusual reflection of the setting sun, followed by a dream. Some theorists might even argue that it was another manifestation of the UFO phenomenon with its continuing links to apocalyptic religion. Whatever the truth of the story is, Constantine's purported vision of a bright light in the sky followed by the appearance of "Jesus" the next night is stated to be the event which pushed Constantine into the arms of apocalyptic Christianity. He issued the famous "Edict of Milan" one year later. The Edict officially granted tolerance to the Christian religion within the Roman Empire, ending almost three centuries of Roman persecution.

Constantine was responsible for other significant changes to Christianity. It was he who convened, and often attended, the Council of Nicea in 325 A.D. At that time, many Christians, such as the Gnostics, strongly resisted efforts by Constantine and others to deify Jesus. The Gnostics simply saw Jesus as an honest spiritual teacher. The Nicene Council met in large part to put an end to such resistance and to create a divine image of Jesus. With this purpose in mind, the Council created the famous Nicene Creed which made belief in Jesus as "the Son of God" a cornerstone of Christian faith. To enforce these often unpopular tenets, Constantine put the power of the state at the disposal of the newly "Romanized" Christian church.

Constantine's reign was notable for another achievement. It marked the beginning of the European Middle Ages. Constantine is credited with laying the foundation for medieval serfdom and feudalism. As in the Hindu caste system, Constantine made most occupations hereditary. He decreed that the "coloni" (a class of tenant farmers) were to be permanently attached to the soil on which they lived. Constantine's "Romanized" Christianity (which came to be known as Roman Catholicism) and his oppressive feudalism caused Christianity to move sharply away from the surviving maverick teachings of Jesus into a nearly complete Custodial system.

As time progressed and official changes to Christian doctrine continued to be made, two new crimes emerged: "heresy" (speaking out against established dogma) and "paganism" (not adhering to Christianity at all). In the earliest days of the Church, Christian leaders felt that people could only be made Christians by appealing to their reason, and that no one could be, or should be, forced. After Constantine, leaders of the new Roman orthodoxies took an entirely different view. They demanded obedience as a matter of law, and belief on the basis of faith alone rather than reason. With those changes came new punishments. No longer was excommunication the severest penalty of the Church, although it was still practiced. Physical and economic sanctions were also applied. Many devoted Christians became victimized by the new laws when they would not agree to the new Roman orthodoxies. Those victims correctly saw that the Church was moving away from Jesus's true teachings.

The new Christian teachings were given a great boost at the end of the fourth century A.D. by East Roman Emperor Theodosius I. Theodosius issued at least eighteen laws aimed at punishing those people who rejected the doctrines established by the Nicene Council. He made Christianity the official state religion and closed down many pagan temples by force. He ordered Christian armies to burn down the famous Alexandrian Library, which was a world book depository and center of learning. The Alexandrian Library contained priceless historical, scientific, and literary records from all over the world—gathered over a period of seven hundred years. Although some of the library had already been ravaged by earlier wars, the destruction by Theodosius's army obliterated what remained. Because most of the documents were one-of-a-kind, a great deal of recorded history and learning was lost.

Matters continued to worsen. By the middle of the sixth century A.D., the death penalty came into use against heretics and pagans. A campaign of genocide was ordered by East Roman emperor, Justinian, to more quickly establish the Christian orthodoxies. In Byzantine alone, an estimated 100,000 people were murdered. Under Justinian, the hunting of heretics became a frequent activity and the practice of burning heretics at the stake began.

Justinian also introduced more changes to Christian doctrine. He convened the Second Synod of Constantinople in 553 A.D. The Synod was neither attended nor, apparently, sanctioned by the Pope in Rome. At that time, in fact, many of the changes to Christian doctrine in the eastern Roman empire had not yet reached the Papacy, although they eventually would. The Second Synod issued a decree banning the doctrine of "past lifetimes," or "reincarnation," even though the doctrine was an important one to Jesus. The Synod decreed:

> If anyone assert the fabulous pre-existence of souls and shall submit to the monstrous doctrine that follows from it, let him be anathema [excommunicated].[2]

In deference to that decree, all but very veiled references to "pre-existence" were taken out of the Bible. Belief in pre-existence was declared heresy. This suppression was enforced throughout the western Christian world and in its sciences. The idea of personal pre-existence still remains, to a very large degree, a Western religious and scientific heresy.

Christianity was shaped into a powerful institution under the East Roman emperors. True to the pattern of history, "Romanized" Christianity was another Brotherhood faction that could be counted on to do battle with other Brotherhood factions, thereby helping to generate nonstop warfare between human beings. The new orthodox Christianity was placed in opposition to all other religions, including the East Roman Mystery Schools, which Justinian banned.

We have just observed a snowballing of historical events triggered by Constantine's vision. This period marked one of mankind's "End of the World" episodes, highlighted by religious "visions," cataclysmic genocides, and the creation of a new world social order promising, but not delivering, utopia. Another important "End of the World" element was also present. A massive plague struck, accompanied by reports of unusual aerial phenomena.

Between 540 A.D. and 592 A.D., when Justinian was carrying out his Christian "reforms," a bubonic plague engulfed the East Roman Empire and spread to Europe. The epidemic began inside Justinian's realm, and so it was named "Justinian's Plague." Justinian's Plague was one of the most devastating plagues of history and many people at the time believed it to be a punishment from God. In fact, the word "plague" comes from the Latin word for "blow" or "wound." Plague has been nicknamed "God's Disease," *i.e.*, a blow or wound from God.

One reason people thought plague to be from God was the frequent appearance of unusual aerial phenomena in conjunction with outbreaks of the plague. One chronicler of Justinian's Plague was the famous historian, Gregory of Tours, who documented a number of unusual events from the plague years. Gregory reports that just before Justinian's Plague invaded the Auvergne region of France in 567 A.D., three or four brilliant lights appeared around the sun and the heavens appeared to be on fire. This may have been a natural "sun dog" effect; however, other unusual celestial phenomena were also seen in the area. Another historian reported a similar event twenty-three years later in another part of France: Avignon. "Strange sights" were reported in the sky and the ground was sometimes as brightly illuminated at night as in the day. Shortly thereafter, a disastrous outbreak of the plague occurred there. Gregory reported a sighting in Rome consisting of an immense "dragon" which floated through the city and down to the sea, followed by a severe outbreak of the plague immediately thereafter.

Such reports chillingly suggest the unthinkable: that Justinian's Plague was caused by biological warfare agents spread by Custodial aircraft. It would be a repetition of similar plagues reported in the Bible and ancient Mesopotamian texts. By the time of Justinian's Plague, however, the Custodians were "invisible." They were hidden behind Brotherhood secrecy and veils of religious myth, yet they were apparently no less concerned about keeping their slave race oppressed. We will see a great deal more evidence of UFO activity associated with plagues in the upcoming chapter on the Black Death.

According to apocalyptic prophecy, an event like Justinian's Plague is supposed to herald the coming of a new "Messiah" or messenger from "God." Sure enough, such a figure did arrive. His name was Mohammed. He was born during Justinian's reign at a time when the Plague was still raging. Proclaimed in adulthood as the new "saviour," Mohammed became the leader of a new monotheistic apocalyptic religion: Islam. Like Moses and Jesus before him, Mohammed appears to have been a sincere man, but his new religion nevertheless became a faction which created new religious "issues" for people to endlessly fight over. Like Moses and Jesus, Mohammed was supported by the corrupted Brotherhood.

# 15

# Mohammed

MOHAMMED WAS BORN circa 570 A.D. As with Jesus, there are gaping holes in the life history of Mohammed, especially in regard to his childhood and early adulthood. To fill in the gaps, some historians hypothesize that Mohammed was an orphan who had been shunted about among relatives during his youth. It is known that at age 25 he married a wealthy widow, and some biographers believe that he worked as a tradesman in her business for the next fifteen years, although that is not entirely certain. At age 40, Mohammed suddenly emerged as a religious prophet and the leader of a powerful new religious movement.

According to Mohammed's own statements, his religious mission was triggered by an apparition. The vision occurred outside a secluded cave to which Mohammed would frequently retire for prayer and contemplation. The apparition was an "angel" bearing a message for Mohammed to spread. This was not just any angel, however. It called itself Gabriel—one of the most important of the Christian angels. Mohammed described the meeting in these words:

*The Koran [the holy book of Islam] is no other than a revelation revealed to him.* One terrible in power taught it to him, endued with wisdom. With even balance stood He in the highest part of the horizon. Then He came nearer and approached, and was at a distance of two bows, or even closer—and he revealed to His servant what He revealed.*

The Koran repeats the story:

*That this is the word of an illustrious Messenger, endued with power, having influence with the Lord of the Throne, obeyed there by Angels, faithful to his trust, and your compatriot is not one possessed by jinn [spirits]; for he saw him in the clear horizon.*

Mohammed was either semiconscious or in a trance when the angel Gabriel ordered him to "Recite!" and record the message that the angel was about to give him. The angel's command to Mohammed was much like the commands given earlier in history to Ezekiel of the Old Testament and to "John" of the *Book of Revelation* by similar Custodial personnel.

When Mohammed awoke, it seemed to him that the angel's words were "inscribed upon his [Mohammed's] heart." This is significant, for it suggests that Mohammed, like Ezekiel, John, and perhaps even Constantine, had been drugged and mentally tampered with so that the message would be more firmly implanted in his mind.

The message given to Mohammed was a new religion called "Islam," which means "Surrender." Followers must "surrender" to God. Members of Mohammed's faith are therefore called "Moslems," which comes from the word "muslim" ("one who submits"). Islam was one more Custodial religion designed to instill abject obedience in humans.

---

* Mohammed uses the third-person "him" when referring to himself.

The Supreme Being of the Islam faith is named "Allah," who was said by Mohammed to be the the same God as the Jewish and Christian Jehovah. Two key themes of the Koran are its Day of Judgment prophecy and its "fire and brimstone" depiction of Hell. Mohammed honored Moses and Jesus as Allah's two previous messengers and proclaimed Islam to be the third and final revelation from God. It was therefore the duty of all Jews and Christians to convert to Islam. Hebrews and Christians tended to be less than cooperative with Mohammed's demand. After all, they had been warned in their own apocalyptic writings about the dangers of "false prophets." The result has been some of the bloodiest fighting in world history.

Like so many Custodial religions before it, Islam did not allow people the luxury of choosing whether or not to become adherents. Mohammed embarked on a program of conquest to make it clear which way the choice was to go. Using the tactics of a generalissimo, the "divinely inspired" Mohammed raised an army and set off to convert "unfaithful ones" ("infidels") to his faith. Mohammed's apocalyptic army cut a wide bloody swath through most of the Middle East, including important Christian centers. The militant Moslem empire eventually stretched as far east as India where elements of Islam were incorporated into the Hindu religion. Untold lives were lost during the Islamic conquests because the Islamic armies were prone to commit fearsome genocides as part of their mission to bring utopia to mankind.

To most "infidel" Christians, Moslems were nothing more than savage "heathens" ("nonbelievers"). This set up an inevitable conflict into which millions of people would be dragged. Five hundred years after the death of Mohammed, the Christian world launched a coordinated military effort to force the Moslems out of the Holy Land. That effort is known as the Crusades.

The Christian Crusades to free Palestine from the Moslems took place between 1099 and 1270 A.D. Skirmishes and minor battles between Christians and Moslems had broken out beforehand, but it was a call-to-arms by Pope Urban II in 1095 that finally turned those skirmishes into an organized war effort involving nearly every Christian ruler of Europe. Hundreds of thousands of Christians enlisted in the Crusades after being promised religious blessings, fiefdoms, and spoils of conquest. Volunteers came from nearly every social class. For many serfs and peasants, the Papal call-to-arms represented a way to escape feudal lords and perhaps to return as wealthy heroes.

The Crusades got off to a good, but bloody, start. The Christians captured Jerusalem in the summer of 1099. Although the knights and peasants who marched under Christian banners were extolled to practice high virtues and chivalry, they frequently degenerated into butchery and other acts of viciousness. When the Crusaders took Jerusalem in 1099, they murdered many of the non-Christian survivors in a slaughter that claimed the lives of more than 10,000 victims.

Not only were the Crusaders killing Moslems, they were also killing Jews, who were considered by many Christians to be as heathen as the Moslems. The slaughter of Jews began even before the first Crusade to the Holy Land. In the year 1095, Christian factions started murdering Jews in Europe. A genocidal wave in the German Rhineland was the first major episode; it was sparked by unsubstantiated rumors that Rhineland Jews were using Christian children in their religious sacrifices. Obliterating the Jews became an important element of the Crusades, and the massacres continued even after the Crusades to Jerusalem had ended.

The Crusades had another important effect on Europe. Several decades before the launching of the First Crusade, Pope Gregory VII had attempted to put the Roman Catholic Church under greater centralized control. Prior to Gregory's effort, the Catholic Church in Europe was a loosely-knit organization run primarily by nonclergymen; the type of organization envisioned by Christianity's earliest founders. After Pope Urban II ascended to the Papacy and rallied all good Christians to fight the unholy Moslems, Christian princes and supporters began pledging allegiance direct-ly to the Pope, thereby hastening the centralization effort attempted earlier by Pope Gregory VII. The power of the Roman Papacy increased as the holy wars dragged on and growing numbers of people proclaimed their Papal loyalty.

Behind the Crusades lay the Brotherhood. The Christian Crusaders were led primarily by two powerful knight organizations with intimate Brotherhood ties: the Knights Hospitaler and the Knights of the Temple ("Knights Templar").

The "Knights Hospitaler" were so named because they operated a hospital in Jerusalem to help pilgrims in distress. The Hospitalers began operations in the year 1048 as a charitable order. Their purpose was aid and comfort. When the first Crusaders successfully captured the Holy City, the Hospitalers began to receive generous financial support from the wealthier Crusaders. In the year 1118, seventy years after their founding, the Knights Hospitaler underwent a change of leadership and purpose. They were made into a military order dedicated to fighting the Moslems who were continually trying to recapture Jerusalem. With this change of purpose came a change in name; the Hospitalers were variously called the "Order of Knights Hospitaler of St. John," "Knights of St. John of Jerusalem," or simply, "Knights of St. John." The Hospitalers had named themselves after John, son of the King of Cyprus. John had gone to Jerusalem to aid Christian pilgrims and knights.

There is some doubt as to whether the Hospitalers were founded as a Brotherhood organization. They reportedly did not function as one at the outset. However, they soon became affiliated with the Brotherhood network by adopting Brotherhood traditions and titles. They became ruled by a Grand Master and developed secret rites and rituals.

By 1119, one year after the Hospitalers had become a fighting order, the Templar Knights were in existence. The Templars originally called themselves the "Order of the Poor Knights of Christ" because they took solemn vows of poverty. Their name was later changed to "Knights of the Temple" after they were housed near the site where Solomon's temple had once stood. Although the Templars and Hospitalers had a common enemy in the Moslems, the two Christian organizations became bitter rivals.

The Templar Knights began their existence as a branch of the Brotherhood. They practiced a deep mystical tradition

and used many Brotherhood titles, notably "Grand Master."
Like the Hospitaler Knights, the Templars received large
sums of money from well-to-do Christian crusaders. The
Templars thereby became enormously wealthy and were
able to transform themselves into an international banking house during the twelfth and thirteenth centuries. The
Templars loaned large sums of money to European kings,
princes, merchants, and to at least one Moslem ruler. Most
of the Templars' riches were stored in strongrooms in their
Paris and London temples, causing those cities to become
leading financial centers.

After the fall of Jerusalem and the final victory of the
Moslems in 1291, the fortunes of both knightly orders
changed. The Knights of St. John (Hospitalers) were forced
to flee the Holy Land. They took up residence on a succession of islands during the ensuing centuries. With the
changes of location came changes in name. They became the
"Knights of Rhodes" after moving to the island of Rhodes.
They were the "Knights of Malta" when they moved to that
island and ruled it. While on Malta, the Knights became a
major military and naval power in the Mediterranean until
their defeat in 1789 by Napoleon. After enjoying temporary
protection under Russian Emperor Paul I, the Knights of
Malta had their headquarters moved to Rome in 1834 by
Pope Leo XIII. Today they are known as the "Sovereign
and Military Order of Malta" (SMOM) and have the unusual
distinction of being the world's smallest nation. Located in
a walled enclave in central Rome, SMOM still retains its
status as a sovereign state, although new Grand Masters
of the Order must be approved by the Pope. SMOM runs
hospitals, clinics, and leper colonies throughout the world.
It also gives active assistance to anti-Communist causes
and is surprisingly influential in political, business, and
intelligence circles today despite its small size.*

---

* Recent American members of SMOM have included the late William
Casey (American C.I.A. director), Lee Iacocca (chairman of the Chrysler
Corporation), Alexander Haig (former U.S. Secretary of State), and
William A. Schreyer (president of Merrill Lynch).

The Templar Knights did not fare as well as the Hospitalers after the Crusades. They were forced to flee with the Hospitalers to the island of Cyprus, whereupon the Templars split up and returned to their many Templar houses ("preceptories") in Europe. The Templars came under heavy criticism for their failure to save the Holy Land and rumors circulated that they engaged in heresy and immorality. Accusations were made that the Templars spat on the cross during their initiations and forced members to engage in homosexual acts. By 1307, the Templar controversy had become so strong that Philip IV the Fair of France ordered the arrest of all Templars within his dominion and used torture to extract confessions. Five years later, the Pope dissolved the Templar Order by Papal decree. Many Templars were executed, including Grand Master Jacques de Molay, who was publicly burned at the stake on March 11, 1314 in front of the cathedral of Notre Dame in Paris. Nearly all Templar properties were confiscated and turned over to the Hospitaler Knights. The long and intense rivalry between the Hospitalers and Templars had finally come to an end. The Hospitalers emerged as the victors. The Hospitalers' victory could not have occurred at a more fortuitous time for there had been serious discussion within Papal circles about merging the two orders—a plan which would have been completely unacceptable to both.

Despite the downfall of the Templar Knights, the organization managed to survive. According to Freemasonic historian, Albert MacKey, the Knights Templar were given a home in Portugal by King Denis after their banishment from the rest of Catholic Europe. In Portugal, the Templars were granted their usual rights and privileges, they wore the same costumes, and they were governed by the same rules they had before. The decree which re-established the Templars in Portugal stated that they were in that country to be rehabilitated. Pope Clement V approved the rehabilitation plan and issued a bull (official proclamation) commanding that the Templars change their name to "Knights of Christ." The Templars, or "Knights of Christ," also changed the cross on their uniform from the eight-pointed Maltese cross to the official Latin cross.

The Templars became quite powerful in their new home. In 1420, King John I gave the Knights of Christ control of Portugese possessions in the Indies. Subsequent Portuguese monarchs expanded the Knights' proprietorship to any new countries which the Knights might discover. The Knights of Christ became so powerful, reports Albert MacKey, that several Portugese kings felt compelled to curtail the Knights' influence by taking over the Grand Master position. The Knights of Christ survived under Portugese sponsorship until well into the eighteenth century, at which time the Templar name re-emerged and took on renewed importance in the stormy political affairs of Europe, as we shall see later.

There was a third Christian knight organization during the Crusades worth mentioning: the Teutonic Knights. The Teutonic Knights were originally called the "Order of the Knights of the Hospital of St. Mary of the Teutons in Jerusalem." Like the Hospitalers, the Teutonic Knights started as a charitable order. They operated a hospital in Jerusalem to aid Christians making pilgrimages to the Holy Land. In March 1198, the Teutonic Knights were given the rank of an order of knights, which made them into a fighting order. Like the Templars, the Teutonic Knights lived a semimonastic lifestyle, practiced initiation rites, and were ruled by a Grand Master. The Teutonic Knights permitted only Teutons [Germans] to become members. They also feuded a great deal with the Hospitalers and Templars.

During the Crusades when Brotherhood military organizations were valiantly leading Christian armies to fight the Moslems, other groups in the Brotherhood network were rallying Moslems to battle the Christians! Of the several Brotherhood branches promoting the cause of Islam, one is of particular interest to us: the sect of the Assassins.

Mohammed died in 632 A.D. A struggle immediately ensued over who was to become his successor. This caused the Islamic religion to break apart into competing sects, each having its own ideas about who was to succeed Mohammed. One such Islamic faction was the "Shia" sect, which adhered to a strong "End of the World" tradition. Shiites believed in the "Millennium": a Day of Judgment followed by a thousand years of peace and spiritual salvation. Eventually the Shia sect itself split apart. One faction to emerge from the Shia split was the Ismaili sect, which gave birth to the Assassins.

The Ismailians broke away from the other Shiites in the eighth century. The Ismaili sect was a Brotherhood secret society with a lodge system similar to Freemasonry and to other Brotherhood organizations. The Ismaili Grand Lodge was situated in Cairo where it practiced step-by-step initiations with all of the attendant symbols and mysteries. Led by a Grand Master, the Ismailians promulgated a very strong apocalyptic message complete with the promise of a coming Messiah.

One Ismaili lodge member was a man named Hasan-i Sabbah. Mr. Sabbah's mystical conversion came about as the result of a "severe and dangerous illness" during which he believed that God had purged him and had given him a spiritual rebirth. In 1078, at the Grand Lodge in Cairo, Mr. Sabbah asked the Ismaili caliph* for permission to spread the Ismaili gospel in Persia. The caliph granted Mr. Sabbah's request on the condition that Sabbah agree to support the caliph's eldest son, Nizar, as the next (ninth) caliph. Sabbah accepted the deal and named his new Ismaili branch the "Nizaris" after the caliph's son. It was not long, however, before Mr. Sabbah's branch became known by its more famous name: the "Assassins."

The Assassins are usually referred to as a religious sect. They were, more accurately, a secret society. According to Masonic historian Albert MacKey, the Assassins adopted the organizational structure of the Ismailians. The Assassins practiced step-by-step initiations and possessed a secret mystical doctrine. Mr. MacKey adds that the Assassins appear to have practiced three of the very same fraternal degrees used in Freemasonry today: Apprentice, Fellow, and Master. The Assassins had a religious code similar to

---

* A "caliph" is a successor to Mohammed. The title "caliph" was given to those Moslem heads of state who claimed to be a successor to Mohammed.

the Hospitaler and Teutonic Knights. The Assassins were an integral part of the Brotherhood network.

A distinguishing feature of the Assassin organization was its use of drugs, primarily hashish, for mystical and other purposes. In fact, the word "assassin" comes from the word "hashshishin," which means "users of hashish." The Assassins and several other Brotherhood groups in history extolled the virtues of mind-altering pharmaceuticals as a way to achieve mystical enlightenment.

The Assassins were also a fighting organization with an army. Grand Master Sabbah chose a fortress located high in the northern mountains of Iran for the headquarters of his new group. This Assassin fortress was known as "Alamut," which means "Eagle's Teaching" or "Eagle's Nest." The Assassins became a formidable military and political power in the region and eventually controlled other fortresses in Persia and Syria. The Assassins feuded with other Moslem organizations and fought against the Knights Templar and other Christian armies during the Crusades. To help win its feuds and wars, the Assassins developed the deadly tool for which they became famous and feared: the tool of the "lone assassin."

Most people today are painfully aware of the phenomenon of the so-called "lone assassin." This is usually a young man in his twenties or thirties who is driven by crazed delusions and who displays little or no concern for his own safety as he murders an important leader in broad daylight, in public, and in front of witnesses. The killing has tremendous shock value and it can greatly affect the political direction of a nation.

Many people believe that so-called "lone assassins" are products of our modern age. It is quite amusing to read ponderous psychiatric tomes to that effect. In truth, the "lone assassin" has been a political institution for over seven hundred years, if not longer. Seven hundred years ago, however, no pretense was made that the "lone assassins" acted alone, as is done today. Back then, the "lone assassin" was known to be an effective and terrifying tool of political and social control. It was a technique used by the Assassin organization to win its wars, increase its political influence, destroy its enemies, and enlarge its coffers by extortion.

How did the Assassin sect get young men to commit the murders? It is not easy to make people kill others, especially when the murderer is likely to be caught and slain himself. The Assassin organization had an effective method for overcoming this natural resistance and programming young men to kill. One of the earliest people to describe the Assassin programming technique was Marco Polo, the famous European traveller of the 13th century who wrote a bestselling book about his journeys. Although Mr. Polo was accused by a few people in his own time of fabricating stories, subsequent investigation has verified nearly everything he described in his famous book.

According to Mr. Polo, a portion of the Assassin fortress in Alamut had been converted into a beautiful secret garden fashioned after the paradise described in Mohammed's visions of Heaven. The garden grew almost every imaginable type of fruit and was watered with streams of wine, milk, and honey. The palaces were beautifully ornamented and had a company of singers, dancers, and musicians. If certain young men in the region showed promise as potential murderers, they were drugged, usually with opium or hashish, and taken to the secret garden. There they were pampered for a few days and nothing was denied them, including women. They were then drugged again and returned to their homes. The young men believed that Assassin leaders had transported them to Heaven and back. Eager to return, the young men would gladly follow the instructions of their Assassin leaders. The heaven-struck underlings were often told that a return to paradise lay in boldly assassinating a targeted enemy leader. The young assassin was instructed to wait in a public place and strike down the victim with a dagger as the victim passed by. Because the young assassins would often be killed on the spot or be later executed, they were made to believe that their death at the scene of the crime or by later execution would result in a return to the paradise they remembered.

The notoriety of the Assassins spread. It was rumored that some European kings were paying tribute to the Assassins to avoid becoming targets. Although the extent of

Assassin activity in Europe is still debated today (some historians assert that the Assassins focused most of their deadly practices on the conflicts going on in the Middle East), the Assassins became famous far and wide. As a result, all people who attempt the murder of a political leader have come to be known as "assassins," or "users of hashish." Although most modern "assassins" have not been hashish users, many have shown evidence of considerable mental tampering, which will be discussed near the end of this book.

By the end of the 13th century, the Mongols had overrun the Middle East and had destroyed major Assassin strongholds. Interestingly, the Mongols were also inspired by mystical beliefs. The Assassins managed to survive the onslaught, and they exist today. Modern Assassin sects are reported to be peacably settled in India, Iran, and Syria. Their titular head is the "Aga Khan," who is the spiritual leader of all Ismailians worldwide. The Ismailians are estimated to number about 20 million people today. As of 1840, the Aga Khans have been operating out of India because of an unsuccessful rebellion in 1838 of Aga Khan I against the Persian Shah. When the rebellion failed, Britain offered sanctuary to the Aga Khan in India, which was then under British rule. Since then, the Aga Khans have been traveling in elite circles of Western society. Recent Aga Khans have received educations at Oxford, Harvard, and in Switzerland. The Aga Khans have also gained a place in the international banking community through their establishment of a central bank in Damascus, Lebanon.

It may be a coincidence that "lone assassins" arose as an important phenomenon in the United States at just about the time that Aga Khan I was establishing a relationship with the British in the early 19th century. The first known "lone assassin" to strike a U.S. President did so in 1835. The intended victim was Andrew Jackson who was, interestingly, a member of a Knights Templar organization in America. Since then, U.S. Presidents have been the targets of "lone assassins" every ten to twenty years. Many other Western leaders and public figures have also been victims. Although I have seen no evidence that the Assassin sect itself is behind modern "lone assassins" episodes, it is clear that their technique has been picked up and used by influential political sources with Brotherhood connections in the Western world, as I shall discuss more fully in a later chapter.

As we have seen, the Crusade era witnessed the birth of institutions which still affect us today. To the list we can add two famous Christian Orders: the Franciscans and the Dominicans. The Franciscans adopted the cord-at-the-loins outfit and bald spot used by ancient Egyptian Brotherhood priests at El Amarna. The Franciscans appeared to be quite humane. The Dominicans, on the other hand, were placed in charge of the most widely-hated by-product of the Crusades: the Catholic Inquisition.

The medieval Inquisition has been universally condemned as one of the most oppressive human institutions ever developed. It was known for its tortures and zealous excesses. The Inquisition arose out of an effort by Pope Innocent II to stamp out a large heretical sect in the south of France known as the "Albigensians." Innocent II had called for a special Crusade in 1208 to enter France and wipe out the sect. The five-year war which ensued devastated the region. Ten years later, a new Pope, Gregory IX, continued the action. He placed the Dominicans in charge of investigating the Albigensians. Gregory gave the Dominican Order full legal power to name and condemn all surviving heretics. Out of this campaign grew the full inhuman machinery of the Catholic Inquisition which sought to stamp out heresy of every type. The Inquisition generated a fearful climate of intellectual and spiritual oppression in Europe for the next six hundred years. Hearsay, innuendo, and honest intellectual disagreement led many decent people to the torture rack and auto-da-fe (death by burning). The social scars are still visible today in the instinctive fear so many people have of expressing nonconforming ideas. The Inquisition helped breed a social reaction of violence to nonconforming ideas that the world has not yet fully escaped.

It is clear that the Christian Church had undergone many changes by the time the Crusades ended. The Church was no longer the humanitarian decentralized religion envisioned by Jesus. The new Catholic ("Undivided") Church headquartered in Rome had succumbed to the "reforms" of the East Roman emperors. It was a religion Jesus would have deplored. Fortunately, after the demise of the Inquisition, the Catholic Church began to improve and it has many good qualities today.

Perhaps the most significant event of the Crusades does not involve the waging of war, the programming of assassins, or the creation of an Inquisition. It entails the making of a peace.

In the year 1228, German emperor Frederick II led a Crusade to Jerusalem. Frederick was not in good graces with the Pope at the time. Frederick has been described as a "strange secular-minded, highly educated prince, a sworn enemy of the papacy on political grounds, who had acquired by marriage the title to what was left of the kingdom of Jerusalem."[1]

Frederick's fight with Pope Gregory IX had begun only one year before his trip to Jerusalem. The conflict between Frederick and Pope Gregory centered around the issue of centralized Papal power. Frederick opposed it and Gregory was striving to hasten it. This dispute caused Frederick to be put under sentence of excommunication—a sentence finally carried out in 1245.

While under the sentence, but not yet excommunicated, the unrepentant Frederick journeyed to his kingdom in Jerusalem at the head of his own crusade. Despite a deep involvement with the Teutonic Knights, Frederick II proved on that trip that he could be a man of peace. Instead of prolonging war with the Moslems, Frederick negotiated a peace treaty. He apparently felt that it was in everyone's best interests to end the religious strife, and that is precisely what he did. Frederick accomplished this feat by negotiating with the reigning Moslem leader, Sultan Kamil. Within a year of starting his talks with the Sultan, and without the approval of the Pope, Frederick concluded a treaty signed in 1229 that gave Jerusalem back to the Christians for ten years provided that the Christians did not arm themselves. The arrangement worked.

Using negotiation and appeals to reason, Frederick had accomplished in one short trip what the Popes had claimed they were trying to do for almost 130 years with warfare and blood. Under Frederick's treaty, Christians were free to inhabit Jerusalem and make pilgrimages there, and the Moslems were freed from the threat posed by Christian armies. Many Christian and Moslem leaders were not at all happy with this arrangement, however, for Frederick had set it up "leaving both parties indignant at so peaceful a settlement. When the truce finally ran out in 1239, the holy war was resumed . . ." [2*]

We might legitimately ask, why was Frederick's treaty not extended or a similar one negotiated? What purpose was served by diving into seventy additional years of bloody warfare? The Christians wound up losing the Holy Land altogether.

So often we hear that wars are a product of basic human nature, yet in one peace effort we saw 130 years of raging conflict end through the effort of one man appealing to the reason and cooperation of another man, resulting in a peace for the duration of the treaty. We can see that the ability of people to have peace is as strong, if not stronger, than a desire for war. What then, drove Moslems and Christians to slaughter one another over a trivial bit of dry real estate?

One answer to this question may be found in what the Moslems and Christians thought they were ultimately fighting for: their spiritual salvation and freedom. They believed that by fighting, and perhaps even dying gloriously, for their faith, they were guaranteed eternal salvation. History has clearly demonstrated that the drive for spiritual freedom is so strong that it can override any human drive, including the urge for physical self-preservation. At some

---

* There is an amusing sideline to the story. After Frederick completed the treaty, he wanted to be crowned monarch of Jerusalem per his inheritance. Because he was under sentence of excommunication, no Catholic authority would perform the ceremony for him. Frederick, however, was not one to be thwarted by technicalities. He simply crowned himself and sailed back home to Germany.

point, people will sacrifice their own physical existences, and even the physical survival of loved ones, if they believe that the sacrifice will ensure their spiritual integrity or that it will bring about their spiritual salvation. When genuine spiritual knowledge is distorted, yet the desire for spiritual salvation continues to be stimulated, a great many people can be led into doing a great many stupid things. One important step to solving the problem of war, then, is to achieve a true understanding of the spirit and an actual way to its rehabilitation.

When we look at the spiritual practices of the Christian knights and the Moslem Ismailians, we discover that participation in warfare was often exalted as a spiritual quest. Warriors on both sides were inspired by corrupted Brotherhood mysticisms which taught that spiritual rewards could be earned by engaging in military endeavors against fellow human beings. This was the mythology of the "spiritually noble" war in which gallant soldiers were promised eternal salvation and a place in Heaven for fighting a noble cause. This mythology still remains vital today for recruiting people to participate in continued warfare. It twists the urge for spiritual freedom into an honoring of war.

What is war, then, if not a noble quest?

Analyzed down to its most basic components, warfare is nothing more than the act of causing solid objects to destructively collide with other solid objects. That might sometimes be fun, but there is not much spiritual benefit to be derived from constantly engaging in it. Although it is true that war has many elements of a game, the destructive nature of war causes it to be little more than a series of criminal acts: primarily arson, battery, and murder. This reveals something of great significance:

*War is the institutionalization of criminality. War can never bring about spiritual improvement because criminality is one of the main causes of mental and spiritual deterioration.*

Societies which exalt criminal actions as a noble quest will suffer a rapid deterioration in the mental and spiritual condition of their inhabitants. "Spiritual" doctrines which exalt combat are doctrines which degrade the human race.

Is not warfare in pursuit of a just cause a good thing?

The biggest problem with using violent force to fight for a cause is that the rules of force operate on competely different principles than do the principles of right and wrong. The victorious use of violent force depends upon skills that have nothing to do with whether or not one's cause is a just one. The man who can draw his six-shooter the fastest is not necessarily the man with the best ideals. We like our heroes when they can outshoot or physically overpower the bad guys, and there is nothing wrong with their being able to do so, but not all of our heroes can. Those who have a legitimate cause should therefore be wary of the temptation to assert the rightness of their beliefs in the arena of violent force since their cause may undeservedly lose. There are many effective methods to promote good causes and make them win, but those methods are seldom used in a world educated to use violence as the ultimate court of appeal.

The Crusades and other religious conflicts have often been fueled by the issue of who is a true "messiah" and who is not. Passions can run strong on this topic. It therefore behooves us at this time to discuss what a "messiah" might or might not be.

# 16

# Messiahs and Means

IN A GLOBAL civilization such as ours where spiritual knowledge and freedom appear to have been tampered with, there would obviously be a place for someone to develop a useful and understandable body of knowledge about the spirit and the spirit's relationship to the universe. Because verifiable spiritual phenomena seem to be consistent from person to person, and from time to time, it is probable that all spiritual realities are rooted in consistent laws and axioms, just like astronomy or physics. If someone were to discover and methodically outline those laws and axioms, he or she would be doing a great service. Such discoveries could open up a whole new science. Would a person who did this be a "messiah"?

Promises of a "messiah" have been put forth by a great many religions, both maverick and Custodial. The word "messiah" has had several meanings, from simply "teacher" to "liberator." A "messiah" could be anyone from a person who develops a successful science of the spirit to someone who is actually able to spiritually liberate the human race.

Throughout history, there have been thousands of people claiming to be a "messiah," or they have been given the label by others even if they did not claim it themselves. Such messianic claims are usually based upon prophecies recorded earlier in history, such as the Buddhist Mettaya legend, the "Second Coming" prophecy of the *Book of Revelation,* the apocalyptic teachings of Zoroaster, or the Hebrew prophecies. Many people look at all messianic claims with outright skepticism; others become avid followers of a leader whom they believe to be the fulfillment of a religious prophecy. This raises the question: has there ever been, or will there ever be, a genuine messiah? How would one identify such a person?

Anyone who successfully develops a functional science of the spirit would obviously have a legitimate claim to the title of "messiah" in the "teacher" sense. There is nothing mystical or apocalyptic about this: a person makes some discoveries and shares them. If this knowledge becomes widely known and results in widespread spiritual salvation, then we enter the realm of the "liberator" or "prophesized messiah." How do we identify such a liberator when there exist so many different prophecies with so many ways to interpret them?

The answer is simple: The would-be liberator must succeed. That person must *earn* the title; it is not God-given.

This is a terribly cold and uncompromising way of looking at it. It strips away the magic and mysticism normally associated with messianic prophecy. It forces any person who would claim the title of messiah to actually bring about peace and spiritual salvation, because such a prophecy is not going to be fulfilled unless someone causes it happen. This compels the would-be liberator to fully overcome the overwhelming obstacles which act against these universal goals. This is one of the most unenviable tasks that any person could ever hope to undertake. We need only look at past "liberators" to appreciate the long hard road that such a person must travel. To date, no one has succeeded, but it is certainly a challenge worthy of the best talent.

When most people envision a messiah, they see a person dressed in spotless white who thinks, speaks and behaves in the saintliest of manner. This may be the wrong image to look for in determining whether or not someone has made the discoveries necessary to achieve spiritual salvation. Developing a successful spiritual science would be no different than developing a successful science of aeronautics: the key scientists may not all be saints—some of them may even be people you would not invite into your home—but their airplanes fly. It is an irony that important discoveries are often made by unsavory personalities. Witness, for example, the Scandinavian vikings who charted vast unknown regions but plundered as they went.

It follows that a person who might discover a route to spiritual salvation may not be a saint. In fact, it is more likely that such an individual would exhibit as many character flaws as any other person. The test to determine if a route to spiritual recovery has been developed is not the personality of the discoverer: the test is whether that route truly and clearly brings about spiritual recovery in others.

There is an idea that proclaiming someone a prophesized messiah is enough to make it true. The logic behind this is that if everyone rallies around a single religious leader, harmony and world peace would automatically result. Such a plan sounds good, but history has clearly shown that it does not work. Even followers of the same religious leader are easily split apart into factions. Witness the Christians and Moslems.

Religion ultimately addresses the survival of the individual spiritual being and, as we shall discuss near the end of this book, the possible survival of a Supreme Being of some sort. It is therefore easy for people to become quite zealous about religion. There is nothing wrong with that zealousness as long as it is guided by compassion and good sense. We have already seen how several religions initially rooted in very humanitarian ideals had betrayed those ideals and became tyrannies far worse than any tyrannies the religions had opposed. This usually happens when religious adherents believe that the means used to achieve an altruistic goal will always be justified as long as the goal is attained. Their logic seems sensible enough, but is it?

It is an unfortunate fact of life that the means will always shape the ends. No matter how noble an end may be, the final result will always resemble the means used to attain it. It is in this way that some of the most stellar goals can create some of the most oppressive and deadly institutions. A frequent character in literature is the altruistic individual who gradually becomes just like the evils he is fighting because he uses the same means that the enemy is using. This results in our finally not being able to tell the difference between an "altruist" and his opponent. We frequently see this phenomenon occur on a larger scale involving organizations and governments.

To judge an individual or organization, therefore, one must do more than merely consider its professed goal or aim. One must also scrutinize the actual day-to-day means being used to reach the goal. No matter how sincere the individuals are, what they eventually create will be determined greatly by the means they are using. Interestingly, a group with less lofty aims can sometimes achieve far more good, even more than its own members may have intended, if it is employing honest, constructive means to attaining its purposes.

As we can see, an organization which justifies killing, defamation, and Machiavellian manipulations to gain influence and defeat opponents in the name of a higher goal is creating a world in which killing, defamation and turmoil are taking place. On the other hand, a person who believes in always telling the truth so that her knitting club will be respected is creating a world in which truth is being told. Ultimately, the best of all worlds combines a lofty goal with lofty means to attain it since the accomplishment of a goal usually requires a conscious effort to achieve it. Second to that, noble means to a lesser goal will benefit the world far more than disreputable means to a higher goal.

# 17

# Flying Gods
# Over America

BY THE TIME of the Crusades, major dramas had unfolded on the opposite side of the globe. Great civilizations had come and gone on the American continents.

It is difficult to study the history of the ancient American civilizations because nearly all original records from those civilizations were destroyed centuries ago. As a result, historians are often confronted with disputes over the most basic facts, such as dates. For example, time estimates regarding the great Mayan civilization have placed it everywhere from 30,000 years ago to 12,000 years ago to only 700 years ago. For the purposes of this book, I will use the dates most commonly accepted by modern historians and archaeologists.

Many archaeologists believe that the first important North American civilization was the Olmec society of Mexico. It is estimated to have flourished from about 800 B.C. until 400 B.C. Very little is known about the Olmecs except that they left behind impressive ruins which included a large pyramid. The existence of the pyramid is strong evidence that there was interaction between the Old and New Worlds in the B.C. years.

The Olmecs are believed to have given birth to the famous Mayan civilization which followed. The Mayan culture extended from Mexico to Central America and lasted from about 300 B.C. until 900 A.D. Like the Olmecs, the Mayans were fond of building pyramids. Surprisingly, some Mayan pyramids were given a limestone facing like the earlier pyramids in Egypt. The Mayans also copied the Egyptians by mummifying bodies and by holding similar beliefs about a physical afterlife. According to historian Raymond Cartier:

> Other analogies with Egypt are discernable in the admirable art of the Mayas. Their mural paintings and frescoes and decorated vases show a race of men with strongly marked Semitic [Mesopotamian] features, engaged in all sorts of activities: agriculture, fishing, building, politics and religion. Egypt alone has depicted these activities with the same cruel verisimilitude [appearance of truth]; but the pottery of the Mayas recalls that of the Etruscans [an ancient civilization of Italy]; their bas-reliefs remind one of India, and the huge steep stairways of their pyramidal temples are like those at Angkor [in Cambodia, dedicated to Hindu worship]. Unless they obtained their models from outside, their brains must have been so constructed that they adopted the same forms of artistic expression as all the other great ancient civilizations of Europe and Asia. Did civilization, then, spring from one particular geographical region and then spread gradually in every direction like a forest fire? Or did it appear spontaneously and separately in various parts of the world? Were some races the teachers and others the pupils, or were they all self-taught? Isolated seeds, or one parent stem giving off shoots in every direction?[1]

The coincidences are far too strong for the American civilizations to have arisen independently of the Old World societies. Jungian theories of a "collective unconscious" are hardly satisfactory. The striking similarities indicate that the American civilizations were part of a global society, even if ancient American inhabitants were not aware of it. A similar situation exists today. In different cities around the world, we find modern skyscrapers that look remarkably alike no matter where on the globe they stand: from Singapore to Africa to the United States. It can be rather a surprise to see in a remote African nation a tall glassy skyscraper that is virtually identical to a skyscraper in Chicago. The surrounding culture, however, may be radically different in each country, indicating that the skyscraper in Africa is not a product of the native African culture, but is the product of an independent global influence. A similar global influence clearly existed more than a millennium ago as evidenced by the remarkable similarities between ancient Mayan and Egyptian cultures. That global influence appears to have been the Custodial society, because as soon as we review ancient American writings, we encounter once again our Custodial friends.

Custodians were worshipped by ancient Americans as humanlike "gods" who hailed from other worlds. As in the Eastern Hemisphere, Custodians in America were eventually disguised by a cloak of mythology. As in Egypt and Mesopotamia, Custodial servants in America were the priests, who held considerable political power because of their special relationship to mankind's reported extraterrestrial masters. It is therefore not surprising to find evidence that the Brotherhood existed in the ancient Americas. For example, the snake was an important religious symbol throughout the ancient Western Hemisphere. Several Freemasonic historians claim evidence of early Masonic rites in pre-Columbian societies. The Brotherhood symbol of the swastika was also prominent, as Professor W. Norman Brown of the University of Pennsylvania points out on page 27 of his book, *The Swastika: A Study of the Nazi Claims of Its Aryan Origin:*

A curious problem lies in the presence of the swastika in America before the time of Columbus. It is frequent in northern, central and southern America, and has many variant forms.

The American civilizations had a history similar to that of the Old World. It was filled with wars, genocides, and calamities. Cities and religious centers in ancient America came and went. One thing that remained consistent was the building of pyramids. The Toltecs, a civilization which arose from the Mayan society, continued the pyramid-building tradition and constructed the fabulous Pyramid of the Sun in Mexico. This pyramid is larger than the Great Pyramid of Egypt in sheer bulk and is crafted with the same stonecutting precision that characterizes its Egyptian counterpart.

When the Spaniards invaded America in the 16th century, they deliberately destroyed nearly everything they could of the ancient American cultures, except for the gold and precious metals which were shipped to Spain. At that time in history, the Inquisition was at its height and Spain was its most zealous advocate. The ancient Americans were considered pagan, and so Christian missionaries engaged in an energetic campaign to destroy all records and artifacts related to the American religions. Unfortunately, those records included priceless history and science texts. The effect of this obliteration was much like the destruction of the Alexandria Library by Christians earlier: it created a substantial "black out" regarding some of mankind's ancient history. This has left a great many unanswered questions about the Mayans. For example, the Mayans built many fabulous religious centers and then abandoned them. Some historians believe that the abandonment was done suddenly and that its cause remains a mystery. Others conclude that it was done gradually as the Mayan society decayed. The Mayans were also known to practice human sacrifice. Some historians believe that the sacrifices were an infrequent ritual; others think that the sacrifices amounted to full scale genocide claiming 50,000 lives per year. Where does the truth lie?

One book has surfaced which purports to be a record of ancient Mayan beliefs. It is known as the *Popol Vuh* ("Council Book"). The *Popol Vuh* is not a genuinely ancient work.

It was first written in the sixteenth century by an unknown Mayan. It was later translated into Spanish by Father Francisco Ximenez of the Dominican Order. Ximenez's translation was first published in Vienna in 1857 and it is the earliest surviving version of the *Popul Vuh*.

The *Popol Vuh* is said to be a collection of Mayan beliefs and legends as they had been passed down orally through the centuries. It is clear, however, that many Christian ideas were incorporated into the work, either by the original unknown Mayan author, by Father Ximenez, or by both. It is also obvious that the *Popol Vuh* contains many tales of pure fiction mixed in with what is said to be the true story of the creation of man. Nevertheless, several segments of the *Popol Vuh* are worth considering because they repeat important religious and historical themes we have seen elsewhere, but with far greater sophistication than is found in Christian writings. Those themes are expressed by the *Popol Vuh* within the context of the multiple gods of the ancient Mayas.

The *Popul Vuh* states that mankind had been created to be a servant of the "gods." The "gods" are quoted:

*"Let us make him who shall nourish and sustain us! What shall we do to be invoked, in order to be remembered on earth? We have already tried with our first creations, our first creatures; but we could not make them praise and venerate us. So, then, let us try to make obedient, respectful beings who will nourish and sustain us."* [2]

According to the *Popul Vuh*, the "gods" had made creatures known as "figures of wood" before creating *Homo sapiens*. Said to look and talk like men, these odd creatures of wood "existed and multiplied; they had daughters, they had sons. . . ."[3] They were, however, inadequate servants for the "gods." To explain why, the *Popul Vuh* expresses a sophisticated spiritual truth not found in Christianity, but which is found in earlier Mesopotamian writings. The "figures of wood" did not have souls, relates the *Popol Vuh*, and so they walked on all fours "aimlessly." In other words, without souls (spiritual beings) to animate the bodies, the "gods" found that they had created living creatures which could biologically reproduce, but which lacked the intelligence to have goals or direction.

The "gods" destroyed their "figures of wood" and held lengthy meetings to determine the shape and composition of their next attempt. The "gods" finally produced creatures to which spiritual beings could be attached. That new and improved creature was *Homo sapiens.**

Creating *Homo sapiens* did not end Custodial headaches, however. According to the *Popol Vuh*, the first *Homo sapiens* were *too* intelligent and had *too* many abilities!

> *They [first* Homo sapiens*] were endowed with intelligence; they saw and instantly they could see far, they succeeded in seeing, they succeeded in knowing all that there is in the world. When they looked, instantly they saw all around them, and they contemplated in turn the arch of heaven and the round face of the earth.*
>
> *. . .*
>
> *But the Creator and the Maker did not hear this with pleasure. "It is not well that our creatures, our works say; they know all, the large and the small," they said.*[4]

Something had to be done. Humans (and by implication, the spiritual beings that animate human bodies) needed to have their level of intelligence reduced. Mankind had to be made more stupid:

> *"What shall we do with them now? Let their sight reach only to that which is near; let them see only a little of the face of the earth! It is not well what*

---

* According to Sumerian texts, *Homo sapiens* resembled Custodial bodies. This may explain why the "gods" of the *Popol Vuh* were successful with *Homo sapiens,* but not with other types of bodies: spiritual beings were more willing to inhabit bodies which resembled those they had already animated before.

*they say. Perchance, are they not by nature simple.
creatures of our making? Must they also be gods?"*[5]

The *Popol Vuh* then tells in symbolism what Custodians
did to early *Homo sapiens* to reduce human intelligence and
intellectual vision:

> *Then the Heart of Heaven blew mist into their eyes,
> which clouded their sight as when a mirror is breathed
> upon. Their eyes were covered and they could see only
> what was close, only that was clear to them.*
> *In this way the wisdom and all the knowledge of the
> four men [first* Homo sapiens*] . . . were destroyed.*[6]

The above passage echoes the Biblical Adam and Eve
story in which "revolving swords" had been placed to block
human access to important knowledge. It also suggests a
Custodial intention that human beings should never learn
about the world beyond the obvious and superficial.

The *Popol Vuh* contains another element worth mentioning because it reflects the "muddling of languages" theme of
the Biblical Tower of Babel story. The *Popol Vuh* relates that
various "gods" spoke different languages which the ancient
Mayan tribes were compelled to adopt whenever they fell
under the rule of a new "god." Even in the New World,
humans were broken into different linguistic groups by the
Custodial "gods."

By the time the Spaniards first landed in the Americas in
the late 15th century, the Custodial "gods" were no longer
directly visible in human affairs, and had not been so for
centuries. Although UFOs continued to be observed around
the world, people no longer viewed them as the vehicles of
the "gods." The Custodial race assumed a low profile which
made it seem as though they had left the Earth and gone
back home. Unfortunately, they still remained, as the next,
and perhaps most ominous, chapter reveals.

# 18

# The Black Death

THE CENTRALIZATION OF Papal power culminated under Pope Innocent IV, who held the Papal reins from 1243 until 1254. Innocent IV attempted to turn the Papacy into the world's highest political authority by proclaiming that the Pope was the "vicar [earthly representative] of the Creator (to whom) every human creature is subjected." It was under Innocent IV that the Inquisition was made an official institution of the Roman Catholic Church.

Despite the oppression of the Inquisition, Europe in the 13th century was beginning to recover from the economic and social disruption caused by the Crusades. Signs of a European renaissance were visible in the widening of intellectual and artistic horizons. Trade with other parts of the world did much to enrich European life. Europe was entering an era in which chivalry, music, art, and spiritual values were playing greater roles. Hardly a century of this progress had passed, however, before a disastrous event abruptly brought it to a temporary halt. That event was the Bubonic Plague, also known as the Black Death.

The Black Death began in Asia and soon spread to Europe where it killed well over 25 million people (about one third of Europe's total population) in less than four years. Some historians put the casualty figure closer to 35 to 40 million people, or about half of all Europeans.

The epidemic first spread through Europe between 1347 and 1350. The Bubonic Plague continued to strike Europe with decreasing fatality every ten to twenty years in short-lived outbreaks all the way up until the 1700's. Although it is difficult to calculate the total number of deaths from that 400-year period, it is believed that over 100 million people may have died from the Plague.

Two types of plague are believed to have caused the Black Death. The first is the "bubonic" type, which was the most common. The bubonic form of plague is characterized by swellings of the lymph nodes; the swellings are called "buboes." The buboes are accompanied by vomiting, fever, and death within several days if not treated. This form of plague is not contagious between human beings: it requires an active carrier, such as a flea. For this reason, many historians believe that flea-infested rodents caused the Bubonic Plague. Rodents are known to carry the disease even today. A number of records from between 1347 and the late 1600's speak of rodent infestations prior to several outbreaks of the Black Death, lending credence to the rodent theory.

The second form of plague contributing to the Black Death is a highly contagious type known as "pneumonic" plague. It is marked by shivering, rapid breathing, and the coughing up of blood. Body temperatures are high and death normally follows three to four days after the disease has been contracted. This second type of plague is nearly always fatal and transmits best in cold weather and in poor ventilation. Some physicians today believe it was this second form, the "pneumonic" plague, which was responsible for most of the casualties of the Black Death because of the crowding and poor hygienic conditions then prevalent in Europe.

We would normally shake our heads at this tragic period of human history and be thankful that modern medicine has developed cures for these dread diseases. However, troubling enigmas about the Black Death still linger. Many outbreaks occurred in summer during warm weather in uncrowded regions. Not all outbreaks of bubonic plague were preceded by rodent infestation; in fact, only a minority of cases seemed to be related to an increase in the presence of vermin. The greatest puzzle about the Black Death is how it was able to strike isolated human populations which had no contact with earlier infected areas. The epidemics also tended to end abruptly.

To solve these puzzles, an historian would normally look to records from the Plague years to see what people were reporting. When he does so, he encounters stories so stunning and unbelievable that he is likely to reject them as the fantasies and superstitions of badly frightened minds. A great many people throughout Europe and other Plague-stricken regions of the world were reporting that outbreaks of the Plague were caused by foul-smelling "mists." Those mists frequently appeared after unusually bright lights in the sky. The historian quickly discovers that "mists" and bright lights were reported far more frequently and in many more locations than were rodent infestations. The Plague years were, in fact, a period of heavy UFO activity.

What, then, were the mysterious mists?

There is another very important way in which plague germs can be transmitted: through germ weapons. The United States and the Soviet Union today have stockpiles of biological weapons containing bubonic plague and other epidemic diseases. The germs are kept alive in cannisters which spray the diseases into the air on thick, often visible, artificial mists. Anyone breathing in the mist will inhale the disease. There are enough such germ weapons today to wipe out a good portion of humanity. Reports of identical disease-inducing mists from the Plague years strongly suggest that the Black Death was caused by germ warfare. Let us take a look at the incredible reports which lead to that conclusion.

The first outbreak of the Plague in Europe followed an unusual series of events. Between 1298 and 1314, seven large "comets" were seen over Europe; one was of "awe-inspiring blackness."[1] One year before the first outbreak of the epidemic in Europe, a "column of fire" was reported over the Pope's* palace at Avignon, France. Earlier that year, a "ball of fire" was observed over Paris; it reportedly remained visible to observers for some time. To the people of Europe, these sightings were considered omens of the Plague which soon followed.

It is true that some reported "comets" were probably just that: comets. Some may also have been small meteors or fireballs (large blazing meteors). Centuries ago, people were generally far more superstitious than they are today and so natural meteors and similar prosaic phenomena were often reported as precursors to later disasters even though there was no real-life connection. On the other hand, it is important to note that almost any unusual object in the sky was called a "comet." A good example is found in a bestselling book published in 1557: *A Chronicle of Prodigies and Portents . . .*** by Conrad Lycosthenes. On page 494 of Lycosthenes' book we read of a "comet" observed in the year 1479: "A comet was seen in Arabia in the manner of a sharply pointed wooden beam . . ." The accompanying illustration, which was based on eyewitness descriptions, shows what clearly looks like the front half of a rocketship among some clouds. The object appears to have many portholes. Today we would call the object a UFO, not a comet. This leads us to wonder how many other ancient "comets" were actually similar rocketlike objects. When we are confronted with an old report of a comet, we therefore do not really know what kind of thing we are dealing with unless there is a fuller description. A report of a sudden increase in "comets" or similar celestial phenomena may, in fact, mean an increase in UFO activity.

The link between unusual aerial phenomena and the Black

---

* This was a second unauthorized pope who assumed the title as the result of a schism within the Catholic Church.
** The complete title is, *A chronicle of prodigies and portents that have occurred beyond the right order, operation and working of nature, in both the upper and lower regions of the earth, from the beginning of the world up to these present times.*

Death was established immediately during the first outbreaks of the Plague in Asia. As one historian tells us:

> The first reports [of the Plague] came out of the East. They were confused, exaggerated, frightening, as reports from that quarter of the world so often are: descriptions of storms and earthquakes: of meteors and comets trailing noxious gases that killed trees and destroyed the fertility of the land. . . .[2]

The above passage indicates that strange flying objects were doing more than just spreading disease: they were also apparently spraying chemical or biological defoliants from the air. The above passage echoes the ancient Mesopotamian tablets which described defoliation of the landscape by ancient Custodial "gods." Many human casualties from the Black Death may have been caused by such defoliants.

The connection between aerial phenomena and plague had begun centuries before the Black Death. We saw examples in our earlier discussion of Justinian's Plague. We read from another source about a large plague that had reportedly broken out in the year 1117—almost 250 years before the Black Death. That plague was also preceded by unusual celestial phenomena:

> In 1117, in January, a comet passed like a fiery army from the North towards the Orient, the moon was o'ercast blood-red in an eclipse, a year later a light appeared more brilliant than the sun. This was followed by great cold, famine, and plague, of which one-third of humanity is said to have perished. *[3]

Once the medieval Black Death got started, noteworthy aerial phenomena continued to accompany the dread epidemic. Reports of many of these phenomena were assembled

---

*I have seen no mention of this plague in any other history book. It may have been a local plague which destroyed not a third of humanity, but a third of the afflicted population.

by Johannes Nohl and published in his book, *The Black Death, A Chronicle of the Plague* (1926). According to Mr. Nohl, at least 26 "comets" were reported between 1500 and 1543. Fifteen or sixteen were seen between 1556 and 1597. In the year 1618, eight or nine were observed. Mr. Nohl emphasizes the connection which people perceived between the "comets" and subsequent epidemics:

> In the year 1606 a comet was seen, after which a general plague traversed the world. In 1582 a comet brought so violent a plague upon Majo, Prague, Thuringia, the Netherlands, and other places that in Thuringia it carried off 37,000 and in the Netherlands 46,415.[4]

From Vienna, Austria, we get the following description of an event which happened in 1568. Here we see a connection between an outbreak of Plague and an object described in a manner remarkably similar to a modern cigar or beam-shaped UFO:

> When in sun and moonlight a beautiful rainbow and a fiery beam were seen hovering above the church of St. Stephanie, which was followed by a violent epidemic in Austria, Swabia, Augsberg, Wuertemberg, Nuremburg, and other places, carrying off human beings and cattle.[5]

Sightings of unusual aerial phenomena usually occurred from several minutes to a year before an outbreak of Plague. Where there was a gap between such a sighting and the arrival of the Plague, a second phenomenon was sometimes reported: the appearance of frightening humanlike figures dressed in black. Those figures were often seen on the outskirts of a town or village and their presence would signal the outbreak of an epidemic almost immediately. A summary written in 1682 tells of one such visit a century earlier:

> In Brandenburg [in Germany] there appeared in 1559 horrible men, of whom at first fifteen and later on

twelve were seen. The foremost had beside their pos-
teriors little heads, the others fearful faces and long
scythes, with which they cut at the oats, so that the
swish could be heard at a great distance, but the oats
remained standing. When a quantity of people came
running out to see them, they went on with their
mowing.[6]

The visit of the strange men to the oat fields was followed immediately by a severe outbreak of the Plague in
Brandenburg.

This incident raises intriguing questions: who were the
mysterious figures? What were the long scythe-like instruments they held that emitted a loud swishing sound? It
appears that the "scythes" may have been long instruments
designed to spray poison or germ-laden gas. This would
mean that the townspeople misinterpreted the movement
of the "scythes" as an attempt to cut oats when, in fact, the
movements were the act of spraying aerosols on the town.
Similar men dressed in black were reported in Hungary:

. . . in the year of Christ 1571 was seen at Cremnitz
in the mountain towns of Hungary on Ascension Day
in the evening to the great perturbation [disturbance]
of all, when on the Schuelersberg there appeared so
many black riders that the opinion was prevalent that
the Turks were making a secret raid, but who rapidly disappeared again, and thereupon a raging plague
broke out in the neighborhood.[7]

Strange men dressed in black, "demons," and other terrifying figures were observed in other European communities.
The frightening creatures were often observed carrying long
"brooms," "scythes," or "swords" that were used to "sweep"
or "knock at" the doors of people's homes. The inhabitants
of those homes fell ill with plague afterwards. It is from these
reports that people created the popular image of "Death" as
a skeleton or demon carrying a scythe. The scythe came
to symbolize the act of Death mowing down people like
stalks of grain. In looking at this haunting image of death,

we may, in fact, be staring into the face of the UFO.

Of all the phenomena connected to the Black Death, by far the most frequently reported were the strange, noxious "mists." The vapors were often observed even when the other phenomena were not. Mr. Nohl points out that moist pestilential fogs were "a feature which preceded the epidemic throughout its whole course."[8] A great many physicians of the time took it for granted that the strange mists caused the Plague. This connection was established at the very beginning of the Black Death, as Mr. Nohl tells us:

> The origin of the plague lay in China, there it is said to have commenced to rage already in the year 1333, after a terrible mist emitting a fearful stench and infecting the air.[9]

Another account stresses that the Plague did not spread from person to person, but was contracted by breathing the deadly stinking air:

> During the whole of the year 1382 there was no wind, in consequence of which the air grew putrid, so that an epidemic broke out, and the plague did not pass from one man to another, but everyone who was killed by it got it straight from the air.[10]

Reports of deadly "mists" and "pestilential fogs" came from all Plague-infested parts of the world:

> A Prague chronicle describes the epidemic in China, India and Persia; and the Florentine historian Matteo Villani, who took up the work of his brother Giovanni after he had died of the plague in Florence, relays the account of earthquakes and pestilential fogs from a traveller in Asia; . . .[11]

The same historian continues:

> A similar incident of earthquake and pestilential fog was reported from Cyprus, and it was believed that

the wind had been so poisonous that men were struck down and died from it.[12]

He adds:

German accounts speak of a heavy vile-smelling mist which advanced from the East and spread itself over Italy.[13]

That author states that in other countries:

. . . people were convinced that they could contract the disease from the stench, or even, as is sometimes described, actually see the plague coming through the streets as a pale fog.[14]

He summarizes, rather dramatically:

The earth itself seemed in a state of convulsion, shuddering and spitting, putting forth heavy poisonous winds that destroyed animals and plants and called swarms of insects to life to complete the destruction.[15]

Similar happenings are echoed by other writers. A journal from 1680 reported this odd incident:

That between Eisenberg and Dornberg thirty funeral biers [casket stands] all covered with black cloth were seen in broad daylight, among them on a bier a black man was standing with a white cross. When these had disappeared a great heat set in so that the people in this place could hardly stand it. But when the sun had set they perceived so sweet a perfume as if they were in a garden of roses. By this time they were all plunged in perturbation. Whereupon the epidemic set in in Thuringia in many places.[16]

Further south, in Vienna:

. . . evil smelling mists are blamed, as indicative of the plague, and of these, indeed, several were observed last autumn.[17]

Direct from the plague-ravaged town of Eisleben, we get this amusing and perhaps exaggerated newspaper account published on September 1, 1682:

In the cemetary of Eisleben on the 6th inst. [?] at night the following incident was noticed: When during the night the gravediggers were hard at work digging trenches, for on many days between eighty and ninety have died, they suddenly observed that the cemetary church, more especially the pulpit, was lighted up by bright sunshine. But on their going up to it so deep a darkness and black, thick fog came over the graveyard that they could hardly see one another, and which they took to be an evil omen. Thus day and night gruesome evil spirits are seen frightening the people, goblins grinning at them and pelting them, but also many white ghosts and spectres . . .[18]

The same newspaper story later adds:

When Magister Hardte expired in his agony a blue smoke was seen to rise from his throat, and this in the presence of the dean; the same has been observed in the case of others expiring. In the same manner blue smoke has been observed to rise from the gables of houses at Eisleben all the inhabitants of which have died. In the church of St. Peter blue smoke has been observed high up near the ceiling; on this account the church is shunned, particularly as the parish has been exterminated.[19]

The "mists" or Plague poisons were thick enough to mix with normal air moisture and become part of the morning dew. People were warned to take the following precautions:

If newly baked bread is placed for the night at the end of a pole and in the morning is found to be mildewed and internally grown green, yellow and uneatable, and when thrown to fowls and dogs causes them to die from eating it, in a similar manner if fowls drink the morning dew and die in consequence, then the plague poison is near at hand.[20]

As noted earlier, lethal "mists" were directly associated with bright moving lights in the sky. Other sources for the stenches were also reported. For example, Forestus Alcmarianos wrote of a monstrous "whale" he had encountered which was:

28 ells [105 feet] in length and 14 ells [33 feet] broad which, coming from the western sea, was thrown upon the shore of Egemont by great waves and was unable to reach the open again; it produced so great a foulness and malignity of the air that very soon a great epidemic broke out in Egemont and neighborhood.[21]

It is a shame that Mr. Alcmarianos did not provide a more detailed description of the deadly whale because it may have been a craft similar to modern UFOs which have been observed entering and leaving bodies of water. On the other hand, Mr. Alcmarianos' whale may have been just that: a dead rotting whale which happened to wash up on shore just before a nearby outbreak of the Plague.

It is significant that foul mists and bad air were blamed for many other epidemics in history. During a plague in ancient Rome, the famous physician Hippocrates (ca. 460-337 B.C.) stated that the disease was caused by body disturbances brought on by changes in the atmosphere. To remedy this, Hippocrates had people build large public bonfires. He believed that large fires would set the air aright. Hippocrates' advice was followed centuries later by physicians during the medieval Plague. Modern doctors take a dim view of Hippocrates' advice on this matter, however, in the belief that Hippocrates was ignorant about the true causes of plague. In reality, huge outdoor bonfires were the only conceivable defense against the Plague if it was indeed caused by germ-saturated aerosols. Vaccines to combat the Plague had not been invented and so the people's only hope was to burn away the deadly "mists" with fire. Hippocrates and those who followed his advice may have actually saved some lives.

Significantly, bubonic and pneumonic plagues were not the only infectious diseases in history to be spread on strange lethal fogs. The deadly intestinal disease, cholera, was another:

> When cholera broke out on board Her Majesty's ship Britannia in the Black Sea in 1854, several officers and men asserted positively that, immediately prior to the outbreak, a curious dark mist swept up from the sea and passed over the ship. The mist had barely cleared the vessel when the first case of disease was announced.[22]

Blue mists were also reported in connection with the cholera outbreaks of 1832 and 1848-1849 in England.

As mentioned earlier, plagues had a very strong religious significance. In the Bible, plagues were said to be Jehovah's method of punishing people for evil. "Omens" preceding outbreaks of the Black Death resembled many of the "omens" reported in the Bible:

> Men confronted with the terror of the Black Death were impressed by the chain of events leading up to the final plague, and accounts of the coming of the 14th-century pestilence selected from among all the ominous events that must have occurred in the years preceding the outbreak of 1348 those which closely resemble the ten plagues of Pharoah: disruptions in the atmosphere, storms, unusual invasions of insects, celestial phenomena.[23]

In addition, the Bubonic form of plague was very similar, if not identical, to some of the punishments inflicted by "God" in the Old Testament:

*But the hand of the Lord was heavy upon the people of Ashdod [a Philistine city], and he destroyed them, and killed them with emerods [painful swellings].*
1 SAMUEL 5:6

*. . . the hand of the Lord was against the city [Gath, another Philistine city] with a very great destruction: and he killed the men of the city, both young and old, and they had emerods in their secret parts.*
1 SAMUEL 5:9

*. . . there was a deadly destruction throughout all the city; the hand of God was very heavy there.*
*And the men that survived were afflicted with the emerods: and the crying of the city went up to heaven.*
1 SAMUEL 5:11-12

The religious aspect of the medieval Black Death was enhanced by reports of thundering sounds in connection with outbreaks of the Plague. The sounds were similar to those described in the Bible as accompanying the appearance of Jehovah. Interestingly, they are also sounds common to some UFO sightings:

During the plague of 1565 in Italy rumblings of thunder were heard day and night, as in a war, together with the turmoil and noise as of a mighty army. In Germany in many places a noise was heard as if a hearse were passing through the streets of its own accord . . .[24]

Similar noises accompanied strange aerial phenomena in remarkable Plague-related sightings from England. The object described in the quote below remained visible for over a week and does appear to be a true comet or planet (such as Venus); however, some of the other objects can only be labeled "unidentified." Historian Walter George Bell, drawing on writings from the period, summarized:

Late into dark December nights of the year 1664 London citizens sat up to watch a new blazing star, with "mighty talk" thereupon. King Charles II and his Queen gazed out of the windows at Whitehall. About east it rose, reaching no great altitude, and sank below the south-west horizon between two and three o'clock. In a week or two it was gone, then letters came from Vienna notifying the like sight of a brilliant comet, and "in the ayr [air] the appearance of a Coffin, which causes great anxiety of thought amongst the people." Erfurt saw with it other terrible apparitions, and listeners detected noises in the air, as of fires, and sounds of cannon and musket-shot. The report ran that one night in the February following hundreds of persons had seen flames of fire for an hour together, which seemed to be thrown from Whitehall to St. James and then back again to Whitehall, whereafter they disappeared.

In March there came into the heavens a yet brighter comet visible two hours after midnight, and so continuing till daylight. With such ominous portents the Great Plague in London was ushered in.[25]

Other less frequent "omens" were also reported in connection with the Black Death. Some of those phenomena were obvious fictions. Significantly, the fictions were not widespread and were rarely reported outside of the communities in which they originated.

The preceding quotes provide evidence that UFOs (*i.e.* the Custodial society) have bombarded the human race with deadly diseases. This evidence is particularly intriguing when we consider claims made by a number of modern UFO contactees who say that they are relaying messages to mankind from the UFO society. Some of them claim that UFOs are here to help mankind and that UFOs will eradicate disease on Earth. The UFO civilization reportedly has no disease. If the Custodial civilization is indeed so healthy, perhaps it is only because it is not bombarding itself with germ weapons. If UFOs truly intended to bring health to the human race, maybe all they needed to do was to stop spraying infectious biological agents into the air.

The Black Death not only killed a great many people, it also caused deep psychological and social wounds. People in the past were convinced that the epidemics were God's punishment for sin, and this caused deep introversion. It was natural for people to accuse themselves and their neighbors of wickedness and to wonder what they had done to "deserve" their punishment. It rarely occurred to the victims that plagues, even if deliberately inflicted, had nothing to do with trying to make human beings more virtuous. After all, the social and psychological effects of the Plague produced the opposite result. The misery and despair generated by the massive death tolls brought about widespread ethical decay. In a dying environment, many people will no longer care about whether their actions are right or wrong; they are going to die anyway. In the fearful climate of the medieval Plague, spiritual values noticably declined and mental aberration sharply increased. The same results are observed during war. Although the Bible and other religious works may preach that plagues and wars are created by "God" to ultimately make the human race more virtuous and spiritually advanced, the effect is always the opposite.

The cataclysmic nature of the Black Death overshadowed another disastrous occurrence of the Plague years: a renewed attempt by Christians to exterminate the Jews. False accusations circulated that Jews were causing the Plague by poisoning wells. These rumors stirred up a fearsome hatred of the Jews inside those Christian communities being devastated by the epidemic. Many Christians participated in the genocides, which may have claimed as many lives, if not more, than the slaughter of Jews by the Nazis in the 20th century. According to *Collier's Encyclopedia:*

> That country [Germany] figured . . . as the site of brutal massacres on the widest possible scale, which periodically swept the country from end to end. These culminated at the time of the terrible plague of 1348-1349, known as the Black Death. Perhaps because their medical knowledge and hygienic way of life rendered them somewhat less susceptible than others, the Jews were preposterously accused of having

deliberately propagated the plague, and hundreds of Jewish communities, large and small, were blotted out of existence or reduced to insignificance. After this, only a broken remnant remained in the country, mainly in the petty lordships which protected and even encouraged them for the sake of financial advantages which they brought. Only a few large German Jewish communities, such as Frankfurt-am-Main or Worms, managed to maintain an unbroken existence from Medieval times onward.[26]

The genocides were often instigated by German trade guilds, which excluded Jews from membership. Many of those guilds were direct offshoots of the ancient Brotherhood guilds. In fact, membership in Brotherhood organizations and European trade guilds still overlapped heavily in the 14th century with leadership in the guilds often being held by men who were members of other Brotherhood organizations. Here again was an instance in which the corrupted Brotherhood network was a significant contributor, if not the primary source, of a major historical genocide.

Germany was not the only nation to host Jewish slaughters. The same occurred in Spain. In 1391, a massacre of Jews was perpetrated throughout much of the Spanish peninsula.

Although frightened Christians supplied the manpower for these terrible genocides, their activities were not always endorsed by the Papacy. To the credit of Clement VI, who served as Pope from 1342 until 1352, he tried almost immediately to protect the Jews from massacre. Clement VI issued two Papal bulls declaring the Jews to be innocent of the charges against them. The bulls called upon all Christians to cease their persecutions. Clement VI did not fully succeed, however, because by that time many of the secretive trade guilds had become a united faction engaged in anti-Papal activity. Pope Clement also did not dismantle the Inquisition, and the Inquisition did much to create the generally oppressive social climate in which such massacres could occur.

The combination of Plague, Inquisition, and genocide

provided all of the elements needed to fulfill apocalyptic prophecy. The Catholic Church was on the brink of collapse due to the many clergymen lost to the Plague and from the loss of popular faith in the Church caused by the Church's inability to bring an end to "God's Disease." A great many people were proclaiming that the "End Days" were at hand. True to prophecy, out of this tumult emerged new "messengers from God" with promises of an imminent utopia. The teachings and proclamations of those new messiahs had an electrifying effect on the ravaged Europeans and brought about an event of major importance: the Protestant Reformation.

---

# 19

# Luther and the Rose

IN THE 14TH century, that region of Europe we know today as Germany consisted of numerous independent principalities and city-states. By that time, several of those principalities had emerged as the primary centers of Brotherhood activity in Europe, with most of that activity concentrated in the central German state of Hesse. In Germany and elsewhere, the Brotherhood and some of its most advanced initiates had become known by a Latin name: the "Illuminati," which means "illuminated (enlightened) ones."*

---

* This Illuminati should not be confused with another lesser "Illuminati" founded in 18th-century Bavaria by Adam Weishaupt. The true Illuminati and Weishaupt's Illuminati are two distinct organizations. Weishaupt's Bavarian Illuminati will be briefly discussed in an upcoming chapter.

One of the Illuminati's most important branches in Germany was the mystical Rosicrucian organization. Rosicrucianism was first introduced to Germany by the emperor Charlemagne in the early ninth century A.D. Germany's first official Rosicrucian Lodge was established in the city of Worms in the German state of Hesse in the year 1100 A.D. Rosicrucians achieved fame for their dedication to alchemy, their complex mystical symbols, and their secret degrees of initiation. The links between the Illuminati and early Rosicrucians were quite intimate in that advancement through the Rosicrucian degrees often resulted in admittance to the Illuminati.

A number of Rosicrucian histories mistakenly state that the Rosicrucians did not begin their existence until the year 1614—the year in which German Rosicrucians published a dramatic pamphlet in Hesse announcing their presence and inviting people to join them. One reason this mistake is so commonly made, and why the Rosicrucian Order has been so difficult to trace as one consecutive existence, is a policy the Order adopted of engaging in 108-year cycles of "activity" and "inactivity." According to the regulation, each major branch of the Rosicrucian Order was required to establish an official date of its founding. From that date, each branch was to then compute successive 108-year periods. The first period would be a time of well-publicized "outward" activity during which the branch's existence would be made widely known to the public and the branch would openly recruit new members. The next period was to consist of concealed, silent activity in which there was to be no publicity and no one outside of the members' immediate families would be admitted to membership. Each Rosicrucian branch would then alternate between these two phases every 108 years. As Rosicrucian bodies switched back and forth between their "outward" and "hidden" phases, it seemed to observers that Rosicrucian Orders were appearing and disappearing in history. According to Dr. Lewis of AMORC, "just why this new regulation was brought into effect is not known."[1]

The Illuminati and Rosicrucians were major powers behind a new wave of religious movements during the

Plague years. One of the earliest of those movements was a mystical religion known as the "Friends of God."

The Friends of God appeared in Germany in the same year that the Black Death first struck Europe. The Friends organization was founded by a banker named Rulman Merswin who had begun his financial career early in life and had made a sizable fortune from it. According to Merswin, in the year 1347 he was approached by a stranger claiming to be a "friend of God." The identity of the mysterious stranger was never revealed by Merswin, leading to suspicion that Merswin had merely invented him. It appears, however, that Merswin's "friend" was quite real, and quite influential, as evidenced by the sudden change in Merswin and by the considerable support that the Friends movement was able to so quickly gather.

During one of their earliest encounters, Merswin's mysterious friend stated that he had had many mystical revelations directly from God and that Merswin had been chosen to disseminate those revelations to the rest of the world. Merswin was deeply impressed. After that meeting, Merswin gave up his banking business, "took leave of the world," and devoted himself and his personal fortune to spreading the new religion which the mysterious stranger was bringing him.

As it turns out, what the stranger caused Merswin to create was another branch of the Brotherhood network. The teachings of the Friends were deeply mystical and were divulged through a system of secret degrees and initiations. History records that "illuminated" mystics and other Illuminati were among Merswin's principle backers.

The teachings of the Friends of God were not only mystical, they were also heavily apocalyptic. The Friends preached a powerful End of the World message to gain converts. Merswin claimed to be the recipient of many supernatural "revelations" in which he was told that God had grown disgusted with the Pope and the Catholic Church. God was now placing His faith in people like Merswin to carry out His sacred plans. According to Merswin, God was planning to severely punish humanity in the near future because of mankind's increased corruption and sin. Merswin had the sacred duty of preaching the need for everyone to therefore become completely obedient to God. Merswin was not alone in spreading this dire message. Similar prophets also found their way into the Friends movement bearing identical warnings. They all emphasized the need to unwaveringly obey God on the eve of the world's destruction. Merswin and his fellow doomsayers were certainly correct about one thing: the world was about to undergo a cataclysm. The Black Death was just getting started.

The Friends of God attracted a large following in Europe. Adherents were taught a nine-step program to become utterly and unquestioningly obedient to God. They were made to believe that this regimen would save them from the plague and resulting social devastation occurring around them.

The first step of the program was a sincere confessional to restore health. A properly-done confessional can have a highly beneficial effect on an individual, although a poorly-done or unnecessary confessional can be damaging. The second step was a resolution by adherents "to give up their own will and to submit to an illuminated Friend of God, who shall be their guide and counselor in the place of God."[2] By the seventh step, a member had completely given up all self-will and had "burned all bridges" to become completely subservient to the Lord. By the final step, all personal desire was to be destroyed, the individual was to be "crucified to the world and the world to them," enjoying only what God does and to wish for nothing else. These teachings were a program to make human beings obedient to an ultimate degree. Members were taught that obedience was a spiritual being's highest calling and something to be striven for as a quest.

Merswin's conversion to his mysterious "friend's" religion was very damaging to Merswin, as it no doubt was to many others. Merswin soon began to suffer strong "manic-depressive" symptoms: the phenomenon of alternately being in a happy state and then inexplicably experiencing mental depression, back and forth. In Merswin, these symptoms became severe and they were erroneously perceived by his followers as a sign of religious transformation. Many people today would recognize such symptoms as an indication that Merswin was connected to a repressive influence—in this case, the corrupted Brotherhood and probably his mysterious "friend."

During his life in the Friends movement, Merswin continued to claim many mystical experiences, including "joint revelations" with his "friend." In one of those revelations, Merswin was told to use his money to buy an island in Strausberg for use as a Friends retreat. Strausberg was Merswin's home city and is located by the southwestern French-German border. Five years later, Merswin had another joint revelation in which he was told to turn the whole Friends operation over to an organization called the Order of St. John, which governed the Friends movement thereafter.*

The Friends of God religion was one of many mystical movements that proliferated during the Plague years. Those movements were usually Christian in nature, but they advertised themselves as an alternative to the Catholic Church and attracted many disgruntled Catholics on that basis. This began to split apart the Christian world. Unfortunately, the split did not mean that Christians were returning to Jesus's maverick teachings. The new mystical religions only strengthened the emphasis on obedience and apocalypticism. This began to drive many people out of religion altogether and helped lay the foundation for the radical materialism which began to arise out of Germany shortly thereafter.

---

*Exactly what the Order of St. John was, and where it came from, is quite a mystery. It has been described in Albert MacKey's *Encyclopedia of Freemasonry* as a 17th-century system of Freemasonry with a secret mission. Is the Order of St. John described by MacKey the same one which had taken over the Friends of God movement three centuries earlier in the 14th century? I do not know.

The Friends of God and other mystical practices of the time became a juggernaut which brought about one of the greatest challenges ever faced by the Catholic Church: the Protestant Reformation of Martin Luther.

Luther began his famous ecclesiastical rebellion in the early 1500's. By that time, the Catholic Church had fallen into the hands of Pope Leo X, son of Lorenzo Di Medici. Lorenzo Di Medici was the head of a wealthy international banking house in Florence, Italy. The Medici family had become involved with the Papacy a generation earlier when the Medicis financed an archbishop who later became the schismatic ("anti-Pope") Pope John XXIII. Under John XXIII, the Medicis were awarded the task of collecting taxes and tithes that were due this Pope. The Medicis operated a far-flung network of collectors and sub-collectors to accomplish this undertaking. The fees earned from this operation helped make the Medici family one of the wealthiest and most influential banking houses in Europe.

The involvement of profit-motivated bankers in Church affairs transformed many spiritual activities of the Catholic Church into business enterprises. For example, Catholics believed in the importance of paying "indulgences." An indulgence is money paid to compensate for sin. When paid in conjunction with a properly-done confessional, monetary penance can often be effective in relieving guilt, especially if the money is used to assist the injured party. Most indulgences, however, went into Church coffers. Medici collectors were more often concerned with how much money a person could pay than whether or not the penitent achieved any spiritual benefit from paying it. Understandably, many Catholics grumbled and their discontent helped pave the way for Martin Luther.

History books tell us that Martin Luther was a German Catholic priest and educator. He had begun his career as a monk in the Augustinian Order and worked his way up to holding the chair of Biblical study at the University of Wittenberg in the German state of Saxony.

As a Catholic priest, Luther was subject to the strict regimen imposed upon all clergy of the Church. That included regular attendance at confessional. In Catholic confessional, a person tells a priest in confidence of wrongs that the confessor has committed. This is designed to help unburden a person spiritually. As already mentioned, a properly done confessional has a positive effect and, interestingly, it does appear to be necessary at some point for nearly everyone's spiritual advancement. By Luther's day, however, confessionals were often done improperly or unnecessarily so that people often felt little relief.

Luther eventually found going to confessional difficult. He had already come to hate the angry condemning God of the Catholic religion and, as a result, he began to lose his faith in the Catholic way to salvation. There was, however, another equally important reason why Luther was having difficulty in confessional: he had committed acts which he felt unable or unwilling to confess. Luther claims that he tried to purge himself of every conceivable sin, but some acts still "eluded" his memory when it came time to divulge them to his confessor. In part because of this, Luther did not feel himself advancing spiritually and he despaired of ever achieving salvation. He felt compelled to seek another path to spiritual recovery that would not force him to endure the uncomfortable confessionals. Although Luther voiced many legitimate criticisms of the Catholic Church and claimed that he was trying to re-establish the primitive Christian Church of Jesus, Luther was, to an extent, a man driven by the demons of unconfessed wrongs. As a result, he helped create a new form of Christianity that only further departed from the true teachings of Jesus.

Despite the East Roman corruption of Jesus's teachings and the brutal methods of the Inquisition, Catholicism during Luther's time still retained several important elements of Jesus's maverick lessons. For example, the Catholic Church continued to preach that salvation was up to the individual to achieve. It taught further the importance of doing good works,* the need to confess sin when sin had been committed, and the importance of rectifying wrongs or compensating for them. The Catholic Church emphasized that man had the free will to either accept or reject salvation, that salvation could not be imposed upon anyone against his or her will (even by a monotheistic God), and that all people were endowed with the right to seek salvation. While Catholic teachings still had many serious flaws and lacked a true science of the spirit, these ideas reflected some of the truth and decency which were at the heart of Jesus's message.

Luther's key to reform would have been to reinforce the good tenets still alive in Catholicism while eliminating the blatant commercialization and the East Roman changes to Christian doctrine. That was not the road Luther chose to take. He taught instead the false idea that a person has no personal control over his spiritual salvation. Luther convinced people that salvation is dependent entirely upon the grace of a monotheistic God. There was only one

---

*Good works are important to the extent that they improve a person's environment and bolster his level of ethics, which in turn helps provide a foundation for an individual's ultimate spiritual recovery. Unfortunately, the Catholic Church used good works as a scorecard. Catholics believed that a person's good works ("merits") were added up like points by God, and once a person had accumulated enough merits in his or her "treasury," the person was guaranteed salvation (provided that a few other requirements were also met). The Church taught that saints had a surplus of merits and that the Pope could transfer merits from the saints' treasuries to other people whose treasuries were lacking. The lucky recipients were naturally expected to contribute money to the Church for the favor. Luther rightly rejected the notion of merits and treasuries, and that became a major issue over which Luther was eventually excommunicated. Unfortunately, Luther did not restore an understanding of the true relationship of good works to salvation, but instead he wrongly eliminated the doing of good works altogether, even though it is one ingredient which can help lay the foundation for a person's spiritual recovery.

action an individual could take to obtain God's grace, said Luther, and that was to believe in Jesus as Saviour and to accept Christ's agony and crucifixion as penance for one's own sins.

Luther's curious notion that Jesus's crucifixion can be the penance for other people's sin is partially based upon the concept of "karma." "Karma" is the idea that all acts in this universe eventually "come back" at a person in the future. People frequently invoke the idea of karma when they ask, "What did I do to deserve this?" In modern science, "karma" has been expressed as: "For every action there is an equal and opposite reaction." In monotheism, "karma" usually comes in the form of God's inevitable punishments for sin and rewards for good. On a personal level, the principle of karma seems to hold true in the sense that the world one creates, good or bad, through action or inaction, is ultimately the world that comes back to one. Poor ethics seem to boomerang in the form of spiritual degredation. A major benefit of a properly-done confessional is that it actually seems to break the negative "boomerang" effect and it will thereby help start a person back on the road to spiritual recovery.

Because Luther's confessionals were unsatisfactory, he felt compelled to invent another way to escape the "karma" cycle enforced by the rewards and punishments of his monotheistic God. Luther therefore developed the idea that God would allow Jesus's pain and suffering on the cross to become the "boomerang" for everybody. In other words, by "believing in" Jesus, you will not spiritually suffer for the bad things you have done in the past because Jesus has already suffered for you. This is a wonderfully magical notion, but it is hardly a philosophy of responsibility, nor is it fair to Jesus that he should be expected to take the brunt for everyone else's wrongs. More importantly, Luther's solution simply does not work. Many people do feel and act better after "proclaiming Christ" because they have acknowledged their spiritual existences in a way they had not done before and they often begin more ethical behavior as a result, but their act of belief has not caused them to overcome the many other barriers which stand in the way of complete spiritual recovery.

Protestants continued to practice confessional, although it was no longer considered vital for achieving salvation. Practical knowledge of the spirit was also largely ignored. Luther's method amounted to "quickie salvation": a simple act of belief. Luther taught that salvation was guaranteed by God for as long as a person continued to adhere to a belief in Jesus as Saviour.

Luther's ideas were clearly mystical. This is not surprising when we consider that Luther had been greatly influenced by some of the mystical religions which were so popular in his country. Luther's primary mentor in the Augustinian Order, Johann von Staupitz, preached a theology containing many elements from the writings of the prominent German mystics Heinrich Suso and Johann Tauler. Tauler was one of the most widely-read mystics of the 14th century and he was associated with the Friends of God movement. Luther became an avid reader of Tauler's works. Evidence of a more direct connection of Luther to the Brotherhood network is found in Luther's personal seal. Luther's seal consisted of his initials on either side of two Brotherhood symbols: the rose and the cross. The rose and cross are the chief symbols of the Rosicrucian Order. The word "Rosicrucian" itself comes from the Latin words "rose" ("rose") and "crucis" ("cross").

Both during his life and after, Luther counted among his supporters important individuals and families who were active in the Illuminati and in Rosicrucianism. One of them was Philip the Magnanimous, head of the powerful royal house of Hesse, whose descendants would later hold important leadership positions in Brotherhood organizations, especially in German Freemasonry, as we shall later see. As one of the prime leaders of the Reformation, Philip the Magnanimous founded the Protestant University of Marburg and organized a political alliance against the Catholic German Emperor, Charles V. After Luther's death, his religion was supported by Sir Francis Bacon (1561-1626), who was at one time the Lord Chancellor of England. Bacon was also the highest executive of the Rosicrucian Order in Great Britain. One of Bacon's greatest contributions to the Reformation arose from his efforts as the coordinator of a project to create an authorized English Protestant Bible under his king, James I. This Bible, known as the "King James Version," was released in 1611 and became the most widely-used Bible in the English-speaking Protestant world.

Luther and his supporters created the single largest schism in Christian history. Enormous power was wrested from the Roman Catholic Church. The Protestant sects today account for about one third of all Christians worldwide, and nearly half of all Christians in North America. The Catholic Church did not allow this to happen without a fight, however. The Catholics launched a Counter-Reformation in an unsuccessful attempt to squelch the Protestant heresies. Leading the Counter-Reformation was, interestingly, a new Brotherhood-style organization created for the purpose: the Society of Jesus, better known as the Jesuits. The Jesuit Order was founded in 1540 by a soldier-turned-cleric named Ignatius of Loyola. The Jesuits were a Catholic secret society with degrees of initiation, periods of probation, and many secret rituals. It was also militant. Jesuits were encouraged to adopt a soldierly spirit of loyalty to their "captain" Jesus. Ignatius was chosen to be the first "general" of the Order in April 1741. The image of Jesus as a quasi-military captain may seem rather humorous to anyone familiar with Jesus's teachings, but the image was helpful in making the Jesuit Order an effective cadre for combating the Protestants.

Although it is true that the Reformation led the human race further away from spiritual understanding, it did have one very beneficial effect: it helped break the back of the Catholic Inquisition. The Inquisition had been one of the most oppressive institutions to burden the human spirit. Inquisitors meddled in nearly every human endeavor—from religion to the sciences to the arts. The Inquisition enforced some of the most hopelessly antiquated scientific thought by threatening people with torture and death. It hindered the development of many of the fine arts, notably theatre. It probably did not greatly matter what the Protestants taught; they would have still been able to bring enormous relief to Europe as long as they were able to reduce the power of the Catholic Inquisition. There was an eventual price to be paid for this benefit, however, and that was the price of an ever-deepening materialism. Philosophies of "humanism," "rationalism," and similar ideologies with a materialistic bent took on renewed vigor in the Reformation climate.

Most importantly, many of the positive effects of the Reformation were offset by the fact that Protestantism was yet one more human faction placed in unresolvable conflict with other factions over erroneous religious issues. Luther himself contributed to this by hinting that the Pope represented the forces of the "anti-Christ." The result has been more war, this time between Catholics and Protestants—notably today in Ireland.

Despite the Brotherhood network's continued pattern of generating conflict during the centuries discussed in this chapter, it is important to note that a maverick influence had manifested itself in the Rosicrucian organization by the early 1600's. The Rosicrucian goal of individual spiritual recovery and some of its teachings were remarkably similar to some earlier maverick goals. Modern Rosicrucian literature from the United States continues to reflect some of this positive influence by attempting to propagate a more scientific view of spiritual phenomena and by teaching that humans can intelligently control their lives. Unfortunately, modern Rosicrucianism still contains many Custodial elements which will prevent adherents from achieving full spiritual rehabilitation.

Although Rosicrucians contributed to the success of the Reformation, they did not achieve much fame until the year 1614 when, as noted earlier, a lodge of German Rosicrucians began a phase of "outward" activity by mass-producing a leaflet announcing the presence of Rosicrucians in Hesse's largest principality, Hesse-Kassel. The pamphlet created a stir by urging all people to abandon their false teachers, such as the Pope, Galen (a popular ancient Greek physician), and Aristotle. The pamphlet also told the story of a fictitious character, "Christian Rosenkruez," to symbolize the founding of the Rosicrucian Order. The pamphlet is best known by its shortened name, the *Fama Fraternitis* ("Noted Fraternity" or "Famous Brotherhood"). The full title of the leaflet, translated to English, is: *Universal and General Reformation of the Whole Wide World, together with the Noted Fraternity of the Rosy Cross, inscribed to all the Learned and Rulers of Europe.*

Despite the quaint high-sounding tone, the leaflet's title revealed a deadly serious intent: to create broad universal changes in human society. By the time of the *Fama Fraternitis*, the Brotherhood network had already launched its program to bring about this transformation. For the next several hundred years, the Brotherhood network supplied the world with leaders who inspired and led violent revolutionary movements in all parts of the world in an effort to bring about a massive transmutation of human society. They succeeded, and we live today in the world they created.

# 20

# A New Aristocracy

REVOLUTION IS AS old as history itself. People have been rebelling against gods, kings, and parents for millennia, and so we hardly look at it as anything out of the ordinary.

Luther's revolt was not a true revolution in the sense of blood being spilled. Luther and the Pope led no armies against one another. The Reformation did, however, lay the groundwork and provide the inspiration for numerous wars and violent political revolutions that were to sweep the globe for centuries to follow.

One of the earliest political struggles to grow out of the Reformation was the Eighty Years War, which got fully underway by 1569. The Eighty Years War pitted Spain against that region of Europe we know today as the Netherlands, which was then under Spanish rule. A new Protestant sect known as "Calvinism" (the origins of which will be discussed in Chapter 22) had emerged by that time. Radical Calvinists from France had migrated to the Netherlands and created an activist Protestant community in Holland. This naturally caused friction between the devout

Catholic rulers of Spain and the emerging Protestant minority of Holland. The Dutch minority not only sought religious freedom, but they soon craved political independence as well. The result was nearly a century of warfare.

Many of the early Dutch struggles against Spain were led by William I the Silent—a German ruler who reigned over the German principality of Nassau (which bordered on Hesse) and over the French region of Orange; hence, William's dynasty was known as the House of Nassau-Orange, or more simply, the "House of Orange." William led the fight in Holland partly because he had inherited large tracts of land there.

The eventual success of the Dutch rebellions brought about the birth of a fully independent Netherlands. With independence came the establishment of a political and economic system that was to provide a model for revolutions in other countries. The Netherlands adopted a parliamentary form of government accompanied by a reduction of the monarch's power. Although the House of Orange became the Dutch royal family, and remains so to this very day, the monarch's role in the new government was reduced to that of "Stadtholder," or chief magistrate. The Stadtholder could not hold office unless approved by the national assembly (the States-General), although this is often a mere formality. One intended effect of the parliamentary system was to prevent any single individual from achieving too much power.

We might puzzle over why the German royal family of Nassau-Orange helped establish a political system in which their own power was reduced. It can be argued that they did so to encourage popular support for the revolt against Spain; after all, the House of Orange did gain a permanent position in the government. This does not fully solve the riddle because, as we shall see, other German royal families led coups and revolutions in which nearly identical political systems were erected, and few of those dynasties were acting entirely from noble impulses. A clue to resolving the puzzle is found in the fact that those German dynasties were deeply involved in Brotherhood organizations. As we shall see in upcoming chapters, the evidence indicates that the families were promoting a Brotherhood agenda from which the royals handsomely profited in other ways.

In light of the role of the Brotherhood network in promoting revolution and reducing monarchies, it might appear at first glance that the Brotherhood was back to its true uncorrupted purpose of opposing Custodial institutions. After all, the institution of monarchy is traceable back to the Custodial "gods" of ancient Sumeria. According to Mesopotamian tablets, the Custodial society was ruled in a unique fashion. At the top was a Council or system of councils. Beneath the top council(s) were planetary subdivisions, such as Earth. Each subdivision was ruled by individual Custodians on a hereditary basis but subject to the laws of the Council(s). According to ancient Sumerians, local hereditary Custodial rulers were Earth's first kings. Those rulers naturally implanted their monarchial system on human society. We see intriguing evidence of this in those ancient Mesopotamian drawings that depict Custodial "gods" bearing two objects which are now universal symbols of monarchy: the sceptre and the tiara.

The Sumerians state that the first human kings on Earth were the offspring of Custodial rulers who mated with human women. Those matings entitled the half-human offspring to become early monarchs on Earth. Thus was born the idea of "royal blood" and the perceived importance of maintaining proper royal "breeding" to ensure continued purity of the human royal blood line. Interestingly, some ancient Custodial "gods" were depicted as either blue-skinned or blue-blooded: this gave us the idea (and some say reality) of royal "blue bloods." Aristocratic breeding practices have persisted through history and remain important to some royalty even today. Human "blue bloods" appear to be the prize Hereford cows of Earth's livestock race, *Homo sapiens*.

In light of the above, it would have been in keeping with the aims of the original uncorrupted Brotherhood to eliminate monarchy and to replace it with a parliamentary form of government in which human beings could choose their leaders. Had the Brotherhood reformed itself by the time of William the Silent?

Unfortunately, no.

As we have seen before, the Custodial influence caused valid aims and teachings of the Brotherhood to acquire fatal twists. Precisely such a twist distorted the otherwise altruistic social and political goals of the Brotherhood revolutionaries. The newly-weakened monarchies and parliamentary governments allowed for greater power to be assumed by a new institution being installed by the revolutionaries: a new banking and monetary system. This new monetary system was a major element of the revolutions of the 16th, 17th, and 18th centuries, yet this fact is only minimally discussed in the majority of history books. Those who ran, and still run, the new monetary system have been aptly labeled by one author, Howard Katz, "the paper aristocracy." The revolutions which began to sweep the world after the Reformation heralded the diminishment of powerful political aristocracies in favor of the less visible, but in many ways equally potent, "monetary aristocracies." This happened because, during the Reformation, banking and moneylending, which were once viewed as lowly occupations, were being forged into a renewed power due to a clever new science of money.* This new money was a type of paper currency that could have its value deliberately and systematically diminished through a process known as "inflation." It is the type of money still in use today. This new money, and the institutions which arose from it, have had an enormous impact on our modern civilization. We cannot fully appreciate the effects of Protestantism and the revolutions which arose out of it without comprehending just how the new money system works.

---

*For a simple and amusing introduction to the history of money and economics, I recommend *The Cartoon Guide to Economics* by Douglas Michael, published in the United States by Harper and Row Publishers, Inc., and in Canada by Fitzhenry & Whiteside Ltd. of Toronto.

# 21

# Funny Money

FEW TOPICS OCCUPY as many minds or stimulate as many emotions as money. This is largely because money is an overwhelming problem to a majority of people. One thing which causes modern money to be a problem is inflation, whether inflation is climbing at 3% annually or 300%. Inflation, of course, is the situation in which the costs of goods and services steadily rise due to the ever-decreasing value of money. This happens when the money supply becomes larger in proportion to the supply of valuable goods and services.

Money itself is not valuable; only the goods and services that can be bought with it are. The wealth of any individual or nation, therefore, is ultimately determined by what it produces in terms of valuable products and services, not by how much money it prints, distributes or holds. A nation could actually survive without any currency at all as long as it was otherwise productive.

The purpose of money is to facilitate the exchange of goods and services. Money is therefore an extension of the barter system. Barter is the act of trading something one possesses or does for something of someone else's. Production and barter are the bases of all economy.

Coins and paper money were originally created to assist in barter. They allowed people to barter without having to carry around actual goods or immediately deliver a service. This permitted individuals to trade more easily and to save the profits of their labors for the future.

Paper money initially began as "promissory notes." A promissory note is a written promise to pay a debt. A person would write a note on a piece of paper promising the bearer of the note a certain quantity of goods or services that the notewriter could provide on demand. To illustrate, let us look at the following fictitious example:

Let us pretend that a chicken farmer was in the village market and wanted to trade for a basket of apples. He did not have his chickens with him, so he might write a note to the apple seller entitling the bearer of the note to come up to the farm at any time to pick out two healthy chickens. The chicken farmer would be able to walk away with his basket of apples and it would be up to the apple grower to visit the farm one day to redeem the note by getting his two chickens. As long as people have faith in the chicken farmer's ability to honor his notes, he will be able to use them for barter.

Let us now pretend that as the day draws to a close, the apple grower decides to have a look around the market. He comes across the cloth merchant. The apple grower's wife has been henpecking him for days to buy some of the new silk that just arrived on a caravan from the Far East. The apple grower's home life has been made miserable by her unceasing demands and her denial of wifely comforts, so he negotiates with the cloth merchant for some silk. The cloth merchant, however, does not need any more apples, so the apple grower, remembering that he has a note for two chickens, asks the merchant if the merchant needs poultry. The merchant says that he does, and the apple grower gives him the note for two chickens in exchange for silk. It is now up to the cloth merchant to trudge on up to the chicken farm to redeem the note. The chickens themselves have never left the coop, yet they have changed ownership twice in one day. This type of exchange was all that paper money was initially created for; but do you see the temptation that it can open up?

If the chicken farmer knows that some time will pass before he must redeem his notes with actual chickens, or that some if his notes will circulate forever and never come in for redemption, he may be tempted to issue more notes than he has in actual chickens, thinking that he will be able to cover all the notes by the time they come back to him.

Temptation now gets the best of the chicken farmer.

The chicken farmer has a big family get-together coming up and he wants to impress his in-laws for once by putting on an opulent feast. Down to the market he goes where he writes notes for chickens not yet hatched and stocks up with an abundance of goods from other merchants. Several things can now happen. The chicken farmer will get away with it if he is always able to meet the demand for chickens when his notes come in for redemption. Another thing that may, and often will, occur is that he has so saturated the marketplace with his chicken notes that most people just do not want any more of them, so he must offer even more hens for each trade to make people feel that it is worth their while. He is now writing notes for two or three chickens in exchange for items for which he previously only had to issue single-chicken notes. As these chicken notes circulate, they become less and less valuable because there are so many of them. A vicious spiral ensues: the more notes the chicken farmer issues, the less valuable they become, and the more he has to issue in order to get what he wants. This is known as inflation.

Now comes the worst part.

With more and more notes outstanding, an increasing number of notes will start coming in for redemption. Soon the farmer will see that his true wealth, which is his supply of chickens, is becoming rapidly depleted even though only a small portion of his outstanding notes have come back. To preserve his chickens, he must decrease the value of his notes by declaring that the outstanding notes are now only good for half of what they say. This is called devaluation.

Since the farmer may find it difficult to admit that he had issued many more notes than he had chickens, he may try to save his reputation by lying, such as by saying that a fierce chicken plague had wiped out half of his flock. That will probably not prevent him from becoming very unpopular. Public faith in his notes will be destroyed. He will either have to revert back to straight barter, or else he will need to acquire someone else's notes in order to continue trading in the market.

As we can see, paper notes, or money, are rooted in actual commodities and are meant to be an expression that the creator of the notes has something valuable to trade.

In contrast to notes are coins, which functioned somewhat differently. Metals have always been considered valuable, and so pieces of metal were convenient trading tools. Metal pieces were imprinted with various designs, thereby becoming coins, and their metallic purity was guaranteed by the imprinter. Coin values were initially determined by the quantity and purity of the metal contained within the coins. Gold was a rare and popular metal, so coins made from gold were more expensive and had a higher barter value than, for instance, copper coins.

Metal coins became a popular tool of barter because they were durable and quantities could be controlled. They did create some problems, however. Realistically, people were only trading pieces of metal for other goods. This created a disproportionate emphasis on metals. The acquisition of coins and coin metals became an obsession to a great many people, and such obsessions tend to drain away energy better spent producing other valuable goods and services. The system also gave a disproportionate amount of power to those who possessed large quantities of coined metals, even though other commodities, such as food, are ultimately more valuable. The person with the coin metals could immediately acquire any good or service, but a farmer first had to go through the intermediate step of exchanging his product for a coin or coin metal before he could have the same spending flexibility.

Coin metals merged with paper notes to create the foundation of our modern monetary system in the 1600's. Those who laid this foundation were reportedly the goldsmiths. Goldsmiths usually owned the strongest safes and lockboxes in town. For this reason, many people deposited their coin metals with the smiths for safekeeping. The smiths issued receipts to the depositors that promised to pay to the receipt holders on demand those quantities of gold or silver shown on the receipts. Every such receipt was actually a note which could be circulated as money until a holder of the note went back to the goldsmith to redeem it for the specified amount of metal.

The goldsmiths made an important discovery. Under normal circumstances, only about 10% to 20% of their receipts ever came back for redemption at any given time. The rest circulated in the community as money, and for good reason. Paper was easier to carry than bulky coin and people felt safer holding receipts in lieu of actual gold and silver. The smiths realized that they could lend out the unredeemed metals and charge interest, and thereby earn money as lenders. In making such a loan, however, the smith would try to convince the borrower to accept the loan in the form of a receipt instead of actual metal. The borrower could then circulate that note as money. As we can see, the goldsmith has now created "money" (his receipts) for double the actual quantity of metal he has in his safe: first to the original depositor, and then to a borrower. The goldsmith did not even own the metal in his safe, yet by simply writing upon a piece of paper, someone now owes him money up to the full value of the gold in his safe. The smith could continue writing his notes as long as the notes coming in for redemption did not exceed his actual deposits of precious metals. Typically, a smith would issue notes four to five times in excess of his actual supply of gold.

As profitable as this operation may have been, there were some pitfalls. If too many of the goldsmith's notes came back for redemption too rapidly, or the smith's borrowers were slow to repay, the smith would be wiped out. The credibility of his notes would be destroyed. If the smith ran his operation cautiously, however, he could become quite wealthy without ever producing anything of value.

The injustice of this system is obvious. If for every sack of gold the smith had on deposit people now owed him the equivalent of four sacks, someone had to lose. As public debt to the goldsmith increased, more and more true wealth and resources were owed to him. Since the goldsmith was not producing any true wealth or resources, but was demanding an ever-increasing share of them because of his paper notes, he easily became a parasite upon the economy. The inevitable result was the enrichment of the careful goldsmith-turned-banker at the cost of the impoverishment of other people in the community. That impoverishment was manifested either in the people's need to give up things of value or in their need to toil longer to create the wealth needed to repay the banker. If the goldsmith was not careful and his monetary bubble burst, the people around him suffered anyway due to the disruption caused by the collapse of his bank and the loss of the value of his notes still in circulation.

Such was the birth of modern banking. Many people feel that it is an inherently dishonest system. It is. It is also socially and economically destabilizing, yet all of the world's major monetary and banking systems today operate on a close variation of the system I just described.

By the 17th century, the Medici banking house of Italy had come up with the idea of using gold as the commodity upon which to base all paper currency. Gold was touted as the perfect basis for paper notes because of the scarcity and desirability of gold. This was the beginning of the "gold standard" in which all other goods and services are valued in relation to gold (and sometimes silver). The gold standard was certainly a terrific idea for those people who owned plenty of gold and silver, but it created an artificial reliance on a commodity that is not nearly as useful as many other products. To base an entire monetary system on a single commodity is better than basing it upon no commodities at all, but even under a gold standard paper notes will far exceed the metals used to back the notes. The best solution is to root a money supply firmly in a nation's *entire* valuable output so that the money acts as an accurate reflection of that output.

Once the gold standard was created, paper notes were thought to be "as good as gold" because people could redeem the notes for actual gold. This created a false sense of security. As more and more gold notes entered the market, they gradually became worth less and less, resulting in a steady inflation. The gold owners/bankers had to keep issuing a constant stream of notes because that is how they earned their profits. As long as the bankers planned carefully and the people retained faith in the notes, the note writers could stay ahead of the inevitable inflation they created and make an enormous profit from it. If, on the other hand, they issued an overabundance and too many of their notes came back for redemption, they could, as a last resort, devalue the notes to save their gold. In this fashion, inflatable paper money, even under a gold standard, became a source of wealth and power to those entitled to create the money. It also generated indebtedness on an enormous scale because most of the "created-out-of-nothing" gold notes were released into the community as loans repayable to the bankers. If people did not borrow from the bankers, little new money would enter the market and the economy would slow down.

This method of creating money clearly destroyed the true purpose of money: to represent the existence of actual tradeable commodities. Inflatable paper money allows a handful of people to absorb and manipulate a great deal of true wealth, which are the valuable goods and services people produce, simply through the act of printing paper and then slowly destroying the value of that paper with inflation. It causes money to become its own commodity which can be manipulated on its own terms, usually to the detriment of the production-and-barter system. Money was meant to assist that system, not to dominate and control it.

The inflatable paper money system described above was the new "science" of money being installed by Brotherhood revolutionaries. An early version of the system was established in Holland in 1609. That was the year in which Dutch and Spanish forces signed a truce suspending the hostilities of the Eighty Years War. The truce marked the birth of the independent Dutch Republic and the founding of the Bank of Amsterdam in the same year.

The privately-owned Bank of Amsterdam operated on the inflatable paper money system described above. It was run by a group of financiers who pooled some of their precious metals to form the asset base of the Bank. By prior agreement with the new Dutch government, the Bank helped Dutch forces resume the wars against Spain by issuing notes four times in excess of the Bank's asset base. The Dutch magistrates were then able to draw on three quarters of the "created-out-of-nothing" money to finance the conflict. This reveals the primary reason why the inflatable paper money system was created: it enables nations to fight and prolong their wars. It also makes the human struggle for physical existence in a modern economy more difficult due to the massive debt and parasitic absorption of wealth that the system causes. Furthermore, steady inflation reduces the value of people's money so that their accumulated wealth is gradually eroded. The Custodial aims expressed in the Garden of Eden and Tower of Babel stories were greatly furthered by the new paper money system.

The initial success of the Bank of Amsterdam encouraged similar banking arrangements in other nations. The most notable offspring was the Bank of England, founded in 1694. The Bank of England established the pattern for our modern-day central banks by refining the inflatable paper money system of Holland. The Bank of England system was subsequently spread from nation to nation, often on the backs of revolutions led by prominent Brotherhood network members. The worldwide reformation announced in the *Fama Fraternitis* was well underway by the end of the 17th century, and the "new money" was a big part of it, as we shall see more of later.

# 22

# Marching Saints

ONE OF THE most important leaders of the Reformation was John Calvin. Calvin was only ten years old when Luther broke from the Catholic Church, but as an adult, Calvin became one of Protestantism's most zealous advocates.

Calvin published his first religious tract in 1536 in Basel, Switzerland—a city by the Swiss-German border. Calvin spent his adult life writing and teaching his own unique interpretations of Protestant doctrine. The result was the creation of a Protestant denomination named after him, "Calvinism," which was headquartered in Geneva.

Calvin continued in the mystical vein of Martin Luther. As we recall, Luther said that spiritual salvation was not something that a human being could achieve through his or her own labors. Instead, salvation required an act of belief. The same idea was promulgated by Calvin, but with a harsher twist. According to Calvin's doctrine, not even an act of faith or belief would ensure a person's spiritual survival. Calvin proclaimed instead that a person's spiritual salvation, or lack of it, was already predetermined before birth by God. Not only had God decided in advance who would achieve spiritual salvation and who would not, but there was absolutely nothing a person could do about God's decision. This unhappy doctrine is known as "predestination." Calvin's predestination teachings offered people little comfort because they stressed that most human beings were spiritually condemned. Those humans favored by God before birth were known as the "Elect." The Elect were few in number and could do nothing to share their good fortune with others. The Elect had only one real duty on Earth, proclaimed Calvin, and that was to suppress the sin of others as a service to "God." Calvin, of course, was one of the Elect.

One might ask: why would "God" condemn nearly every soul before birth and then continue to punish them after birth? It seems rather cruel. According to Calvin, the human race was still being punished for the "original sin" of Adam and Eve. As we recall, the "original sin" was early man's attempt to gain knowledge of ethics and spiritual immortality.

Calvin did not attempt to justify predestination, despite its obvious unfairness. He preached instead that predestination was a mystery to which all people should be humbled. Many things of "God" were never meant to be understood by human beings, he said.

Calvinism was more than a Sunday religion. It was a way of life. It demanded of its adherents a pragmatic and austere lifestyle in which a person's highest duty was to glorify God in his or her daily actions. People were taught that their positions in life, no matter what those positions happened to be, were their "callings" by God. A life should be lived as though it were a Supreme Being's will that a person was where he or she was. Calvinism was clearly a philosophy of feudalism for the modern age.

On religious grounds, Calvin forbade drunkenness, gambling, dancing, and singing flippant tunes. Those were among the sins that the Elect had been put on Earth to stamp out. To no one's surprise, Calvinists quickly developed a reputation for being dour and colorless. They also grew violent. Calvin was not a man of tolerance and he adopted some of the vicious practices of the East Roman emperors. For example, Calvin encouraged the death penalty for heresy against his new doctrines and he demanded that "witches" be burned to death at the stake.

Calvinism traveled from its stronghold in Switzerland to other countries. In the Netherlands, Calvinists had played a very large role in agitating and bringing about the Eighty Years War, which gave us the Bank of Amsterdam. In Great Britain, Calvinism was the basis of the Puritan religion.

Like their Calvinist brethren in Holland, some English Puritans decided to assert their gloomy beliefs and material self-interests through violent revolution. In the year 1642, a group of wealthy and prominent British Puritans led a full-scale civil war against the English king, Charles I. In Puritan eyes, Charles had committed crimes against God by marrying a Catholic and by being tolerant of Catholicism. After winning the civil war and beheading Charles, the victorious Puritan armies placed their own dictator in charge of Britain: Oliver Cromwell.

Under Cromwell, the Puritans were able to assert their religious beliefs into the arena of foreign policy. English Puritans believed strongly in the concept of Armageddon, *i.e.,* the Final Battle. They believed that the great Final Battle had begun and would climax in the latter 17th century, and that the Puritans' civil war against Charles I was a part of that Battle. The Pope was labeled the anti-Christ and Catholicism was considered Satan's tool. Cromwell tried to shape English foreign policy around these beliefs by working to solidify international Protestant unity and by waging war against Catholics in various parts of Europe. Cromwell believed that the English Puritans were God's "second chosen" people* and that his actions were all part of Biblical prophecy.

Calvinist cosmology did much to shape Puritan ideas about war. Engaging in war was glorified. The Puritans believed that tension and struggle were permanent elements

---

* The Hebrews were considered God's "first chosen," but they had fallen out of favor.

of the cosmic scheme because of the eternal struggle between God and Satan. Professor Michael Walzer, in his intriguing book, *Revolution of the Saints: A Study in the Origins of Radical Politics,* explains their belief this way:

> As there is permanent opposition and conflict in the cosmos, so there is permanent warfare on earth . . . This tension was itself an aspect of salvation: a man at ease was a man lost.[1]

It is vital to understand this Puritan idea because it exalts war *as a necessary step to spiritual salvation*. It was also one of the seeds which gave us the Marxist philosophy of "dialectical materialism."[2] This Puritan belief is one of the most pernicious ideas ever taught by the Custodial religions. It caused Puritans to view peace as an affront to God because peace meant that the struggle against "Satan" had ceased! "The world's peace is the keenest war against God," wrote Thomas Taylor in 1630.* The highest calling of a Puritan man was to march off to war for the glory of God. When there were (heaven forbid) no wars in progress, men were encouraged to attend military drills for recreation:

> And in religious respects, since every man will have recreations, that be best which is freest from sin, that best which strengtheneth a man . . . then abandon your carding, dicing, chambering, wantonness, dalliance, scurrilous discoursing and vain raveling out of time, to frequent these exercises [military drills] . . . [3]

The Puritans' ennoblement of war, coupled with their austere pragmatism, helped bring about major changes in the manner of fighting wars. Generations earlier, the

---

* Dialectical materialism is the philosophy which states that conflicts between social classes are inevitable and that such conflicts are the first stage of a process that will ultimately bring about a classless utopia on Earth.

Renaissance had had a very interesting effect on warfare in Europe. War had become a "gentleman's" activity—ornate and full of bluster. European rulers expended considerable sums of money to create aesthetic and colorful armies. Bright uniforms, flapping banners, and fancy armor were the order of the day. Significantly, pageantry replaced combat on the battlefield. More often than not, the dazzling Renaissance armies engaged in endless maneuverings against one another with little actual contact. After a great deal of pomp and show, a military stalemate would often occur followed by an elegant cavalry maneuver known as the caracole. Each side could then declare itself the winner with few or no casualties, and march colorfully home to the adulation of its people. Young male soldiers survived to quicken their lovers' pulses with noble tales of gallantry and honor in the field.

In today's jaded, ultrapragmatic world, the above activities might seem rather silly, like something from *The Wizard of Oz*. They were, however, an exceptionally important phenomenon because the Renaissance style of warfare revealed the true nature of the human spirit. The majority of people will gravitate away from war when given the chance. They will turn arenas of conflict into theatres of pageantry. They will choose life, color, and artistry over death, pallor, and decay. The Renaissance was a short period of history revealing that when repression is eased, when intolerance and war-inducing philosophies diminish in importance, and when people are able to think and act more freely, human beings as a whole will naturally and automatically move away from war.

Puritan austerity and glorification of war helped make European wars bloodier. Puritan armies operated on the idea that wars were meant to be fought effectively, not colorfully. With that in mind, Puritans eliminated military glitter and developed efficient fighting units through rigorous drilling. This pragmatic way of fighting quickly spread when other nations discovered that a beautifully embroidered banner could not win against an effectively pointed cannon. While most military organizations today still engage in some pageantry, it is noticably absent in the actual conduct of war. We observe instead austere fighting uniforms, curt efficiency, and military strategists who coldly calculate nuclear megadeath with percentage points and probability factors. They are all reflections of the pragmatism reintroduced into war by the Puritans and other Protestants. As we survey the war-mangled bodies of our fellow humans who have been killed more efficiently and more pragmatically, perhaps we realize that Renaissance pageantry was not so silly after all.

Despite its early successes, the new Puritan government under Cromwell did not last very long. The Stuart dynasty regained the British throne in 1660 with the crowning of Charles II (son of the beheaded Charles I). Charles II died 25 years later in 1685 without an heir, and so his brother, James II, took the throne. James ruled a mere three years, after which a second English revolution was launched in 1688 known as the "Glorious Revolution." Although a big issue was still Protestantism versus Catholicism, the Puritans did not lead the Glorious Revolution. In fact, a great many Puritans had fled England to establish colonies in North America after Charles II assumed the throne. The Glorious Revolution was led, in part, by none other than the House of Orange-Nassau. By the time of the Glorious Revolution, the House of Orange was firmly seated on the Dutch throne. How Orange also came to take the British throne and reign over three nations at once is a fascinating story of political intrigue.

# 23

# William and Mary Have a War

KING CHARLES II of England and his brother/successor, James II, had a sister, Mary, who had married the Dutch Prince of Orange. This marriage created a family tie between the royal houses of Britain and Holland. This tie was further strengthened by the marriage of James II's daughter, Mary II, to the son of the Prince of Orange, William III. Royal marriages in those times were not only matters of "breeding," they were also designed to secure political advantages and were often arranged with all of the sophistication and cunning of an espionage coup. Several German royal families were masters at the game. They were notorious for marrying into foreign royal families as a stepping stone to seizing power in those other nations. The House of Orange-Nassau was a member of that treacherous German clique. The Stuart family, after its hard-won struggle to regain the English throne, fell into the trap. Its marriages into the House of Orange helped bring the Stuart monarchy to a permanent end during the Glorious Revolution of 1688. To understand how this happened, and why all of this is important to us, let us briefly review the Glorious Revolution.

A powerful group of Englishmen and Scots had formed a Protestant political faction in England known as the Whigs. The Whigs were actually headquartered in Holland which, of course, was under the monarchy of the House of Orange. From their Dutch base, the Whigs launched the Glorious Revolution of 1688 and quickly unseated James II in a bloodless coup. The Whigs then placed James II's son-in-law, William III of Orange, on the British throne. The House of Orange now reigned over both Holland and England, as well as over their original German homeland.

Behind this intrigue we see the shadow of the Brotherhood. William III is reported to have been a Freemason.[1] In fact, in 1688, a militant secret society was formed to support William III. It was called the Order of Orange after William III's family, and it patterned itself after Freemasonry. The Orange Order was anti-Catholic and its purpose was to ensure that Protestantism remained the dominant Christian religion of England. The Orange Order has survived the centuries and is today strongest in Ireland where it has over 100,000 members. It is perhaps best known for its annual public parade to commemorate the successes of William III in England.

Upon his assumption of the British throne, William III quickly undertook to erect the same institutions in England as those which had been established by his dynasty in Holland: a strong parliament with a weakened monarchy and a central bank operating on an inflatable paper currency. William and his queen, Mary II, also promptly launched England into expensive wars against Catholic France.

The man chosen to organize the English central bank under William III was a mysterious Scottish adventurer named William Paterson, of whom very little was apparently known. The British House of Commons (parliament) was at first reluctant to accept Paterson's central bank scheme, but relented as the British national debt continued to skyrocket from the conflicts launched by the very warlike William III. The paper money system with its built-in inflation was touted as the way to finance the costly wars. Taxes were already as high as they could reasonably go and so the House of Commons felt that it had no alternative but to institute the scheme. The Bank of England was thereby born and warfare could continue, just as war could continue in Holland after the Bank of Amsterdam had been created there.

The Bank of England has been labeled by some economists the "Mother of Central Banks." It became the model for all central banks which followed it, including the central banks of today. Under the Bank of England scheme, the central bank was to be the nation's primary bank, and it would lend exclusively to the national government. The central bank's entire purpose was to put the government into debt and to be the government's major creditor. The central bank's notes would be lent to the government and those notes would then circulate as a national currency. This would cause the nation and its people to rely on those notes as money. The establishment of the Bank of England caused Britain to go deeply into debt to a monetary elite (the "paper aristocracy") which could then influence the use of the nation's resources. This is the modus operandi of every central bank today.

Like most modern central banks, the Bank of England was a privately-owned or privately-operated bank with quasi-governmental status. In accordance with Paterson's plan, the financiers who pooled their resources to create the Bank of England received approval from the government to issue gold and silver notes in a quantity many times exceeding the financiers' pooled holdings. The standard practice of bankers during that period was to issue notes four to five times in excess of their precious metals. The Bank of England, however, issued an incredible multiplication of $16\frac{2}{3}$. The British government agreed to borrow those notes and honor them as legal money for use in its purchases. The government accepted this plan because the government was not required to repay the initial loan, only the interest on the loan. Would not the Bank of England lose money on such a deal?

Not at all.

The face value of the loan notes were many times in excess of the value of the actual assets on which the notes were based. The *interest* on the loan in just one year surpassed the total value of the precious metals of the Bank of England! Specifically, the financiers had put together a total base of 72,000 pounds of actual gold and silver. By issuing notes valued at 16⅔ times the base, the bank was able to make a loan to England of 1,200,000 Pounds in paper money. The yearly interest rate was 8⅓%, which equaled 100,000 Pounds. This amounted to a profit of 28,000 Pounds, or 39% in just one year!

Twenty-two years after the Bank of England was established, an identical bank was set up in France in 1716. The founder of the French version was John Law, who became the Finance Minister of France. Law has been dubbed the "Father of Inflation" for his efforts. This title is not accurate, of course, because the practice of inflation had begun earlier. However, the spectacular inflation which occurred in France after Law's central bank was nationalized gave Law the dubious honor of the title.

As the son of a goldsmith-turned-banker, John Law was an interesting character in many ways. He was deeply devoted to the schools of Brotherhood mysticism that were behind many of the important social changes occurring in his time. Biographer Hans Wantoch, writing in his book *Magnificent Money-Makers*, describes Law as "one of the last of the alchemist-mystics, of the astrologers who were dying out in the time of Voltaire, but in his pursuit of the stone of wisdom he invented inflation."[2] Another interesting fact is that Law was a Scotsman with an obscure background, just like his earlier counterpart in England, William Paterson. The Scottish link between Law and Patterson may be significant when we later review evidence that Scotland was an important center of secret, but far-reaching, Brotherhood activity in Europe.

Law had played upon France's justifiable paranoia of England in order to convince the French government to establish a central bank identical to that of Britain. The warfare which had earlier been instigated by William III was causing a serious drain on the French treasury. Law's proposal seemed an attractive solution and so it was finally adopted.

At first, the new French currency issued under Law's plan appeared to revitalize the French economy. This happened because the banknotes could be redeemed for coins in which the people had faith. After the Bank of France became nationalized, however, it issued a severe overabundance of notes, not just a careful and gradual increase. People quickly realized that there were far more paper notes in circulation than there were coins to back them up. The result was a shattering of popular confidence in the notes and a consequent upheaval of the French economy.

The Glorious Revolution of 1688 not only gave us the Bank of England, which is still Great Britain's central bank today, it also gave us England's current royal family: the House of Windsor. The House of Windsor is directly descended from the royal family of German Hannover*, which had intimate ties to the House of Orange and to other German principalities in the treacherous marry-and-overthrow clique. After William III of Orange/England died, his sister Anne was seated on the British throne. By prior arrangement, upon Anne's death, the British throne was relinquished by the Orange family to the rulers of the German state of Hannover, who had also earlier married into the British Stuart family. Hannover's first elector [prince], Duke Ernest Augustus (1629-1698), had married a granddaughter of England's King James I. As was true with the House of Orange, the Hannoverian nuptials to the Stuart family did not legally entitle any of the Hannoverians to sit on the British throne, but with the overthrow of James II by the Whigs and House of Orange, the rules were changed to suit the victors.

The first Hanoverian king to take the British throne was George Louis, who became George I of England. George I could not speak English and he viewed England as a temporary possession. He continued to devote most of his attention and care to his German homeland. As generations of Hanoverians ascended to the British throne, they became permanently entrenched in British society. The Hanoverians provided England with all of its mon-

---

* In Germany, Hannover was spelled with two "n's." In Britain, the spelling had only one "n." I will use the British spelling "Hanover" when referring to the family in Britain, and the German spelling "Hannover" when specifically referring to the German state.

archs through 1901, and Hanoverian descendants from Queen Victoria's side have furnished the rest all the way up until today. During all of that time, the dynasty continued to maintain strong ties to other German noble families. During the first century and a half of Hanoverian rule in England, for example, the British Hanoverian kings married only the daughters of other German royal families.

Not surprisingly, there was widespread opposition in England to the Hanoverians after they took over. Many Englishmen understandably felt that German monarchs had no business reigning over British subjects. Anti-Hanoverian factions arose seeking to put the Stuarts back on the throne of England. Because of this, the Hanoverians decided not to allow a large standing army of native Britons, fearing they might stage a coup. Instead, whenever England required a large number of troops, the Hanoverians used money from the British treasury to rent mercenaries from their German friends and from their own German principality of Hannover, all at a most handsome fee. The greatest number of mercenaries were provided by the royal family of Hesse, which had close and friendly ties to the German House of Hannover. A curious aspect of the mercenary arrangement is that some important members of those German families, especially from Hesse, later emerged as leaders of a new type of Freemasonry which had been created to topple the Hanoverians from the English throne!

Before we study this remarkable situation, we should look to see what was happening with Freemasonry at that time. Major changes were unfolding that were about to make Freemasonry the single largest branch of the Brotherhood network.

# 24

# Knights' New Dawn

As HUMAN HISTORY entered the eighteenth century, changes were occurring. The Inquisition was almost dead and the Bubonic Plague was dying with it.

Students of Masonic history know that the early 1700's were an important period for Freemasonry. Masonic lodges in England had attracted many members who were not masons or builders by trade. This happened because Freemasonry was evolving into something other than a trade guild. It was becoming a fraternal society with a secret mystical tradition. Many lodges were quietly opening their doors to non-masons, especially to local aristocrats and men of influence. By the year 1700, an estimated 70% of all Freemasons were people from other occupations. They were called "Accepted Masons" because they were accepted into the lodges even though they were not masons by trade.

On June 24, 1717, representatives from four British lodges met at the Goose and Gridiron Alehouse in London and created a new Grand Lodge. The new Grand Lodge, which was called by some "The Mother Grand Lodge of the World," officially dropped the guild aspect of Free-masonry ("operative Freemasonry") and replaced it with a type of Freemasonry that was strictly mystical and fraternal ("speculative Freemasonry"). The titles, tools and products of the mason's trade were no longer addressed as objects that members would use in their livelihoods. Instead, the items were transformed entirely into mystical and frater-nal symbols. These changes were not made suddenly, but were the result of a trend which had already begun well before 1717.

A number of histories incorrectly state that the Mother Grand Lodge of 1717 was the beginning of Freemasonry itself. As we have seen, Freemasonry's roots were firmly established long before then, even in England. For example, one Masonic legend relates that Prince Edwin of England had invited guilds of Freemasons into his country as early as 926 A.D. to assist the construction of several cathedrals and stone buildings. Masonic manuscripts dating from 1390 and 1410 have been reported. Handwritten minutes from a Masonic meeting from the year 1599 are reproduced in Albert Mackey's *History of Freemasonry*. Freemasonry was so well-established in England by the 16th century that a well-documented schism in 1567 is on record. The schism divided English Freemasons into two major factions: the "York" and "London" Masons.

The new Grand Lodge system established at the Goose and Gridiron Alehouse in 1717 consisted at first of only one level (degree) of initiation. Within five years of the Lodge's founding, two additional degrees were added so that the system consisted of three steps: Entered Apprentice, Fellow Craft, and Master Mason. These steps are commonly called the "Blue Degrees" because the color blue is symbolically important in them. The three Blue Degrees have remained the first three steps of nearly all Masonic systems ever since.

The Mother Grand Lodge issued charters to men in England, Europe and the British Empire authorizing them to establish lodges practicing the Blue Degrees. The colorful fraternal activities of the lodges provided a popular way for men to spend their time and Freemasonry soon became quite the rage. Many lodge meetings were held in taverns where robust drinking was a featured attraction. Of course, many members were also drawn into the lodges by promises of fraternity and spiritual enlightenment.

The new Mother Grand Lodge was reportedly very strict in its rule forbidding political controversy within the lodges. Ideally, Freemasonry was to be independent of political issues and problems. In practice, however, the Mother Grand Lodge, which was established only three years after the coronation of the first Hanoverian king, supported the new German monarchy at a time when many Englishmen were strongly opposed to it. One of the earliest and most influential Grand Masters of the Mother Lodge system was the Rev. John T. Desaguliers, who was elected Grand Master in 1719. Desaguliers had earlier written a tract stating that the Hanoverians were the only legitimate sovereigns of England under the "laws of nature." On November 5, 1737, he conferred the first two Masonic degrees on Frederic, Prince of Wales—a Hanoverian. During the ensuing generations, members of the Hanoverian royal family even became Grand Masters.* The English Grand Lodge was decidedly pro-Hanoverian and its proscription against political controversy really amounted to a support of the Hanoverian status quo.

In light of the Machiavellian nature of Brotherhood activity, if we were to view the Mother Grand Lodge as a Brotherhood faction designed to keep alive a controversial political cause (*i.e.*, Hanoverian rule in Britain), we would expect the Brotherhood network to be the source of a faction supporting the opposition. That is precisely what happened. Shortly after the founding of the Mother Grand

---

*Augustus Frederick (1773-1843), the ninth son of George III, was Grand Master for the thirty years before his death. Prior to that, his older brother, who became King George IV, had held the Grand Master position. A later royal Grand Master was King Edward VII, son of Queen Victoria; Edward served as Grand Master for 27 years while he was the Prince of Wales. The most recent royal Grand Master to become a king was the Duke of York, who afterwards became King George VI (r. 1936-1952).

Lodge, another system of Freemasonry was launched that directly *opposed* the Hanoverians!

When James II was unseated by the Glorious Revolution of 1688, he fled England. His followers promptly formed organizations to help him recover the British throne. The most effective and militant group was the Jacobite organization. Headquartered in Scotland and Catholic Ireland, the Jacobites were able to rally widespread support for the Stuarts. They staged many uprisings and military campaigns against the Hanoverians, although they were ultimately unsuccessful in recrowning the Stuarts. When the unsuccessful James II died in 1701, his son, the self-proclaimed James III, continued the family struggle to regain the British throne. A new branch of Freemasonry was created to assist him. That branch was patterned after the old Knights Templar.

The man who reportedly founded Knights Templar Freemasonry was one of James III's loyal supporters, Michael Ramsey. Ramsey was a Scottish mystic who had been hired by James III to tutor James' two sons in France.

Ramsey's goal was to re-establish the disgraced Templar Knights in Europe. To accomplish this, Ramsey adopted the same approach used by the Mother Grand Lodge system of London: the resurrected Knights Templar were to be a secret mystical/fraternal society open to men of varied occupations. The old knightly titles, uniforms, and "tools of the trade" were to be used for symbolic, fraternal and ritual purposes within a Masonic context. In keeping with these aims, Ramsey dubbed himself the Chevalier [Knight] Ramsey.

Ramsey did not work alone. He was assisted by other Stuart supporters. Among them was the English aristocrat, Charles Radcliffe. Radcliffe was a zealous Jacobite who had been arrested with his brother, the Earl of Derwentwater, for their actions in connection with the failed rebellion of 1715 to place James III on the British throne. Both brothers were sentenced to death. The Earl was beheaded, but Radcliffe escaped to France.

In France, Radcliffe assumed the title of Earl of Derwentwater. He presided over a meeting in 1725 to organize a new Masonic lodge based on the Templar format being revealed by Ramsey. The Derwentwater lodge was instrumental in getting the new Templar system of Freemasonry going in Europe. Derwentwater claimed that the authority to establish his Lodge came from the Kilwinning Lodge of Scotland—Scotland's oldest and most famous lodge.* Templar Freemasonry is therefore often called Scottish Freemasonry because of its reputed Scottish origin.

Ramsey's Scottish Masonry attracted many members by claiming that the Templar Knights had actually secretly created the Mother Grand Lodge system. According to Ramsey, the Knights Templar had rediscovered the "lost" teachings of Freemasonry centuries earlier in the Holy Land during the Crusades. They brought the teachings back to Europe and, after their disgrace and banishment, secretly kept the teachings alive for hundreds of years in France, England, and Scotland. After centuries of living in the shadows, the Templars cautiously re-emerged by releasing only the Blue Degrees through the vehicle of the Mother Grand Lodge. Ramsey claimed that the three Blue Degrees were issued only to test the loyalty of Freemasons. Once a Freemason proved his loyalty by reaching the third degree, he was entitled to advance to the "true" degrees: the fourth, fifth, and higher degrees released by Ramsey. Ramsey stated that he was authorized to release the higher degrees by a secret Templar headquarters in Scotland. According to his story, the

---

* There is some debate as to whether Lord Derwentwater had also received a charter from the Mother Grand Lodge of England to start his new French lodge. Many histories state that he did, but some Masonic scholars aver that no record of such a charter exists and that Lord Derwentwater's lodge was an unofficial ("clandestine") lodge. It has been argued that the Mother Grand Lodge of England would not have granted Derwentwater a charter because his pro-Stuart political leanings were well known.

As a footnote, Lord Derwentwater continued to remain politically active and he tried to join Charles Edward during the Jacobite rebellion of 1745. The ship on which Derwentwater sailed was captured by an English cruiser. The Earl was taken to London where he was beheaded in December 1746.

Scottish Templars were secretly working through the lodge at Kilwinning.

To effect their pro-Stuart political aims, the Scottish lodges changed the Biblical symbolism of the third Blue Degree into political symbolism to represent the House of Stuart. Ramsey's "higher" degrees contained additional symbolism "revealing" why Freemasons had a duty to help the Stuarts regain the throne of England. Because of this, many people viewed Scottish Freemasonry as a clever attempt to lure Freemasons away from the Mother Grand Lodge system which supported the Hanoverian monarchy and turn the new converts into pro-Stuart Masons.

The Stuarts themselves joined Ramsey's organization. James III adopted the Templar title "Chevalier St. George." His son, Charles Edward, was initiated into the Order of Knights Templar on September 24, 1745, the same year in which he led a major Jacobite invasion of Scotland. Two years later, on April 15, 1747, Charles Edward established a masonic "Scottish Jacobite Chapter" in the French city of Arras. Charles Edward later denied ever having been a Freemason in order to squelch damaging rumors that Scottish Masonry was nothing more than a front for the Stuart cause (which it largely was), even though he had been a Grand Master in the Scottish system. Proof of his Grand Mastership was discovered in 1853 when someone found the charter issued by Charles Edward to establish the above-mentioned lodge at Arras. The charter states in part:

> We, Charles Edward, King of England, France, Scotland, and Ireland, and as such Substitute Grand Master of the Chapter of H., known by the title of Knight of the Eagle and Pelican . . .[1]*

We have just discussed the founding of two systems of Freemasonry. Each one supported the opposite side of an

---

* "Chapter of H" is believed to have been the Scottish lodge at Heredon. Charles Edward is denoted as the "Substitute" Grand Master because his father, as King of Scotland, was considered the "hereditary" Grand Master.

important political conflict going on in England—a conflict which affected other European nations, as well. Both systems of Freemasonry were launched within less than five years of one another. Ramsey's story of how the two systems came into existence therefore contains some rather stunning implications. His story implies that a small hidden group of people belonging to the Brotherhood network in Scotland deliberately created two opposing types of Freemasonry to encourage and support both sides of a violent political controversy. This would be a startlingly clear example of Machiavellianism.

How true is Ramsey's story?

To answer this question, we must first take a brief look at the history of Freemasonry in Scotland.

Scotland has long been an important center of masonic activity. The earliest of the old masonic guilds in Scotland had been founded at Kilwinning in 1120 A.D. By 1670, the Kilwinning Lodge was already practicing speculative Freemasonry (although, in name, it was still an operative lodge).

The Scottish lodges were unique in that they were independent of, and were never chartered by, the English Grand Lodge even after they began to practice the Blue Degrees of the English Grand Lodge system. The Kilwinning Lodge itself had been granting charters since the early 15th century. It ceased doing so only in 1736 when it joined other Scottish lodges in elevating the Edinburgh Lodge to the position of Grand Lodge of Scotland. The new Grand Lodge of Scotland at Edinburgh adopted the speculative system of the English Grand Lodge, yet it still remained independent of the English Grand Lodge and issued its own charters. About seven years later, in 1743, the Kilwinning Lodge broke away from the Grand Lodge of Scotland over a seemingly trivial dispute. Kilwinning set itself up as an independent Masonic body ("Mother Lodge of Kilwinning") and once again issued its own charters. In 1807, the Kilwinning Lodge renounced all right of granting charters and rejoined the Grand Lodge of Scotland. We therefore see substantial periods of time in which the Kilwinning Lodge was independent of all other Lodges and when it could very well have granted charters to Templar Freemasons. It was independent at the time Ramsey and Derwentwater claimed to have received authorization from Kilwinning to establish Templar degrees in Europe.

Some masonic historians argue that the Kilwinning Lodge and other Scottish lodges still had nothing to do with creating the so-called "Scottish" degrees. They state that the Scottish degrees were all created in France by Ramsey and his Jacobite cohorts. Some Masonic writers contend that Templarism did not even reach Scotland until the year 1798—decades after it had already caught on in Europe. Those writers further claim that the Kilwinning Lodge had never practiced anything but the Blue Degrees of the English system. Others believe that Ramsey, who was born in the vicinity of Kilwinning, claimed a Scottish origin to his degrees out of nationalistic pride and to help build a base of political support for the Stuarts in Scotland. These arguments sound persuasive, but historical documentation proves that they are all false.

First of all, we have already seen that Scotland was providing this era with important historical figures contributing to some of the changes being wrought by Brotherhood revolutionaries. Michael Ramsey is the third mysterious Scotsman of obscure origin we have seen help bring important changes to Europe. The other two were discussed earlier: William Paterson, who helped German rulers set up a central bank in England, and John Law, who was the architect of the central bank of France.

Secondly, the Scottish masonic lodges were a natural place for pro-Stuart Templar degrees to arise. Scotland was strongly pro-Stuart and the Jacobites were headquartered there. Decades before the English Grand Lodge was created, many Masons in Scotland were already known to be helping the Stuarts. These Scottish loyalists used their lodges as secret meeting places in which to hatch political intrigues. Pro-Stuart Masonic activity may go as far back as 1660—the year of the Stuart Restoration (when the Stuarts took the throne back from the Puritans). According to some early Masons, the Restoration was largely a Masonic feat. General Monk, who played such a pivotal role in the Restoration, was reported to be a Freemason.

Finally, there is incontroverted evidence that the Scottish lodges, including the one at Kilwinning, were involved with Templarism decades before 1798. Masonic historian Albert Mackey reports in his *History of Freemasonry* that in 1779, the Kilwinning Lodge had issued a charter to some Irish Masons who called themselves the "Lodge of High Knights Templars." More than a decade earlier, in 1762, St. Andrew's Lodge of Boston had applied to the Grand Lodge of Scotland for a warrant (which it later received) by which the Boston lodge could confer the "Royal Arch" and Knight Templar degrees at its August 28, 1769 meeting. It is significant that St. Andrew's Lodge had applied to the Grand Lodge of Scotland for the right to confer the Templar degree, not to any French lodge.

We have thus confirmed two elements of Ramsey's story: 1) that Scottish lodges practiced Templar Freemasonry, and 2) that a Scottish Grand Lodge was granting Templar charters at least as early as 1762. We can safely assume that the Scottish Grand Lodge was involved with Templarism before that year because the Lodge would have had to establish the Templar degree before another lodge could apply for it. Unfortunately, there are no apparent records surviving to indicate just when Templarism began in the Scottish lodges. Ramsey and Derwentwater, of course, claim that the Templar degrees already existed in the early 1720's. The Scottish lodges may well have been involved with some form of Templarism at that time.

Understandably, the Scottish lodges were highly secretive about their Templar activities. We only know about the 1762 Templar charter to St. Andrew's Lodge from records found in Boston. One need only consider the fates of the two Earls of Derwentwater to appreciate the dangers awaiting those people, including Freemasons, who engaged in pro-Stuart political activity.

Not every element of Ramsey's Templar story was backed by evidence. For example, Freemasonry itself was not started by the Templar Knights as Ramsey implied. The masonic guilds which gave birth to Freemasonry existed long before the Templar Knights were founded. On the other hand, there is circumstantial evidence that Templar Knights may indeed have been the ones who brought the Blue Degrees to England.

As mentioned in Chapter 15, it is thought that the three Blue Degrees were already being practiced centuries earlier by the Assassin sect of Persia. The Templar Knights had frequent contact with the Assassins during the Crusades. During those periods when they were not fighting against one another, the Assassins and Templars established treaties and engaged in other amicable relations. One treaty even allowed the Templars to build several fortresses on Assassin territory. It is believed by some historians that during those peaceful interludes, the Templars learned about the Assassins' extensive mystical teachings and incorporated some of those teachings into the Templar system. It is therefore quite possible that the Templars did indeed have the Blue Degrees long before they were established by the English Mother Grand Lodge.

Further circumstantial evidence is that during the Crusade era, the Templars were at the height of their power in Europe. They owned properties throughout the Continent. Their holdings and preceptories in Scotland were especially numerous. When the Templars abandoned the Holy Land after the Crusades, they eventually returned to their preceptories around the world, including Scotland. After the Templar Order was suppressed throughout Europe, many Templars refused to abandon their Templar traditions and so they conducted their activities in secrecy. Some secretly-active Templars joined Masonic lodges, including lodges in Scotland and England. It is therefore conceivable that Templars were the conduit through which the three Blue Degrees traveled from the Assassin sect, through Scotland, to the Mother Grand Lodge of 1717.

Some Freemasons may view any attempt to connect the Blue Degrees with the Assassin sect as an effort to discredit Freemasonry, even though the connection was suggested by one of Masonry's most esteemed historians. In discussing such a link, it is important to keep in mind that the assassination techniques employed by the Assassins were never taught in the Blue Degrees. The Assassins possessed an extensive mystical tradition that extended well beyond their controversial political methods. Furthermore, the Assassins had borrowed many of their mystical teachings from earlier Brotherhood systems. The Blue Degrees may have therefore begun even earlier than the founding of the Assassin organization.

Whatever the ultimate truth of the origins of the Blue Degrees and Scottish Degrees may have been, both systems gained great popularity. The Scottish Degrees eventually came to dominate nearly all of Freemasonry. On continental Europe, the center of Scottish Freemasonry proved to be Germany, where the same small clique of German petty princes we have been observing soon emerged as leaders in the new Templar Freemasonry.

---

## 25

# The "King Rats"

---

THROUGHOUT ALL OF history, small groups of political and economic elites belonging to the mystical Brotherhood network have profited from the conflicts generated by the network. If ancient Mesopotamian, American and biblical writings are correct, then those human elites are really only at the top of a prisoner hierarchy. We might label those elites the "King Rats" of Earth.

The term "King Rat" comes from a James Clavell novel which was later made into a Hollywood movie starring George Segal. The story *King Rat* concerns a group of American and British soldiers being held captive in a Japanese prisoner-of-war camp during World War II. Through clever bargaining and organization, one of the American prisoners, Corporal King, manages to amass a wealth of material goods desperately craved by the other prisoners of war. As a result, he sits at the top of the prisoner hierarchy and is often able to buy loyalty with a cigarette or fresh egg. The other prisoners simply call him King, for that is what he is inside the prison. When he embarks on a venture to breed rats as food, he earns the title "King Rat," which somehow seems to fit him.

King Rat enjoys every luxury craved by the other prisoners, yet the fact remains that he is still a prisoner himself. King Rat can only remain at the top of the pecking order so long as everyone remains imprisoned. At the end of the film, when the war is over and the camp is liberated, he no longer has the prison environment he relied on to stay on top. In freedom, he is lost, wondering if he really welcomes the liberation. In the final scene of the movie we see him being driven off in a truck, just another corporal. We sense, however, even if King Rat does not, that he is better off liberated since the fragile fiefdom he had built could have been easily toppled at any time by the Japanese prison keepers. King's life as a liberated corporal is far more secure than his precarious existence at the top of an oppressed prison population.

The King Rat of cinema was ultimately a sympathetic character. Those whom we might label the "King Rats" of Earth are not so endearing for we will use the term to describe only those individuals who acquire their profits and influence not by breeding rats, but by helping to breed war and suffering for human consumption.

For thousands of years, Earth has had endless successions of "King Rats." In this chapter, we will look at a particularly interesting group of them: the petty princes of 18th-century Germany. They and their relationship to Brotherhood mysticism provide a fascinating look at a curious element of 18th-century politics—politics which have done much to shape the social, political and economic world we live in today.

Germany became the center of Templar Freemasonry on continental Europe. The Knight degrees took on a unique character in the German states where the degrees were made into a system of Freemasonry called the "Strict Observance." The "Strict Observance" was so named because every initiate was required to give an oath of strict and unquestioning obedience to those ranking above him within the Order. The vow of obedience extended to a mysterious figure known as the "Unknown Superior," who was said to be the secret leader of the Strict Observance and who was reportedly residing in Scotland.

Members of the Strict Observance first passed through the Blue Degrees before they were initiated into the higher degrees of "Scottish Master," "Novice," "Templar," and "Professed Knight." The "Unknown Superior" went by the title "Knight of the Red Feather." Although secrecy in the Strict Observance was very strong, several leaks revealed that the Strict Observance was true to the Scottish degrees by agitating against the House of Hanover in favor of the Stuarts.

The Strict Observance spread quickly throughout the German states and became the dominant form of Freemasonry there for decades. It also became influential in other countries such as France, which was the second largest center of Freemasonry in Europe. (Germany was the largest.) In all nations, Strict Observance members pledged obedience to the "Unknown Superior" of Scotland. According to J. M. Roberts, writing in his book, *The Mythology of the Secret Societies:*

> The Strict Observance evoked suspicion and hostility in France because of its German origins and great excitement was aroused by the implied recognition by the Grand Orient [France's supreme Masonic body] of the authority of the unknown superiors of the Strict Observance over French freemasons.[1]

One of the earliest Grand Masters of the Strict Observance was G. C. Marschall. Upon Marschall's death in 1750, the position was assumed by a German from Saxony: the Baron Von Hund. The Strict Observance degrees had nearly all been created by the beginning of Von Hund's Grand-Mastership, but Von Hund has been given credit for doing the most to put them into recognizable form. Von Hund stated that he had been initiated into the Order of the Temple (*i.e.* the Templar Knights) by Lord Kilmarnock, a prominent nobleman from Scotland. Von Hund also claimed that he had met both the "Unknown Superior" and Charles Edward.

Like Michael Ramsey, Von Hund was on a mission to re-establish the Templar Knights in Europe. Von Hund sought to raise money to repurchase the lands which had been seized from the Templars centuries earlier. Although Von Hund had many successes, he was branded a fraud by his enemies and he eventually fell into disgrace.

The Strict Observance gained a strong following among the German royal families (although some opposed it and remained loyal to the English Masonic system). This is a puzzle. Some royal families involved in the Strict Observance were politically allied to Hanover. Why would they participate in a form of Freemasonry which secretly opposed the English House of Hanover?

In some cases, it appears that the royal members had joined the Strict Observance after it ceased to be virulently pro-Stuart. Certainly the Stuart cause was waning by the 1770's when some of those German princes emerged as Strict Observance leaders. On the other hand, there is another important factor to be considered:

The woes of England caused by the Stuart rebellion and by other conflicts were a source of immense profit to those German principalities, including to Hannover! That same small clique of German royal dynasties which had been marrying into foreign royal families and then overthrowing them, made big money from the conflicts which they helped to create—conflicts which were also being stirred up by the Brotherhood network.

To better understand this situation, we must briefly digress and review the history of the Teutonic Knights after they were defeated in the Crusades.

When the Crusades ended, the Teutonic Knights, like the Templar and Hospitaler Knights, found work elsewhere. In 1211, while under the leadership of Grand Master Hermann von Salza, the Teutonic Knights were invited to Hungary to aid a struggle going on there. For their services, they were awarded the district of Burzenland in Transylvania, which was then under Hungarian rule. The Knights outlived their welcome, however, and were expelled because they demanded too much land. After their ouster from Transylvania, the Knights were invited by Conrad, Polish

Prince of Masovia, to help fight heathen Slavs in Prussia. The Knights were again rewarded with land. This time they received large sections of Prussia.

The Knights gained another benefactor: German Emperor Frederick II—the man who made the ten-year peace treaty we discussed in Chapter 15. Although Frederick had acted as a man of peace, he was unfortunately also associated with this organization of war. In 1226, Frederick empowered the Knights to become overlords of Prussia. Frederick awarded to Grand Master von Salza the status of a prince of the German Holy Roman Empire. Frederick was also responsible for a reorganization of the Order.

The Teutonic Knights were thoroughly entrenched in Prussia by the year 1229. They built solid fortresses and imposed Christianity on the native Prussian populace with an energetic military campaign. By 1234, the Knights were politically autonomous and served under no authority except the Pope. The Knights surrendered their extensive Prussian holdings to the Pope in name and received them back as fiefs. In reality, the Teutonic Knights were the true rulers of Prussia, not the Pope.

With Papal support, the ranks of the Teutonic Knights ballooned rapidly. Many Germans traveled to Prussia to enter the new and potentially lucrative theatre of war. This migration eventually brought about the complete "Germanization" of Prussia. Commerce and industry eventually replaced armed conflict and Prussia became a major commercial center. By the early 1300's, the dominion of the Teutonic Knights extended over most of the southern and southeastern coastline of the Baltic Sea. The Teutonic Knights had two centuries in which to leave their indelible mark on central and western Europe. Before losing power, the Knights had established the militant character of Prussia that would define that region for centuries to follow.

By the early 1500's the fate of the Teutonic Knights had worsened. They were driven out of West Prussia by Poland and were forced to rule East Prussia as a Polish fief. By 1618, Prussia fell completely under the rule of the Hohenzollern dynasty. This effectively marked the end of autonomous Teutonic Knight rule.

Despite continuing friction between the Knights and the Hohenzollerns over control of Prussia, the Hohenzollerns kept significant elements of the Knight organization alive. At least one Hohenzollern, Albert of Brandenburg-Anspach, had been a Grand Master of the Order around 1511. Hohenzollern Prussia adopted the colors of the Teutonic cloaks (black and white) as the official hues of the land. The two-headed Teutonic bird became Prussia's national symbol.

Like the other knightly organizations of the Crusades, the Teutonic Knights were eventually turned into a secret fraternal society, this time under the sponsorship of the royal Hapsburg family of Austria. The Teutonic Knights still survive in that form today.

Under the rule of the Hohenzollerns, the power and influence of Prussia grew. Prussia became a formidable player in the tangled political arena of Europe. By the eighteenth century, the Hohenzollerns had also become extensively intertwined with their German royal neighbors through marriage. For example, history's most famous Hohenzollern, Frederick II (better known as "Frederick the Great"), had been set up by his father in 1733 to marry Elizabeth Christina of the northwestern German principality of Brunswick. (In 1569, the Brunswick dynasty had founded the Brunswick-Luneburg family line which later became the Hannover family.) Frederick's mother was Sophia Dorothea, sister of Hanoverian King George II. Generations earlier, Frederick the Great's great grandfather had married Henrietta, daughter of the Prince of Orange.

Political marriages, because they were usually loveless, were often unsatisfactory to those who were wed. This proved true in the joining of Frederick the Great to Elizabeth Christina of Brunswick. Frederick had wanted to marry one of the Hanoverians, but his father's stern will prevailed. Despite this unhappy arrangement, Frederick still had amicable ties to others in the Brunswick family. It was in Brunswick that Frederick, not yet the King of Prussia, was secretly initiated into Freemasonry on August 14, 1738 against his father's wishes. The initiation had been authorized by the Lodge of Hamburg in Hannover. The Lodge practiced the Blue Degrees of English Freemasonry.

Two years after his initiation, Frederick II became the king of Prussia. He then publicly revealed his Masonic membership and initiated others into the Order.* At Frederick's command, a Grand Lodge was established in Berlin called Lodge of Three Globes. Its first meeting was held on September 13, 1740. This Lodge began as an English system lodge and it had the authority to grant charters.

How long Frederick remained active in Freemasonry is still debated today. Some historians believe that he ceased his Masonic activities in 1744 when the demands of war occupied his full attention. His general cynicism later in life eventually extended to Freemasonry. Nevertheless, Frederick's name continued to appear as the authority for Masonic charters even after he was reportedly inactive. It is uncertain whether Frederick merely lent his name to the granting of charters or was personally involved in the process.

Within about a decade of Frederick's Masonic initiation, the Strict Observance and its Scottish degrees were in the process of almost completely taking over German Masonry. Frederick's Lodge of Three Globes became decidedly "Strict Observance" when its new statutes were adopted on November 20, 1764. On January 1, 1766, Baron Von Hund, Grand Master of the Strict Observance, constituted the Three Globes as a Scots or Directoral Lodge empowered to warrant other Strict Observance Lodges. All lodges already warranted by the Three Globes except one (the Royal York Lodge) went over to the Strict Observance (Scottish) system.

Whatever Frederick's masonic involvement may or may not have been, he and his Prussian kingdom profited from the conflicts of England that Scottish Masonry had been

---

* In 1740, Frederick initiated several other important German nobles into Freemasonry: his brother, Prince William; the Margrave (Prince) Charles of Brandenburg (whose family was also married into the House of Hanover through Caroline of Brandenburg as wife to King George II); and Frederick William, the Duke of Holstein.

An ancient Mesopotamian depiction of one of their female extraterrestrial "gods." The "gods" were very humanlike with male and female bodies. The eyewear, form-fitted clothing, and body apparatus on the above "god" are strongly reminiscent of modern aviator's goggles, airtight suit, and modern gadgetry.

(Reproduced by permission from *The Twelfth Planet*, by Zecharia Sitchin.)

The Great Pyramid is also pointed precisely along the four compass directions. This postage stamp issued by Egypt in 1959 shows an airplane flying in direct alignment with the Great Pyramid, as though to suggest that the pilot is using the pyramid to guide the airplane.

Egypt's Custodial "gods" were said to participate in the upbringing of the pharaohs. In this Egyptian illustration we see Pharaoh Thutmose III being given an archery lesson by one of his "gods." Thutmose became famous for his military exploits. This illustration suggests that Custodians had a role in training humans to be warlike.

The Custodial "gods" of ancient Egypt were very often depicted wearing aprons.

The Zoroastrian "God," Ahura Mazda, was depicted in ancient Persia as a humanlike creature who flew in a circular object. The object is depicted with stylized wings and bird's tail to indicate that it flies. It also had bird's feet that look like landing struts. Depictions such as these were not meant to be literal images of the "God," but were meant to portray the "God" in such a way so as to reveal its attributes. Zoroaster's "God" had the attributes of being humanlike and flying about in a circular craft.

Grand Master of the Templar Knights, Jacques de Molay, is led to a stake where he will be burned. Three other Templar Knights also await execution. The burning took place in Paris; in the background one can see the Cathedral of Notre Dame.

*Christianity has been closely associated with Brotherhood mysticism since the lifetime of Jesus. This painting by Jan Provost (ca. 1465–1529) is entitled, "A Christian Allegory." It features Christian symbols—among them the "All-Seeing Eye" of God and the lamb. Both of these symbols were used by the Brotherhood long before the advent of Christianity. The "All-Seeing Eye" of God was derived from the "Eye of Horus" symbol used in ancient Egypt. Horus was one of Egypt's Custodial "gods." The lamb was already symbolically important during the reign of Melchizedek centuries before the birth of Jesus. It was Melchizedek's branch of the Brotherhood that reportedly first began to use lambskin for its ceremonial aprons.*

*The extraordinary similarities between the ancient civilizations of Egypt and America are too striking to be coincidence. Above is the ancient Mexican Pyramid of the Sun, which resembles the first step pyramid of Egypt.*

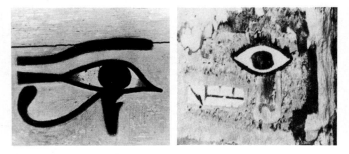

ABOVE LEFT AND RIGHT: *The similarities between ancient Old and New World civilizations are also seen in some of the symbols used by both. Above left is the Eye of Horus symbol found in ancient Egypt. Above right is a similar eye found on an ancient American artifact.*

*Centuries ago, almost any unusual flying object was called a "comet." The above is an illustration published in 1557 of a "comet" observed in 1479 in Arabia. The comet was described as looking like a sharply pointed wooden beam. The artist's concept, which was based on eyewitness testimony, looks like a rocketship with numerous port holes. Many other ancient reports of "comets" may well have been of similar objects.*

(Reproduced from *A Chronicle of Prodigies and Portents*...
by Conrad Lycosthenes.)

*Depiction of George Washington wearing his Masonic regalia.*

ABOVE AND BELOW: *Many proposed designs were submitted for a flag for the new Confederacy. These two proposals, which are preserved today in the United States National Archives, prominently feature the Brotherhood's symbol of the All-Seeing Eye. The Confederate leaders eventually opted for a simple cross bars and stars design.*

*Evidence that Martin Luther was a Rosicrucian or member of another Brotherhood secret society is found in the symbols Luther chose for his personal seal:*

ABOVE LEFT: *Martin Luther's personal seal. It contains his initials "M.L." and a cross inside a rose. The rose and cross were the two main symbols used by Rosicrucians in Martin Luther's homeland (Germany) and elsewhere.*

ABOVE MIDDLE AND RIGHT: *Variations of the rose and cross symbol still used by Rosicrucians in the 20th century.*

*Postage stamp issued by Ethiopia in 1977. It depicts the Marxist regime's emblem. Note the prominence of the Brotherhood "All-Seeing Eye" symbol in the middle.*

*The seal used by George Washington after a design by Charles Thompson. The long-necked bird is the image of a phoenix. The phoenix was unofficially the first national bird of the United States, but was later replaced by the bald eagle.*

contributing to. Despite his domestic liberalism and professed anti-Machiavellian beliefs, Frederick proved by his actions to be as warlike and as shrewdly manipulative in the complex web of European politics as any man of his day. His goal was the militaristic expansion of the Prussian kingdom. He was not above aiding insurrection and being fickle in his alliances to achieve his goal. In the 1740's, Frederick had a political alliance with France. France was actively supporting the Jacobites against the Hanoverians and rumors circulated in London that Frederick was helping the Jacobites prepare for their big invasion of England in 1745.

Frederick afterwards shifted his alliance back to England and continued to profit from England's woes. He not only gained territory, but money as well. Sharing in Frederick's monetary profits were other German principalities, including Hannover itself. They all made their money by renting German soldiers to England at exhorbitant prices. Hannover had already been engaged in this enterprise for decades.

The rental of German mercenaries to England was perhaps one of the great "scams" of European history: a small clique of German families overthrew the English throne and placed one of their own upon it. They then used their influence to militarize England and to involve it in wars. By doing so, they could milk the British treasury by renting expensive soldiers to England to fight in the wars they helped to create! Even if the Hanoverians were unseated in England, they would go home to German Hannover with a handsome profit made from the wars to unseat them. This may be one key to the puzzle of why some members of this German clique supported Scottish Templar Freemasonry and later took on leadership positions within it.

England rented German mercenaries through the signing of "subsidy treaties," which were really business contracts. England began entering into subsidy treaties almost immediately after the German takeover of their country by the House of Orange in 1688. As we recall, one of the first things that William and Mary did after taking the English throne was to launch England into war.

The German mercenaries were a constant burden to England. One early mention of them is found in the correspondence of the Duke of Marlborough.* Marlborough was an English leader fighting on the European continent against France during the War of Spanish Succession (1701-1714).** Hannover was renting troops to England at that time—years before Hannover took the British throne. On May 15, 1702, Marlborough discussed the need to pay the Hannoverian troops so that they would fight:

> If we have the Hanover troops, I am afraid there must be one hundred thousand crowns given them before they will march, so that it would be very much for the Service if that money were ready in Holland at my coming.[2]

Four days later, 22,600 pounds were allocated by the English government to pay the mercenaries.

Prussia and Hesse were also supplying mercenaries to Britain during that war. Marlborough's woes in getting them paid continued. Writing from the Hague on March 26, 1703, he lamented:

> Now that I am come here [the Hague] I find that the Prussians, Hessians, nor Hanoverians have not received any of their extraordinaries [fees] . . .[3]

England's next major European war was the War of Austrian Succession (1740-1748). Frederick the Great was allied with France against England this time. This did not stop other German principalities from continuing their business relationship with England, especially Hannover and Hesse. Although Hannover now sat on the British

---

* Letters written by the Duke of Marlborough are translated here into modern English.
** Wars of "succession" were wars sparked by disputes over who should succeed to a royal throne. The major European powers often got involved in these frays and turned them into large-scale conflicts which could drag on for years.

throne, it was not about to cease its profitable enterprise. If anything, Hannover's British reign gave that German principality greater leverage to drive even harder bargains with England for Hannoverian mercenaries. A letter written on December 9, 1742 by Horace Walpole, Britain's former Prime Minister, discussed the enormous fee England was asked to pay for renting 16,000 Hannoverian troops:

> . . . there is a most bold pamphlet come out . . . which affirms that in every treaty made since the accession [to the British throne] of this family [Hanover], England has been sacrificed to the interests of Hanover . . .[4]

The pamphlet mentioned by Warpole contained these amusing words:

> Great Britain hath been hitherto strong and vi[g]orous enough to bear up Hanover on its shoulders, and though wasted and wearied out with the continual fatigue, she is still goaded on . . . For the interests of this island [England] must, for this once, prevail, or we must submit to the ignominy of becoming only a money-province to that electorate [Hannover].[5]

In the end, opposition to the subsidy treaties failed. England truly became Hannover's "money-province." Lamented Walpole:

> We have every now and then motions for disbanding Hessians and Hanoverians, alias mercenaries; but they come to nothing.[6]

The subsidy treaties were indeed lucrative. For example, in the contract year beginning December 26, 1743, the British House granted 393,733 pounds for 16,268 Hannoverian troops. This may not seem like much until we realize that the value of the pound was very much higher than it is today. To raise some of this money, the Parliament went as far as to authorize a lottery.

At the same time that England was fighting the War of Austrian Succession, it was also fighting the Jacobites. More German troops were needed on that front.

On September 12, 1745, Charles Edward of the Stuart family led his famous invasion of England by way of Scotland. "Bonnie Prince Charlie," as Charles Edward was called, captured Edinburgh on September 17 and was approaching England with the intent of taking London. That meant more money for Hesse. On December 20, 1745, Hanoverian King George II announced that he had sent for 6,000 Hessian troops to fight in Scotland against Charles Edward. King George presented Parliament with a bill for the Hessian troops. It was approved. The Hessians landed on February 8 of the following year. Meanwhile, back on the European front, England hired more soldiers from Holland, Austria, Hannover, and Hesse to pursue England's "interests" there. The bills were staggering.

The war on the Continent finally ended. It was not long, of course, before the rulers of Europe were involved in another one. This time it was the Seven Years War (1756-1763)— one of the largest armed conflicts in European history up until that time.* Frederick of Prussia had switched his allegiance back again to England, and the two nations (England and Prussia) were pitted against France, Austria, Russia, Sweden, Saxony, Spain, and the Kingdom of Two Sicilies. Frederick did not ally himself to England this time out of fickle love for Britain. England was paying him. By the Treaty of Westminster effective April 1758, Frederick received a substantial subsidy from the English treasury to continue his fighting, much of it to defend his own interests! The treaty ran from April to April and was renewable annually.

During the Seven Years War, England also paid out money

---

* The Seven Years War was actually an expansion of the French and Indian War being fought in North America between England and France. The expansion of the war into Europe had been triggered by Frederick the Great himself when he invaded Saxony.

to help Hannover defend its own German interests. France had attacked Hannover, Hesse, and Brunswick. Some of the subsidy money paid to Hannover and Hesse was used by those principalities to defend their own borders. The treaty with Hesse, signed on June 18, 1755 (shortly before the Seven Years War erupted) was especially generous. In addition to "levy money" (money used to gather an army together) and "remount money" (money used to acquire fresh horses), Hesse was granted a yearly subsidy of 36,000 Pounds when its troops were under German pay, and double that when they entered British pay. An additional 36,000 Pounds went directly to the coffers of the Landgrave of Hesse.

Many English Lords did not feel that German troops were worth the money. While discussing a possible French invasion of England, Warpole joked, "if the French do come, we shall at least have something for all the money we have laid out on Hanoverians and Hessians!"[7] William Pitt, another influential English statesman, added these amusing words to the debate:

> The troops of Hanover, whom we are now expected to pay, marched into the Low Countries, where they still remain. They marched to the place most distant from the enemy, least in danger of an attack, and most strongly fortified had an attack been designed. They have, therefore, no other claim to be paid than that they left their own country for a place of greater security. I shall not, therefore, be surprised, after such another glorious campaign . . . to be told that the money of this nation cannot be more properly employed than in hiring Hanoverians to eat and sleep.[8]

The German principality to profit most from the soldiers-for-hire business was Hesse.

In taking a quick look at the history of Hesse, we find that after Philip the Magnanimous died in 1567, Hesse was divided between Philip's four sons into four main provinces: Hesse-Kassel (often spelled Hesse-Cassel),

Hesse-Darmstadt, Hesse-Rheinfels, and Hesse-Marburg. The most important and powerful of these four Hessian regions became Hesse-Kassel, into which Hesse-Rheinfels and Hesse-Marburg would later be reabsorbed.

Renting mercenaries to England became the Hessian royal family's most lucrative enterprise. Although Hesse itself was scarred during some of the European conflicts, the Hessian dynasty built an immense fortune from the soldier business. In fact, Landgrave Frederick II of Hesse-Kassel (not to be confused with Frederick II of Prussia or with the German emperor Frederick II of the Crusade era) made Hesse-Kassel the richest principality in Europe by renting out mercenaries to England during Britain's next great struggle: the War for American Independence, also known as the American Revolution. Also benefiting from the American Revolution was the royal House of Brunswick. Its head, Charles I, rented soldiers to England at a very handsome price to help fight the rebelling colonists.

As we can see, Hesse, Hannover and a few other German states profited handsomely from the conflicts which had beset England. The problems of Britain gave them the opportunity to plunder the British treasury at the expense of the English people. This had the additional effect of pushing England into ever-deepening debt to the new bankers with their inflatable paper money.

The populace of Germany also suffered. Most of the mercenaries rented to England were young men involuntarily conscripted and forced to fight where their leaders sent them. Many were maimed and killed so that their rulers could live in greater luxury. The wealth and influence of a small clique of German dynasties had been built upon the blood of the young.

Lurking behind these activities we continue to find the presence of the Brotherhood network. As the years progressed, members of the royal families of Hesse and Brunswick emerged as leaders of the Strict Observance. In 1772, for example, at a Masonic congress in Kohlo, Duke Charles William Ferdinand of Brunswick was chosen to succeed Von Hund as Grand Master of the Strict Observance.* Several years after his election to the Grand Master position, Duke Ferdinand succeeded Charles I as the ruler of Brunswick and inherited the money from Brunswick's rental of mercenaries.

Sharing leadership duties in the Strict Observance with the Duke of Brunswick was Prince Karl of Hesse, son of Frederick II of Hesse-Kassel. According to Jacob Katz in his book, *Jews and Freemasons in Europe, 1723-1939,* Prince Karl was later "accepted as the head of all German Freemasons."9 Karl's brother, William IX, who later inherited the principality and immense fortune of Hesse-Kassel from their father, was also a Freemason. William IX had provided mercenaries to England when he earlier ruled Hesse-Hanau.

How important a role did the Brotherhood itself really play in manipulating these affairs? To determine if there truly was active Brotherhood involvement of a Machiavellian nature, it would help to discover if there was any single Brotherhood agent who participated first in one faction and then in another. We would require a Brotherhood agent traveling in all circles: from the Jacobites to the electors of Hesse, from the King of France to Prussia.

Interestingly, history records just such an individual. We would not normally learn of such an agent because of the secrecy surrounding Brotherhood activity. This particular person, however, by virtue of his flamboyant personality, his remarkable artistic talents, and his flair for drama, had attracted so much attention to himself that his activities and travels were noted and recorded for posterity by many of

---

* With the election of Duke Ferdinand, the Strict Observance underwent several changes. The Strict Observance was informally called the "United Lodges." Another congress was held ten years later in 1782 in Wilhelmsbad (a city near Hanau in Hesse-Kassel). There the name "Strict Observance" was dropped altogether and the Order was thereafter called the "Beneficent Knights of the Holy City." The Wilhelmsbad congress officially abandoned the story that the Templar Knights were the original creators of Freemasonry. However, the Knight degrees were retained, as was the idea of leadership by an "Unknown Superior."

the people around him. Deified by some and declared a charlatan by others, this flamboyant agent of the Brotherhood was best known by a false appellation: the Count of St. Germain.

# 26

# The Count of
# St. Germain

A CONTROVERSIAL FIGURE IN the intrigues of 18th-century
Europe was a secretive and colorful individual known as
the Count of St. Germain.* St. Germain's life has been the
subject of many articles and at least one book. Ever since his
reported death in 1784, there has been a tendency to either
deify him or to dismiss him as an unimportant charlatan.
Neither characterization seems to accurately reflect what he
truly was.

St. Germain's activities are important because his movements provide a fascinating link between the wars going on in
Europe, the deeper levels of the Brotherhood, and the clique
of German princes—particularly the House of Hesse.

The first of many mysteries concerning St. Germain is
the circumstance of his birth. Many researchers believe him

---

*Not to be confused with the French general of the same name, nor
Claude Louis de St. Germain, an 18th-century mystic.

to have been the offspring of Francis II, ruler of the once powerful principality of Transylvania. Transylvania, famous in cinema as the home of the mythical human vampire, Dracula, and other assorted literary ne'er-do-wells, had ties to the dynasty in Hesse. Francis II of Transylvania had married sixteen-year-old Charlotte Amalie of Hessen-Reinfels on September 25, 1694 at the cathedral of Cologne in Germany.

Out of this union came two known children. However, when the will of Francis II was published in 1737, a third unnamed son was mentioned as a beneficiary. This third child proved to be Leopold-George, eldest son and heir to the Transylvanian throne. Leopold-George was born in either 1691 or 1696, depending upon which theory of his birth one accepts. Because of the uncertainty of his birthdate, it is not known if he was the son of Charlotte of Hesse or of Francis II's prior wife. What does appear certain is that Leopold-George's early "death" in 1700 had been staged to save him from the deadly intrigues which were about to destroy the Transylvanian dynasty and end the independence of Transylvania.

Leopold-George is believed to have been the Count of St. Germain.

St. Germain first appeared in European society in 1743 when he would have been a man in his forties. Little is known about his life before that year. A dossier on the mysterious Count had been created by order of French Emperor Napoleon III (r. 1852-1870) but, unfortunately, all of the documents were destroyed in a fire that engulfed the house in which the dossier was stored. This resulted in the loss of irreplaceable information about St. Germain. St. Germain's own secretiveness only deepens the mystery about his life. The surviving information indicates that St. Germain was raised to become one of the most active, colorful, and successful secret political agents of the Brotherhood in the 18th century.

Of St. Germain's early life, Strict Observance leader Prince Karl of Hesse wrote that St. Germain had been raised in childhood by the last of the powerful Medici family of Italy. The Duke of Medici, like some earlier Medicis, was engrossed in the mystical philosophies prevalent in Italy at the time, which may account for St. Germain's deep involvement in the Brotherhood network as an adult. While under Medici care, St. Germain is believed to have studied at the university in Siena.

St. Germain's first documented appearance in European society occurred in England in 1743. At that time, the Jacobite cause was very strong and the 1745 invasion of Scotland was only two years away. During those two crucial years prior to the invasion, St. Germain resided in London. Only glimpses of his activities during that time are available. St. Germain was a gifted musician and several of his musical compositions were publicly performed in the Little Haymarket Theatre in early February 1745. St. Germain also had several of his trios published by the Walsh company of London.

British authorities did not believe that St. Germain was in London to pursue a musical career, however. In December 1745, with the Jacobite invasion underway, St. Germain was arrested by the British on suspicion of being a Jacobite agent. He was released when rumored letters from Charles Edward, leader of the Stuart invasion, were not found on his person. Horace Walpole wrote of the arrest afterwards:

> . . . t'other day they seized an odd man, who goes by the name of Count St. Germain. He has been here these two years, will not tell who he is or whence, but professes two very wonderful things, the first that he does not go by his right name, and the second, that he never had any dealings, or desire to have any dealings, with any woman—nay, nor with an succedaneum [substitute]. He sings, plays on the violin wonderfully, composes, is mad, and not very sensible.[1]

After his release, St. Germain departed England and spent one year as the guest of Prince Ferdinand von Lobkowitz, first minister to the Austrian emperor. The War of Austrian Succession was still raging at the time, in which Austria and England were allied against France and Prussia. During this visit to Austria, St. Germain was introduced to the French

Minister of War, the Marshal de Belle-Isle, who, in turn, introduced St. Germain to the French court.

This is an intriguing sequence of events. Here we have a man arrested as a suspected enemy of England during a time of war, who then immediately went to stay with a top minister of a nation (Austria) which was allied to England. During that stay, this same man befriended the Minister of War of a nation (France) which was an enemy of Austria! St. Germain's political contacts on all sides of a raging war were remarkable.

What St. Germain did for the next three years after leaving Austria is not certain.

St. Germain reappeared in European society again in 1749, this time as a guest of King Louis XV of France. France, a Catholic nation, actively supported the Jacobite cause against the Hanoverians of England. France was also involved in many other foreign intrigues. According to a lady of the French court who later wrote of St. Germain in her memoirs:

> From 1749, the King [Louis XV] employed him [St. Germain] on diplomatic missions and he acquitted himself honorably in them.[2]

King Louis had gained fame as an architect of 18th-century secret diplomacy. The acceptance of St. Germain into the French Court and his work for the French king as a political agent is significant for several reasons:

First, it points to the important role that Brotherhood members have played in the creation and operation of national and international intelligence networks throughout history; a matter we will consider in more detail in later chapters.

Secondly, as a Catholic, King Louis XV adhered to Papal decrees. The papacy was hostile to Freemasonry. Indeed, Roman Catholicism and Freemasonry are both factions with origins in the Brotherhood which have long opposed one another. In 1737, Louis XV issued an edict forbidding all French subjects to have anything to do with Freemasonry.

During the ensuing decades, the French government actively repressed the French Freemasons with police raids and imprisonment. Louis XV's edict of 1737 was followed a year later by Pope Clement's Papal Bull which forbade Catholics everywhere from participating in or supporting Freemasonry under penalty of excommunication; yet here was the Count of St. Germain, who would later reveal a life-long involvement in the Brotherhood, residing as a guest of the King. The likely explanation, based upon the known facts of St. Germain's life, is that he was not so much a Freemason as he was an agent of the higher Brotherhood. It is also unlikely that the French King understood St. Germain's role in the Brotherhood network.

St. Germain's exact activities from 1749 through 1755 are largely unknown. In 1755, he made a second trip to India. He went with English Commander Robert Clive who was on his way there to fight the French! India was a major theatre of war in which a great deal was at stake. Commander Clive was an important leader on the British side. This trip highlighted once again St. Germain's remarkable political contacts and his ability to travel back and forth between important leaders of warring camps. One biographer has suggested that the Count may have been acting as a secret agent of King Louis XV of France when he went to India with Clive, for when St. Germain returned, he was awarded in 1758 with an apartment in the French royal palace at Chambord. He was also given laboratory facilities for his chemical and alchemical experiments, in which Louis XV sometimes participated.

St. Germain was clearly a flamboyant and multifaceted character. One of the talents for which he achieved fame was his considerable knowledge of alchemy. (Alchemy mixes mysticism with chemistry and was a staple of Rosicrucian practice.) St. Germain became a topic of gossip in the French court because he claimed to possess the alchemical Elixir of Life. The Elixir was said to be a secret formula which made people physically immortal. This was the same Elixir many European Rosicrucians claimed to possess. St. Germain may have had tongue slightly in cheek when he made the claim, however. He is quoted as saying to King Louis XV, "Sire, I sometimes amuse myself not by making it believed, but by allowing it to be believed, that I have lived in ancient times."[3]

In 1760, St. Germain left France for the Hague in Holland. This trip was made during the height of the Seven Years War. Holland was a neutral country during that conflict. Exactly what St. Germain was trying to accomplish in Holland remains debated even today. After declaring himself to be a secret agent of King Louis XV, St. Germain tried to gain an audience with the English representative at the Hague. St. Germain claimed that he was there to negotiate a peace between England and France. However, the French Foreign Minister, the Duke of Choiseul, and the French ambassador to Holland, Count D'Affry, had not been notified by their king about St. Germain's purported mission. The Duke of Choiseul therefore branded St. German a charlatan and ordered his arrest. To avoid imprisonment by Dutch authorities, St. Germain fled to London in the same year. St. Germain's escape was aided by his influential friend, Count Bentinck, the President of the Dutch Council of Deputy Commissioners.

As a result of this debacle and the unwillingness of Louis XV to publicly acknowledge St. Germain as his agent, St. Germain was unable to openly return to French royal society until 1770—the year in which his enemy, the Duke of Choiseul, was disgraced and removed from power.

St. Germain had a second, and perhaps even more compelling, reason for making that ill-fated trip to Holland. A letter written on March 25, 1760 by Prince de Galitzin, Russian Minister to England, offered this insight into St. Germain's aborted activities in Holland:

I know the Count de St. Germain well by reputation. This singular man has been staying for some time in this country, and I do not know whether he likes it. There is someone here with whom he appears to be in correspondence, and this person declares that the object of the Count's journey to Holland is merely some financial business.[4]

The financial business mentioned by de Galitzen was very secret. It appeared to be the true purpose of St. Germain's visit. St. Germain was in Holland to exploit the marriage of a Princess Caroline to the German prince of Nassau-Dillenburg for the purposes of establishing a "Fund" for France. St. Germain wanted to negotiate the formation of the Fund with Dutch bankers. According to French ambassador D'Affrey, "his objective in general was to secure the credit of the principal bankers there for us."[5] In another letter, D'Affry stated that St. Germain "had come to Holland solely to complete the formation of a Company adequate to the responsibility of this Fund. . . ."[6]

The formation of the Fund was probably the true reason for St. Germain's (and perhaps King Louis's) extreme secrecy. France already had important financiers to the royal Court: the wealthy Paris-Duverney Brothers. The Paris Brothers had salvaged France's financial standing after the disastrous Bank of France episode involving the inflated money of John Law. St. Germain was quite hostile to the Paris Brothers and he did not want them to gain control of the Fund. St. Germain is quoted by Monsieur de Kauderbach, a minister of the Saxon court in the Hague:

> . . . he [King Louis XV of France] is surrounded only by creatures placed by the Brothers Paris, who alone cause all the trouble of France. It is they who corrupt everything, and thwarted the plans of the best citizen in France, the Marshal de Belle-Isle. Hence the disunion and jealousy amongst the Ministers. All is corrupted by the Brothers Paris; perish France, provided they may attain their object of gaining eight hundred millions.[7]

St. Germain may well have had legitimate grounds for objecting to the undue influence of the Paris Brothers. St. Germain's mission in the Hague, however, was only an attempt to covertly wrest financial control from the Paris Brothers and put it back into the hands of the same clique of financiers whose predecessors had institutionalized the inflatable paper money system to begin with—the very system which had brought financial ruin to France and the consequent intervention of the Paris Brothers. Because of St. Germain's sudden forced departure from Holland, he was never able to complete his financial mission.

Upon arriving in London after fleeing Holland, St. Germain was once again arrested and released. During this short stay in England, St. Germain published seven violin solos.

St. Germain continued his covert political activities after leaving London. In 1760, he returned secretly to Paris. There St. Germain is believed to have stayed with his friend, the Princess of Anhalt-Zerbst. Anhalt-Zerbst was another German state which rented mercenaries to England, although it never accumulated the same wealth as some of its German neighbors.

The Princess of Anhalt-Zerbst had a daughter, Catherine II. On August 21, 1744, Catherine II had married Peter III of Russia. This marriage had been arranged by Frederick the Great of Prussia, who was a friend of the Anhalt-Zerbst family and, at least for a time, of St. Germain.

In 1762, two years after St. Germain's quiet return to Paris, Peter III assumed the Russian throne. St. Germain traveled immediately to the Russian capital of St. Petersburg where he helped Catherine overthrow Peter and establish her as the Empress of Russia. Assisting in the coup d'etat was the Russian Orloff family. The Orloffs are believed to have murdered Peter by strangling him in a phony brawl. For his assistance in the coup, St. Germain was made a general of the Russian army and he remained a close friend of the Orloff family for many years. Catherine, who later became known as "Catherine the Great," went on to rule Russia for twenty-nine years.

With this bold coup, St. Germain had helped put Russia under the rule of the same small clique of German royal families under which other European countries had fallen. The same modus operandi was used: the marriage of a royal German into the victim dynasty followed by a revolution or coup. Here we find evidence of direct Brotherhood involvement in the person of St. Germain.

What St. Germain did between 1763 and 1769 after leaving Russia is a mystery. He is known to have spent approximately one year in Berlin and was a short-term guest of Friedrich August of Brunswick. From Brunswick, St. Germain continued his travels around Europe. He returned to France in 1770. In 1772, St. Germain again acted as an agent for Louis XV, this time during negotiations in Vienna over the partition of Poland. Unfortunately for St. Germain, Louis XV died on May 10, 1774 and Louis's nineteen-year-old grandson, Louis XVI, took the throne. The new king brought Choiseul back to power and took a personal dislike to St. Germain. The Count was forced to leave French society for the last time.

St. Germain immediately departed for Germany where, only eleven days after the death of Louis XV, he was a guest of William IX of Hesse—the prince who was to inherit the vast Hesse-Kassel fortune. According to J. J. Bjornstahl, writing in his book of travels:

> We were guests at the court of the Prince-Hereditary Wilhelm von Hessen-Cassel (brother of Karl von Hessen) at Hanau, near Frankfort.
>
> As we returned on the 21st of May 1774 to the Castle of Hanau, we found there Lord Cavendish and the Comte de St. Germain; they had come from Lausanne, and were travelling to Cassel and Berlin.[8]

After his visit to the home of the Hessian prince, St. Germain traveled about Europe some more. He was welcomed as a guest of the Margrave of Brandenburg and by others. Finally, in 1779, St. Germain was taken in by Prince Karl of Hesse, who was a top leader of the Strict Observance. St. Germain spent the last five years of his known life with Karl.

In 1784, St. Germain reportedly died. The church register of Eckenforde contained the entry:

Deceased on February 27, buried on March 2, 1784,
the so-called Compte de St. Germain and Weldon*—
further information not known—privately deposited in
this Church.[9]

It was after his reported death that St. Germain's true
status within the Brotherhood emerged. Not only was St.
Germain portrayed as one of the highest representatives
of the Brotherhood, he was also deified as a physically
immortal being who did not age or die. A number of his
contemporary admirers claimed that they saw St. Germain
at times when it should have been impossible for them to
do so because of St. Germain's age. For example, Baron
E. H. Gleichen, writing in his memoirs published in 1868,
stated:

> I have heard Rameau and an old relative of a French
> ambassador at Venice testify to having known St.
> Germain in 1710, when he had the appearance of a
> man of fifty years of age.[10]

If St. Germain was fifty years old in 1710, then he would
have been 124 years old when he reportedly died. There
are, however, those who claim that St. Germain did not
die in 1784. A German mystical magazine published in
1857, *Magazin der Beweisfuhrer fur Verurtheilung des
Freimaurer-Ordens,* stated that St. Germain was one of
the French representatives to the 1785 Masonic convention
in Paris, one year after his reported death. Another writer,
Cantu Cesare, in his work, *Gli Eretici d'Italia,* stated that St.
Germain was present at the famous Wilhelmsbad Masonic
conference which was also held in 1785.

These reports are viewed by some people as evidence that
St. Germain's death had been staged (perhaps for the second
time in his life) to enable him to escape the controversy which
surrounded him so that he could live out the rest of his life in
relative quiet.

---

* St. Germain used many aliases. Weldon was one of them.

St. Germain's alleged appearances after death did not end in 1785, however. Countess D'Adhemar, a member of the French court who wrote her memoirs shortly before her death in 1822, alleged seeing St. Germain many times after his reported death, usually during times of upheaval. She claimed that St. Germain had sent warnings to the King and Queen of France (his enemy Louis XVI and Marie Antoinette) just prior to the outbreak of the French Revolution which occurred in 1789. She also claimed that she saw him in 1793, 1804, 1813, and 1820. A Rosicrucian writer, Franz Graeffer, stated that St. Germain had made appearances in Austria after his reported death, and was honored there as an advanced Adept of the Brotherhood. In the late 1800's, Madame Helena Blavatsky, one of the cofounders of the Theosophical Society, declared that St. Germain was one of the Hidden Masters of Tibet who secretly controlled the destiny of the world. In 1919, a man claiming to be St. Germain appeared in Hungary at a time when a successful communist-led revolution was underway in that country. Finally, in 1930, a man named Guy Ballard claimed that he met St. Germain on Mount Shasta in California, and that St. Germain had helped him establish a new Brotherhood branch known as the "I AM." We will look at the "I AM" in a later chapter.

Were all of these witnesses lying? Probably not. The Brotherhood occasionally sponsored "resurrections" as a way to deify select members. That is what had been done with Jesus. In fact, those Brotherhood branches which deify St. Germain (which is certainly not all of them) often give St. Germain the same spiritual status as Jesus. Why St. Germain was chosen for deification may never be fully understood. Perhaps his successes on behalf of the Brotherhood were far more numerous than we know. Whatever the reason might have been, it is clear that St. Germain was mortal. He did die, if not on the reported date of his demise, then surely within a decade of it.

During his lifetime, and still today, many people have labeled St. Germain a fraud and charlatan. Some critics contend that St. Germain was nothing more than a glib con artist of common birth whose entry into royal society came about solely through his wiles and colorful personality. The evidence we have looked at clearly does not support this argument. It was not easy for an outsider to enter so many royal circles and remain there. St. Germain's involvement in the overthrow of Peter of Russia was not a petty scam; it was a major coup which altered the political landscape of Europe. Yes, St. Germain was a charlatan on a number of matters, but that made his political activities and connections no less significant. St. Germain's color and flamboyance obscured a deadly serious side to his life. His travels and activities tied the Brotherhood to the Hessian princes, the intrigues of France, the wars of Europe, and the paper money bankers.

The personality of St. Germain reveals that when we discuss "behind-the-scenes" influences, we are not necessarily talking about eerie characters who skulk about in shadows doing incomprehensible things. We are usually discussing people who are as lively and colorful as the rest of us. They succeed and they fail. They have their charms and their quirks like everyone else. They exercise influence over people, but not puppetlike control. They are affected by the same things that everyone else is affected by. These observations lead to an important point:

When some writers describe the influence of the Brotherhood network in history, and when some readers read about it, they envision strange subterranean "occult" forces at work. This is an illusion generated by the mysticism and secrecy of the Brotherhood itself. Changes in society, whether for good or bad, are caused by people doing things. The Brotherhood network has simply been an effective channel to get people to act, and to keep much of what they do secret. The influence of the Brotherhood network only appears mysterious and "occult" because so many actions have gone unrecorded and unknown to outsiders. The corrupted Brotherhood network does not have today, nor has it ever had, effective "occult" powers. The world can therefore be remade for the better by people simply acting and doing. No magic wand is needed. Just some elbow grease.

# 27

# Here a Knight,
# There a Knight . . .

EVEN AFTER THE collapse of the Stuart cause, the Knight
degrees remained popular and spread rapidly. The pro-Stuart
slant vanished in favor of an antimonarchial philosophy
in some Templar organizations, and a pro-monarchial
sentiment in others. Freemasons practicing the Templar
degrees played important political roles on both sides of
the monarchy vs. antimonarchy battles going on in the 18th
century, thereby helping to keep that issue alive in such a
way that people would find it something to continuously
fight over. For example, King Gustavus III of Sweden
and his brother, Karl, the Duke of Sodermanland, had
been initiated into the Strict Observance in 1770. In
the following year, one of Gustavus's first acts upon
assuming the Swedish throne was to mount a coup
d'etat against the Swedish Riksdag [parliament] and re-
establish greater powers in the Crown. According to
Samuel Harrison Baynard, writing in his book, *History
of the Supreme Council*, Gustavus was assisted largely by
fellow Freemasons.

The Knight degrees also found a home in Ireland where they attached themselves to the Order of Orange. As we recall, the Orange Order was a militant organization patterned after Freemasonry. It was founded to ensure that Protestantism remained England's dominant religion. Members of the Orange Order vowed to support the Hanoverians as long as the Hanoverians continued their support of Protestantism. The Knight degrees were grafted onto the Order of Orange in the early 1790's, by which time the Stuart cause was nearly dead. The Orange Order's Templar degrees were, and still are today, called the "Black Preceptory." Although the Orange Order and the Black Preceptory are supposed to be equal in status and rank, entry into the Black Preceptory is accomplished only after a person has first passed through the degrees of the Orange Order. According to Tony Gray, writing in his fascinating book, *The Orange Order,* the Black Preceptory today has eleven degrees and "a great deal of secrecy still shrouds the inner workings of this curious institution."[1] Approximately 50% to 60% of all Orange members become members of the Preceptory. The Orange Order itself continues to be strongly Protestant and anti-Catholic, and in this way it contributes to some of the conflicts between Catholics and Protestants in Ireland today.

Another interesting chapter in the history of the Templar Degrees concerns the creation of a bogus "Illuminati." "Illuminati," as we recall, was the Latin name given to the Brotherhood. In 1779, a second "Illuminati" was started in the Strict Observance Lodge of Munich. This second bogus "Illuminati" was led by an ex-Jesuit priest named Adam Weishaupt and was structured as a semiautonomous organization. Openly political and antimonarchial, Weishaupt's "Illuminati" formed another channel of "higher degrees" for Freemasons to graduate into after completing the Blue Degrees. Weishaupt's "Illuminati" had its own "hidden master" known as the "Ancient Scot Superior." The Strict Observance members who were initiated into this "Illuminati" apparently believed that they were being initiated into the highest echelons of the real Illuminati, or Brotherhood. Once initiated under strict vows of secrecy, members were "revealed" a great deal of political and antimonarchial philosophy.

Weishaupt's "Illuminati" was soon attacked, however. Its headquarters in German Bavaria were raided by the Elector of Bavaria in 1786. Many radical political aims of the Illuminati were discovered in documents seized during the raid. The Duke of Brunswick, acting as Grand Master of German Freemasonry, finally issued a manifesto eight years later, in 1794, to counteract Weishaupt's bogus "Illuminati" after the public scandal could no longer be contained. Joining in the suppression of Weishaupt's Bavarian "Illuminati" were many Rosicrucians. Despite the repression, this "Illuminati" survived and still exists today.

Many people have mistakenly believed that Weishaupt's "Illuminati" was the true Illuminati and that it took over all of Freemasonry. This error is caused by Weishaupt's express desire to have his degrees become the only "higher degrees" of Freemasonry. One can still find books today which theorize that Weishaupt's "Illuminati" was, and still is, the source of nearly all of mankind's social ills. A careful study of the evidence indicates that Weishaupt's "Illuminati" is actually a red herring in this respect. Although Weishaupt's "Illuminati" did contribute to some of the revolutionary agitation going on in Europe, its impact on history does not appear to have been as great as some people believe, despite the enormous publicity it received. The social ills which have sometimes been blamed on Weishaupt's "Illuminati" existed long before the birth of Adam Weishaupt. What did take over nearly all of Freemasonry in the eighteenth century were the Templar degrees, which were not the same thing as Weishaupt's "Illuminati." The true significance of the Bavarian Illuminati is that is was an antimonarchy faction allowed to operate out of Strict Observance lodges; meanwhile, the Strict Observance was generally considered pro-monarchy and it supported pro-monarchy causes, as in the Swedish Ricksdag overthrow mentioned earlier. This made the Strict Observance a source of secret agitation on *both* sides of the monarchy-versus-antimonarchy conflicts for a number of years—another example of Brotherhood Machiavellianism.

The worldwide transformation of human society announced in the Rosicrucian *Fama Fraternitis* gained momentum as Freemasons and other mystical network members led numerous revolutions around the world. The uprisings were not confined to Europe; they spilled across the Atlantic Ocean and took root in the European colonies in North America. There they gave birth to the single most influential nation on Earth today: the United States of America.

# 28

# American Phoenix

WHEN EUROPEAN COLONISTS sailed to North America, the Brotherhood organizations sailed with them. In 1694, a group of Rosicrucian leaders from Europe founded a colony in what is today the state of Pennsylvania. Some of their picturesque buildings in Ephrata still stand as a unique tourist attraction.

Freemasonry followed. On June 5, 1730, the Duke of Norfolk granted to Daniel Coxe of New Jersey one of the earliest known Masonic deputations to reach the American colonies. The deputation appointed Mr. Coxe provisional Grand Master of New York, New Jersey, and Pennsylvania. It also allowed him to establish lodges. One of the earliest official colonial lodges was founded by Henry Price in Boston on August 31, 1733 under a charter from the Mother Grand Lodge of England. Masonic historian Albert MacKey believes that lodges probably existed earlier, but that their records have been lost.

Freemasonry spread rapidly in the American colonies just as it had done in Europe. The early lodges in the British colonies were nearly all chartered by the English Mother Grand Lodge, and members of the early lodges were loyal British subjects.

Englishmen were not the only people to colonize America. England had a major rival in the New World: France. The competition between the two nations caused frequent spats over colonial boundaries. This brought about a number of violent clashes on American soil, such as Queen Anne's War during the first decade of the 18th century, and King George's War in 1744. Even during times of peace, relations between the two superpowers were anything but smooth.

One of Britain's loyal military officers in the colonies was a man named George Washington. He had been initiated into Freemasonry on November 4, 1752 at the age of 20. He remained a member of the Craft for the rest of his life. Washington became an officer in the colonial army, which was under British authority, by the time he reached his mid-twenties. Standing six feet three inches tall and weighing nearly two hundred pounds, Washington was a physically impressive figure.

One of Washington's military duties was to keep an eye on French troops in tense border regions. The Treaty of Aix-la-Chapelle executed in 1748 had ended King George's War and had returned some territories to France. Both England and France benefited from this pause in hostilities because the wars were driving the two into debt. Even the inflatable paper currencies the two nations used to help pay for their wars did not prevent the serious financial difficulties that wars always bring.

Unfortunately, the peace lasted less than a decade. It was broken, according to some historians, by George Washington during one of his military forays into the Ohio Valley. Washington and his men sighted a group of French soldiers, but were not spotted by the French in return. On the command of Washington, his troops opened fire without warning. It turned out that Washington's soldiers had ambushed credentialed French ambassadors traveling with a customary military escort. The French alleged afterwards that they were on their way to confer with the British to settle some of the disputes still existing over the Ohio regions. Washington justified his attack by stating that the French soldiers were "skulking" and that their claim to diplomatic immunity was a pretense. Whatever the truth might have been, the French felt that they had been the victims of unprovoked military aggression. The French and Indian War was soon underway. It spread to Europe as the Seven Years War.

The renewed warfare was disastrous. According to Frederick the Great, the Seven Years War claimed as many as 853,000 military casualties, plus hundreds of thousands of civilian lives. Heavy economic damage was inflicted upon both England and France. When the war ended, England faced a national debt of 136 million pounds, most of it owed to a banking elite. To repay the debt, the English Parliament levied heavy taxes in its own country. When this taxation became too high, duties were placed on goods in the American colonies. The duties quickly became a sore point with the American colonists who began to resist.

Another change caused by the War was Hanover's abandonment of their policy of keeping a small standing army in Britain. England's armed forces were greatly expanded. This brought about a need to tax citizens even more. In addition, nearly 6,000 British troops in America needed housing and they often encroached upon the property rights of colonists. This generated yet more colonial dissent.

The fourth adverse consequence of the War (at least in the minds of the colonists) was England's capitulation to the demands of several American Indian nations. The American Indians had fought on the side of the French because of the encroachment of British colonists on Indian lands. After the French and Indian War, the Crown issued the Proclamation of 1763 commanding that the vast region between the Appalachian Mountains and the Mississippi River was to be a widespread Indian reservation. British subjects were not permitted to settle there without approval from the Crown. This sharply reduced western expansion.

The first of Britain's new colonial tax measures went into effect in 1764. It was known as the Sugar Act. It placed duties on lumber, food, rum and molasses. In the following year a new tax, the Stamp Act, was instituted to help pay for the British troops stationed in the colonies.

Many colonists strongly objected to the taxes and the manner in which they were collected. Under British "writs of assistance," for example, Crown custom agents could search wherever they pleased for goods imported in violation of the Acts. The agents had almost unlimited powers to search and seize without notice or warrant.

In October 1765, representatives from nine colonies met at a Stamp Act Congress in New York. They passed a Declaration of Rights expressing their opposition to taxation without colonial representation in the British Parliament. The Declaration also opposed trials without juries by British Admiralty courts. This act of defiance was partially successful. On March 17, 1766, five months after the Stamp Act Congress met, the Stamp Act was repealed.

Despite sincere efforts by the British Parliament to satisfy many colonial demands, a significant independence movement was developing in the American colonies. Under the leadership of a man named Samuel Adams, a secret organization calling itself the "Sons of Liberty" began to commit acts of violence and terrorism. They burned the records of the Vice Admiralty court and looted the homes of various British officials. They threatened further violence against stamp agents and other British authorities. The Sons of Liberty organized economic boycotts by urging colonists to cancel orders for British merchandise. These acts hurt England because the colonies were very important to Britain as a trade outlet. Therefore, in 1770, Britain bowed once again to the colonists by repealing all duties except on tea. By that time, however, the revolutionary fervor was too strong to be halted. The result was bloodshed. On March 5, 1770, the "Boston Massacre" occurred in which British troops fired into a Boston mob and killed five people. Tensions continued to mount and more secret revolutionary groups were formed. Britain would still not repeal the tax on tea. On October 14, 1773, three years after the Boston Massacre, colonists dressed as Indians crept onto a British ship anchored in Boston harbor and threw large quantities of tea into the water. This incident was the famous "Boston Tea Party."

These acts of rebellion finally caused Parliament to enact trade sanctions against the colonists. The sanctions merely fueled the rebellion. In 1774, a group of colonial leaders convened the First Continental Congress to protest British actions and to call for civil disobedience. In March 1775, Patrick Henry gave his famous "Give me liberty or give me death" speech at a convention in Virginia. Within less than a month of that speech, the American Revolution got under way with the Battle of Concord, where an organized colonial militia called "the minute men" suffered eight casualties while inflicting 273 on the British. In June of that same year, George Washington, the man who some historians believe had gotten the entire snowball rolling two decades earlier when he had ordered his troops to fire on the French in the Ohio Valley, was named commander-in-chief of the new ragtag Continental Army.

Historians have noted that economic motives were not the only ones propelling the American revolutionaries. This became obvious after the British Parliament repealed nearly all of the tariffs they had imposed. King George III, despite being a Hanoverian, was popular at home and he initially thought of himself as a friend to the colonists. The sharp attacks against King George by revolutionary spokesmen quite upset him because the attacks seemed out of proportion to his actual role in the problems complained of by the colonists. More of the revolutionary rhetoric should have been aimed at Parliament. There was clearly something deeper driving the revolutionary cause: the rebels were out to establish a whole new social order. Their revolt was fueled by sweeping philosophies which encompassed much more than their disputes with the Crown. One of those philosophies was Freemasonry.

A "Who's Who" of the American Revolution is almost a "Who's Who" of American colonial Freemasonry. Freemasons fighting on the revolutionary side included George Washington, Benjamin Franklin (who had been a Mason since at least 1731), Alexander Hamilton, Richard Montgomery, Henry Knox, James Madison, and Patrick Henry. Revolutionaries who were also Masonic Grand Masters included Paul Revere, John Hancock, and James Clinton,

in addition to Washington and Franklin. According to Col.
LaVon P. Linn in his article "Freemasonry and the National
Defense, 1754-1799,"[1] out of an estimated 14,000 officers
of all grades in the Continental Army, one seventh, or 2,018,
were Freemasons. They represented a total of 218 lodges.
One hundred of those officers were generals. Col. Linn
remarks:

> In all our wars, beginning with the French and Indian
> Wars and the War for American Independence, the
> silhouettes of American military Masons have loomed
> high above the battles.[2]

Europe provided the Americans with two additional Freemasons of importance. From Germany came the Baron von
Steuben, who personally turned Washington's ragged troops
into the semblance of a fighting army. Von Steuben was a
German Freemason who had served in the Prussian Army
as an aide-de-camp to Frederick the Great. He had been
discharged during the 1763 Prussian demobilization after
the Seven Years War. At the time that von Steuben's
services were procured in France by Benjamin Franklin,
von Steuben was a half-pay captain who had been out of
military work for fourteen years. Franklin, in order to get
the approval of Congress, faked von Steuben's dossier by
stating von Steuben to be a Lieutenant General. The decep-
tion worked, much to the ultimate benefit of the Continental
Army.

The second European was the Marquis de La Fayette.
La Fayette was a wealthy French nobleman who, in his
very early twenties, had been inspired by news of the
American Revolution while serving in the French army
in Europe, so he sailed to America to aid the revolutionary
cause. In 1778, during his service with the Continental
Army, La Fayette was made a Freemason. Later, after
the war, La Fayette revealed just how important Free-
masonry was to the leadership of the revolutionary army.
In his address to the "Four of Wilmington" Lodge of
Delaware during his last visit to America in 1824, La
Fayette said:

At one time [while serving under General Washington] I could not rid my mind of the suspicion that the General harboured doubts about me; this suspicion was confirmed by the fact that I had never been given a command-in-chief. This thought was an obsession and it sometimes made me very unhappy. After I had become an American freemason General Washington seemed to have seen the light. From that moment I never had reason to doubt his entire confidence. And soon thereafter I was given a very important command-in-chief.[3]

When we consider the prominence of Freemasons in the American Revolution,[*] it should come as no surprise that revolutionary agitation came from Masonic lodges directly. According to Col. Linn's article, the famous Boston Tea Party was the work of Masons coming directly out of a lodge:

On December 6, 1773, a group disguised as American Indians seems to have left St. Andrew's Lodge in

----

[*] Two important Revolutionary leaders who are thought *not* to have been Freemasons are Samuel Adams and Thomas Jefferson. According to John C. Miller, writing in his book, *Sam Adams, Pioneer in Propaganda:*

**It is surprising to find that Sam Adams, who belonged to almost every liberal political club in Boston and carried the heaviest schedule of "lodge nights" of any patriot, was not a Mason. Many of his friends were high-ranking Masons and the Boston lodge did much to foster the Revolution, but Sam Adams nev~ joined the Masonic Society.[4]**

Thomas Jefferson's name was recorded in the Proceedi~ Grand Lodge of Virginia in 1883 as a visitor to the C Lodge No. 60 on September 20, 1817. The *Pittsbur~ Vol. I, August 4, 1828, mentions Jefferson as a N~ his lifetime, he was even accused of being Bavarian "Illuminati." More recently, s~ Jefferson as a member of their frate~ records of Jefferson's membershi~ appears to be either missing or none~ visitor to the Charlottesville Lodge. F~ historians believe that Jefferson was ei~ was not a member at all.

Boston and gone to Boston Harbor where cargoes of tea were thrown overboard from three East Indiamen [ships from the East Indies]. St. Andrew's Lodge closed early that night "on account of the few members in attendance."[5]

Sven G. Lunden, in his article, "Annihilation of Freemasonry," states that St. Andrew's Lodge was the leading Masonic body in Boston. He adds:

And in the book which used to contain the minutes of the lodge and which still exists, there is an almost blank page where the minutes of that memorable Thursday should be. Instead, the page bears but one letter—a large T. Can it have anything to do with Tea?[6]

In *Sam Adams, Pioneer of Propaganda,* author John C. Miller describes the hierarchy of the anti-British mobs which played such an important role in the conflict. The mobs were not just random aggregates of disgruntled colonials. Mr. Miller explains the important role of Freemasons in those mobs:

A hierarchy of mobs was established during Sam Adam's rule of Boston: the lowest classes—servants, negroes, and sailors—were placed under the command of a "superior set consisting of the Master Masons carpenters of the town"; above them were put the merchants' mob and the Sons of Liberty . . .[7]

Masonic Lodges were not johnny-come-lately's to the revolutionary cause. There is evidence that they were the initial instigators. At least one lodge engaged in agitation from very beginning. Letters and newspapers from the early 's reveal that the Boston Masonic Society was stirring -British sentiment at the end of the Seven Years War, ten years before the Revolution actually began:

ston Masonic Society peppered [governor Hutchinson and the royal government from its meeting place in "Adjutant Trowel's long Garret," where it was said more sedition [inciting to revolt], libels, and scurrility were hatched than in all the garrets in Grubstreet. Otis and his Masonic brethren became such adept muckrakers that Hutchinson's friends believed they must have "ransak'd Billingsgate and the Stews" for mud to sling at the Massachusetts aristocracy.[8]

We might wonder how American lodges became sources of revolt when they were nearly all chartered under the English system which, as we recall, was pro-Hanoverian and forbade political controversy within the lodges. It must be kept in mind that by the 1760's, the anti-Hanoverian Templar degrees had become firmly established in Europe and had also traveled secretly to many of the lodges in the American colonies. For example, as mentioned in an earlier chapter, St. Andrew's Lodge of Boston, which had perpetrated the Boston Tea Party in 1773, conferred a Templar degree already on August 28, 1769 after applying for the warrant in 1762 from the Scottish Grand Lodge in Edinburgh. That application was made almost a decade before the American Revolution began. Some Templars were not only anti-Hanoverian, they sought the abolition of all monarchy.

The philosophical importance of Freemasonry to the American Revolutionaries can also be seen in the symbols which the revolutionary leaders chose to represent the new American nation. They were Brotherhood/Masonic symbols.

Among a nation's most significant symbols is the national seal. An early proposal for the American national seal was submitted by William Barton in 1782. In the upper right-hand corner of Barton's drawing is a pyramid with the tip missing. In place of the tip is a triangular "All-Seeing Eye of God." The All-Seeing Eye, as we recall, has long been one of Freemasonry's most significant symbols. It was even sewn on the Masonic aprons of George Washington, Benjamin Franklin, and other Masonic revolutionaries. Above the pyramid and eye on Barton's proposal are the Latin words *Annuit Ceoptis*, which means "He [God] hath prospered our beginning." On the bottom is the inscription *Novus Ordo Seclorum:* "The beginning of a new order of the ages." This bottom inscription tells us that the leaders of the Revolution were pursuing a broad universal goal which encompassed much more than their immediate concerns as colonists. They were envisioning a change in the entire world social order, which follows the goal announced in the *Fama Fraternitis*.

Barton's pyramid and accompanying Latin inscriptions were adopted in their entirety. The design is still a part of the American Great Seal which can be seen on the back of the U.S. $1.00 bill.

The main portion of Barton's design was not adopted except for one small part. In the center of Barton's proposal is a shield with two human figures standing on either side. Perched atop the shield is a phoenix with wings outstretched; in the middle is a small phoenix burning in its funeral pyre. As discussed earlier, the phoenix is a Brotherhood symbol used since the days of ancient Egypt. The phoenix was adopted by the Founding Fathers for use on the reverse of the first official seal of the United States after a design proposed by Charles Thompson, Secretary of the Continental Congress. The first die of the U.S. seal depicts a long-necked tufted bird: the phoenix. The phoenix holds in its mouth a banner with the words *E. Pluribus Unum* ("Out of many, one"). Above the bird's head are thirteen stars breaking through a cloud. In one talon the phoenix holds a cluster of arrows; in the other, an olive branch. Some people mistook the bird for a wild turkey because of the long neck; however, the phoenix is also long of neck and all other features of the bird clearly indicate that it is a phoenix. The die was retired in 1841 and the phoenix was replaced by the bald eagle— America's national bird.

Freemasons consider their fraternal ties to transcend their political and national divisions. When the War for American Independence was over, however, the American lodges split from the Mother Grand Lodge of London and created their own autonomous American Grand Lodge. The Scottish degrees soon became dominant in American Free- masonry. The two major forms of Freemasonry practiced in the United States today are the York Rite (a version of the original English York Rite) and the Scottish Rite. The modern York Rite has a total of ten degrees: the topmost is "Knights Templar." The Scottish Rite has a total of thirty-three degrees, many of which are Knight degrees.

The influence of Freemasonry in American politics remained strong long after the Revolution was over. About one third of all U.S. Presidents have been Freemasons, most of them in the Scottish Rite.*

The influence of Freemasonry in American politics extended beyond the Presidency. The U.S. Senate and House of Representatives have had a large Masonic membership for most of the nation's history. In 1924, for example, a Masonic publication listed sixty Senators as Freemasons.[9] They constituted over 60% of the Senate. More than 290 members of the House of Representatives were also named as lodge members. This Masonic presence has waned somewhat in recent years. In an advertising supplement entitled, "Freemasonry, A Way of Life," the Grand Lodge of California revealed that in the 97th Congress (1981-1983), there were only 28 lodge members in the Senate and 78 in the House. While that represents a substantial drop from the 1920's, Freemasonry still has a good-sized representation in the Senate with more than a quarter of that legislative body populated by members of the Craft.

---

* In addition to George Washington and James Madison, Freemasons in the Presidency have been: James Monroe (initiated November 9, 1775), Andrew Jackson (in. 1800), James Polk (in. June 5, 1820), James Buchanan (in. December 11, 1816), Andrew Johnson (in. 1851), James Garfield (in. November 22, 1861 or 1862), William McKinley (in. May 1, 1865), Theodore Roosevelt (in. January 2, 1901), William Howard Taft (in. February 18, 1908), Warren Harding (in. June 28, 1901), Franklin D. Roosevelt (in. October 10, 1911), Harry S. Truman (in. February 9, 1909), and Gerald Ford (in. 1949). The list of prominent American Freemasons also includes such people as the late J. Edgar Hoover, founder of the F.B.I., who had attained the highest (33rd) degree of the Scottish Rite, and presidential candidate Jesse Jackson (in. 1988). Famous American artists have also been members, such as Mark Twain, Will Rogers and W. C. Fields.

The American Revolution was more than a local uprising. It involved many nations. France was a secret participant in the American cause long before the actual outbreak of war. As early as 1767, the French Foreign Minister, Duke of Choiseul, had sent secret agents to the American colonies to gauge public opinion and to learn how far the seeds of revolt had grown. France also dispatched agent provocateurs to the colonies to secretly stir up anti-British sentiment. In 1767, Benjamin Franklin, who was not yet committed to armed warfare with England, accused France of attempting to blow up the coals between Britain and her American subjects. After Choiseul was deposed in 1770, his successor, Compte de Vergennes, continued Choiseul's policy and was instrumental in bringing about France's open military support for the American cause after the War for Independence began.*

Frederick the Great of Prussia was another to openly support the American rebels. He was among the first European rulers to recognize the United States as an independent nation. Frederick even went as far as closing his ports to Hessian mercenaries sailing to fight against the revolutionaries. Just how deeply Frederick was involved in the American cause may never be known, however. There is no doubt that many colonists felt indebted to him and viewed him as one of their moral and philosophical leaders. Decades after the Revolution, a number of Masonic lodges in America adopted several Scottish degrees which had reportedly been created by Frederick. The first American Lodge of the Scottish Rite, which was established in Charleston, South Carolina, published a circular on October 10, 1802 declaring

---

* Interestingly, Vergennes was also a Freemason. He supported some of the French Freemasons, such as Voltaire, who were creating the fervent intellectual climate that led to the French Revolution. The French Revolution overthrew Vergennes' king, Louis XVI, within a decade of Vergennes' death. It is ironic that while he was alive, Vergennes had opposed all deep-seated reforms to French society. He thereby helped create the popular discontent which did so much to make the French Revolution successful.

that authorization of its highest degree came from Frederick, whom they still viewed as the head of all Freemasonry:

> On the 1st of May, 5786 [1786], the Grand Constitution of the Thirty-Third Degree, called the Supreme Council of the Sovereign Grand Inspectors General, was ratified by his Majesty the King of Prussia, who as Grand Commander of the Order of Prince of the Royal Secret,* possessed the Sovereign Masonic power over all the Craft. In the New Constitution this Power was conferred on a Supreme Council of Nine Brethren in each nation, who possess all the Masonic prerogatives in their own district that his Majesty individually possessed, and are Sovereigns of Masonry.[10]

Some scholars argue that Frederick was not active in Freemasonry in the late 1700's. They feel that his name was simply used to lend the Rite an air of authority. This argument may well be true, or at least partially so. The significance of the Charleston pamphlet lies in the loyalty that the early American Scottish Rite openly proclaimed to German Masonic sources so soon after the founding of the new American republic.

While some German Freemasons from Prussia were aiding the American cause, other German Masons were helping Great Britain, and at an enormous profit. Nearly 30,000 German soldiers were rented to Great Britain by six German states: Hesse-Kassel, Hesse-Hanau, Brunswick, Waldeck, Anspach-Bayreuth, and Anhalt-Zerbst. More than

---

*Degrees in the Scottish Rite are grouped together in sections, and each section is given a name. *Order of Prince of the Royal Secret* is today called the *Consistory* [Council] *of Sublime Princes of the Royal Secret* and contains the 31st and 32nd degrees of the Scottish Rite. Another indication of the early Scottish Rite's admiration for things Prussian is found in the title of the 21st degree, which is called *Noachite*, or *Prussian Knight*.

half of those troops were supplied by Hesse-Kassel; hence, all of the Germans soldiers were known as "Hessians." Hesse-Kassel's troops were considered to be the best of the mercenaries; their accurate gunfire was feared by the colonial troops. In many battles, there were more Germans fighting for the British than there were British soldiers. In the Battle of Trenton, for example, Germans were the only soldiers against whom the Americans fought. This does not mean that the German soldiers were especially loyal to Britain, or even to their own German rulers. Almost one sixth of the German mercenaries (an estimated 5,000) deserted and stayed in America.

The use of German mercenaries created a stir in both England and America. Many British leaders, including supporters of the monarch, objected to hiring foreign soldiers to subdue British subjects. For the Germans, the arrangement was as lucrative as ever. The Duke of Brunswick, for example, received 11,517 pounds 17 schillings 1½ pence for the first year's rental, and twice that figure during each of the following two years. In addition, the Duke received "head money" of more than seven pounds for each man, for a total of 42,000 pounds for Brunswick's six thousand soldiers. For each soldier killed, Brunswick was paid an additional fee, with three wounded counting as one dead. The Prince of Hesse-Kassel, Frederick II, earned about 21,000,000 thaler for his Hessian troops, amounting to a net total of approximately five million British pounds. That was an almost unheard of sum during his day and it accounted for more than half of the Hesse-Kassel fortune inherited by William IX when his father died in 1785. The Hesse-Kassel treasury became one of the largest (some say *the* largest) princely fortunes in Europe because of the American Revolution.

The American Revolution followed the pattern of earlier revolutions by weakening the head of state and creating a stronger legislature. Sadly, the American revolutionaries also gave their new nation the same inflatable paper money and central banking systems that had been erected by revolutionaries in Europe. Even before the American Revolution was won, the Continental Congress had gotten into the inflatable paper money business by printing money known as "Continental notes." These notes were declared legal tender by the Congress with nothing to back them. The Continental Congress used the notes to buy the goods it needed to fight the Revolutionary War. Cooperative colonists accepted the money on the promise that the notes would be backed by something after the war was won. As the Continental notes continued to come off Ben Franklin's press, inflation set it. This caused more notes to be printed, which triggered a hyperinflation. After the war was won and a new "hard" currency (currency backed by a metal) was established, the Continental notes were only redeemable for the new currency at the rate of one cent to the dollar. It was another clear and painful lesson on how paper money, inflation and devaluation can be effective tools to help nations fight wars.

Ironically, some American Founding Fathers used the experience of the Continental notes to urge the creation of a central bank patterned after the Bank of England to better control the currency of the new American nation. The proposed central bank was a hot issue of debate with strong emotions running for and against the plan. The pro-bank faction won. After several years of controversy, America's first central bank, the Bank of the United States, was chartered in 1791. The charter expired twenty years later, was renewed after a five-year lapse, was vetoed by President Andrew Jackson in 1836, regained its charter twenty-seven years later (in 1863), and finally became the Federal Reserve Bank, which is America's central bank today. Although considerable opposition to a central bank has always existed in the United States, the country has had one, under one name or another, for most of its history.

The Founding Father credited with creating America's first central bank was Alexander Hamilton. Hamilton had joined the revolutionary movement in the early 1770's and rose to the rank of lieutenant colonel and aide-de-camp on Washington's staff by 1777. Hamilton was a good military commander and became a close friend of George Washington and the Marquis de La Fayette. After the war ended, Hamilton studied law, was admitted to the bar, and in February 1784, founded and became director of the Bank of New York.

Hamilton's goal was to create an American banking system patterned after the Bank of England. Hamilton also wanted the new U.S. government to assume all state debts and turn them into one large national debt. The national government was to continue increasing its debt by borrowing from Hamilton's proposed central bank, which would be privately owned and operated by a small group of financiers.

How was the American government going to repay all of this debt?

In an act of supreme irony, Hamilton wanted to place taxes on goods, just as the British had done prior to the Revolution! After Hamilton became Secretary of Treasury, he pushed through such a tax on distilled liquor. This tax resulted in the famous Whiskey Rebellion of 1794 in which a group of mountain people refused to pay the tax and began to speak openly of rebellion against the new American government. At Hamilton's insistence, President George Washington called out the militia and had the rebellion crushed militarily! Hamilton and his backers had managed to establish in the United States a situation identical to England before the American Revolution: a nation deeply in debt which must resort to taxing its citizens to repay the debt. One might legitimately ask: why did Messrs. Hamilton and Washington bother participating in the American Revolution? They simply used their influence to create the very same institutions in America that the colonists had found so odious under British rule. This question is especially relevant today as the United States faces an astounding national debt of over two trillion dollars, and an enormous tax burden on its citizens far higher than anything ever conceived of by Britain to impose on the colonists in the 18th century.

Although Hamilton's plans were largely successful, they did not go without very considerable opposition. Leading the fight against the establishment of a privately-owned central bank were James Madison and Thomas Jefferson. They wanted the government to be the issuer of the national currency, not a central bank. In a letter dated December 13,

1803, Jefferson expressed his strong opinion about the Bank of the United States:

> This institution is one of the most deadly hostility existing, against the principles and form of our constitution.[11]

He added:

> . . . an institution like this, penetrating by its branches every part of the Union, acting by command and in phalanx [unison], may, in a critical moment, upset the government. I deem no government safe which is under the vassalage of any self-constituted authorities, or any other authority than that of the nation, or its regular functionaries.[12]

Although one of Jefferson's objections to the central bank rested on his concerns that such a bank might be an *obstruction* during times of war, he was nonetheless quite farsighted about some of the effects that such an institution would have. Not only did the U.S. central banks create major financial panics in 1893 and 1907, but the financial fraternity operating the U.S. central bank has exerted, and continues to exert today, a strong influence in U.S. affairs, especially foreign affairs, just as Jefferson had warned. It was Jefferson's powerful influence, incidentally, which caused the five-year delay in the renewal of the bank's charter in 1811.

We have just finished viewing the American Revolution in a less than rosy light. There was, however, a powerful humanitarian influence at work inside the circle of Founding Fathers that must be acknowledged. The United States is one of the freer countries today as a direct result of that influence, even if Americans are still far from being a completely free peoples. The American founders affirmed important freedoms, especially those of speech, assembly and religion. An excellent Constitution was created for the United States that has proven highly workable in such a large and diverse society. The genocide which seemed to go along with earlier Brotherhood political activity is conspicuously absent in the American Revolution. American Freemasons today are proud of the role that their Brethren played in creating the American nation, and just so. The spark of humanitarianism which periodically resurfaces in the Brotherhood network surely did so again during the founding of the American republic.

If we were to name a few of the most important humanitarians among the Founding Fathers, we might list such well-known figures as Thomas Jefferson, James Madison, Patrick Henry, and Richard Henry Lee. One of the most important of the Founding Fathers is rarely mentioned, however. He is the one in whose memory no large monuments have ever been erected in Washington, D.C. His portrait does not grace any U.S. currency and he did not even have a postage stamp issued in his honor until 1981. That man was George Mason.

George Mason was described by Thomas Jefferson as "one of our really great men, and of the first order of greatness."[13] Mason is the most neglected of the Founding Fathers because he ignored political glory, shunned office, and was never famous for his oratory; yet he stands as one of the most far-sighted of the men who created the American nation. After the Revolution, George Mason opposed the plans of Hamilton and declared that Hamilton had "done us more injury than Great Britain and all her fleets and armies."[14] It was George Mason who pushed hardest for the adoption of a federal Bill of Rights. The ten Amendments to the U.S. Constitution which constitute the Bill of Rights are based upon Mason's earlier Virginia Declaration of Rights written by him in 1776. The Bill of Rights almost did not make it into the American Constitution, and it would not have done so had not Mason engaged in a heated battle to ensure its inclusion. Despite his chronic ill health, Mason published influential pamphlets denouncing the proposed Constitution because it lacked specified individual rights. Most drafters of the Constitution, including Alexander Hamilton, declared a Bill of Rights unnecessary due to the balance and limitation of powers imposed on the federal government by the Constitution. Mason persisted and was supported by Richard Henry Lee and Thomas Jefferson. With the backing of James

Madison, the Bill of Rights was finally pushed through to ratification in the final hours. When we consider how the federal government has grown since then and how crucial the Bill of Rights have become, we can appreciate what a man of vision George Mason truly was. His far-sightedness and humanitarianism were also manifested in his attempts to completely abolish slavery. At a time when even his friends George Washington and Thomas Jefferson were slave owners, George Mason denounced the slave trade as a "disgrace to mankind" and worked to have it outlawed throughout all of the states. George Mason did not succeed in this quest during his lifetime, but his dream did come true less than a century later when slavery was abolished in the United States by the thirteenth amendment to the Constitution.* Although most American schoolchildren do not hear much about George Mason in their history lessons or have his portrait hanging in their classrooms, he was one of the great heroes of human freedom.

The renewed spark of humanitarianism which arose during the American Revolution was soon overshadowed. The establishment of the inflatable paper money system in the United States was a clue that something was still badly amiss in the Brotherhood network. As similar revolutions led by Freemasons erupted around the world, the old horrors reemerged. One of those horrors was calculated genocide.

---

* La Fayette and a few other Freemasons also deserve credit for the success of the anti-slavery movement. They belonged to a Masonic organization known as the *Societé des Amis des Noirs* (Society of the Friends of the Blacks) which worked to bring about the universal emancipation of blacks. Unfortunately, Aryanism still remained very much alive in other Brotherhood branches.

# 29

# The World Afire

ONE SIGNIFICANT BY-PRODUCT of the American Revolution was a philosophical reshaping of how people viewed revolution. When Benjamin Franklin was in France to win French military support for the American cause, he engaged in an intensive public relations campaign. He vigorously promulgated the idea of "virtuous revolution"—a concept which had already found increasing favor in the Masonic lodges. The public at that time tended to view violent revolution as a crime against society. Franklin was successful in changing this perception by encouraging people to accept violent revolutions as steps in the progress of mankind. Revolutionaries were no longer to be frowned upon as criminals, he argued, because they were idealists fighting for freedom and justice. A new motto was coined: "Revolution against tyranny is the most sacred of duties."[1] These bold ideas electrified Paris and helped to win open French support for the American cause, but at a terrible long-term cost to human society. The ideas expressed by Franklin have helped to stimulate endless bloody revolutions ever since.

The American Revolution was followed by many other revolutions and/or the establishment of republican-style governments throughout the western world and South America. The success of the American Revolution had made it easy to rally people to fight. We witness during this era the French Revolution, the creation of the Batavian Republic in the Netherlands (1795-1806), the Helvetic Republic in Switzerland (1798-1805), the Cisalpine Republic in northern Italy (1797-1805), the Ligurian Republic in Genoa (1797-1805), and the Parthenopean Republic in southern Italy. Between 1810 and 1824, the Spanish colonies in South America took up arms and won their political independence. In 1825, the Decembrist revolt broke out in Russia. A second revolution erupted in France in 1830. In that same year, a revolt in Holland brought about the sovereignty of Belgium. A Polish revolution in 1830 and 1831 was successfully stamped out by Russia. In 1848, a major wave of revolutionary activity swept Europe spurred by an international collapse of credit caused in good part by the new inflatable paper money system, bad harvests, and a cholera epidemic.

In nearly all of those revolutions, we continue to see important revolutionary leadership positions held by Freemasons. During the first French Revolution, a key rebel leader was the Duke of Orleans, who was the Grand Master of French Masonry before his resignation at the height of the Revolution. Marquis de La Fayette, the man who had been initiated into the Masonic fraternity by George Washington, also played an important role in the French revolutionary cause. The Jacobin Club, which was the radical nucleus of the French revolutionary movement, was founded by prominent Freemasons. According to Sven Lunden's article, "The Annihilation of Freemasonry":

Herbert, Andre Chenier, Camille Desmoulins and many other "Girondins" [moderate French republicans supporting republican government over monarchy] of the French Revolution were Freemasons.[2]

Freemasons were the primary leaders of the 1825 Decembrist revolt in Russia. Some of the planning for that revolt took place within their lodges.

In South America, according to Richard DeHaan, writing in *Collier's Encyclopedia:*

The order [Freemasonry] played an important role in the spread of liberalism and the organization of political revolution in Latin America. Like French Freemasonry, the Latin American movement was also generally anti-clerical. In Mexico and Colombia, Masons helped win independence from Spain, while in Brazil they worked against Portuguese domination.[3]

Mr. Lunden agrees:

In Latin America, too, the process of liberation from the Spanish yoke was the work of Freemasons, in large measure. Simon Bolivar was one of the most active of Masonry's sons, and so were San Martin, Mitre, Alvear, Sarmiento, Benito Juarez—all hallowed names to Latin Americans.[4]

Regarding other revolutions, Mr. Lunden adds:

Many of the leaders in the great year 1848, which saw so many uprisings against feudal rule in Europe, were members of the Order; among them was the great Hungarian hero of democracy, Louis Kossuth, who found a temporary refuge in America.[5]

The 1800's also witnessed the wars of Italian unification led by Giuseppe Garibaldi (1807-1882), who was a thirty-third degree Mason and the Grand Master of Italy. The victorious Garibaldi placed Victor Emmanuel, another Freemason, on the throne.

The Italian wars of unification left two important legacies: a united Italy and the modern Mafia. The Mafia was a loosely-knit secret society founded in Sicily in the mid 1700's. At first, the Mafia was a resistance movement formed to oppose the foreign rulers who controlled Sicily at the time. The early Mafiosi were popular heroes who specialized in criminal acts against the hated foreigners. The Mafia built an underground government in Sicily and held power by extortion. The Mafia assisted Garibaldi when he invaded Sicily in 1860 and declared himself dictator of the island. After the foreign rulers were ousted and Italy was unified, the Mafia became the violent criminal network we know today.

Freemasonry was clearly an important catalyst in the creation of modern Western-style government. The vast majority of Freemasons who participated in the revolutions were well-intended. The representative form of government they helped to create was certainly an improvement over some of the governments they replaced.* Regrettably, the lofty ideals of those Freemasons were in the process of a speedy betrayal by sources within the Brotherhood network itself.

One consequence of the French Revolution was a severe disruption of the French economy. Food production had dropped severely and the new regime was in deep political trouble because the majority of Frenchmen were still loyal to the monarchy. Under this cloud, the revolutionary government decided to solve the problems of political opposition, hunger and distribution of wealth by reducing the human population of France. Rather than increase food production to meet the demand, it was decided to reduce the demand to match the lessened amount of food. Throughout the French nation, a program of mass murder was launched as an official program of the revolutionary council. This program was

---

*This is not to say that monarchy is always bad. History has seen a few benevolent monarchs who ruled well, who could act for peace, and who were popular with their people. Hereditary or life-term leadership has the advantage of stability. It can work if the monarch is accountable for his or her actions and can be removed for chronic incompetence or abuse of power. Monarchies have rarely functioned well on Earth because monarchs have usually ruled by so-called "divine right" and have therefore not been accountable to the people they governed.

known as the Reign of Terror. People were put to death by all means available, including guillotine, mass drowning, bludgeoning, shooting, and starvation. Although not as many people were murdered as the council had planned, it has been estimated that over 100,000 people died.

We have noted that genocides are committed by grouping people into superficial categories usually based upon race, religious belief, or nationality. The victims are then targeted for slaughter even though they may be guilty of no crimes against their murderers. The French revolutionaries took the process to an extreme. During the Reign of Terror, people were grouped simply according to their economic and vocational standing. Those who fell into the wrong categories were deemed members of an undesirable social class and were killed. This was certainly as superficial a distinction as one can make, yet grouping people in this fashion has been extremely successful in factionalizing human beings.

The French Revolution dragged nearly all of the major powers of Europe into a war. Initially benefiting from this was William IX, the prince who had inherited the immense Hesse-Kassel fortune. William IX rented out, at a handsome fee, 8,000 soldiers to England to fight against the French during the first half of the 1790's. When Napoleon Bonaparte later became emperor of France, William IX seemed to gain even more. After Napoleon's troops occupied German regions west of the Rhine River, including some Hessian properties, Napoleon compensated William IX by awarding him a large section of Mainz and by conferring upon William the title of Elector—a status higher than prince. The cordiality between Napoleon and Elector William did not last very long, however. William IX tried to play the old trick of courting both sides of the conflict in order to make a fortune by renting soldiers. William foolishly leased mercenaries to the Prussian king for a quarter of a million Pounds to fight Napoleon and then tried to claim "neutrality." True to the warning of Machiavelli, this double-dealing finally caught up and backfired on the House of Hesse. Hesse-Kassel was soon annexed and made part of Napoleon's "Kingdom of Westphalia." It was not until after Napoleon's defeat at the Battle of Leipzig in 1813 that William IX was able to regain Hesse-Kassel. Hesse-Kassel remained under the control of his dynasty until 1866, when it was taken over by Prussia. Although the Hessian royal family has remained influential in German society until well into the twentieth century, it never regained exclusive rule over its territory. Hesse merged into what has become modern Germany— a country that was unified in large part by the Prussian Hohenzollern dynasty.

Despite the reversals suffered by Hesse-Kassel, the upheavals in France proved to be a boon for one of William IX's financial agents: Mayer Amschel Rothschild (1743-1812), founder of one of the most influential banking houses of Europe.

Mayer Amschel was an ambitious and hard-working merchant who began his career in the Jewish ghetto of Frankfurt-am-Main in Hesse. In 1765, two decades before the French Revolution, Rothschild managed to gain a hard-won audience with Prince William IX, who was still at that time living in Hesse-Hanau. Mayer Amschel strove to ingratiate himself with the Hessian prince by selling antique coins to William at extremely low prices. William, who always had an eye open to increasing his material fortunes in any way possible, was delighted to take advantage of Rothschild's generous bargains. As a reward, William granted Rothschild's request to be appointed a "Crown Agent to the Prince of Hesse-Hanau." This appointment, made in 1769, was more honorary than substantial, but it gave Mayer Amschel a big boost in his community standing and aided his efforts to create a successful banking house.

During the twenty years following his appointment, Mayer Amschel continued to keep in close contact with Prince William IX. Rothschild's goal was to become one of the Prince's personal financial agents. Rothschild's perseverance finally paid off. In 1789, the year in which the French Revolution began and four years after William IX inherited the wealth of Hesse-Kassel, Mayer was given his first financial assignment on behalf of Prince William. This, in turn, led to the coveted position as a personal financial agent to the Prince.

Rothschild made a fortune from various activities while serving under William IX. The French Revolution and the wars it triggered created many shortages throughout Hesse. Rothschild capitalized on this situation by sharply raising the prices of the cloth he was importing from England. Rothschild also struck a deal with another of William IX's chief financial agents, Carl Buderus. The deal enabled Rothschild to share in the profits from the leasing of Hessian mercenaries to England. Virginia Cowles, writing in her excellent book, *The Rothschilds, A Family of Fortune*, described the arrangement:

> At this point Mayer made a proposition to the enterprising Carl Buderus. England was paying the Landgrave [William IX] large sums of money for the hire of Hessian soldiers; and the Rothschilds were paying England large sums of money for the goods they were importing. Why not let the two-way movement cancel itself out, and pocket the commissions both ways on the bills of exchange? Buderus agreed, and soon this extra string to the Rothschild bow was producing an impressive revenue.[6]

Out of those beginnings rose the House of Rothschild, named after the red shield ("roth" [red] and "schild" [shield]) used as its emblem. The Rothschild family soon became synonymous with wealth, power, and banking. For generations, the Rothschild house was Europe's most powerful banking family and it remains influential in the international banking community today. Sharing the Rothschild house in Frankfurt during its early days was the Schiff family. The Schiffs also became a major banking family and they have done business with the Rothschilds all the way up until our own time.

Control of the Rothschild house, as well as many other banking houses, passed from father to son(s) over the generations. The Rothschilds, Schiffs, and other banking families were truly part of a hereditary "paper aristocracy" to which Brotherhood revolutionaries had given a great deal of power when they established the inflatable paper money system and its attendant central banks.

Many historians writing about the Rothschild family focus on the fact that Mayer Amschel was Jewish. The Rothschilds have been important supporters of Jewish causes throughout the family's history. Less frequently mentioned is the fact that the Rothschilds were also associated with German Freemasonry. This association apparently began with Mayer Amschel, who accompanied William IX on several trips to the Masonic lodges. Whether or not Mayer actually became a member is uncertain. It is known that his son, Solomon (founder of the Rothschild bank in Vienna), had become a Freemason. According to Jacob Katz, writing in his book, *Jews and Freemasons in Europe, 1723-1939,* the Rothschilds were one of the rich and powerful Frankfurt families appearing on a Masonic membership list in 1811.

The Scottish degrees used in the German lodges were Christian in nature. This created problems for Jewish men like Rothschild who may have wanted to participate. To solve the dilemma, efforts were made in Jewish communities to change certain rituals in order to make Freemasonry acceptable to Jews. Special Jewish lodges were created, such as the "Melchizedek" lodges named in honor of the Old Testament priest-king whose importance we discussed in an earlier chapter. Those who belonged to the Melchizedek lodges were said to be members of the "Order of Melchizedek." This was an extremely interesting development, for across the Atlantic Ocean the name of Melchizedek was about to be resurrected on the American continent during what some people believe to have been a series of significant UFO episodes. Those episodes gave the world a new religion: the Church of Jesus Christ of Latter Day Saints, better known as the Mormon Church.

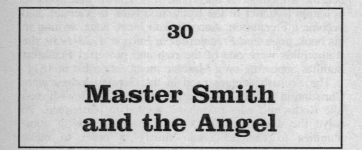

# 30

# Master Smith
# and the Angel

WE HAVE SEEN many instances in which religious agitation
and revivalism were associated with the UFO phenomenon:
the Hebrew rebellions in Egypt under Moses, the Christian agitations under Jesus, the Islamic militancy under
Mohammed, and the religious activism during the UFO-
plagued years of the Black Death.

In the early 20th century, a particularly interesting bout
of intense religious fever overtook some communities in
British Wales. This incident is known as the Welsh Revival
of 1904-1905, in which a preacher driven by "inner voices"
electrified the countryside with his sermons. People were
reporting all manner of unusual phenomena during the
Revival years, including bright moving lights in the sky
that we would today label UFOs. For example, we read

the following personal eyewitness accounts gathered by the Society for Psychical Research (SPR) and published in its *Proceedings* of 1905:*

> First of all my attention was drawn to it by a person in the crowd, and I looked and saw a block of fire as it was rising from the mountain side, and it followed along the mountain side for about 200 to 300 yards, before it gradually rose to heaven. Then a star, as it were, shot out to meet it, and they clapped together and formed a ball of fire. It also grew brighter as it rose higher, and then it seemed to sway about a lot; then it seemed to form into something like the helm of a ship. The size of it at this time would be about the size of the moon, but very much brighter, and lasted about a quarter of an hour.[1]

> . . . the star appeared, like a ball of fire in the sky, glittering and sparkling, and as it went up it seemed to be bubbling over. This continued for about 20 minutes . . .[2]

> Firstly, there appeared in the heavens a very large and bright ball of fire. It was of a much more brilliant lustre than an ordinary star—very much the colour of a piece of iron white-heated. It had two brilliant arms which protruded towards the earth. Between these arms there appeared a further light or lights resembling a cluster of stars, which seemed to be quivering with varying brightness. . . . It lasted for ten minutes or more.[3]

It is interesting that in some regions of Wales, the lights arrived at the very same time as the Revival. The *Proceedings* report:

*For the SPR's complete report on the Welsh Revival, please see "Psychological Aspects of the Welsh Revival" by A. T. Fryer, which was published in the *Society for Psychological Research, Proceedings, 19:80,* 1905. A copy of the complete article may be ordered from The Sourcebook Project. (Please see Bibliography for address.)

In reply to questions about his experiences, Mr. M. stated that he had never seen such lights before the Revival, nor before he had heard of others seeing them. . . . They [the lights] were seen "high up in the sky, where no houses or anything else could lead us to make any mistake" (*i.e.* to mistake ordinary lights for them); they were seen both on very dark nights and also when the moon and stars were visible.[4]

The lights were seen at least once near a chapel, and also leaving an area where a prominent preacher lived, thereby hinting at a direct UFO involvement with some of those people who were responsible for the Revival:

We happened to reach Llanfair about 9:15 P.M. It was a rather dark and damp evening. In nearing the chapel, which can be seen from a distance, we saw balls of light, deep red, ascending from one side of the chapel, the side which is in a field. There was nothing in this field to cause this phenomenon—*i.e.* no houses, etc. After that we walked to and fro on the main road for nearly two hours without seeing any light except from a distance in the direction of Llanbedr. This time it appeared brilliant, ascending high into the sky from amongst the trees where lives the well-known Rev. C. E. The distance between us and the light which appeared this time was about a mile. Then about eleven o'clock, when the service which Mrs. Jones conducted was brought to a close, two balls of light ascended from the same place and of similar appearance to those we saw first. In a few minutes afterwards Mrs. Jones was passing us home in her carriage, and in a few seconds after she passed, on the main road, and within a yard of us, there appeared a brilliant light twice, tinged with blue. In two or three seconds after this disappeared, on our right hand, within 150 or 200 yards, there appeared twice very huge balls of similar appearance as that which appeared on the road. It was so brilliant and powerful this time that we were dazed for a second or two. Then immediately there appeared a brilliant light ascending from the woods where the Rev. C. E. lives. It appeared twice this time. On the other side of the main road, close by, there appeared, ascending from a field high into the sky, three balls of light, deep red. Two of these appeared to split up, whilst the middle one remained unchanged. Then we left for home, having been watching these last phenomena for a quarter of an hour.[5]

Included among the Welsh aerial phenomena were music and sound effects coming from out of the sky. It seems that the sound effects were designed to more firmly implant the Revivalist message in people by making them believe that they were witnessing visitations from heaven:

E. B., on Wednesday previous, heard about four o'clock what appeared to him to be a thunder clap, followed by lovely singing in the air.

. . .

E. E., on Saturday evening, between seven and eight, while returning home from his work, heard some strange music, similar to the vibration caused by telegraph wires, only much louder, on an eminence, the hill being far from any trees and wires of any kind, and it was more or less a still evening.

J. P. heard some lovely singing on the road, about half a mile from his home, on Saturday evening, three weeks ago, which frightened him very much.[6]

It is interesting that these UFO phenomena were debunked in 1905 in an identical way that modern UFOs are debunked today, revealing that debunking is by no means a late 20th-century phenomenon. One investigator, in his report of February 21, 1905, dismissed all of the Welsh phenomena as farm lanterns, marsh gas, the planet Venus, and "phantasies of overwrought brains." Such explanations were no more helpful in 1905 than they are today in shedding light on some genuinely remarkable phenomena.

The Welsh Revival was not an isolated event. It followed a similar occurrence in New York state almost a century earlier. The events in New York included a vision leading to the founding of the Mormon Church by a teenaged youth named Joseph Smith. His story is worth looking at.

Joseph Smith described it as a beautiful clear day in the spring of 1820. Master Joseph was 14 or 15 years of age and his mind was in a state of confusion. In his hometown of Manchester, New York, intense quarreling had broken out between various Christian sects, all of which were vying for members. To sort out the controversies in his mind, Joseph climbed a lonely hill near his home, prayed aloud, and hoped that God would answer him. What happened next was probably more than he had bargained for:

> . . . immediately I was seized upon by some power which entirely overcame me, and had such an astonishing influence over me as to bind my tongue so that I could not speak. Thick darkness gathered around me, and it seemed to me for a time as if I were doomed to sudden destruction.
>
> JOSEPH SMITH 2:15*

Just as Joseph was about to give in to despair, he saw:

> . . . a pillar of light exactly over my head, above the brightness of the sun, which descended gradually until it fell upon me.
>
> It no sooner appeared than I found myself delivered from the enemy which held me bound. When the light rested upon me I saw two Personages, whose brightness and glory defy all description, standing above me in the air. One of them spake unto me, calling me by name, and said, pointing to the other—This is My Beloved Son. Hear Him!
>
> JOSEPH SMITH 2:16-17

---

*The words of Joseph Smith are quoted from the book, *Pearl of Great Price*.

So began a series of appearances by an "angel" whose reported dictates and pronouncements are the foundation of the Church of Jesus Christ of Latter Day Saints, also known as the Mormon Church. This church is, without doubt, an important institution. Its membership in 1985 totaled approximately 5.8 million people and the Church has extensive business and land holdings. Beginning with a teenaged boy on a hill in New York State, the Church has grown to influence the lives of many people.

Joseph's vision on the hill was the first of several visits that he would receive from his "angel" friend. The second visit occurred three and a half years after the first. Joseph Smith had just gone to bed, was in the act of praying, when:

> I discovered a light appearing in my room, which continued to increase until the room was lighter than at noonday, when immediately a personage appeared at my bedside, standing in the air, for his feet did not touch the floor.
>
> He had on a loose robe of most exquisite whiteness beyond anything earthly I had ever seen; nor do I believe that any earthly thing could be made to appear so exceedingly white and brilliant.
>
> JOSEPH SMITH 2:30-31

The figure in Joseph's room had naked hands, wrists, feet and ankles. It also had a bare head, neck and exposed chest. The figure introduced itself as Moroni, the angel of a man who had lived centuries earlier. The resurrected "Moroni" imparted a message to Joseph consisting of quotes from Final Judgment prophecies in the Old Testament. Moroni stated that the prophecies were about to be fulfilled. Moroni also informed Joseph about the existence of ancient metal plates which contained some of the history of the early North American continent. Joseph was told that he must later dig up the plates, have them translated, and present the translation to the world. After this message, the image of Moroni vanished in a unique way:

. . . I saw the light in the room begin to gather immediately around the person of him who had been speaking to me, and it continued to do so until the room was again left dark, except just around him; when, instantly I saw, as it were, a conduit open right up into heaven, and he ascended till he entirely disappeared . . .

JOSEPH SMITH 2:43

Joseph did not have long to ponder the curious phenomenon. The mysterious light and visitor soon re-entered his room. Of this second visit that night, Joseph relates:

He [the angel] commenced, and again related the very same things which he had done at his first visit, without the least variation; which having done, he informed me of great judgments which were coming upon the earth, with great desolations by famine, sword, and pestilence; and that these grievous judgments would come on the earth in this [Joseph Smith's] generation. Having related these things, he again ascended as he had done before.

JOSEPH SMITH 2:45

The apparition in Joseph's bedroom came and went repeatedly the full night. On the following day, while he was out in the field, the exhausted young Smith abruptly lost his strength while trying to climb a fence and he fell unconscious to the ground. Upon regaining awareness, Joseph observed above him the same angel repeating the same message. A new postscript had been added, however: the angel instructed Joseph to tell his father of the visions.

Some critics dispute the accuracy of Joseph Smith's stories, pointing out that Smith did not record his first vision on paper until nineteen years after it had happened. Under the circumstances at the time, this delay is understandable when we consider Joseph's youth and minimal education.

To the degree Smith's accounts are accurate, they are worth looking at. Did he have a true religious vision as his followers believe, or was he, as others suggest, a victim of UFO tampering?

Joseph's angel, Moroni, was different than the angels described by Ezekiel and John in the Bible. Smith's angel did not wear items that could be interpreted as a helmet and boots. Moroni was a figure in a true robe. However, Joseph appears to have been looking at a recorded image projected through the window into his room. The clue to this lies in Joseph's words that Moroni had repeated the second message "without the least variation." This suggests a recorded message. The manner in which Moroni disappeared indicates a projected light image from a source in the sky outside the house. When Moroni returned for a third time that same night, Smith "heard him rehearse or repeat over again . . . the same things—as before. . . ." (*Joseph Smith 2:48-49*). If Smith's account is accurate and UFO-related, there would be tremendous humor in it. Today we can go to Disneyland and marvel at remarkable, life-like, projected images of talking heads in the Haunted House ride. A similar projection viewed by a young country bumpkin in the 19th century would no doubt be considered nothing less than a true vision from God. Certainly young Smith's narrative resembles earlier Custodial encounters in many respects: a bright light descends from the sky followed by the appearance of "angels." Joseph's testimony that he felt seized and unable to move is identical to several modern UFO close encounters in which eyewitnesses report being immobilized, especially before an abduction.

Other Mormon writings also tend to support the likelihood that Joseph Smith had had a UFO encounter. The Mormon doctrines revealed by Smith state that there are many inhabited planets in the universe. This was quite a daring idea for an uneducated man of the nineteenth century. Smith added that God inhabits a human flesh-and-bones body (see, *e.g.*, *Doctrines and Covenants 130:22*) and that God lives near a star called Kolob (see *Abraham 3:1-3*). In other words, God is a humanlike extraterrestrial living on another planet. What we seem to clearly have in Joseph Smith's experience is another appearance of our Custodial friends pretending that they are God and meddling in human affairs by implanting yet another apocalyptic religion on Earth.

Harsh criticism is often aimed at the "bible" of Smith's religion: the *Book of Mormon*. The *Book of Mormon* is said to be a translation of the ancient metal plates that Smith had dug up at the command of his angel. The stories contained in the *Book of Mormon* are remarkable, and to many, unbelievable.

The *Book of Mormon* is written in a style of prose resembling the Old Testament. It ties the history of ancient North America to the history described in the Old Testament. According to *Mormon,* people from Palestine were transported in saucerlike submarines to the Americas under the guidance of "God" in the year 600 B.C. "God" was sending them to the New World largely because of the Tower of Babel incident. Somewhere in the Americas (perhaps Mexico or Central America) the refugees built magnificent cities rivaling those of the Old World. They fought wars and were obedient to the same "God" and "angels" worshipped in the Middle East. The *Book of Mormon* tells of regular visits by "angels" and of their deep involvement in the affairs of ancient America. The angels encouraged their human servants to practice important virtues, the foremost being, of course, obedience.

The *Book of Mormon* tells us that many other remarkable events took place in ancient America as time went by. In the first century A.D., Jesus Christ reportedly made an appearance in the Americas immediately following his crucifixion on the other side of the world. The Christ vision described in *Mormon* is complete with glorious rays of light in the sky from which Jesus emerged.

Although many scholars take the Old Testament seriously as an historical record, little such deference is given the *Book of Mormon. Mormon* stories seem so outrageous, and the manner in which Joseph Smith reportedly obtained and translated the plates appears so suspect, that scant academic heed is paid to them. The question is: should the *Book of Mormon* be dismissed out of hand?

In truth, the *Book of Mormon* may well be one of the most significant historical records to come out of the Custodial religions. Based upon all that we have already studied in this book, the history of ancient America as told in *Mormon* is precisely the type of history we would expect. Earth is small. We would anticipate that an "ancient astronaut" (*i.e.*, the Custodial) race would rule human society in the same fashion everywhere, on every continent. We would expect them to exhibit the same brutality and to promote identical religious fictions. The dates extrapolated from the *Book of Mormon* for the arrival of the Palestinians to America are especially interesting because they coincide with the dates that historians have assigned to the emergence of the ancient civilizations of Mexico and Central America. The *Book of Mormon* might therefore explain why those civilizations abruptly arose in North and Central America so long after similar civilizations had already come and gone on the opposite side of the world.

This still leaves a puzzle unsolved.

If *Mormon* is at least partially true, where are the ruins of the cities it names? Many magnificent American ruins have been found, of course, but not all of the key cities identified in the *Book of Mormon*. *Mormon* offers a chilling answer: some were utterly destroyed by "God" in a frightening cataclysm.

As elsewhere, it was very difficult for humans in ancient America to please their Custodial masters. *Mormon* tells us that some ancient Americans did an especially poor job of it. As a result, a massive punishment was inflicted upon a large American region reportedly around the year 34 A.D., coincident with the crucifixion of Jesus on the other side of the world. The *Mormon* account of this American cataclysm is extraordinary. It accurately describes a nuclear holocaust:

> . . . *in the thirty and fourth year, in the first month, on the fourth day of the month, there arose a great storm, such an—one as never had been known in all the land.*
>
> *And there was also a great and terrible tempest [violent wind]; and there was terrible thunder, insomuch that it did shake the whole earth as if it was about to divide asunder.*

*And there were exceeding sharp lightnings, such as never had been known in all the land.*

*And the city of Zarahemla did take fire.*

*And the city of Moroni did sink into the depths of the sea, and—inhabitants thereof were drowned.*

*And the earth was carried up upon the city of Moronihah that in the place of the city there became a great mountain.*

*And there was a great and terrible destruction in the land southward.*

*But behold, there was more great and terrible destruction in the land northward; for behold, the whole face of the land was changed, because of the tempest and the whirlwinds and the thunderings and the lightnings, and the exceeding great quaking of the whole earth;*

*And the highways were broken up, and the level roads were spoiled, and many smooth places became rough.*

*And many great and notable cities were sunk, and many were burned, and many were shaken till the buildings thereof had fallen to the earth, and the inhabitants thereof were slain, and the places were left desolate.*

*And there were some cities which remained; but the damage thereof was exceeding great, and there were many of them who were slain.*

*And there were some who were carried away in the whirlwind; and whither they went no man knoweth, save they know that they were carried away.*

*And thus the face of the whole earth became deformed, and because of the tempests, and the thunderings, and the lightnings, and the quaking of the earth.*

*And behold, the rocks were rent in twain; they were broken up upon the face of the whole earth, insomuch that they were found in broken fragments, and in seams and in cracks, upon all the face of the land.*

*And it came to pass that when the thunderings, and the lightnings, and the storm, and the tempest, and the quakings of the earth did cease—for behold, they did last for about the space of three hours;*

*and it was said by some that the time was great-
er; nevertheless, all these great and terrible things
were done in about the space of three hours—and
then behold, there was a darkness upon the face of
the land.*

*And it came to pass that there was thick darkness upon
all the face of the land, insomuch that the inhabitants
thereof who had not fallen [died] could feel the vapor
of darkness;*

*And there could be no light, because of the darkness,
neither candles, neither torches; neither could there be
fire kindled with their fine and exceedingly dry wood,
so that there could not be any light at all;*

*And there was not any light seen, neither fire, nor
glimmer, neither the sun, nor the moon, nor the stars,
for so great were the mists of darkness which were
upon the face of the land.*

*And it came to pass that it did last for the space of
three days that there was no light seen; and there was
great mourning and howling and weeping among all
the people continually; yea, great were the groanings
of the people, because of the darkness and the great
destruction which had come upon them.*

3 NEPHI 8:5-23, BOOK OF MORMON

The rumblings, flashes of lightning, rapid incineration
of cities, all within three hours, followed by three days
of thick heavy darkness combine to accurately depict a
nuclear strike followed by the inevitable thick lingering
cloud of soot and debris. The above passage is especially
remarkable when we remember that it was first published
over a century ago—long before nuclear weapons were
developed by man. It gives added credence to the Mormon
Church's claim that Joseph Smith had not invented the
*Book of Mormon* as some critics have charged. It is highly
unlikely that any person in Smith's day could have accidentally imagined an event so closely mirroring a nuclear
holocaust.

Some Mormons stress that the spiritual teachings found
in Mormon texts are more important than the historical

information. Mormon spiritual beliefs are indeed significant because they are quite forthright about Custodial intentions.

The basic spiritual beliefs of the Mormon Church can be summarized as follows:

Humans are immortal spiritual beings occupying human bodies. The spirit is the true source of intelligence and personality, not the body. As spiritual beings, we existed before birth and will continue to exist after death. The true goal of life is to improve spiritually, and everyone can eventually achieve a rehabilitated spiritual state that mirrors the state of a Supreme Being. Ethics are an important step to achieving such a state. Everyone is endowed with free will.

These beliefs sound like the teachings of a maverick religion. We can at once understand why so many people are drawn to Mormonism and remain devoted adherents. Members are told important truths. When we read further into Mormon works, however, we find that the above truths are given many fatal twists which actually prevent people from ever attaining their spiritual salvation.

Mormon texts state that people are actually immortal spirit *bodies* which inhabit human bodies. Spirit bodies are made of matter and look just like human bodies. Joseph Smith said that "spirit is a substance; that it is material, but that it is more pure, elastic and refined matter than the body." (HC, IV. p. 575.) A Supreme Being (God) is said to be a similar material being who inhabits a perfect and immortal flesh-and-bones body. The ultimate goal of Mormonism is to achieve the same state as "God" and dwell in a perfect immortal human body for the rest of eternity. Mormon teachings, which are alleged to have come from ancient plates and Custodial "angels," therefore encourage humans to welcome the grim fate of endless entrapment in human bodies. The *Book of Mormon* expresses that objective this way:

> *The spirit and the body shall be reunited again in its*
> *perfect form; . . . their spirits united with their bodies,*
> *never to be divided; . . .*
>
> ALMA II:43, 45

Ancient Mesopotamian texts told us that mankind's Custodial "gods" wanted to permanently join spiritual beings to human bodies so that the Custodians would have a slave race. Maverick religions have argued that a spirit's enmeshment in a human body is the primary cause of suffering. To counteract this maverick teaching and to promote Custodial aims, Mormonism falsely declares that a spiritual being can only achieve ultimate happiness and Godliness when it has been permanently joined to matter:

> *For man is spirit. The elements are eternal, and spirit and element, inseparably connected, receive a fulness of joy;*
> *And when separated, man cannot receive a fulness of joy.*

DOCTRINES AND COVENANTS 93:33-34

Only where true spiritual understanding has been lost can such a teaching take hold, as it has on a widespread scale on Earth.

Mormonism teaches that everyone lived with the Heavenly Father (God) before coming to Earth. As part of God's grand plan, people are sent to Earth in order to learn right from wrong, and to demonstrate to God that they prefer doing good over evil. However, something is done to all spiritual beings who are sent to Earth: they are induced with amnesia about their prebirth existences. According to a pamphlet published by the Mormon Church:

> . . . though we might sometimes sense intimations of our premortal existence [spiritual existence before taking on a body] as "through a glass darkly" [vaguely], it would be effectively blocked from our memory.[7]

This is a remarkable claim, for it suggests that memory of pure spiritual existence is in some way deliberately blocked from human memories by the Custodial society as part of its effort to weld spiritual beings to human bodies. The Custodial society does seem to have effective methods for occluding memory, as demonstrated in modern UFO abduction cases where human victims are apparently caused to suffer almost complete amnesia regarding their abduction experiences.

The forced amnesia described in *Mormon* had several purported purposes, one of which was:

> . . . to ensure that our choice of good or evil would reflect our earthly desires and will, rather than the remembered influence of our All-Good Heavenly Father.[8]

This is also an astonishing admission. It alleges that spiritual memory is dimmed so that people will base their actions on their concerns as material beings rather than upon their knowledge and remembrance of spiritual existence. This can only hamper the ability of individuals to attain a high level of ethics because true ethics must ultimately take into account a person's spiritual nature when confronted with an ethical dilemma. By reducing all questions of ethics to strictly earthly concerns, people are prevented from fully resolving those ethical questions that will start them on the road to full spiritual recovery. This restriction is precisely what the Custodians wanted, as revealed in the Old Testament: "God" did not want Adam and Eve to "eat" from the "tree of knowledge of good and evil" because it would lead to knowledge of how to regain spiritual immortality.

The above passage further suggests that there exists a Custodial intention to block human remembrance of a Supreme Being. The implication is that people not only have buried memories of prior spiritual existence, but they also hold hidden recollections of contact with a Supreme Being. If such memory exists, we can at once understand why the Custodians would try to veil it. By blocking such memory, the Custodial society further deepens spiritual ignorance and is better able to promote its religious pretenses and fictions.

This is not to say that the Custodial society would alone be guilty of causing spiritual deterioration and amnesia. Such deterioration would have probably begun long before the formation of the Custodial civilization. Mormon writings would only suggest that Custodians took advantage of such deterioration and hastened it to suit their own ends.

We have noted the use of breeding war as a Custodial tool for maintaining control over the human population. According to the *Book of Mormon*, this tool was used in the ancient American civilizations where "God" was held responsible for the outbreak of many wars:

> *And it came to pass that I beheld that the wrath of God was poured out upon the great and abominable church [Satan's church], insomuch that there were wars and rumors of wars among all the nations and kindreds [families] of the earth.*
>
> 1 NEPHI 14:15

*Mormon* states that wars would continue to be bred over the generations as "God's" tool for maintaining control:

> *Yea, as one generation passeth to another there shall be bloodsheds, and great visitations [disasters] among them; wherefore, my sons, I would that ye would remember; yea, I would that ye would hearken to my words.*
>
> 2 NEPHI 1:12-13

In light of the above, it is not surprising to discover that Mormonism is another branch of the Brotherhood network, even though the Mormon Church has traditionally been opposed to other secret societies, such as Freemasonry. Mormon opposition to Freemasonry is based upon passages in the *Book of Mormon* which seem to suggest that God opposes secret societies. For example, we read in *2 Nephi 26:22-23*:

> *And there are also secret combinations, even as in times of old, according to the combinations of the devil, for he is the foundation of all these things . . .*

Many people object to interpreting the above passage as being directed against societies like Freemasonry. After all, did not Joseph Smith himself create a multileveled priesthood patterned after Freemasonry, complete with secret ceremonies and a ceremonial apron?

The Mormon priesthood is divided into two sections: the Priesthood of Aaron (named after Moses' brother) and the High Priesthood, better known as the Priesthood of Melchizedek (named after the Biblical king Melchizedek). According to *Alma 13:1-14,* the Mormon high priesthood is precisely the same one over which Melchizedek had reigned many centuries earlier. The Mormon Priesthood today continues to follow the step-by-step initiation process of other Brotherhood organizations. Its highest ceremonies are performed in secret and initiates are required to take vows of silence. During such ceremonies, initiates often wear ceremonial aprons as various "mysteries" are revealed to them through the use of symbols and allegory.

Joseph Smith claimed that he patterned the Mormon priesthood according to the dictates of an angel. He did not rely entirely on his extraterrestrial friend, however. Smith also became a Freemason for a short period of time in order to borrow from the Craft. According to Thomas F. O'Dea, writing in his book, *The Mormons:*

Joseph went to Masonry to borrow many elements of ceremony. These he reformed, explaining to his followers that the Masonic ritual was a corrupted form of an ancient priesthood ceremonial that was now being restored.[9]

Joseph Smith was made a Master Mason on March 16, 1842 at a lodge in Illinois. That same lodge was joined by other top Mormons. Perhaps the most famous Mormon Freemason was Brigham Young—the man who led the Mormon exodus across America to Utah and established the headquarters of the Church in that state, where it remains today.

The above facts do not mean that Mormonism was a branch of Freemasonry. Organizational ties between the

Mormon Church and Freemasonry were severed quite early on. Smith and the early Mormons went to Freemasonry to borrow, not truly to join. The Mormon Church was but another faction at war with other Brotherhood factions. Mormons were told that their religion was "the only true and living church upon the face of the whole earth, with which I, the Lord, am well pleased. . . ." *(Doctrines and Covenants 1:30.)* This proclamation naturally conflicts with every other Custodial religion which declares the same thing, thereby setting in motion more senseless "religious" disputes to keep people fighting and disunited. Some people are still fighting the Mormons now. Joseph Smith suffered for it when he was murdered by an angry mob in 1844.

Throughout the Church's embattled history, Mormons have found solace in the future Judgment Day promised by Smith's angel. Smith's writings clearly indicated that the Judgment Day was to arrive during his own generation. Perhaps the predicted Great Conflagration did arrive: the American Civil War broke out in 1861. Many of Smith's personal followers were still alive to witness that brutal conflict which must have seemed like an Armageddon to many Americans.* As always, the promised millennium of peace and spiritual salvation did not follow that Armageddon, so

---

* Interestingly, the Southern secessionist and pro-slavery movements which had caused the Confederacy to split from the Union, and thereby set the stage for the Civil War, were greatly influenced by the Brotherhood network. We see this, for instance, in two of the many proposed flag designs for the new Confederacy: the designs prominently feature the Brotherhood's "All-Seeing Eye" of God. Before the outbreak of the War, a group of Southerners had created an influential pro-slavery secret society called the Knights of the Golden Circle. Those fraternal Knights were committed to the preservation of slavery in the lands bordering the Caribbean Sea—the so-called "Golden Circle." The seal of the Knights featured a cross similar to the Maltese cross used by the old Knights of Malta. The Knights of the Golden Circle eventually vanished and were replaced by the Knights of the Ku Klux Klan. The Klan was a crude Brotherhood-style secret society which arose in the turbulence of the postwar South. Reportedly founded as a joke, the Klan quickly grew and became a powerful social and political force in the South. Klan teachings are deeply racist and rooted in Aryanism.

Mormons did what so many other apocalyptic religions have done: they reinterpreted their Judgment Day prophecy to keep it alive even though it had clearly failed.

One great project of the Mormon Church today is the maintenance of a vast genealogical library—the world's largest. "Genealogy" is the study of family lineage and ancestry. It tells who gave birth to whom, as well as the racial and social characteristics of a person's family tree. The Mormon genealogical vaults are housed in a mountain in the Rocky Mountains about twenty miles south of Salt Lake City. The vaults are protected by 700-foot thick mountain granite and a 14-ton steel door. The library is clearly meant to survive almost anything. According to a Mormon pamphlet, ongoing record collection produces more than 60,000 rolls of microfilm each year containing data from deeds, marriage licenses, family Bibles, registers, cemetery lists, and other sources.

This remarkable activity began during the first half of the twentieth century. It is ostensibly carried out because Mormons believe that families go on forever. Mormons are taught that they need to trace family lines so that all those who lived and died in the past can be blessed in ceremonies performed in the present by modern Mormons. The Mormons, however, do not limit their genealogical research to just Mormon families. Their goal is to "perform the necessary genealogical research so that all those now or ever in the spirit world can be vicariously baptized."[10] Since every human being who has ever lived fits the above category, we must conclude that the Mormon objective is a complete genealogical record of the entire human race! According to the Mormon Church, that is precisely the goal of the project, to the degree that it can be accomplished.

This activity understandably concerns some people. Many individuals living today witnessed the racial madness of the German Nazis and might shudder at the devastating impact that the Mormon genealogical collection could have in the hands of racists. This unease is increased by early Mormon doctrines which had placed dark-skinned people in a greatly inferior position to whites. Aryanism was an important element of early Mormon philosophy. In *2 Nephi*

5:21-24, we read that dark skin was created by "God" as a
punishment for sin:

> . . . wherefore, as they (those being punished) were
> white, and exceeding fair and delightsome, that they
> might not be enticing unto my people the Lord God
> did cause a skin of blackness to come upon them.
>
> ·And thus saith the Lord God: I will cause that they
> shall be loathsome unto my people, save they shall
> repent of their iniquities.
>
> And cursed shall be the seed [sperm] of him that
> mixeth with their seed; for they shall be cursed even
> with the same cursing. And the Lord spake it, and it
> was done.
>
> And because of their cursing which was upon them
> they did become an idle people, full of mischief and
> subtlety, and did seek in the wilderness for beasts
> of prey.

Much to their credit, Mormons have recently dropped
these racist beliefs and now admit black people to the
priesthood. Mormons must nevertheless be alert to ensuring
that their genealogical records are never permitted to fall
into the hands of those who might desire them for racial
"purification" purposes.

Modern Mormon activities do exhibit many humanitarian
leanings. The Church, for example, encourages strong family
units. In 1982, I was gratified to see a television advertise-
ment produced by the Mormon Church that expresses the
importance of not ignoring a child's accomplishments. This
brings up a very important point:

No individual or organization is purely good or purely
bad. In our crazy universe, "absolute" good and "absolute"
evil just do not appear to exist. In the worst of people one
will always find a tiny ember of good (e.g., the psychopath
Adolf Hitler was kind to children), and in the best of
individuals there is always at least one thing that should
change. The majority of people who join a group or follow
a leader do so for the right reasons: they have heard an
element of truth or they seek the solution to a genuine

problem. The real trick in judging a person or group is to determine whether more good is being done than bad, and how the bad may be corrected without destroying whatever good there might be. The task is not usually an easy one.

Mormon writings declare that "God" (*i.e.,* Earth's Custodial management) intends to eventually eliminate the "spirit world" entirely as part of "God's" great utopian plan for mankind. In other words, nothing but the material universe is to ever exist as far as the people of Earth are concerned. This can be translated to mean total spiritual entrapment in physical matter. Such intentions would require that philosophies of strict materialism be created and imposed upon the human race so that humans do not look beyond the material universe. Such philosophies would teach that there is no spiritual reality and that all life, thought, and creation arise solely out of physical processes. Such ideas have become very fashionable and they are, sadly, helping to push the human race into an ever-deepening spiritual sleep. Leading this trend for many years was a political philosophy which had gained its initial momentum in 19th-century Germany. I am speaking, of course, of "communism"— that ever-so-curious mix of apocalypticism, materialism, and Protestant work ethic which was such a significant force in the 20th century.

# 31

# Apocalypse of Marx

THE FIRST FRENCH Revolution of 1789 marked the beginning of a long series of uprisings in France. A new Duke of Orleans, Louis-Philippe, became the figurehead of a July 1830 revolt which placed him on the throne of France as the ruler of a constitutional monarchy. Assisting him was the Marquis de La Fayette. Another of Louis-Philippe's important backers was a man named Louis-Auguste Blanqui, who was decorated by the new government for helping to make the 1830 revolution a success.

Blanqui remained an active revolutionary after 1830 and provided significant leadership for a long string of uprisings. According to Julius Braunthal, writing in his book, *History of the International,* "Blanqui was the inspiration of all uprisings in Paris from 1839 to the Commune* in 1871."[1]

---

*The Commune was a revolutionary group which governed Paris from March 18 to May 28, 1871

Blanqui belonged to a network of French secret societies which organized and planned the revolutions. Nearly all of those secret societies were outgrowths of Brotherhood activity and were patterned after Brotherhood organizations. Each society had a different function and ideological foundation for drawing people into the revolutionary cause. Although the revolutionary societies sometimes differed in matters of ideology and tactics, they had one objective in common: to bring on the revolution. Many revolutionary leaders participated in several of these organizations simultaneously.

One of the most effective of the secret French revolutionary groups was the Society of the Seasons, over which Blanqui shared leadership. This society was designed explicitly for the purpose of hatching and carrying out political conspiracies. One of the Society's allied organizations was the "League of the Just." The League of the Just was founded in 1836 as a secret society and it aided Blanqui and the Society of the Seasons in at least one revolt: the uprising of May 1839. A few years after that uprising, the League was joined by a man who would later become the revolutionaries' most famous spokesperson: Karl Marx.

Karl Marx was a German who lived from 1813 until 1883. He is considered by many to be the founder of modern communism. His writings, especially the *Communist Manifesto*, are an important cornerstone of communist ideology. As some historians have pointed out, however, Karl Marx did not originate all of his ideas. He was acting largely as a spokesperson for the radical political organization to which he belonged. It was during his membership in the League of the Just that Marx penned the *Communist Manifesto* with his friend, Friedrich Engels. Although the *Manifesto* contained many of Marx's own ideas, its true accomplishment was to put into coherent form the communist ideology which was already inspiring the secret societies of France into revolt.

Because of his intellect, Marx gained considerable power within the League of the Just, and his influence caused a few changes within that organization. Marx did not like the romantic conspiratorial character of the secret society network to which he belonged and he was able to do away with some of those traits within the League. In 1847, the name of the League was changed to "Communist League." Associated with the Communist League were various "workers" organizations, such as the German Worker's Educational Society (GWES). Marx founded a branch of the GWES in Brussels, Belgium.

At this point, we can see the extraordinary irony in these events. The same network of Brotherhood organizations which had given us the United States and other "capitalist" countries through revolution, was now actively creating the ideology (communism) which would oppose those countries! It is crucial that this point be understood: both sides of the modern "communist vs. capitalist" struggle were created by the same people in the same network of secret Brotherhood organizations. This vital fact is almost always overlooked in history books. Within a short one hundred year period, the Brotherhood network had given the world two opposing philosophies which provided the entire foundation for the so-called "Cold War": a conflict that lasted nearly half a century.

Considering the affiliation of Karl Marx to the Brotherhood network, it should come as no surprise that Marx's philosophy follows the basic pattern of Custodial religion. Marxism is strongly apocalyptic. It teaches a "Final Battle" creed involving forces of "good" and "evil" followed by a utopia on Earth. The primary difference is that Marx molded those beliefs into a nonreligious framework and tried to make them sound like a social "science" rather than a religion. In Marx's scheme, the forces of "good" are represented by the oppressed "working classes," and "evil" is represented by the ownership classes. Violent conflict between the two classes is portrayed as natural, inevitable, and ultimately healthy because such conflict will eventually result in the emergence of a utopia on Earth. Marx's idea of inevitable class tension reflects the Calvinist belief that conflict on Earth is healthy because it means that the forces of "good" are actively battling the minions of "bad."

Marx tried to make his "inevitable conflict" idea sound scientific by fitting it into a concept known as the "dialectic." The "dialectic" was a notion espoused by another

German philosopher, Hegel (1770-1831). Hegel's idea of the "dialectic" can be explained this way: from a thesis (an idea or concept) and an antithesis (a contradictory opposite) one can derive a synthesis (a new idea or concept which is different than the first two, but is a product of them). Marx took this seemingly scientific idea and incorporated it into his theory of social history. In the communist model of "dialectical materialism," social, economic, and political change arises out of the clash of contradictory, and often violent, opposites. In this way, the endless wars of history and the unceasing array of opposing factions on Earth are said to be a natural part of existence out of which all social change must occur. This makes endless social conflict seem desirable, and that is precisely the illusion Marx tried to convey in his "class struggle" theory.

The communist vision of utopia is a curious, but significant one. In it, everyone is a worker equal to every other worker. No one owns anything but everyone together owns everything; everybody gets everything they need but not necessarily everything they want; but before this utopia occurs, everyone must first live in a dictatorship. Whew! This bizarre vision of utopia seems clearly designed to maintain mankind as a work race and to encourage humans to accept conditions of social repression (*i.e.,* dictatorship).

By Marx's lifetime, spiritual knowledge had reached a severe state of decay. The "quickie salvation" of the Protestants and the embarrassing rituals practiced by nearly all religions were understandably driving many rationally-minded people out of religion altogether. It is not surprising that the validity of all spiritual reality began to be questioned. This questioning led many people to lean towards a strictly materialist outlook on life, and Marx provided a philosophy for many of those people to step into. Although Marx acknowledged the reality of spiritual existence, he erroneously stated that spiritual existence was entirely the product of physical and material phenomena. In this way, Marx's teachings helped promote the Custodial aims expressed in the *Book of Mormon* and in ancient Sumerian tablets of bringing about a permanent union between spiritual beings and human bodies. Marx's writings gave this union "scientific" acceptability by suggesting that spirit and matter could not be separated at all. Marxist philosophy added that "supernatural" reality (*i.e.*, reality existing outside the bounds of the material universe) is not possible. Marx's utopia therefore amounts to a Biblical Eden: a materialistic paradise in which everyone is a worker with no route to spiritual knowledge and freedom; in other words, a pampered spiritual prison.

During the same era in which communism was being shaped into an organized movement, the practice of banking was undergoing important developments. By the late 19th century, the new system of inflatable paper money was the established norm throughout the world. This money system was not adequately organized on an international scale, however, and that was the next step: to create a permanent worldwide central banking network which could be coordinated from a single fixed location.

One scholar to write about this development was the late Dr. Carroll Quigley, professor at Harvard, Princeton, and the Foreign Service School of Georgetown University. Dr. Quigley's book, *Tragedy and Hope, A History of the World in Our Time*, achieved a degree of fame because it was used by some members of the John Birch Society to prove their "Communist Conspiracy" ideas. Putting this notoriety aside, we find that Dr. Quigley's book is exhaustively researched and well worth reading. Dr. Quigley was not a "conspiracy buff," but was a highly-respected professor with outstanding academic credentials. Dr. Quigley's book describes in great detail the development and workings of the international banking community as it established the inflatable paper money system throughout the world.

Let us take a brief look at what Dr. Quigley had to say.

# 32

# Funny Money Goes International

IN HIS BOOK, *Tragedy and Hope,* Dr. Quigley divides the history of "capitalism" into several stages. The third stage, which is described as the period from 1850 until 1931, is defined by Dr. Quigley as the stage of Financial Capitalism. Dr. Quigley states:

> This third stage of capitalism is of such overwhelming significance in the history of the twentieth century, and its ramifications and influences have been so subterranean and even occult, that we may be excused if we devote considerable attention to its organizations and methods. Essentially what it did was to take the old disorganized and localized methods of handling money and credit and organize them into an integrated system, on an international basis, which worked with incredible and well-oiled facility for many decades.[1]

Dr. Quigley described the overall intent of the new integrated system:

. . . the powers of financial capitalism had another far-reaching aim, nothing less than to create a world system of financial control in private hands able to dominate the political system of each country and the economy of the world as a whole. This system was to be controlled in a feudalist fashion by the central banks of the world acting in concert, by secret agreements arrived at in frequent private meetings and conferences. The apex of this system was to be the Bank for International Settlements in Basel, Switzerland, a private bank owned and controlled by the world's central banks which were themselves private corporations. Each central bank . . . sought to manipulate foreign exchanges, to influence the level of economic activity in the country, and to influence cooperative politicians by subsequent economic rewards in the business world.[2]

In the English-speaking world, the newly-organized central banks exerted significant political influence through an organization they supported known as the Round Table. The Round Table was a "think tank" designed to affect the foreign policy actions of governments.

The Round Table was founded by an Englishman named Cecil Rhodes (1853-1902). Rhodes had created a vast diamond and gold-mining operation in South Africa and in the two African nations named after him: Northern and Southern Rhodesia (today Zambia and Zimbabwe, respectively). Rhodes, who was educated at Oxford, did the most of any Englishman to exploit the mineral resources of Africa and to make the southern African continent a vital part of the British Empire.

Rhodes was more than a man driven to make a personal fortune. He was very concerned with the world and where it was headed, especially in regard to warfare. Although he lived almost a century ago, he envisioned a day when weapons of great destruction could destroy human civilization. His farsightedness inspired him to channel his considerable talents and personal fortune into building a world political system under which it would be impossible for a war of such magnitude to occur. Rhodes intended to create a one-world government led by Britain. The world government would be strong enough to stamp out any hostile actions by any group of people. Rhodes also wanted to unify people by making English the universal language. He sought to diminish nationalism and to increase awareness among people that they were part of a larger human community. It was with these goals in mind that Rhodes established the Round Table. In his last will, Rhodes also created the famous "Rhodes Scholarship"—a program still in operation today. The Rhodes scholarship program is designed to promote feelings of universal citizenship based upon Anglo-Saxon traditions.

Rhodes' heart was clearly on the right track. If successful, he would have undone many of the harmful effects caused by purported Custodial actions and by the corrupted Brotherhood network. A universal language would have undone the damaging effects described in the Tower of Babel story of dividing people into different language groups. Promoting a sense of universal citizenship would help overcome the types of nationalism which help generate wars. Something went wrong, however. Rhodes committed the same error made by so many other humanitarians before him: he thought that he could accomplish his goals through the channels of the corrupted Brotherhood network. Rhodes therefore ended up creating institutions which promptly fell into the hands of those who would effectively use those institutions to oppress the human race. The Round Table not only failed to do what Rhodes had intended, but its members later helped create two of the 20th century's most heinous institutions: the concentration camp and the very thing that Rhodes had dedicated his life to preventing: the atomic bomb.

Rhodes' idea for the Round Table had begun in his early twenties. At the age of 24, while a student at Oxford, Rhodes wrote his second will, which described his plans by bequeathing his estate for:

> . . . the establishment, promotion and development of a Secret Society, the true aim and object whereof shall be the extension of British rule throughout the world . . .

and finally the foundation of so great a power as to hereafter render wars impossible and promote the best interests of humanity.[3]

Rhodes' secret society, the Round Table, was finally born in 1891. It was patterned after Freemasonry with its "inner" and "outer" circles. Rhodes's inner circle was called the Circle of Initiates and the outer was the Association of Helpers. The organization's name, the Round Table, was an allusion to King Arthur and his legendary round table. By implication, all members of Rhodes' Round Table were "knights."

It was inevitable that Rhodes' success and political influence would bring him into contact with other "movers and shakers" of English society. Among them, of course, were the major financiers of Britain. One of Rhodes' chief supporters was the English banker, Lord Rothschild, head of the powerful Rothschild branch in England. Lord Rothschild was listed as one of the proposed members for the Round Table's Circle of Initiates. Another Rhodes associate was the influential English banker, Alfred Milner.

After Rhodes died in 1902, the Round Table gained increased support from members of the international banking community. They saw in the Round Table a way to exert their influence over governments in the British Commonwealth and elsewhere. In the United States, for example, according to Dr. Quigley:

> The chief backbone of this [Round Table] organization grew up along the already existing financial cooperation running from the Morgan Bank in New York to a group of international financiers led by the Lazard Brothers.[4]

From 1925 onward, major contributions to the Round Table came from wealthy individuals, foundations, and companies associated with the international banking fraternity. They included the Carnegie United Kingdom Trust, organizations associated with J. P. Morgan, and the Rockefeller and Whitney families.

After World War I, the Round Table underwent a period of expansion during which many subgroups were created. The man responsible for getting many of the subgroups started was Lionel Curtis. In England and in each British dominion, Curtis established a local chapter (in Quigley's words, a "front group") of the Round Table called the Royal Institute of International Affairs. In the United States, the Round Table "front group" was named the Council on Foreign Relations (CFR).

Many Americans today are familiar with the New York-based Council on Foreign Relations. The CFR is usually thought of as a "think tank" from which come a great many political appointees at the Federal level. Under the Presidential administration of Ronald Reagan, for example, more than seventy administration members belonged to the Council, including a number of top cabinet members. The CFR has dominated earlier Presidential administrations as well, and it dominates the present administration. The chairman of the CFR for many years has been banker David Rockefeller, former chairman of the Chase Manhattan Bank. Another Chase executive chaired the CFR before that. The warning of Thomas Jefferson has come true. The banking fraternity has exercised a strong influence on American politics, notably in foreign affairs, and the Council on Foreign Relations is one channel through which it has done so. Regrettably, that influence has helped to preserve inflation, debt and warfare as the status quo.

When Cecil Rhodes was alive, he gained considerable power in South Africa and served for a number of years as colonial governor there. He had a unique and effective way of delegating power. According to one of Rhodes' closest friends, Dr. Jameson, Rhodes gave a great deal of autonomy to his trusted men. Dr. Jameson once wrote:

> . . . Mr. Rhodes left the decision [on what to do in a situation] to the man on the spot, myself, who might be supposed to be the best judge of the conditions. This is Mr. Rhodes' way. It is a pleasure to work with a man of his immense ability, and it doubles the pleasure when you find that, in the execution of his

plans, he leaves all to you; although no doubt in the last instance of the Transvaal business he has suffered for this system, still in the long run, the system pays. As long as you reach the end he has in view he is not careful to lay down the means or methods you are to employ. He leaves a man to himself, and that is why he gets the best work they are capable of out of all his men.[5]

This can be an effective style of leadership, except when the means used to achieve an end create their own problems. Some of the methods used by Rhodes' men did more long-term harm than immediate good. In South Africa, for example, a struggle between Dutch settlers (the "Boers") and the English erupted into the Boer War. During that conflict, one of the British officers under Rhodes, Lord Kitchener, established concentration camps to hold captured Boers. The camps were decreed by Kitchener on December 27, 1900 and over 117,000 Boers were eventually imprisoned within forty-six camps. Conditions were so inhumane that an estimated 18,000 to 26,000 people died, primarily from disease. It was tantamount to mass murder. Today we associate concentration camps with Nazi Germany and communist Russia, but their 20th-century usage actually began with the English under Lord Kitchener.

Perhaps the greatest irony in the story of the Round Table was the role of that organization in creating the atomic bomb. After Rhodes' death, the Round Table groups went on to establish other organizations. One of them was the Institute for Advanced Study (IAS) located in Princeton, New Jersey. The IAS greatly assisted the scientists who were developing the first atomic bomb for the United States. Institute members included Robert Oppenheimer, who has been dubbed the "Father of the A-Bomb," and Albert Einstein, to whom the Institute was like a home.

As we have seen, the world was undergoing many important developments as it entered the 20th century. Central banking was being organized into an international network. Bankers gained great influence in British and American foreign affairs through such groups as the Round Table and the Council on Foreign Relations. Meanwhile, the communist movement was gaining increasing momentum in Europe. This momentum bore fruit in 1917 when communist revolutionaries established their first "dictatorship of the proletariat" in Russia.

Once again, the world was on the road to a Biblical utopia.

# 33

# The Workers' Paradise

TO MANY PEOPLE then living, the period from 1914 until the mid-1930's was a full-blown fulfillment of Apocalyptic prophecy. Those years witnessed a devastating world war, a sudden worldwide influenza epidemic which killed tens of millions of people within a short period of time, and an international financial collapse marked in Germany by a hyperinflation of its currency.

Sudden meteorological changes also occurred. Portions of the United States became arid "Dust Bowls." This brought about large-scale crop destruction and the loss of many family farms to foreclosure. This was a period in which reports of spectacular "fireballs" (brilliant blazing meteors) were published by the *New York Times* with increasing frequency. Some fireballs seemed to bring with them violent storms, earthquakes and other natural disasters. New messiahs were appearing throughout the world. Surely, believed many, God was ushering in the Day of Judgment.

The beginning of the 20th century witnessed many changes in Germany. The autonomous principalities were being merged into a single German nation. Leading this unification effort was the Prussian Hohenzollern dynasty, which was also in the process of forging a large German war machine. This machine was commanded by the Kaiser William, a Hohenzollern, who helped plunge Europe into World War I.

Behind the German militarization lay the Brotherhood network. In the early 1900's, a number of mystical organizations in Germany were espousing a curious mix of Aryan Master Race ideas and mystical concepts about the future glories of Germany. This concoction resulted in the notion of a German Master Race. One of the most prominent writers in that genre was Houston Stewart Chamberlain, an Englishman raised in Paris and tutored as a young man by a Prussian. His most important work, *Die Grundlagen des Neunzehnten Jahrhunderts* ("The Foundation of the Nineteenth Century"), was published in 1899. In that work, Chamberlain extolled the glories of "Germanism" and announced that Germany was the nation best suited to bring about a "new order" in Europe. He indicated that Germans belonged to the western Aryan group of peoples and were therefore racially superior to all others. From Germany would arise a new race of "Supermen," he declared. Chamberlain believed in eugenics (improving the human race by carefully choosing natural parents) and he proclaimed that all Aryan Germans had a duty to breed the superrace from their Aryan seed. Chamberlain also did not hesitate to express his anti-Semitism. He stated that Jews introduced an alien influence to Europe and that they debased all cultures into which they became assimilated.

Emperor (Kaiser) Wilhelm of Germany and many members of the German Officer Corps were deeply inspired by Chamberlain's writings. The Kaiser invited Chamberlain to the royal court and reportedly greeted Chamberlain with the words, "It was God who sent your book to the German people and you personally to me."[1] Chamberlain remained a guest at the emperor's palace at Potsdam where he became a spiritual mentor to the Kaiser. The mystical ideas espoused by Chamberlain did much to push the Kaiser and other German leaders into the megalomania that brought about World War I.

World War I itself was triggered by a series of crises caused by the assassination of Austrian Archduke Franz Ferdinand, heir apparent to the Austrian throne. He and his wife, Duchess Sofia, were shot on June 28, 1914 in Sarajevo by Serbian assassins who belonged to a secret occult society called the "Black Hand." A political chain reaction followed the killing, and World War I got underway when the German Chief of Staff, General Helmuth von Moltke (himself a mystic, although by some accounts not as fanatical about German destiny as the Kaiser), ordered full military mobilization, followed by an invasion of France on August 1, 1914.

Members of the mystical network had once again started a brutal and senseless war.

There is another story from World War I worth sharing. It is the tale of an unusual peace. It was told in *Parade* magazine by the writing team of Irving Wallace, David Wallichinsky, and Amy Wallace in their "Significa" column. Here is the story as they wrote it:

> Amid the horrors of World War I, there occurred a unique truce when, for a few hours, enemies behaved like brothers.
>
> Christmas Eve in 1914 was all quiet on France's Western Front, from the English Channel to the Swiss Alps. Trenches came within 50 miles of Paris. The war was only five months old, and approximately 800,000 men had been wounded or killed. Every soldier wondered whether Christmas Day would bring another round of fighting and killing. But something happened: British soldiers raised "Merry Christmas" signs, and soon carols were heard from German and British trenches alike.
>
> Christmas dawned with unarmed soldiers leaving their trenches, as officers of both sides tried unsuccessfully to stop their troops from meeting the enemy in the middle of no-man's land for songs and conversation. Exchanging small gifts—mostly sweets and cigars—they passed Christmas Day peacefully along miles of the front. At one spot, the British played soccer with the Germans, who won 3-2.

In some places, the spontaneous truce continued the next day, neither side willing to fire the first shot. Finally the war resumed when fresh troops arrived, and the high command of both armies ordered that further "informal understandings" with the enemy would be punishable as treason.[2]

The above is another one of those small, but noteworthy, episodes revealing that human beings do not seem to be naturally prone to war. Given the chance, they will lay down their arms and engage in far more constructive and lighthearted pursuits. What caused those soldiers to fight again were the pressures of an artificial social structure arising out of many of the factors described in this book.

One major event of World War I was the Russian Bolshevik Revolution of 1917. This was the revolution which turned Russia into the communist nation we knew for most of the 20th century. The Revolution occurred one year before the end of World War I. It was led in large part by Vladimir Ilyich Ulyanov, who is better known by his code name, "Lenin."

At the time of the Revolution, Russia was an enemy of Germany. The grimness of World War I had aroused in the Russian people a strong anti-German sentiment. Opponents of Bolshevism were able to use this sentiment against the Bolsheviks by accusing Lenin of being a German agent. To some degree, this accusation was true. Sir Winston Churchill, Prime Minister of Great Britain during World War II, wrote, "They [the Germans] transported Lenin in a Sealed Train like a plague bacillus from Switzerland to Russia."[3] Churchill was referring to the train on which Lenin and his entourage traveled from their revolutionary headquarters in Switzerland through Germany to Russia in order to lead the Revolution which had already gotten underway. The German military guaranteed safe passage for Lenin's train through Germany, but would not permit Lenin or his followers to step off the train while it was on German soil. At the train's first stop in Germany after crossing the border from Switzerland, it was met and boarded by two German officers who provided a silent escort for the revolutionary party. The officers had been briefed earlier by General Erich Ludendorff, Chief of Staff of the German 8th Army on the Eastern Front. Ludendorff later became one of Germany's most powerful political figures and a prominent supporter of Adolf Hitler.

Michael Pearson, author of an excellent book, *The Sealed Train*, presents evidence that the Germans continued to support the Bolsheviks even after the Russian Revolution was over. The German military wanted to ensure that the Bolsheviks were able to retain their power in Russia. According to German Foreign Office records released after World War II, the Foreign Office had allocated by February 5, 1918 a total of 40,580,997 German marks for Russian "propaganda" and "special purposes." Most of that money is believed to have been sent directly to the new communist regime. According to the same documents, fifteen million marks had been released to Russia by the German Treasury just one day after Lenin officially assumed power in November of 1917. A telegram sent December 3, 1917 by Richard von Kuhlman, German Foreign Secretary, stated:

> . . . it was not until the Bolsheviks had received from us a steady flow of funds through various channels that they were in a position to build up their main organ Pravda, to conduct energetic propaganda and appreciably to extend the originally narrow base of their party.[4]

Three months later, another telegram sent by von Kuhlman revealed:

> . . . the Bolshevik movement could never have attained the scale or the influence which it has today without our continual support.[5]

Lenin understandably denied accusations that he had received any assistance from Germany. Germany was Russia's enemy, and Lenin would have been considered a traitor to Russia. After all, why would capitalist Germany assist communists? The oppressive Russian Tsar had already abdicated before the Revolution and the Provisional Government set up in his place was a republican form of government patterned after the United States.

Most people believe that Germany helped Lenin overthrow the Provisional Government in order to end Russian involvement in World War I. German military leaders wanted nothing more than to disengage from the Eastern Front so that badly-needed soldiers and supplies could be moved elsewhere. The Provisional Government had continued the war against Germany, whereas the Bolsheviks did indeed pull Russia out of World War I after they took power.

The question is then raised: why did Germany aid *communist* revolutionaries? There were other political groups in Russia which could have been supported.

For one thing, the Bolsheviks probably stood the best chance at success. A more important factor is that some very prominent German industrialists and financiers with influence into the German military were supporters of the communist movement. Their support had begun long before World War I. One of Karl Marx's most visible backers had been the wealthy German industrialist Friedrich Engels. Engels even co-authored the *Communist Manifesto* with Marx. Significant support for communism also came from the German banking community. Max Warburg, a top leader in German finance, lent his assistance to the Bolsheviks, as did banker Jacob Schiff who, though an American, came from the same German family which had shared a house in Frankfurt generations earlier with the Rothschild family. According to Schiff's grandson, Schiff had loaned about twenty million dollars to the early communist government in Russia. The combined infusion of Western loans and German treasury money was the only thing that enabled the early Bolshevik regime to survive.

There were many reasons why Western bankers financed the Bolsheviks. The common origins of communism and the inflatable paper money system in the same mystical network is one factor to be considered. Marxism closely followed the basic philosophical pattern of Christianity and other Custodial religions with their "final battle" and utopian messages. Perhaps the most important fact about modern communism to explain Western banking support is the fact that communism is actually capitalism taken to an extreme. To understand this, we must take a look at what "capitalism" really is.

"Capitalism" and "free enterprise" are often equated. They should not be. "Free enterprise" is unfettered economic activity; it occurs where there is a free and open market for the production and barter of goods and services. Entrepreneurs (people who start businesses and take the risks) are the backbone of "free enterprise" systems.

"Capitalism," on the other hand, has two basic definitions. The first definition elates to so-called "capital goods." Those are goods that are used to manufacture other products. A typical capital good would be a machine used on an assembly line. A "capitalist" can therefore mean a person who buys capital goods and uses them to manufacture other products for a profit. This type of capitalist is usually found in a "free enterprise" system, but he or she does not require a free enterprise system to survive. He or she can exist in almost any type of political or economic system so long as a profit is made. In fact, this type of capitalist often survives best in a closed enterprise system where there is little or no competition.

Governments are capitalists when they own and invest in capital equipment.

The second type of capitalist is the "financial capitalist." Financial capitalism is the control of resources through the investment and movement of money. It may or may not involve the purchase of capital goods. A financial capitalist usually invests his money in company stocks and influences the use of resources by determining what enterprises he will invest in. A financial capitalist may also be a banker who is entitled to create inflatable paper money to lend, and who is able to influence the use of resources by how he lends out his "created out of nothing" money. The financial capitalist also does not require a free enterprise system to survive and often benefits from monopolies.

As we can see, capitalism is not the same creature as free enterprise, even if they often co-exist. Free enterprise and capitalism frequently come into conflict with one another because capitalism tends to move in the direction of monopoly and free enterprise tends to favor free and open markets accessible to any entrepreneur.

In 1989 and the early 1990's, Russia and most Eastern European nations voluntarily dismantled communism in their nations to replace it with Western-style democracy. The Soviet Union was abolished and most of the Soviet republics became independent countries united in a loosely-knit confederation called the "Commonwealth of Independent States." Private ownership of land and business was restored to a large extent. Nevertheless, it is still useful to discuss what the Soviet Union was like under communism to understand how this important Brotherhood faction did so much to perpetuate significant problems within our own lifetime. Furthermore, communism still dominates other nations and continues to inspire revolutionary conflict in the Third World.

The economic system of communist Russia was an ultra-capitalist one because its industry was even more monopolized, and the nation's economy was even more dominated, by the same institutions which dominate capitalist nations. The most significant of those institutions was the Soviet central bank, which operated just like the central banks of Western nations. The major difference was that the Russian central bank had, and still has at the time of this writing, an even more intrusive role in the country's economic life.

The Soviet Union's central bank is called the Gosbank. It is both a central bank and commercial bank rolled into one. As of 1980, the Gosbank had approximately 3,500 branches and 150,000 employees. Major Soviet enterprises, which were all government owned, depended upon the Gosbank for loans to tide them through periods when their outlays were greater than their incomes. In other words, communist government enterprises in the Soviet Union also operated on a profit-loss basis and they had to borrow money from the Gosbank when they suffered a loss. As in non-communist nations, Soviet enterprises paid interest on the money they borrowed. The only difference was that the Gosbank charged a fixed interest rate whereas many Western banks have a fluctuating rate.

The Gosbank was, and still is, a "bank of issue"; *i.e.*, it is empowered to issue money. Gosbank creates money "out of nothing" just as Western banks do. Although the Gosbank was ostensibly under government control in communist Russia, it was in fact a semi-autonomous institution to which Soviet enterprises were, and still are, deeply in debt.

The Gosbank was even more dominant in Soviet financial affairs than are central banks in Western nations because all transactions between Soviet enterprises had to go through the Gosbank. This allowed the Gosbank to oversee all day-to-day financial transactions involving Soviet enterprises. The Gosbank was also in charge of dispersing wages to all of the workers. It was an enormous bureaucracy which regulated Soviet economic activity to a remarkable degree.

As we can see, communist Russia was a financial capitalist's dream. The Marxist idea that everything is owned "collectively" under communism simply meant that a select elite in banking and government had complete authority to direct the use of all exploitable resources in the country. Soviet workers were paid wages with which they could buy personal goods, but under Soviet law they could not own land, buildings, businesses, or any large industrial equipment. Soviet citizens could sell only "used" or personally-produced items, but they could not hire others for personal profit or engage in middleman activities. Although there existed limited exceptions to these restrictions and a flourishing black market, Soviet laws nevertheless created an effective monopoly in which Russian workers were highly exploited in a rigid feudalistic system; we need only compare communist Russia to medieval feudalism to appreciate that fact:

As in old European feudalisms, the majority of the Soviet citizens were forced to suffer chronic scarcities of goods and services, and they were told that they had to endure it as a sacrifice for the good of mother Russia.

As in old feudalisms, the Soviet people were effectively "tied to the land" by a rigid bureaucracy which forbade people from moving without government approval. That regulation existed to control the economic and political life of the Soviet Union by deciding where people lived and worked. That was the same motive used to tie people to the land under old feudal lords. This caused the Soviet people to become, to some degree, serfs. Emigration to nations outside of the Iron Curtain was severely restricted which, again, added up to a form of serfdom because the people were anchored to the land on which they were born.

As in old feudalisms, the "elite" of communist Russia were accorded special luxuries and privileges denied by law to the "masses." In the communist U.S.S.R., such privileges included fancy stores in which only a relative handful were permitted to shop. The "elite" also found it easier to travel outside of the Soviet Union and to send their children abroad to be educated.

The old feudal lords maintained the system by offering a fortified castle into which the serfs could retreat when attacked by marauders or foreign armies. The Soviet system also stayed alive by encouraging xenophobia and by regularly reminding the Russian people about the invasions of Russia by Napoleon and Nazi Germany. The Soviet state promised its people protection against a frightening and dangerous outside world.

As we can perhaps see, Marxist glorification of the laborer fit the Soviet communist system very well. Because the system put such severe limitations on ownership, the vast majority of people were only valuable as workers and bureaucrats. Communism is also openly atheist, *i.e.,* it denies the existence of any spiritual reality. The Soviet communist system thereby satisfied the Custodial intentions expressed in ancient texts of preserving *Homo sapiens* as a creature of toil whose existence from birth until death shall be one long struggle for physical existence with no access to the spiritual knowledge which might set him free.

A significant aspect of the Russian Revolution was the role of espionage services in that upheaval. By the time of the Russian revolution, the international intelligence community had grown into a large and sophisticated affair with considerable influence. Throughout all of history, Brotherhood network members in positions of political power found intelligence services an ideal conduit for promoting Brotherhood social and political agendas because of the secrecy which typically surrounds intelligence activities. As a result, many intelligence services turned into sources of manipulation, upheaval, and betrayal. This behavior was already evident in Russia at the time of the Russian Revolution.

Before the Provisional Government was established, Russia was ruled by a Tsar (emperor). The last Tsar had at his disposal a vast intelligence network known as the "Okhrana." The Okhrana consisted of several intelligence organizations which performed all of the usual espionage functions with their secret agents, double-agents, agents provocateurs, and secret dossiers. The Okhrana spied on Tsarist friends and enemies alike and acted as Russia's internal security police. Inside Russia, the Okhrana engaged in extensive anti-subversive activities. The unpopular domestic activities of the Okhrana were a major issue used by the Bolsheviks to attack the Tsar.

The Tsar, of course, was eventually unseated. That must mean that the Okhrana had failed.

Or had it?

Historians have noted that the Okhrana had heavily infiltrated and assisted the Bolshevik movement. The Okhrana did this through spies known as "agent provocateurs." An agent provocateur is someone who deliberately agitates others into committing illegal or disruptive acts, usually in order to discredit or arrest the manipulated victim. In America and other nations today, agent provocateurs are often used by police agencies to entrap or compromise targeted people. These activities are sometimes called "sting" operations.

There seems to be an obvious reason for engaging in agent provocateur activities. If a targeted person does not commit an act for which he can be defamed, compromised, or imprisoned, he must be made to commit one. Because most provocateur actions are aimed against alleged criminals or subversives, it would appear that provocateurism is a useful tool for battling crime and subversion. In actual fact, it is not.

Upon careful analysis, a researcher soon discovers that provocateur actions are almost invariably carried out by people within intelligence and police agencies who are criminal or subversive themselves. Provocateurism proves to be a frequent cover for officially-sanctioned subversion or criminality. Provocateur actions are the best way for police and intelligence services to disguise their secret support of criminal and subversive elements. A clear example of this was the Russian Okhrana.

The Okhrana sent many agents to join the growing communist movement in Russia. Okhrana agents insinuated themselves into the innermost circles of the Bolshevik Party and directed many Bolshevik activities. This infiltration was so great that in the years 1908-1909, Okhrana agents constituted four out of five members of the Bolshevik Party's St. Petersburg Committee. Although arrests of revolutionaries were frequent, the Okhrana did far more to assist the Russian Bolsheviks under the guise of provocateurism than it did to harm them. The Okhrana provided regular monies and badly needed materials to the revolutionaries. It worked to stamp out two rival parties to the Bolsheviks: the Social Democratic Party and the Mensheviks. The Okhrana helped launch the Bolsheviks' major propaganda publication, *Pravda*. When *Pravda* was founded in 1912, Okhrana agents served as editor (Roman Malinovskii, who was also a member of the Bolshevik Central Committee and Lenin's chief lieutenant in Russia) and treasurer (Miron Chernomazov).

The Okhrana may have also supplied the Russian communists with the infamous dictator Joseph Stalin. Biographer Edward Ellis Smith, writing in his book, *The Young Stalin*, suggests that Stalin—a revolutionary who later rose to the top position of the Soviet government—may have entered the communist movement as an agent provocateur. Historians have pointed out that Stalin was a main contact between the Bolsheviks and the Tsarist police and he was able to get many badly needed items from the Okhrana.

After the Tsar abdicated in early 1917, the Provisional Government disbanded the entire Okhrana network. Bolshevik propaganda had loudly denounced the Okhrana and one would therefore have expected the victorious communists to leave the Russian intelligence apparatus dismantled. The Bolsheviks did just the opposite. Within six weeks of their overthrow of the Provisional Government, the Bolsheviks reestablished the intelligence network. This is perhaps not so surprising when we consider the heavy Okhrana involvement in the Bolshevik Party. Lenin merely did some organizational reshuffling, gave the Okhrana a new name, and made the intelligence arm of government even more dominant and oppressive than it had been under the Tsar. By 1921, only four years after the Revolution, the Bolshevik secret police employed ten times as many people as the Okhrana had done under the Tsar. It was an open secret in Russia that the Okhrana was back, more terrible than ever.

The name given to the reorganized Russian intelligence apparat was the "Extraordinary Commission to Combat Counterrevolution and Sabotage," better known as the "Checka." The Checka changed its name and form several times during the ensuing decades. In 1922 it became the GPU, then the OGPU, and in 1934 it was reorganized into the "Peoples Commission of Internal Affairs" (the "NKVD"). It was finally transformed into the modern KGB—history's largest intelligence organization. In 1992, the KGB employed approximately 90,000 staff officers for internal security and the political prison system alone. The KGB operated its own army of 175,000 border troops and carried out most of the espionage and agent provocateur actions for which the Soviet regime had been so well known. An organization the size of the KGB was obviously expensive to run. The enormous resources required to maintain this immense intelligence bureaucracy were factors which helped keep the Soviet economy so dismal. Soviet workers paid for the massive KGB every day with a lower standard of living which they are still struggling to raise. As of this writing, the KGB continues to exist within the Commonwealth of Independent States, but there has been some restructuring to reflect the breakup of the Soviet Union and some of the KGB's functions have changed.

One person to write about the Russian Revolution was Arsene de Goulevitch, a former general in the anti-Bolshevik

"White" Russian army. Although Goulevitch can hardly be considered impartial, he did have some interesting things to say in his book, *Tsarism and the Revolution*.

According to Goulevitch, English secret agents were numerous in Russia before and during the Revolution. In fact, some financial support for the Leninist cause was rumored to have come from English banking sources. One of those rumored sources was Alfred Milner. As we recall, Milner was one of the organizers of the Round Table. He was also a major political figure in South Africa during the Boer War. It was during the Boer War that the English created the modern concentration camp. If Goulevitch's allegation contains any truth, then we might better understand where the Bolsheviks got the idea to establish a massive concentration camp system as part of the new communist economic system: namely, from the English.

The early Soviet concentration camp system was a large-scale affair that reached its height under Lenin's successor, Joseph Stalin. Under the brutal Stalin, a crash program was launched to industrialize Russia, beginning with Russia's first so-called "Five Year Plan." The Plan required large quantities of inexpensive labor. To acquire it, a widespread concentration camp network was set up in Russia. The camps were administered by Russia's secret police, the NKVD. Concentration camp inmates were slave laborers who worked under brutal conditions. Nearly all of the laborers were native Russians who had been imprisoned under various pretexts.

The camps were an integral part of the Soviet economy for many decades. In 1941, for example, 17% of the capital construction fund for Russia was allocated to the NKVD to help it operate the camps. Almost half of the chrome and two-thirds of Russia's gold production were carried out by camp inmates. Tens of millions of people passed through the camps and about 10% of them died there. An estimated three to four million people perished in the camps from the time of the camps' inception to 1950 alone.

The Soviet concentration camps were decidedly "capitalist" institutions in that they were designed to callously exploit human labor to an ultimate degree. The "downtrodden working classes" had became even more downtrodden under their communist "liberators." With the ongoing reforms in Russia, it remains to be seen what will happen with the concentration camps. As of this writing, they are still in use as prison labor camps.

The imposition on the Russian people of communism and its far-flung concentration camp system occurred during an already tumultuous era. World War I was a brutal conflict. It had claimed about ten million military casualties and millions more in civilian losses. When the war ended in late 1918, another catastrophe struck: a worldwide influenza epidemic. The epidemic lasted less than a year but managed in that surprisingly short time to kill over twenty million people; it was as sudden and nearly as devastating as the 14th-century Bubonic Plague. In Russia, these events were keenly felt. A famine, coupled with the influenza, killed about twenty million Russians between 1914 and 1924. The famine was caused largely by the communist revolution and the consequent economic upheavals.

For the beleaguered Russian people, these events were just the beginning of a growing nightmare.

Under the Five Year Plan begun in 1928 by Stalin, all privately-owned land was to be "collectivized," *i.e.*, it was to be put under government ownership. Many peasants and landowners understandably resisted. Stalin's government responded by launching a program of mass murder similar to the French Reign of Terror. Peasants and landowners were targeted for physical extermination in order to seize their land and remove them as obstacles to communist utopia. This extermination campaign lasted from 1929 until 1934. Millions of people were murdered for no other crime than that they happened to own land. In response, a rebellion broke out between 1932 and 1934 in which defiant peasants destroyed half of Russia's livestock. This rebellious act, coupled with the communist regime's attempt to bring in outside money by overexporting wheat (3.5 million tons within two years) resulted in another famine that claimed an additional five million Russian lives.

The total death count between 1917 and 1950 as a direct

and indirect result of the establishment of communism in Russia is estimated at roughly 35 to 40 million people. This is one of the largest mortality rates from any single episode in history. To this figure we should add the deaths associated with the establishment of communism in other countries, such as the two million land owners murdered in China during Mao Tse-Tung's crash industrial program of the 1950's, and the millions butchered in Cambodia in the early 1970's under the Khmer Republic. In terms of the sheer number of lives lost, communism was one of the single most catastrophic events in human history.

My purpose in this discussion is not to beat a drum for rabid anti-Communism. It is simply to indicate that the historical patterns we studied have continued to recur in the 20th century. Communism is little more than a rehash of a worn-out theme which has been repeated over and over again with the same tragic consequences. "Communism" is but another in a long line of destructive artificialities arising out of the mystical Brotherhood network that has helped keep people fighting, suffering, and dying for absolutely no purpose whatsoever. "Communism" was not an alternative to the enemies it claimed to fight, namely monopolistic "capitalism" and End-of-the-World religions. Modern communism was their natural outgrowth.

The dismantling of Soviet and European communism has been a cause for genuine elation throughout the world. Brotherhood factions have been coming and going throughout history, and the passing of each often brings about a period of resurgence. Unfortunately, East European reformers currently plan to preserve the inflatable paper money system and erect a graduated income tax scheme to help pay for it. Severe ethnic and nationalistic strife in several former communist nations reveals that other warring factions have been regenerated or created to mar the peace that should have come from the end of the Cold War.

# Robo-Sapiens

THE DEGRESSION FROM spiritual knowledge to materialist
ideology appears to follow a graduated path from one into
the other. We can chart this process beginning at the top
with how an accurate spiritual perspective might define
spiritual and physical realities, and proceed down to how
a materialist perspective would define them:

| *Spiritual Reality* | *Physical Reality* |
|---|---|
| Everyone is a spiritual being. Spiritual existence is ultimately independent of all material processes. Spiritual processes are senior to and effective upon the material universe. There is no known limit to the potential ability of any spiritual being. | Material realities are entirely the product of spiritual processes, and those realities can ultimately be created, changed, or vanished through spiritual processes. Full knowledge of all material and spiritual processes is possible. |

| *Spiritual Reality* | *Physical Reality* |
| --- | --- |
| Everyone is a spiritual being, but different classes of spiritual beings exist which cannot be changed. | Spiritual beings are subject to some "inevitable" or "unchangeable" laws governing the workings of the physical universe. |
| Everyone is a spiritual being, but there are senior spiritual beings to whom all other spiritual beings are inferior. | Material processes are primarily the result of the activities of "senior" spiritual beings to whom all other beings are inferior. |
| Everyone has a spiritual side to them, but there is only one purely spiritual being, usually a "one-only" God. | The material universe was created by a "one-only" God. There exist many "inevitable" laws of the universe that people can never hope to understand. |
| Spiritual reality exists, but it is dependent upon and arises out of the material universe. If there is a Supreme Being, it is probably either a material being or a scientific law. | Material processes alone account for any spiritual phenomena. Spiritual abilities, such as "ESP," "clairvoyance," etc., if they exist, are solely the result of as-of-yet undiscovered principles of the material universe. |
| Spiritual reality does not exist at all. Everything can be explained as products of material processes. | There is no reality other than the physical universe. Spiritual abilities, such as "ESP," etc., do not exist. |
| "Life" does not exist. All motion is the product of lifeless physical processes which cause the illusion of "life" and "thought." | |

Modern Western culture appears to be situated somewhere around the lower middle of the above chart. Leading the trend towards the bottom is a practice known as "scientific psychiatry." There are many fine people working in psychiatry, but the field as a whole has become increasingly politicized due to its use by governments in a variety of settings, and it has come to promote a strict materialist view. Modern psychiatry has sadly obliterated the last vestige of spiritual reality acknowledged even by Marx. To understand this development, let us briefly survey the history of scientific psychiatry.

Efforts to cure people of mental affliction are as old as history. It is to the ancient Greeks and Romans that modern psychiatry traces many of its origins. More than two thousand years ago, the Greek physician, Hippocrates (ca. 400 B.C.), had classified various forms of mental illness and rejected the popular notion that mental ills were caused by angry gods or demonic possession. In later Rome, physician Galen (2nd century A.D.) was one of the first to theorize a connection between the brain and mental functioning. After Galen, Western psychology reverted back to a belief in demons and witches for many centuries.

Perhaps the most important breakthrough in psychiatry occurred in Austria. Between 1880 and 1882, Viennese physician Josef Breuer discovered that he was able to cure a girl of severe hysteria by having her remember and relive under hypnosis a traumatic incident from her past. Her symptoms disappeared for good. Dr. Breuer had discovered that a person could actually be cured of mental ills simply through the act of remembering and confronting past incidents which may remain hidden from conscious memory without the assistance of a therapist. In some way, mind-aberrating pain is relieved through this process. Dr. Breuer had stumbled onto something extraordinarily significant, yet his discovery, though utilized to some extent in the psychoanalysis developed by Sigmund Freud, was never fully explored in psychiatry. Even Freud's psychoanalysis failed to take the next step, which was to develop precision methods for helping people accurately pinpoint aberrational incidents from the past and discharge the mental, physical and emotional pain contained in those incidents. Freud strayed off into his sloppy "free-association" methods which made the remembering process less precise. He also over-emphasized sexual incidents.

Breuer's vital breakthrough was dealt an even mightier blow by what was happening in neighboring Germany during his day. "Scientific psychiatry" was emerging.

One of the earliest centers of "scientific psychiatry" was Leipzig, Germany. There a man named Wilhelm Wundt (1832-1920) established the world's first psychological laboratory in 1879. Until that time, universities usually placed the study of psychology in their philosophy departments because of a lingering belief that there exists a spiritual side to man. It was Wundt's contention, however, that psychology belonged in a biological laboratory. To Wundt, human beings were only biological organisms to which there were no spiritual realities attached. He therefore considered his approach "scientific" rather than philosophical.

Wundt's theory about the mind was that human thought is caused by external stimulation bringing about bodily identification with other stimuli which the body had received and recorded in the past. When this identification occurs, the body, or brain, mechanically creates an act of "will" which responds to the new stimulus. There is no such thing as self-created thought or free will. To Wundt and his followers, man was but a sophisticated robot-type organism.

Wundt's ideas were based upon experiments conducted in his laboratories and elsewhere. Some of those experiments revealed that one could produce the physiological manifestations of different emotions by applying electronic stimulation to different parts of the brain. Experimenters erroneously concluded that the brain must therefore be the source of personality because it triggers the physical manifestations of emotion and thought. The fallacy in this reasoning is obvious. The person conducting the experiment is applying external stimulation. In other words, the brain centers are not self-triggering except in a very limited sense. The experiments proved that it takes something else, something external, to trigger those brain centers. What, then, triggers those centers when the experimenter is no longer applying his electrodes? There must be another external source—a missing element. That missing element appears to be the spiritual entity which produces its own energy output. Although Wundt and others used the experiments to "prove" a pure biological basis to human thought, the results were, in fact, subtly pointing in the opposite direction.

Erroneous or not, the stimulus-response model of behavior developed at Leipzig quickly became the "new wave" in psychiatry and received considerable support from the German government. Wundt himself remained the most influential figure in scientific psychiatry for 40 years. The Leipzig labs attracted many students from around the world, many of whom later became prominent names in psychiatry. For example, one Leipzig student from Russia was Ivan Petrovich Pavlov (1849-1936), who gained fame for his experiments with bells and salivating dogs. Duane P. Schultz, writing in his book, *A History of Modern Psychology*, sums it up well:

> Through these students, the Leipzig Laboratory exercised an immense influence on the development of psychology. It served as the model for the many new laboratories that were developing in the latter part of the nineteenth century. The many students who flocked to Leipzig, united as they were in point of view and common purpose, constituted a school of thought in psychology.[1]

By redefining the nature of thought and behavior, scientific psychiatry also redefined the nature of mental abnormality and its cure. Methods to bypass human free will and intellect (behavior modification) were explored and developed. Because human beings were viewed as strictly biological-chemical-electrical organisms, all mental illnesses were said to be the result of physiological processes somehow going "out of kilter." Experimenters theorized that mental illness could be cured by strictly physiological means, such as with drugs, shock treatment, or brain surgery. It was believed that such treatments could remedy the chemical or electrical "imbalances" and thereby cure the mental illness itself.

Out of these theories arose a multibillion dollar drug industry which pours out huge quantities of mood-altering drugs every year. These drugs are designed to relieve every mental ill from "can't get to sleep at night" to violent psychosis. In addition, many psychiatrists use special machines to send electrical shocks through a person's brain. Some may even resort to brain surgery. Now that we have had almost half a century to observe these cures in action, we can ask: have they benefited mankind? Is the world a saner place today than it was 50 years ago? To answer these questions, we might do well to analyze the cure most often prescribed by psychiatrists: psychotropic ("mind-affecting") drugs.

Psychotropic drugs are a mammoth industry. They comprise a large portion of the total prescription drug trade which in 1978 amounted to an estimated $16.7 billion wholesale value in global sales by U.S. manufacturers alone. This figure does not even include sales by Swiss and other European manufacturers. An excellent book, *The Tranquilizing of America,* revealed that the most frequently-prescribed psychotropic drug, Valium (Roche Laboratories), was prescribed over 57 million times in 1977, refills included. According to an advertisement published by Roche in 1981, almost eight million people, or about five percent of the adult U.S. population, would use Valium in that year! Add to that enormous figure the tens of millions of prescriptions for other psychotropic medications and we discover that an enormous quantity of mind and mood altering drugs are being consumed every year. In 1977, for example, the total number of U.S. prescriptions for twenty major psychotropic drugs amounted to over 150 million. That amounted to approximately 8.35 billion pills! These medications are being prescribed in similar quantities today.

This epidemic drug use is not an accident. Powerful psychotropic medications are energetically promoted to the medical community in glossy Madison Avenue advertisements in such publications as the *American Journal of Psychiatry* and through workshops and seminars sponsored by the drug companies.

Justified criticism has been leveled against drug-oriented psychiatry because of the number of patients who actually deteriorate as a result of their psychiatric treatment. For example, a surprisingly large number of people who commit apparently senseless acts of violence, such as shooting sprees and other grisly headline-grabbing acts, are people who were previously treated with psychotropic drugs. John Hinckley, Jr., for example, was under the influence of Valium when he attempted to assassinate U.S. President Ronald Reagan in 1981. Such coincidences are usually explained as an indication that those people were already mentally deranged before the violent episodes and, at worst, the drugs were simply not able to help them. On the other hand, critics point out that such individuals were often not violent before their treatment, but became violent only afterwards. Did psychiatric treatments actually worsen their mental states to the point of their going completely psychotic?

One of the great feathers in the cap of the U.S. Food and Drug Administration is its requirement that all drug manufacturers must list the side effects, or "adverse reactions," that their drugs have been known to cause. This mandatory disclosure warns physicians of possible dangers and guides them in knowing when to take a patient off a drug. Unfortunately, by the time an adverse reaction is visible to the doctor, the damage may already be done. Most adverse reactions do vanish when the medication is discontinued, but some side effects can be permanent and cause lasting complications. This is especially worrisome when we discover that many adverse reactions are psychological.

A person opening a copy of the *American Journal of Psychiatry* and seeing the drug ads for the first time may react with shock at not only the slick sales pitches, but also at the small print. Every advertised psychotropic medication has a long list of potential physical and psychological adverse reactions. Most of the listed side effects are in medical terms incomprehensible to the layman; however, many of them are quite understandable. Here is a sampling of some listed potential adverse reactions to popular psychotropic medications that have been advertised and prescribed in the 1980's:

The drug Surmontil (Ives Laboratories), which is promoted as a drug for helping a person overcome symptoms of depression, lists among its possible side effects:

Confusional states (especially in the elderly) with hallucinations, disorientation, delusions, anxiety, restlessness, agitation, insomnia and nightmares, hypomania [abnormal excitement]; exacerbation [intensification] of psychosis.[2]

Haldol (McNeil Pharmaceutical) is advertised as a way of handling an acutely agitated patient. It can cause:

Insomnia, restlessness, anxiety, euphoria, agitation, drowsiness, depression, lethargy, headache, confusion, vertigo, grand mal seizures, and exacerbation of psychotic symptoms including hallucinations, and catatonic-like behavioral states . . .[3]

Thorazine, which is promoted as a medication for handling psychotic adults and children, belongs to a class of drug which has been known to cause the following:

. . . psychotic symptoms, catatonic-like states, cerebral edema [excess brain fluid], convulsive seizures, abnormality of the cerebrospinal fluid proteins. . . . NOTE: Sudden death in patients taking phenothiazines [the drug classification to which Thorazine belongs] (apparently due to cardiac arrest or asphyxia due to failure of cough reflex) has been reported but no causal relationship has been established.[4]

The last sentence in the above quote is a remarkable bit of doublespeak. It states that giving someone this class of drug has coincided with their suddenly dying, but the manufacturer denies that there is any evidence that the drugs were responsible for the deaths! No doubt it was just an extraordinary coincidence that some people have had cardiac arrests or cough reflex failures at the time of taking the drug. Fate must indeed work in mysterious ways.

Stelazine, another Smith Kline drug, lists many of the same adverse reactions as Thorazine, and adds "hypotension (sometimes fatal); cardiac arrest"[5] to its long list of medical adverse reactions. The drug is advertised as "A Classic Antipsychotic."

Norpramin (Merrel Dow Pharmaceuticals, Inc.) lists the same adverse reactions quoted earlier for the drug Surmontil, but adds "heart block, myocardial infraction, stroke."[6]

Even the relatively "mild" drug, Valium, so widely prescribed today, warns:

> Paradoxical reactions, such as acute hyperexcited states, anxiety, hallucinations, increased muscle spasticity, insomnia, rage, sleep disturbances and stimulation have been reported; should these occur, discontinue drug.[7]

The above drugs are only a sample. Nearly every medication advertised in the *American Journal of Psychiatry* has a long list containing identical or similar potential adverse reactions. The implications of this are significant. These drugs have been known to sometimes seriously worsen a person's mental state or cause mental problems far more severe than those the patient began with!

As noted, physicians prescribe these drugs because the severe adverse reactions reportedly occur only in a minority of cases, and many side effects are reversible by discontinuing the drug. However, the road back from many adverse reactions can be a long one. A person suffering a psychotic break, whether from emotional stress or a drug, may take a long time to recover. In the meantime, he may do considerable damage to himself or to others. When we consider the enormous scale on which these drugs are prescribed, even a small percentage of patients suffering a severe psychological reaction will amount to a large number of individuals. This immediately explains the puzzle of why some mental patients seem to truly "go off the deep end" after treatment. Regrettably, few people will blame the drug even in cases where the drug may be the cause, but will instead blame the patient ("he was always teetering near the edge anyway") or society ("look at what society has done to this poor crazed individual"). The great tragedy is that some children may be affected by this. Many schools and treatment centers are quick to give powerful psychotropics to problem children and adolescents.

It is argued that the number of people who are helped by the drugs far exceed those who are worsened. Advocates cite statistics showing that drugs enable many patients to leave psychiatric institutions sooner and return to the community. Psychotropic drugs seem to enable some people to keep their psychological symptoms under control enough for them to lead useful lives in society. The question is: at what cost are these apparent benefits being obtained?

As many psychiatrists acknowledge, psychotropic drugs rarely cure mental illness. They simply suppress the symptoms. In this respect psychotropics are like cold medicines which can make a person feel better and appear healthier, but they rarely cure the underlying illness itself. When a person is removed from the medication, the symptoms usually recur. The patient functions no better than he or she did before, and may even be worse off from having suffered side effects from the drug. Many psychiatrists therefore do not speak of "cure," but of "maintenance." Psychiatry boasts a low "cure" rate, but a high "maintenance" rate. As long as factories churn out pills, drug "maintenance" can continue.

Is this fair to the patient? In the long run, is society really being helped?

The danger with maintenance-oriented psychiatry is that mental illness is in a sense "contagious." This fact is most obvious in the phenomenon of "mob psychology," as well as in other circumstances. If people are not actually being cured of mental ills but are only having their symptoms masked, and meanwhile mental aberration spreads from other causes, it follows that mental illness will probably increase in any society relying upon drug therapy. If psychotropics are also slamming thousands of people every year into a deeper psychological morass because of dangerous side effects, we can see that drug-oriented psychiatry risks pushing a society to ruin; yet psychotropics constitute the main form of therapy in most psychiatric institutions today.

The dangers of heavy psychotropic drugs are increased by another factor. A large problem facing today's psychiatric community is the abnormally high suicide rate of its practitioners. Psychiatrists in the United States have a suicide rate about six times that of the general population. The highest percentage of those self-inflicted deaths occur among practitioners working in mental hospitals. This high suicide rate is often viewed as an occupational hazard caused by frustration and by a psychiatrist's continuous contact with mental illness. Whatever the cause of it may be, this suicide statistic is a reason to be concerned for the welfare of mental patients. Suicides are usually preceded by a period of declining mental health. One rarely finds a genuinely stable and well-adjusted person committing suicide. One of the major duties of a psychiatrist is accurate diagnosis and proper treatment, yet one of the most common manifestations of mental illness is the visualization of one's own problems in other people. A psychiatrist in a pre-suicidal state therefore risks being the source of grievous misdiagnosis because he may diagnose a patient as having what the doctor is actually suffering from. Because wrong diagnosis and mistreatment can ruin a person's life, especially in a hospital setting where strong psychotropics, shock therapy and psychosurgery are used, it is vital that the treating psychiatrists and technicians be genuinely sane, social, and well-adjusted. Sadly, a statistically large minority of them are not.

The epidemic use of psychotropic drugs creates yet another significant problem. Drug abuse is considered one of today's major social ills. Law enforcement agencies spend an enormous amount of time and money to combat it. The fight against drug abuse is based on the philosophy that people should not take illegal drugs to alter their moods or mental states. Modern psychiatry defeats this campaign. Drug-oriented psychiatry tells us: Feeling depressed? Take a drug. Feeling too happy (manic)? Take a drug. Feeling unable to cope? Take a drug. Feeling too able to cope (megalomaniacal)? Take a drug. Feeling confused and uncertain? Take a drug. Feeling too certain (delusional)? Take a drug. Can't sleep? Take a drug. Too sleepy? Take a drug. Seeing things that aren't there (hallucinations)? Take a drug. Not seeing things that are there? Take a drug. Maintenance-oriented psychiatry promotes the very attitude upon which the illegal drug trade flourishes: want to feel better mentally and emotionally? Take a drug. The great irony is that some of the very same "conservative law-and-order" judges and lawmakers who demand stiffer penalties against illegal drug pushers are among those who are quickest to set up the legal machinery for committing people involuntarily to mental institutions where drugs as powerful as anything on the illegal market are routinely and openly used.

The purpose of this discussion is not to impugn the general mental therapy field. As I mentioned earlier, there are many fine psychiatrists in practice today. It should also be noted that many therapists and counselors who specialize in communication-oriented ("talk") therapy without drugs achieve excellent results and do much to help their clients. To understand the specific problems of scientific psychiatry, it is perhaps wise to remember that psychiatrists (but not most psychologists) are people with medical degrees. Doctors are trained in medical schools to cure physical problems by physical means: bombard an infection with antibiotics or fix a broken leg with a cast. Where many doctors stray is in their belief that a mental problem is the same as a broken leg or viral infection, and so they bombard the "mental illness" with a drug, or they shock it with electricity. Such an approach misses the mark because a "broken mind" must be healed under an entirely different set of rules. This is well recognized by the fact that most nations permit people to become therapists and counselors without a medical degree.

Have philosophies of strict materialism brought about a flourishing psychiatric profession which is bringing about greater sanity to patients, practitioners, and the world as a whole? Sadly, the answer seems to be no. Psychiatry started on the right track when it discovered that the mind could be cured of its inorganic ills by confronting past hidden traumas, but it failed to develop that discovery beyond the crude and haphazard techniques used today in psychotherapy. Psychiatry was derailed when it began to mask mental problems with chemicals, and when it developed bizarre methods for bypassing individual free will in favor of stimulus-response manipulation (behavior modification).

It is perhaps time to move away from the strict materialist perspective, to get off the drugs, and to begin restoring a sense of respect for the free will and intellect of human beings. We may then be able to truly start back on the road to genuine mental, social, and spiritual recovery for the human race.

# 35

# St. Germain Returns

THE UPHEAVALS OF the early 20th century convinced many people of that era that the Judgment Day was at hand. Many Christians and mystics anticipated an imminent Second Coming of Christ. True to prophecy, it came.

Heralding Jesus's "Second Coming" was the resurrected Count of St. Germain—the mysterious Brotherhood agent of the 18th century whose activities we followed in Chapter 26. After St. Germain's reported death in 1784, he was made to seem physically immortal. In the early 1930's, a man named Guy Warren Ballard claimed that St. Germain had spoken to him on a mountain in California. That conversation gave birth to an interesting new branch of the Brotherhood that would not only sponsor the return of St. Germain, but also the reappearance of "Jesus Christ."

Guy Warren Ballard was a mining engineer. In 1930, he went on a business trip to Mount Shasta in northern California. Ballard had become interested in mysticism before his trip and he wanted to use his off-duty hours at Mount Shasta to unravel rumors about the existence of a secret branch of the Brotherhood called the "Brotherhood of Mount Shasta." The Shasta Brotherhood was said to have a secret underground headquarters inside the famous California mountain.

The legends which had caught Mr. Ballard's interest began circulating before the turn of the century. Persistent rumors told of secret dwellers living inside Mount Shasta who practiced a profound mystical tradition. The secret dwellers were said to be descended from inhabitants of the ancient lost continent of "Lemuria" in the Pacific Ocean.

Whatever the truth behind such legends may or may not be, it is unquestioned that Mount Shasta has long been a focus of mystical activity. Associated with that mystical activity has been a significant UFO phenomenon. For example, in the May 1931 issue of the *Rosicrucian Digest* (published in the year following Mr. Ballard's trip to Shasta and a decade and a half before UFOs were popularized in the media), we read the following description of a flying "boat" in an article about the Shasta mystics:

> Many testify to having seen the strange boat, or boats, which sail the Pacific Ocean, and then rise at its shores and sail through the air to drop again in the vicinity of Shasta. This same boat was seen several times by the officials employed by the cable station located near Vancouver, and the boat has been sighted as far north as the Aleutian Islands . . .[1]

According to the same article, the boat "has neither sails nor smokestacks."[2]

Against this background, Mr. Ballard's experience on Mount Shasta takes on added significance.

Mr. Ballard writes that he had hiked up the side of the mountain and paused by a spring. As he bent down to fill a cup with water, he felt an electrical current passing through his body from head to foot. Looking around, he saw behind him a bearded man who looked to be in his 20's or 30's.

The stranger later introduced himself as the Count of St. Germain.*

As a result of this meeting, Mr. Ballard began a full-time career spreading the teachings of the new St. Germain. Ballard established the "I AM Foundation"—an organization with secret initiations and step-by-step teachings. Mr. Ballard claims that he had been introduced to members of the highest levels of the Brotherhood, under which the I AM was founded.

The tales Mr. Ballard tells of his experiences with St. Germain are so extraordinary that many people have derided them as fantasy. Surprisingly, when we strip away the interpretations which both Mr. Ballard and his critics give to his experiences, we find that his stories present a picture not only consistent with the rest of history as we have been viewing it, but they add remarkable new claims with rather startling implications for our own time.

The initial meetings between Ballard and "St. Germain" took place between August and October 1930. During the earliest of those meetings, St. Germain had Ballard drink a liquid which caused a strong physical reaction and made Ballard go "out of body." (This same out-of-body phenomenon is often reported by people taking strong drugs.) After imbibing this fluid on several occasions, Ballard said that he was able to go "out of body" without the drink. This testimony is consistent with other evidence indicating that once a person learns to go "out of body," it can become easy to do for a time.

Ballard alleges that while he was in some of his "out-of-body" states, St. Germain, who was also "out of body," took him to some rather remarkable places. One locale was a mountain in the Teton Range of Wyoming—a mountain Mr. Ballard calls the "Royal Teton." According to Ballard, there was a sealed tunnel entrance near the top of the

---

* The physical appearance of St. Germain on Mount Shasta was considerably different than the St. Germain of the 18th century. The earlier St. Germain was in his 40's, black-haired and clean-shaven. The Mount Shasta St. Germain is depicted as a younger brown-haired man sporting a beard.

mountain that led to elevators. The elevators took their occupants to a location two thousand feet down into an underground complex of huge halls, storage spaces, and mines.

In one of the large underground rooms, Mr. Ballard claims that he saw an All-Seeing Eye symbol on the wall. There was also a large machine, which Ballard described as:

> . . . a disc of gold—*at least twelve feet in diameter. Filling it so that the points touched the circumference— blazed a seven pointed star—composed entirely of yellow diamonds—a solid mass of brilliant golden Light.[3]

Around the main disc were seven small discs, which Ballard gave symbolic meaning to. Mr. Ballard quickly revealed, however, that this large machine was not a mere symbol:

> As I learned later, at certain times for special purposes—Great Cosmic Beings pour through these discs—their powerful currents—of force.[4]

"Great Cosmic Beings" was the term used by Ballard to denote leaders at the highest echelons of the Brotherhood. In his writings, Mr. Ballard claims that some of the Brotherhood's "Great Cosmic Beings" are of extraterrestrial origin.

Ballard was told that the currents of force emitted by the machine were directed "to the humanity of earth."[5] The purpose?

> This radiation affects—the seven ganglionic centers [nerve centers outside the brain and spinal cord] within

---

*Ballard breaks up his sentences with dashes (—). I have included the dashes as they appear in the original texts.

every human body on our planet—as well as all animal and plant life.[6]

This is an astonishing claim, for it would mean that powerful electronics were used by the Brotherhood's "Great Cosmic Beings" to affect the human nervous system on a widespread scale. According to an I AM Foundation magazine, the purpose of the radiation was behavior modification designed to "consume and purify the vortices of force, produced by the discordant and vicious activities of mankind."[7]

The idea of behavior modification through electronic radiation is by no means an absurd one. In recent years, the Soviet Union has been developing and using electronic tranquilizing machines to behaviorally affect large populations. Such devices are also being proposed for classroom use in the United States. We will discuss those devices in an upcoming chapter.

Although the alleged purpose of the Royal Teton radiation machine was to reduce discordant human activity, such radiation will usually have the opposite long-term effect because the emanations are actually irritants to the central nervous system, even if they do cause a superficial sedation. It is perhaps ironic that within less than a decade after Ballard wrote of his experience, the world exploded into one of its bloodiest conflicts: World War II. Either the machine of the "Great Cosmic Beings" did not work . . . or it did.

In his first books, Mr. Ballard claims to have visited four secret underground locations altogether: two of them while "out of body" and two by regular human means. Interestingly, each location corresponded to a region in which there existed earlier in history a major civilization worshiping the Custodial "gods." The Teton location coincided with the ancient North American civilizations. A similar underground location in South America went hand-in-hand with the Incan civilization on that continent. A trip by boat and automobile resulted in a stopover at a reputed underground location on the Arabian peninsula, which matched the ancient Mesopotamian and Egyptian civilizations. The fourth location in the mountains above the city of Darjeeling, India, corresponded to the ancient Aryan civilizations of the Indian subcontinent.

The underground locations were reportedly quite expansive and served a number of functions. In addition to holding electronic gadgetry, the caves were reportedly filled with enormous quantities of precious metals and gems. This is interesting because we know that most of the ancient civilizations worshiping the Custodial "gods" regularly made substantial offerings of gold, silver, gems, and other precious minerals to those "gods." Mr. Ballard alleged that the treasures he viewed came from some of those civilizations:

> In these containers, gold is stored from the lost continents—of Mu and Atlantis—the ancient civilizations of the Gobi and Sahara Deserts*—Egypt—Chaldea—Babylonia—Greece—Rome—and two others.[8]

It has generally been assumed by historians that the ancient offerings went to the priest class. If, however, we take the existence of the Custodial "gods" seriously, it is more likely that the "gods" really did carry the stuff away.

---

* The "ancient civilizations of the Gobi and Sahara Deserts" were major civilizations which are believed to have once existed respectively in the Sahara Desert of northern Africa and the Gobi Desert of east-central Asia. Like Mu and Atlantis, these two civilizations are said to have existed before Sumeria and are therefore relegated to the status of fiction by most historians. The Gobi and Saharan civilizations are said to have been technologically advanced, and the deserts on which they sat are believed to have once been lush with vegetation. The legends state that the Saharan and Gobi civilizations were destroyed in a cataclysmic war. Modern geologists have discovered traces of atomic explosion in those regions, but the traces are usually explained as being caused by the spontaneous combustion of natural radioactive elements a long time ago. Others believe that the traces are more likely the result of atomic weapons used thousands of years ago which destroyed the ancient civilizations and surrounding vegetation, causing the areas to become deserts.

Mr. Ballard's testimony would indicate that a great many of the precious stones and metals were stored by the "gods" in inaccessible underground locations on Earth, perhaps to help finance Custodial activities and to keep the corrupted Brotherhood functioning.

Precious metals and stones are expensive largely because of artificial scarcity. When Cecil Rhodes developed his near-monopoly on diamond mining in southern Africa, he was able to maintain the high price of diamonds by creating a very rigid channel through which his diamonds were sold. This is still true of the diamond trade today. According to Mr. Ballard, the "Ascended Masters" of the Brotherhood intended to keep precious metals and gems scarce. Said Mr. Ballard:

> If all this gold were to be released into the outer activity of the world—it would compel sudden readjustment— in every phase of human experience. At present—it would—not—be part of wisdom.[9]

St. Germain reportedly stated that the huge quantities of gold and treasure would be released into the outer world "when mankind has transcended its—unbridled—selfishness."[10]

The implication is that these precious gems and minerals exist in sufficient quantities on Earth to cause a dramatic drop in their value if they should all be released into the public domain. A further implication is that they are hoarded and made scarce to preserve the wealth of the Brotherhood. If the treasures do indeed exist, then the Brotherhood is a sizable hidden economic power on Earth. According to Mr. Ballard, this hidden economic might does exist and has been used to influence human activities. During his tour of the Teton location, St. Germain reportedly told Ballard:

> No one—in this world—ever accumulated a great amount of wealth—without the assistance and radiation of some—Ascended Master. There are occasions—

in which individuals can be used as a focus of great wealth—for a specific purpose—and at such times—greatly added power is radiated to them—for through it—they can receive personal assistance. Such an experience is a—test—and opportunity—for their growth.[11]

It is certainly true that wealth has traditionally been concentrated in the hands of a small minority. It is also true that many members of that minority throughout history have been affiliated with the mystical Brotherhood network. The problem with this state of affairs would not be the narrow control of wealth, it would be that this control has so often been used to breed war and spiritual decay.

During his trips to the alleged underground locations, Ballard was also shown some radio-type gadgets. One such gadget could reportedly tune in on conversations taking place in various parts of the world—including in the offices of the Bank of England! As we recall, the Bank of England was one of the earliest institutions founded on the inflatable paper money system. That system was largely the creation of mystics and revolutionaries affiliated with the Brotherhood network. The Bank of England has continued to be a principle center of that system up until today. The alleged eavesdropping capability of Mr. Ballard's "Ascended Masters" is therefore remarkable because it would indicate a direct monitoring of a principle central bank in the international paper money system by top echelons of the Brotherhood. This becomes even more interesting in the next chapter when we consider the assistance that the Bank of England's director, Montague Norman, gave to Adolf Hitler and the German Nazi movement during the very time that this electronic snooping was reportedly occurring.

Earlier in this book, we noted the large-scale destruction of irreplaceable religious and historical records in the Eastern and Western Hemispheres by zealous Christians. Historians have been able to piece together much of human history anyway; but is that history complete? According to Mr. Ballard, it is not. Mankind lost additional records to Brotherhood leaders who had deliberately removed and hidden the writings. Ballard claims that he saw some of those ancient historical works inside the underground mountain complex north of Darjeeling, India. He added that the records would not be released to the human race until the "Ascended Masters" so ordered:

> These records are not brought forth into the use of the outer world at the present time, because of lack of spiritual growth and understanding of the people. The race has a restlessness and critical feeling, that is a very destructive activity, . . . the Ascended Masters of the Great White Brotherhood, have always foreseen such destructive impulses, and have withdrawn all important records of every civilization, and preserved them, then left the less important to be destroyed by the vicious impulse of the vandals.[12]

If true, the above quote is a stunning admission. Mankind's "lack of spiritual growth" has been caused by the very organizations to which these alleged "Ascended Masters" belong. It was the Brotherhood that turned spiritual knowledge into incomprehensible symbols, unfathomable mysteries, superstitious rites, savage apocalypticisms, and all of the other ills which ensue therefrom. In such circumstances, it is not surprising that human beings would experience a "restlessness and critical feeling." The "solution" of withholding knowledge would certainly not correct those human deficiencies. Such a "solution" can only deepen the problem. The claim that important records must be hidden to prevent their destruction is spurious. In Ballard's day, book printing was a well-established art. Any important records could be easily duplicated and mass produced with the originals safely stored away. If indeed such hidden records existed, we must conclude that the only purpose for hiding them was to keep mankind ignorant about the past.

The I AM movement created by Mr. Ballard preached a Judgment Day philosophy and strong anti-Communism. Despite attacks from the press and U.S. government, the I AM movement attracted a large following during the late 1930's and early 40's. The I AM taught that communism was the final evil in the world and that it would soon be destroyed by the Ascended Masters. Interestingly, no mention was made of Naziism, which was rapidly growing in Germany at the time.

The "Ascended Masters" and their followers were clearly political creatures. According to Mr. Ballard, members of the Brotherhood were deeply involved in espionage and police organizations in the 1930's. Brotherhood members reportedly served in the American Secret Service, and Mr. Ballard claims that he had met agents of the French Secret Service (France's national intelligence organization) who were members of the Brotherhood and who called themselves "Brothers of Light."

As if the reappearance of "St. Germain" in 1930 was not enough, the I AM movement hosted another most distinguished speaker: "Jesus Christ." Jesus was a featured guest in New York on October 24, 1937, and in Oakland, California on February 15, 1939. Whether this "Jesus" was actually a person claiming to be Christ or was simply Mr. or Mrs. Ballard acting as mediums to channel the "spirit voice" of Jesus, I have not been able to discover. Whichever it may have been, may I respectfully submit that this was as bona fide a "Second Coming" of Jesus as the Custodial religions will probably ever deliver? This "Second Coming" in the 1930's was sponsored by the same Brotherhood network which had sponsored and betrayed Jesus centuries before, and which has kept alive apocalyptic teachings predicting Jesus's return ever since. Naturally, this newest "Second Coming" did not result in a thousand years of peace and spiritual salvation. It merely helped set the stage for World War II.

The I AM movement died down rather quickly after

its peak in the 1940's. It is quite small today.* It never gained the following or influence that so many other Brotherhood branches had attained. To most people, today's I AM Foundation is little more than a curiosity run primarily by retired people. Indeed, the I AM is not important to us for what it is now; it is significant for what it was in the 1930's and '40's.

Was Ballard's I AM Foundation the concoction of blatant spiritual quacks offering a home-brewed spiritual elixir to people seeking a ray of hope in a world gone awry? Or did Mr. Ballard really meet someone that afternoon in 1930 on Mount Shasta? Was the I AM simply a bit of mystical razzle-dazzle designed to make money for the Ballard family as critics have maintained, or did Mr. Ballard's reported experiences offer a rare glimpse into some of the activities of the Brotherhood in the 20th century? It is a pity that Mr. Ballard is not here today to make his confession.

---

*The I AM has inspired several splinter groups. One such group is the "Summit Lighthouse," which is currently the largest of the I AM groups, even though it is not recognized by, nor formally affiliated with, the original I AM organization discussed in this chapter. Headquartered in Malibu, California, the Summit Lighthouse is currently led by its cofounder, Elizabeth Claire Prophet, who, along with her late husband, Mark Prophet, had reportedly been a member of another I AM splinter group called the "Bridge to Freedom" before founding the Lighthouse. Like Ballard's I AM, the Summit Lighthouse believes St. Germain to be an Ascended Master. The Summit Lighthouse is worth mentioning because Ms. Prophet teaches that many UFOs are hostile to human well-being.

# Universe of Stone

*People will not die for business but only for ideals.*
        —Adolf Hitler in *Mein Kampf*

"ST. GERMAIN" AND "Jesus" were not the only messiahs to appear in the 1930's bearing promises of an imminent utopia. Another messiah was gaining a large following in Germany. His "Coming" was said to be the beginning of the Millennium. Using one of the Brotherhood's most important symbols, the swastika, that German Messiah's name was Adolf Hitler.

Adolf Hitler, of course, was the strutting man with the toothbrush mustache who became absolute dictator of Germany and instigated World War II. Hitler and his entourage would look comical to us today were not the consequences of their lunacy so tragic.

During his young adulthood before rising to power, Hitler lived in Vienna. One of Hitler's friends during that period was Walter Johannes Stein. During World War II, Dr. Stein became an advisor to England's Prime Minister, Sir Winston Churchill. Much of what Dr. Stein had to say about Hitler's early life found its way into a book entitled, *Spear of Destiny*, by Trevor Ravenscroft.

*Spear of Destiny* reports that Hitler had become a devotee of mysticism during his poverty-stricken days in Vienna. Between 1909 and 1913, when Hitler was in his early twenties, Hitler was convinced that he had achieved:

> . . . higher levels of consciousness by means of drugs . . . [Hitler] made a penetrating study of medieval occultism and ritual magic, discussing with him [Stein] the whole span of the political, historical and philosophical reading through which he formulated what was later to become the Nazi Weltanshauung [a special concept of human history].[1]

In his autobiography, *Mein Kampf*, Hitler affirmed the importance of this period in shaping his ideas.

Hitler did not develop his ideology in a vacuum. One of his most influential mentors was a Viennese bookstore owner named Ernst Pretzsche. Pretzsche was described by Dr. Stein as a malevolent-looking man with a somewhat toad-like appearance. Pretzsche was a devotee of the Germanic mysticism that was preaching the coming of an Aryan superrace. Hitler frequented Pretzsche's store and pawned books there when he needed money. During those visits, Pretzsche indoctrinated Hitler in Germanic mysticism and successfully encouraged Hitler to use the hallucinogenic drug peyote as a tool for achieving mystical enlightenment.

As it turns out, Pretzsche was associated with a man named Guido von List. Von List was a founding member and leading figure in an occult lodge which used a swastika instead of a cross in its rituals. Before he was disgraced and forced to flee from Vienna, von List had gained a large audience for his Germanic mystical writings. Hitler became a member of that audience through Pretzsche.

Back in his Viennese flophouse room, young Hitler avidly pored through pamphlets and books expounding on the mystical destiny of Germany and the coming of the Aryan superrace. According to some of those tracts, Aryans were created by an extraterrestrial "superrace" of giants. Hitler became an ardent believer in those ideas as he hawked his watercolors on the street to support his meager existence and to pay for his drug-induced enlightenments.

The notion that Hitler was a "druggie" in his youth seeking mystical enlightenment through chemicals should come as no surprise. Drugs were a major factor in shaping the persona of Adolf Hitler. Hitler remained a user of powerful narcotics his entire life. According to the diaries of Hitler's personal physician, Dr. Theodore Morell, which surfaced in the U.S. National Archives, the German dictator was repeatedly injected with various painkillers, sedatives, strychnine, cocaine, a morphine derivative, and other drugs during the entire four years of World War II.

The mystical philosophy so eagerly adopted by the young Hitler was the same one which had already deeply affected the Kaiser and other German leaders. In fact, Houston Stewart Chamberlain, the mystic who had so influenced the Kaiser, years later declared Hitler to be the prophesized German Messiah. On September 25, 1925, the Nazi newspaper, *Volkischer Beobachter,* celebrated Chamberlain's seventieth birthday and declared his work, *Foundations of the Twentieth Century,* to be "The Gospel of the Nazi Movement." As we recall, the Kaiser considered the same book to have been sent by God.

Hitler's road to politics began as a German soldier during World War I. When that war broke out, Hitler enlisted. He remained very concerned about the mystical destiny of Germany and continued to ponder the Aryan question while fighting in the fields. This made him very unpopular with his fellow soldiers, who were more concerned with food, leave, women, and an end to the war which nearly all of them detested. Hitler, on the other hand, flourished in the war-torn environment and distinguished himself as a soldier. He won the highest award a soldier of his rank (corporal) could earn: the Iron Cross, First Class.

About two months after winning the Iron Cross, Hitler was blinded by mustard gas during a battle. He was taken to the Pasewalk military hospital in northern Germany where he was mistakenly diagnosed as suffering from "psychopathic hysteria." (The symptoms were probably caused by the mustard gas.) Hitler was consequently placed under the care of a psychiatrist, Dr. Edmund Forster. What exactly was done to Hitler while under Dr. Forster's care is uncertain because years later, in 1933, Hitler's secret police, the Gestapo, rounded up all psychiatric records related to Hitler's treatment and destroyed them. Dr. Forster "committed suicide" in that same year.

The mystery of what was done to Hitler at Pasewalk is deepened by Hitler's own statements. According to Hitler, he had experienced a "vision" from "another world" while at the hospital. In that vision, Hitler was told that he would need to restore his sight so that he could lead Germany back to glory. Hitler's latent anti-Semitism, which had already been planted by his mystical readings in Vienna, emerged at Pasewalk.

What *did* happen at that hospital?

In a shrewd piece of detective work published in the journal, *History of Childhood Quarterly,* psychohistorian Dr. Rudolph Binion suggests that Hitler's visions may have been deliberately induced by the psychiatrist, Edmund Forster, as a means of helping Hitler recover from his blindness. Hitler's mystical beliefs were well known, and they would certainly have come out in his psychiatric interviews. Dr. Binion cites a book completed in 1939 entitled, *Der Augenzeuge* ("The Eyewitness"), written by a Jewish doctor named Ernst Weiss who had fled Germany in 1933. In *Der Augenzeuge,* the author tells a thinly fictionalized story of a man, "A.H.," who is taken to Pasewalk hospital for psychiatric care. A.H. claims that he had been hit by mustard gas. At Pasewalk, the psychiatrist in charge deliberately induces visionary ideas into the mind of the hysterical "A.H." in order to effect a cure. The "miracle cure" is successful and years later, in the summer of 1933, the psychiatrist attempts to send the records of the treatments abroad to keep them out of the hands of the Gestapo. In his article, Dr. Binion points out that Hitler's psychiatrist, Edmund Forster, had been abroad in Paris that summer, and it is Dr. Binion's guess that Forster may have revealed the facts of Hitler's treatment to someone at that time, resulting in the book, *Der Augenzeuge.* Forster may have also been the person who revealed that two other very high-ranking Nazis, Bernhard Rust (Prussian Minister of Education) and Herman Goering, both had histories of severe mental problems. Rust was a certified psychopath and Goering was a former morphine addict.

After Hitler's discharge from Pasewalk in November of 1918, he traveled back to Munich. He remained in the army and, in April of 1919, he was assigned to espionage duties. A communist revolution had just occurred in southern Germany and a Soviet Republic had been declared there after the regional government collapsed. Hitler was one of the soldier-spies selected to remain behind in Munich and circulate among the pro-Communist soldiers to learn the identities of their leaders. When a German Reichswehr force from Berlin moved in and crushed the rebellion, Hitler walked down the ranks of captured soldiers and singled out the ringleaders. The German soldiers who were identified by Hitler were taken away for immediate execution without trial. Hitler watched as many of his victims were put before the wall and shot.

Hitler's stellar performance in Munich earned him a promotion. He was assigned to the highly secret Political Department of the Army District Command. Hitler's new unit was an intelligence operation that engaged in acts of domestic terrorism. The unit refused to accept Germany's defeat in World War I and so it assassinated some of the German leaders who had negotiated Germany's surrender.

A prominent leader of the District Command was Captain Ernst Rohm. Rohm was a professional soldier who served as liaison between the District Command and the German industrialists who were directly funding the District Command to help it fight communism. Captain Rohm and many other members of the District Command were members of a mystical organization known as the "Thule Society." The Thule believed in the "Aryan superrace" and it preached the coming of a German "Messiah" who would lead Germany to glory and a new Aryan civilization. In *Spear of Destiny*, we learn from Dr. Stein that the Thule group was financed by some of the very same industrialists who supported the District Command. The Thule was also directly supported by the German High Command.

Many assassinations perpetrated by the District Command may have been inspired by the Thule. According to Dr. Stein, the Thule was a "Society of Assassins." It held secret courts and condemned people to death. It is likely that many victims murdered by the District Command had been condemned earlier in the secret courts of the Thule. Many prominent Germans supported this violence and were documented members of the Thule. For example, the Police President of Munich, Franz Gurtner, was a reported member of the innermost circle of the Thule. He later became Minister of Justice of the Third Reich.

After joining the District Command, corporal Adolf Hitler became a good friend of Ernst Rohm. It was Rohm who took Hitler to see Dietrich Eckart, a morphine addict who headed the German Thule Society. Rohm had a purpose for arranging this meeting. He felt that Hitler had strong leadership potential and that Hitler was the man the Thule was looking for. Eckart agreed, and Hitler's career as the new German Messiah was launched.

The vehicle used by Hitler to gain political power was a small socialist organization known as the German Worker's Party. In September 1919, Hitler was sent by the District Command to attend a meeting of the Party. Hitler was subsequently invited by the Party to join it, and within a year he became the Party's leader. At a 1920 Party rally held in a Munich beer hall, Hitler announced that the German Worker's Party was to be renamed the *Nationalsozialistische Deutsche Arbeiterpartei,* or "Nazi" Party for short.

In *Mein Kampf,* Hitler stated that he had made an agonizing decision to quit the District Command in order to participate in the German Worker's Party. Many historians strongly doubt that Hitler had left the District Command, and believe instead that the German Worker's Party was the vehicle used by the District Command to covertly further its political aims. There is good evidence to support this conclusion. Ernst Rohm, Hitler's mentor in the District Command, had already joined and started shaping the German Worker's Party before Hitler became a member. Rohm greatly assisted Hitler in transforming the German Worker's Party into Hitler's political tool. Rohm grew with the fledging Nazi Party and later became the leader of the Nazi S.A. organization—better known as the "brown shirts."* Thule leader Dietrich Eckart, who was also closely affiliated with District Command leaders, became the editor-in-chief of the new Nazi newspaper, *Volkischer Beobachter*. Hitler had by no means abandoned his District Command friends. They were all in there turning the German Worker's Party into the Nazi Party.

Although the Thule was probably the most important mystical organization behind the formation of Naziism, it was not the only one. Another was the "Vril" Society, which had been named after a book by Lord Bulward Litton—an English Rosicrucian. Litton's book told the story of an Aryan "superrace" coming to Earth. One member of the German Vril was Professor Karl Haushofer—a former employee of German military intelligence. Haushofer had been a mentor to Hitler as well as to Hitler's propaganda specialist, Rudolph Hess. (Hess had been an assistant to Haushofer at the University of Munich.) Another Vril member was the second most powerful man in Nazi Germany: Heinrich Himmler, who became head of the dreaded SS and Gestapo. Himmler incorporated the Vril Society into the Nazi Occult Bureau. Yet another mystical group was the Edelweiss Society, which preached the coming of a "Nordic messiah." Nazi financial dictator, Herman Goering, had become an active member of the Edelweiss Society in 1921 while living and

---

* Rohm eventually lost his political power when the S.A. was reduced and Himmler's SS organization rose to supremacy. Rohm's usefulness to the Thule Society and to the German intelligence apparat was outlived by 1934 when Nazi officers went to Rohm's home to arrest him for allegedly conspiring to overthrow his former underling, Hitler. Rohm was reportedly found in his bedroom in a compromising position with one of his top aides. He was offered a chance to commit suicide, but he refused, so the Nazis shot him in a Munich prison. It is interesting that Rohm did not suspect the fate which awaited him because Hitler had personally traveled to Munich to meet and escort him. Hitler was a master at using other people's trust to betray them in extraordinarily treacherous ways—it was one of the methods used to send Jews and other "undesirables" to their deaths in Nazi slave labor camps.

working in Sweden. Goering believed Hitler to be the Nordic messiah.

Naziism was clearly more than a political movement. It was a powerful new Brotherhood faction steeped in Brotherhood beliefs and symbols. The emblem chosen to represent the Nazi party was the swastika—an important Brotherhood symbol since antiquity. Hitler was proclaimed not only a political messiah, but also a religious messiah whose Coming signaled the fulfillment of the apocalyptic philosophies espoused by German mystical groups. Hitler's Coming was to bring about the "Thousand Year Reich"— a millennium in which mankind would be "purified" and reach its highest state of existence. Naziism was a Custodial religious philosophy as much as it was a political ideology. In a speech he gave at the Nazis' 1934 Nuremburg Rally, Hitler said about the Party, "its total image, however, will be like a holy order."*

The brutal Nazi Party as a holy order? The idea seems laughable in hindsight, until we note that this would not be the first time in history that a holy order was responsible for massive atrocities. The Dominicans who ran the Catholic Inquisition during the Middle Ages were another example.

World War II lasted from 1939 until 1945. It took a terrible toll on human life. Much of that toll was the result of the Nazis' most horrific accomplishment: a massive German concentration camp system in which eleven million people died. Six million of the victims were Jews. By that time in history, concentration camps had become quite the fashion, beginning with the British in Africa, continuing with the Bolsheviks in Russia and the American internment of Japanese-Americans during World War II, and sink-

---

* Nazis were not the only people involved in World War II for whom mysticism was important. Many top military leaders of Japan, which was allied to Germany, were members of a secret mystical society known for its Black Dragon symbol. In the United States, President Franklin D. Roosevelt, a staunch anti-Nazi, was a Freemason, as was his successor, Harry S. Truman, who ordered the dropping of atomic bombs on two Japanese cities (Hiroshima and Nagasaki) near the end of the war.

ing to their lowest levels of barbarity in Nazi Germany.

Most people know the Nazi concentration camps for their gas chambers, grisly human experiments, and the deliberate starvation of inmates. The camps were a part of the Nazis' so-called "Final Solution." The Final Solution was not just an attempt to racially "purify" the human race by physically exterminating all Jews and other "undesirables"—it was an effort to kill them in accordance with a grand economic plan. As in Russia, the Nazi concentration camps were designed to be a vital part of the national economy. More than 300 camps were constructed in Germany alone. Many of them were located near large factories specially designed to be run on the slave labor provided by the camps. The infamous Auschwitz camp, for example, was constructed next to an enormous industrial plant for processing and refining oil and rubber. The intent of the "Final Solution" was to destroy non-Aryans (which the Nazis thought of as human "mutations") by reducing them to the lowest common denominator: camp inmates became expendable economic units forced to work to their maximum limit while slowly starving to death. After death, the physical components of their bodies were often used for other purposes. Gold tooth fillings were extracted and sent to the German treasury. Human hair was sometimes woven into blankets. Even human skin was fashioned into lampshades and other decorative items. The Nazi concentration camp system reduced human beings quite literally to the level of livestock.

Most of the concentration camp factories were operated by the giant German chemical combine, I. G. Farben. In fact, one of Farben's subsidiaries manufactured the poison gas used in concentration camp gas chambers. A remarkable book, *The Crime and Punishment of I. G. Farben,* by Joseph Borkin, documents how the Farben companies, in cooperation with the Nazi SS, ran the concentration camps and adjacent factories as a business enterprise. Mr. Borkin's book reproduces a settlement of accounts made between I. G. Farben and the SS for the work of concentration camp inmates. The receipt is neatly handwritten with slave labor rates priced in a very businesslike fashion. When the war ended, all twenty-four top executives of I. G. Farben were charged with crimes against humanity at the Nuremburg War Crime Trials. The few Farben executives who were convicted of slavery and mass murder for their part in running the camp system were given very light sentences. Otto Ambros, an expert on poison gas and a member of the I. G. Farben managing board, served only eight years for his conviction. Heinrich Buetefisch was sentenced to six years. After World War II, the I. G. Farben combine was restructured under different names and remains an international giant to this day.

The Nazi organization which oversaw the concentration camp system was the Schutzstaffel ("SS"). The SS was a ruthless military/intelligence organization run by a chicken farmer-turned-policeman named Heinrich Himmler. Himmler, like so many other top Nazis, was a devotee of German mysticism. We noted his membership in the Vril society earlier in this chapter. Himmler ran the SS as a secret society with initiations. SS members were taught a mystical tradition which included a catechism declaring that Hitler had been sent to the German people by God. Mystical symbology was also taught, with a special emphasis on the occult meanings of the swastika. Himmler dreamed that the SS would build the foundation of the new Aryan utopia. Those admitted into the SS were therefore only to be of the purest Aryan stock.*

As an elite organization, the SS had a great deal of autonomy. Although Himmler remained personally loyal to Hitler out of a belief in Hitler as the Messiah, a number of historians agree that, in many respects, Himmler was as powerful, and certainly as feared, as Hitler. Himmler's dream was to create a fully independent nation in Burgundy, France, run entirely by the SS on SS principles. It was Himmler's goal to make his SS nation the "envy" of the world. The autonomy of the SS was also apparent from the direct funding of it by important German industries. One of those contributors was, of course, I. G. Farben. Others included

---

* Near the end of the war, SS racial standards were considerably lowered as the German military became desperate for manpower.

the German subsidiaries of I.T.T. and General Electric. As had been true earlier of the District Command, this direct funding enabled the SS to act outside the purse strings of the larger national party. It also permitted the industrialists to have a more direct influence into SS activities.

Naziism and all of its atrocities could never have happened without the support of the German banking fraternity. Banking, industry, and government were as tightly interwoven in Nazi Germany as they are in nearly every nation today. In Germany, many bankers held management positions in other companies, not the least of which was I. G. Farben. For example, Max and Paul Warburg, who ran major banks in Germany and the United States (and who, incidentally, had been instrumental in establishing the Federal Reserve system in the United States), were I. G. Farben directors. H. A. Metz of I. G. Farben was a director of the Bank of Manhattan, which was a Warburg bank in the United States that later became part of the Chase Manhattan Bank managed by the Rockefeller family.* One director of American I. G. Farben was C. E. Mitchell, who was also director of the Federal Reserve Bank of New York and of National City Bank. Most significantly, Herman Schmitz, President of I. G. Farben in Germany, had served on the boards of the Deutsche Bank and the Bank for International Settlements. As we recall, the Bank for International Settlements was the apex of the international central banking community and the interlocking inflatable paper money systems. Schmitz was one of the few I. G. Farben executives sentenced to a prison term at Nuremburg. He received a ten-year sentence.

Perhaps the most surprising support for Hitler in the international banking fraternity came from the director of the Bank of England, Montague Norman. England, of course, was an enemy of Nazi Germany during World War II. According to Dr. Quigley's book, *Tragedy and Hope,* Mr. Norman was the "commander in chief of the world system

---

* Another Rockefeller company, Standard Oil of New Jersey, had been a cartel partner with I. G. Farben prior to the war.

of banking control"[3] during his governership of the Bank of England from 1920 until 1944. Said Dr. Quigley:

> . . . many wealthy and influential persons like Montague Norman, and Henri Detering [owner of Shell Oil] directed public attention to the danger of Bolshevism while maintaining a neutral, or favorable, attitude toward Naziism.[4]

Montague Norman apparently felt more than mere neutrality towards Naziism, however. According to a Chicago newspaper story dated November 3, 1938:

> In the spring of 1934, a select group of city financiers gathered around Montague Norman in the windowless building of the Bank of England, in Threadneedle Street. Among those present were Sir Alan Anderson, partner in Anderson, Green & Co.; Lord (then Sir Josiah) Stamp, chairman of the L.M.S. Railway System; Edward Shaw, chairman of the P. & O. Steamship lines; Sir Robert Kindersley, a partner in Hambros Bros.; C. T. Tiarks, head of J. Shroeder Co. . . . But now a new power was established on Europe's political horizon—namely, Nazi Germany. Hitler had disappointed his critics. His regime was no temporary nightmare, but a system with a good future, and Mr. Norman advised his directors to include Hitler in their plans. There was no opposition and it was decided that Hitler should get covert help from London's financial section until Mr. Norman had succeeded in putting sufficient pressure on the Government to make it abandon its pro-French policy for a more promising pro-German orientation.[5]

The Bank of England continued to support Hitler even after the Nazi dictator embarked on his program of conquest. After Hitler invaded Czechoslovakia in violation of the non-aggression pact between then-Prime Minister Chamberlain of England and Hitler, the Bank of England gave Nazi

Germany six million Pounds of Czech gold reserves held by the Bank.

In the same way that a small clique of German petty princes had made a fortune from war in the 18th century by renting soldiers to warring nations, a small clique of banks and multinational corporations made a large profit by providing goods and services to both sides fighting in World War II. After giving early support to Hitler, the Bank of England naturally provided loans to Britain to fight Hitler. At the same time that the German subsidiaries of I.T.T. and General Electric were giving money to the SS and providing needed services to Nazi Germany, other branches in America and elsewhere were aiding Germany's enemies. As I. G. Farben fueled Hitler's war machine in Germany, one of its old cartel partners, Standard Oil, fueled the allied effort against Germany. While the Ford Motor Company produced materials for the American army to fight Germany, Ford plants in Germany were turning out military vehicles for the Nazis. No matter who won the war, those banks and companies would profit and find favor with whoever emerged victorious.

The overwhelming role that various bankers and industrialists played in propping up Hitler and in building the Nazi war machine has caused some historians to view those bankers and industrialists as the true powers behind Naziism. They were indeed highly significant, but were they actually the ultimate sources that gave us Naziism?

As we have already noted, Naziism arose out of the mystical Brotherhood network. Some researchers have erroneously concluded that radical Brotherhood organizations have been the tools of political, military and economic leaders, rather than vice versa. This mistake is usually made because few historians have dared consider that the Brotherhood network has been senior in power and influence to human elites. Once that influence is acknowledged, one must then ask: who is the power behind the Brotherhood? We have, of course, already answered that question in a manner unacceptable to a great many people: members of an extraterrestrial race, *i.e.*, the Custodial society. Once we begin to take such

an extraordinary possibility seriously, we must return our
gaze to the pages of history for confirmation—in this case
to Nazi Germany. When we do so, we discover something
quite remarkable:

*The Nazis themselves claimed that an extraterrestrial
society was the source of their ideology and the power
behind their organization!*

Throughout history, Brotherhood organizations have been
pledging ultimate loyalty to assorted "gods," "angels,"
"Cosmic Beings," "Ascended Masters" from other planets,
and similar nonterrestrials, nearly all of which appear to
be Custodians disguised by veils of myth. The Thule
Society, and Nazi mysticism itself, also claimed that its
true leadership came from extraterrestrial sources. The
Nazis referred to their hidden extraterrestrial masters as
underground "supermen." Hitler believed in the "supermen"
and claimed that he had once met one of them, as did other
members of the Thule leadership. The Nazis said that their
"supermen" lived beneath the Earth's surface and were the
creators of the Aryan race. Aryans therefore constituted the
world's only "pure" race and all other people were viewed
as genetic mutations. The Nazis planned to "re-purify"
humanity by murdering everyone who was not an Aryan.
Top Nazi leaders believed that the underground "supermen"
would return to the surface of the Earth to rule it as soon
as the Nazis began their racial purification program and
established the Thousand Year Reich.

These Nazi beliefs are very similar to other Custodial
religions which teach people to prepare for the future return
of supernatural or superhuman beings who will reign over
a utopian Earth. As in other Custodial religions, the coming
of the Nazi "supermen" would coincide with a great final
"divine judgment." Of the "divine judgment," Hitler had
declared in court during his early Nazi days:

The [Nazi] army we have formed is growing from day
to day. I nourish the proud hope that one day the hour
will come when these rough companies will grow into
battalions, the battalions to regiments, the regiments
to divisions, that the old cockade [ribbon or rosette

worn on a hat as a badge] will be taken from the mud, that the old flags will wave again, that there will be a reconciliation at the last great divine judgement which we are prepared to face.[6]

It would seem that the Nazi "supermen" were not extra-terrestrials at all, but were Earthly in origin because they allegedly hailed from beneath our planet's surface. However, Hitler and his mystical compatriots had a curiously inverted view of the universe. To their way of thinking, the universe consists of infinite rock which is broken by numerous hollow areas. In other words, the universe is like an infinite piece of swiss cheese—solid with many holes in it. The concave surfaces of the hollow areas are the surfaces of "planets," including Earth. Humans are therefore not living on the outer surface of a round ball: they are being pushed by gravity against the inner surface of a hollow area. According to the Nazis, the sun hangs suspended in the middle of the hollow area, the sky is made of blue gas, and the stars are tiny objects (perhaps ice crystals) which hang suspended in a similar fashion to the sun. In this infinite "swiss cheese" universe of stone there are many fissures and cracks that allow travel between the hollow areas. In an adjoining hollow area, according to Naziism, lives the race of Aryan "supermen." Hitler's underground "supermen" were therefore true extraterrestrials, but in a curiously inverted fashion. Lest it be assumed that the Nazi swiss cheese model of the universe was one of Hitler's "Big Lies," there is evidence that the Nazi leadership took the idea quite seriously. For example, an attempt was made to locate the British fleet during World War II with infrared rays pointing toward the sky. The Nazis believed that the rays would hit the opposite side of the "concave" Earth. If for no other reason, we can be glad the Nazis lost the war so that we were spared their astronomy lessons.

It is unfortunate that the Nazi defeat and reported deaths of Adolf Hitler and Heinrich Himmler did not end Nazi influence in the world. After World War II, Nazis participated in many important spheres of activity:

The American Central Intelligence Agency (CIA) accepted the offer of Reinhart Gehlen, Chief of Russian Intelligence operations in the Nazi Secret Service, to help build the American intelligence network in Europe after the war. Gehlen's organization was staffed by many former SS members. The Gehlen organization became a significant element of the CIA in Western Europe and it also provided the foundation for the intelligence apparat of modern West Germany. The CIA also extracted information about Nazi psychiatric techniques from Nuremburg war crime trial records for use in the CIA's infamous mind control experiments decades later.

INTERPOL, the private international police organization which is supposed to combat international criminals and drug traffickers, was headed by former Nazi SS officers several times up until 1972. This is not surprising when we consider that Interpol was controlled by the Nazis during World War II.

Prince Bernhard of the House of Orange in the Netherlands had been a member of the SS before the war, followed by a stint as an employee of I. G. Farben. He then married into the House of Orange and assumed his position as chairman of Shell Oil. Prince Bernhard founded the international "Bilderberg" meetings, which are still held every year. The Bilderberg meetings are meant to be informal get-togethers of the world's top bankers, industrialists, political figures, and other prominent people for the purpose of discussing world conditions and reaching an occasional informal consensus. Prince Bernhard personally chaired these meetings until 1976, when a corruption scandal forced him to resign.

To younger people today, World War II is an episode from the distant past, much as World War I is ancient history to people in their thirties and forties. The conflict most young people understand now is the former Cold War between the United States and Soviet Union. World War II did much to set the stage for that confrontation. During World War II, Russia was an ally of the United States, Great Britain and France in the war against Nazi Germany. Russian troops fought against the Germans in many of the Balkan nations which bordered Russia. In the ensuing instability, communist movements gained considerable power in those Balkan countries, and Russian troops remained there after the Germans were defeated. The allies were not about to prolong the war by turning against the Soviet Union, and so the communist Eastern bloc was born.

The Nazi experience is an extraordinarily important one because it happened within the lifetime of a great many people living today. Incredibly, Nazi groups have been revived in America, Germany, and other nations. It is hard to imagine that anyone would join a movement of such proven madness, yet it is happening. The German Nazi experience revealed to us that the world is still being pushed into war, ignorance and repeated genocides in the same manner that it has been for thousands of years: by a mystical network with organizations pledging ultimate loyalty to an extraterrestrial race. The Nazi experience revealed again a key channel through which Brotherhood network influence has been exerted: namely, through a community of national intelligence organizations whose activities are kept secret by law and whose activities are often outside of the law. Naziism was but another brutal faction set up in opposition to so many other factions which arose out of the Brotherhood network; this helped guarantee more war, more suffering, and the continued imprisonment of mankind on a small planet behind walls of ignorance. In Naziism we saw all of the elements we have looked at in this book come together: the Brotherhood network, apocalypticism, a paper money banking elite, genocide, and an extraterrestrial race worshipped as "gods" and owners of Earth. Naziism should have happened two thousand years ago, but it occurred only decades ago. All of the history we have looked at in this book may still be happening today.

These closing observations require us to look once again at the UFO phenomenon itself. If we hypothesize that human society is still being manipulated by a Custodial society in the same manner that it was thousands of years ago, then we must determine that UFOs continue to behave now as they did in the distant past. Two questions we might pose to make this determination are: are UFOs still spreading the same corrupted Brotherhood mysticisms today as they did earlier in history? Are they still implanting the false idea that they are God? If we are to believe the testimony of recent UFO abductees, the answer to both queries is yes.

# 37

# Modern "Ezekiels"

*I've known some people who claim they've had UFO
experiences and have said they were very pleasant,
very dreamlike and wonderful. But invaders don't
always come armed to the teeth and threatening!
Sometimes they come with happy smiles, waving flags,
bearing Bibles and crosses.*[1]
—On the street interview, courtesy of *UFO* magazine

UFO abduction cases tend to follow a distinct pattern:
a human being is involuntarily taken aboard a UFO,
is given a comprehensive physical examination, and is
then released. An abductee's memory of the event is
usually buried because of apparent mental tampering by
the alien captors. Some researchers compare these abduction
cases to human biologists who tranquilize wild animals,
inspect them, and then release the creatures back into
nature.

Many recent UFO abduction cases have another recur-
ring characteristic of great significance. Dr. Thomas E.
Bullard of Indiana University, whose words appear in the
*MUFON UFO Journal* dated February 1988, had this to say
after conducting his own studies into the abduction phenomenon:

The commonest sequel to the examination [of a human abductee by UFO occupants] is a conference, a more or less formal period of conversation between the witness and his captors. . . . Warnings that certain human behaviors are dangerous and prophecies of coming events are also common. The prophecies usually predict coming disasters and even apocalyptic changes on earth, events the aliens or an enlightened witness may mitigate.[2]

The documented cases reviewed by Dr. Bullard provide fascinating evidence that Custodians continue to spread the same apocalyptic messages today that they have been implanting for thousands of years. Conversely, these modern cases add weight to the historical evidence that many ancient apocalyptic messages, such as those found in the Bible, did indeed come from the same extraterrestrial sources. Dr. Bullard's findings suggest that Custodians are still being highly manipulative by, in effect, saying, "You humans are all behaving badly (although we are not going to tell you that we might be the ones who are stirring you up) and there will be catastrophe. Fear not, however, for we angelic souls will save you. Look to us and to our appointed messengers for your salvation." It is straight out of Machiavelli.

UFO occupants still come right out today and imply that they are God. One abduction episode in which this occurred involved a woman named Betty Ann Andreasson, whose well-documented and exhaustively-researched experience was the subject of an intriguing book entitled *The Andreasson Affair,* by Raymond Fowler.

Mrs. Andreasson's abduction occurred on January 25, 1967. Later, while under hypnosis, Mrs. Andreasson recalled that she had been kidnapped out of her home, was taken aboard an apparent alien aircraft and flown to an unknown location where she was led through what seemed to be a number of unusual red and green underground passages within some sort of city. Mrs. Andreasson then had an experience which makes her story unbelievable to many people; but to us, it is the experience which may give her story the most credence.

According to Mrs. Andreasson, her abductors took her to a special room. There she underwent what her investigators described as "the most painful and emotional segment of her total experience."[3] In the room, Mrs. Andreasson saw a large bird about fifteen feet in height. The bird resembled an eagle, but it had a longer neck. It was, in fact, a replica of a phoenix, and it had the illusion of being alive. As Mrs. Andreasson stood and watched it, the phoenix began to undergo a transformation. Mrs. Andreasson felt an intense heat so powerful that she cried out in pain during her hypnosis session while recounting the incident. The strange alien room abruptly cooled off. Where the "Great Bird" had stood there now burned a small fire. The fire died down to a pile of gray ash with a few red embers. As the pile continued to cool, Betty saw something in the ashes: "Now, looks like a worm," she recalled under hypnosis, "a big fat worm. It just looks like a big fat worm—a big gray worm just lying there."[4]

What Mrs. Andreasson had witnessed was a re-enactment of the legend of the phoenix, clearly staged for her benefit. The phoenix, as we recall, is a Brotherhood symbol which has been used to promote apocalypticism and justify endless human suffering. Although Mrs. Andreasson's "vision" of the phoenix constituted only a small portion of her total abduction experience, the investigators concluded:

> . . . it is only too obvious that the aliens had brought Betty to the bird as the focal point of her whole experience; it seemed to be the purpose for her travel through the red and green spaces.[5]

Mrs. Andreasson testified under hypnosis that after being implanted with this mystical vision, the following conversation ensued between her and her captors:

> They called my name, and repeated it again in a louder voice. I said, "No, I don't understand what this is all about, why I'm even here." And they—whatever it was—said that "I have chosen you."
> "For what have you chosen me?" Betty asked.
> "I have chosen you to show the world."

"Are you God?" Betty asked, "Are you the Lord God?"

"I shall show you as your time goes by."[6]

At the time of her abduction, Mrs. Andreasson was already a Christian. As a result of her experience, she began to include UFOs in her own Christian apocalyptic belief system. Researcher Raymond Fowler probed those beliefs:

RAYMOND FOWLER: Have they [UFOs] anything to do with what we call the second coming of Christ?
BETTY: They definitely do.
RAYMOND FOWLER: When is this going to occur?
BETTY: It is not for them to tell you.
RAYMOND FOWLER: Do they know?
BETTY: They know the Master is getting ready, and very close.[7]

If real, Betty Andreasson's experience was a remarkable one. It would indicate that she was but one in a very long line of reluctant prophets forcibly implanted with an apocalyptic religious message by members of the Custodial society. Like the "Ezekiels" who preceded her in history, Betty Andreasson's testimony suggests that she suffered considerable mental tampering at the hands of her abductors. This tampering may account for some of the unusual perceptual phenomena she experienced during her abduction episode. Unlike past "Ezekiels," however, Mrs. Andreasson's vision will probably not be added to the Bible, nor will it cause her to rally an army and embark on a campaign of religious conquest. Her courageous testimony will simply offer the world additional evidence that the 20th century has not seen a change in the methods by which a Custodial race appears to maintain a hold on the human race.

Does Mrs. Andreasson's experience mean that human society will be required to undergo yet another "End of the World" episode? The political, social, and economic structure of the world certainly makes it possible. The Brotherhood network is alive and active, as are the many institutions it created. They may well bring to our world yet another senseless "Final Battle."

# 38

# The New Eden

A NEW EDEN IS being built today, or perhaps it is merely a new face being put on the old Eden. Today's Eden is characterized by sterile architecture and stylistic homogeneity. Inhabitants of modern Eden are offered many ways to cope with the stresses of living in Eden; among them are drugs that promise to change or control nearly every negative human attribute (and every positive one, too). The new Edenites are taught philosophies which promise a materialist utopia within a spiritual wasteland. Despite all of these "advances," Edenites still commit suicide at a surprisingly high rate. Tragically, a great many suicide victims are young people. What are some of those victims telling us? Perhaps it is that today's Eden is still Eden: a gilded cage, a pampered prison. Many young people sense it and rebel by changing clothing or hairstyle, but they find that they are still trapped not really understanding how or why. Like Adam and Eve, many individuals, no matter how successful or pampered they have been in life, find that they want to escape.

Today's Eden continues to be strongly influenced by the

Brotherhood network and its outgrowths. Any discussion of the Brotherhood in today's world is, however, a delicate matter. We are no longer talking about people and groups that reside comfortably in the past, but we must now confront people and organizations that are very much a part of today's world. Please allow me to therefore reiterate two very important points:

1. The vast majority of people who join movements and organizations do so for the right reasons, including those who join Brotherhood branches and Custodial religions. They have heard a bit of truth or they have seen a solution to a genuine problem. They work in those organizations to disseminate that truth or to solve that problem. *As has been true throughout all of history, almost none of them, including most of their top leaders, are knowingly engaged in Machiavellian activities.* They only know that they have been given a just cause to pursue against some other human group, unaware that somewhere else, in similar organizations, other people have been given a just cause to pursue against *them*. The corruption within the Brotherhood network, and the violence emanating from it, are as upsetting to them as they are to everyone else.

2. My purpose is correction, not condemnation. There are no saints on Earth, and probably nowhere else, for that matter. Yes, there are a great many very fine people who deserve to be helped, but there is probably no being on Earth who has not at some time, in some way, contributed to what we have discussed in this book. To engage in blame, punishment, or recrimination at this stage of the game can only make affairs worse. I hope to encourage the idea that no matter what we have done in the past, it is the present and future that truly count. My purpose in writing this book is only to ask that we take a moment's pause to step back and look at what we may all be caught up in. Perhaps each of us can then carefully determine what we need to do (or stop doing) to help bring about the changes required to set things straight, without disrupting our lives or cherished institutions. What is needed now from everyone is cooperation, not recrimination.

As we survey the modern organizations and religions which arose out of the Brotherhood network, we discover something rather ironic. As the world continues its intellectual flirtation with materialism, Brotherhood organizations and Custodial religions are among the few sources which keep alive any idea that man might be a spiritual being. As a result, many Brotherhood organizations and Custodial religions attract some very fine people within whom the spiritual spark has not died. It is difficult to find a Jesuit father, an American Freemason, a Presbyterian minister, or a Jewish rabbi who is not a very decent person. The overwhelming majority of them emphasize the truly benign and uplifting aspects of their theologies. It is equally difficult not to feel good at a Catholic mass on Christmas Eve, or to be stimulated by a conversation with an articulate Rosicrucian about the meaning of life. It is equally impossible not to appreciate the smile of a young child basking in the warmth of a successful family unit held together by the Hebrew religion, or to savor the aesthetics of an exceptional Hindu artwork. Children and elderly people are helped every day through the kind works of Freemasons, Oddfellows, and Shriners. Fascinating political discussions can be had with an avowed Marxist and one can learn some of the most astonishing facts from a dyed-in-the-wool "right-winger." Nevertheless, most of the institutions that arose out of the Brotherhood network continue to cause serious problems today.

In this book, we looked closely at the inflatable paper money system. In the United States today, over 75% of the money supply is created by commercial banks. When you deposit a dollar in a commercial bank, that dollar becomes the bank's to lend out, and the bank creates an additional dollar which becomes the dollar in your bank account. That dollar in your bank account, however, is not a guaranteed dollar. It is simply a debt owed by the bank to you. That debt, however, quickly turns into money because you can spend it right away, and the bank still has your original dollar. In this way, the bank has created money "out of nothing." Banks make most of their profit by being allowed to create money in this fashion. The interest banks charge on loans merely pays some of the administrative expenses and, more importantly, it compensates for the inflation that the banks inevitably cause by creating money in the manner that they do. There are, of course, legally-mandated limits to how many dollars a bank may create. A commercial bank must maintain a minimum base of cash (central bank notes) for every dollar deposited, but it is only a small percentage. As long as people use their checking accounts and do not demand too much actual cash, a bank will be safe. A bank can go "broke," however, if enough of its loans default or if too many depositors demand actual cash and thereby wipe out a bank's small asset base.

The result of this whole system is massive debt at every level of society today. The banks are in debt to the depositors, and the depositors' money is loaned out and creates indebtedness to the banks. Making this system even more akin to something out of a maniac's delirium is the fact that banks, like other lenders, often have the right to seize physical property if its paper money is not repaid.

At the national and international levels, we read today of Third World nations staggering under huge debts. Most of those debts are "illusionary" in the sense that the bulk of the loans come from banks which generate or channel "created-out-of-nothing" money. Some of those banks, such as some represented by the International Monetary Fund (IMF), have the right to dictate economic policies and demand austerity measures within the indebted nations to get the loans repaid. In Brazil, for example, the IMF imposed austerity measures in the early 1980's. The measures included large scale wage cuts for Brazilian workers, higher prices on all goods, devaluation of the currency, and increased exports—all to pay back a debt founded mainly on illusion. The result was a tremendous drop in the well-being of the Brazilian people, and riots. The destruction of Brazilian rain forests that we are witnessing today is being caused in large part by Brazil's need to repay loans based on illusionary money. Studies prepared by the World Bank blame population growth for depletion of the rain forests, but conveniently leave out the major role that the World Bank itself has played in causing Brazil's indebtedness.

Another example is the Dominican Republic, which had a $3 billion debt as of the mid-1980's. The country would like to spend its scarce income on better housing for its people. In 1985, however, the nation was faced with having to expend more money to repay its loans than it could earn in foreign currency. The IMF nevertheless demanded strict austerity measures, including large price increases on basic goods, thereby triggering riots. The IMF also mandated a devaluation of the Dominican currency; this increased exports, but made imports much more expensive. Who were the real losers in all of this? The Dominican people.

In the United States under the recent presidential administration of Ronald Reagan, the American national debt was doubled. Most of the loan money, of course, traces back to the "created-out-of-nothing" money of large banks. Nevertheless, interest on this money must now be paid. To pay it, federal social services were cut under Reagan, thereby hurting the standard of living of many Americans. What was much of this extra loan money used for? Military needs.

On a smaller scale, the inflatable paper money system causes farmers to lose farms. Most farmers do not lose their way of life because they fail to work hard or because they do not produce something of great value. They lose because they cannot meet the demands of the paper money system. This allows large agribusinesses to step in and buy up the farmland, resulting in the concentration of food production in an ever-dwindling number of hands.

As we can see, the modern monetary system has had the effect of destroying many benefits that mass production and advances in science and technology would have offered the human race. By now, the need for all-consuming toil for physical existence should be largely ended; but the inflatable paper money system has helped to preserve that need by creating massive debt, chronic inflation, and general economic instability. The vast majority of people in all nations today must still continue to spend the major portion of their prime waking hours working to meet their financial needs. The Custodial goal expressed in the Biblical Adam and Eve story of making people toil from birth until death is still being fulfilled.

Another significant by-product of the modern money system is taxation. Most Americans believe that the U.S. government creates its own money. If that is true, then why would the government need to tax anyone? Why does not the government simply allocate to itself the money it needs to operate? That would obviously be far more sensible than erecting enormous tax-collecting bureaucracies which can drive people to despair and greatly diminished productivity.

The answer is that the U.S. government does not create money—the Federal Reserve and commercial banks do, and they are not public entities. To obtain some of the money those banking entities create, the government must either tax or borrow. It does both, and the citizens pay. Taxation, especially in nations with graduated income tax schemes, makes it harder for people to save money and thereby contributes to the need for most people to spend the majority of their lives toiling for physical existence.

Despite the welcome political reforms now transforming Russia and the Eastern bloc, communism remains a power in other nations where it has inspired fearful oppressions in recent decades, as the people of Ethiopia and Kampuchea have learned to their great sorrow:

On September 12, 1974, the monarchy of Ethiopia was overthrown in a military coup. Six months later, the monarchy was entirely abolished by the revolutionary government and Ethiopia was made a Marxist state complete with collective farms and government-owned industry. The new Marxist rulers soon found themselves opposed by an independence movement in the Ethiopian provinces of Eritrea and Tigre. That independence movement was, and still is, kept alive to a large extent by another Marxist group: the Popular Liberation Front. The resulting battles between the Marxist regime and the Marxist liberation have brought about a great loss of life. The Ethiopian famines we hear so much about today have been caused primarily by the Ethiopian government's attempt to squelch the Eritrean liberation movement by hindering relief shipments to drought regions. This amounts to an act of genocide. People have died horrible deaths as they found themselves caught between two equally brutal factions. Behind all of this we find once again evidence of the Brotherhood network: the emblem of the Marxist regime prominently features the Brotherhood symbol of the "All-Seeing Eye."

On April 17, 1975, the capital of Kampuchea (formerly Cambodia) fell to communist revolutionary forces. A virtual news blackout followed. The stories that leaked out were horrifying beyond description. After the election of communist leader Pol Pot as premier in April 1976, Kampuchea suffered what some experts believe to have been the worst genocide since World War II. At least one million, and as many as three million, Kampucheans died. Out of a population of 7.5 million, that represents a substantial portion. This genocide was part of a grand economic plan formulated by highly-educated Kampuchean leaders who boasted advanced degrees in economics and social science from universities in France. Those leaders decided that their nation should have an agrarian economy . . . immediately. The capital of Kampuchea, Phnom Penh, was forcibly evacuated and its residents were compelled to enter the countryside where rural "production cooperatives" awaited them. Private property was abolished. Citizens who were perceived as standing in the way of the new Kampuchean utopia by virtue of their occupations or education, and those people who objected to being forced into slavery, were murdered. Children were often recruited to carry out the murders, thereby helping to breed in the young generation of Kampuchea a higher than normal incidence of psychopathology. This grand Kampuchean scheme under Pol Pot was a virtual carbon copy of the brutal programs launched earlier in history by the revolutionary council of 18th-century France, by the regime of Joseph Stalin in Russia, and by the Cultural Revolution of Mao Tse-Tung in China. The Pol Pot regime collapsed in January 1979 when Kampuchea was invaded by the communist North Vietnamese, who were hardly models of civility themselves. By 1990, Pol Pot and the Khmer Rouge re-emerged. They were part of a coalition seeking to retake power by military force. The coalition was supported by the United States and, according to several eyewitnesses, CIA-provided weapons continued to reach the still-brutal Khmer Rouge troops.

Prior to the dismantling of the Soviet Union, many communist movements in the world were supported by the Soviet KGB and other Eastern bloc secret services as part of their mission to foment wars of "liberation" around the world. Interestingly, Western intelligence services had also assisted in the establishment of communist regimes just as the German military had done in 1917. The United States initially backed Fidel Castro in Cuba and Ho Chi Minh in Vietnam, both of whom afterwards established communist regimes in their respective nations. Both nations still remain communist as of this writing. The United States had also initially backed Pol Pot and helped him achieve power in Kampuchea. The Communist world, both past and present, was very much a product of Western activity.

Behind today's political factionalism we continue to find evidence of direct Brotherhood network involvement. The Sovereign Military Order of Malta (SMOM), for example, was strongly anti-Communist and instilled anti-Communism in its adherents as a spiritual goal. There is nothing wrong with that until it becomes another justification to breed more violence, oppression and strife. One of SMOM's Knights in America, the late William Casey, headed the American CIA from January 28, 1981 until January 29, 1987. During his tenure as CIA chief, Casey did much to increase CIA covert operations, especially in Central America. There, CIA-backed "Contra" rebels and right-wing "death squads" committed horrible atrocities against civilians in the name of fighting communism. Other SMOM Knights in national intelligence organizations have included James Buckley of Radio Free Europe/Radio Liberty, John McCone (former director of the CIA under President John Kennedy), and Alexandre de Marenches (chief of French Intelligence under President Giscard d'Estaing, who was also an SMOM Knight).

The American CIA is also influenced by Mormonism, Freemasonry, and other lesser known Brotherhood organizations. Mormons are often sought by CIA recruiters due to the overseas experience many Mormons receive in their missionary work, and a few have reached very high positions within the American intelligence community. Some Masonic groups provide special scholarships for young members to attend the Foreign Service School in Washington, D.C. That school provides the nation with many of its State Department personnel, diplomats, and spies. All of these Brotherhood influences have combined to create an ideological hotbed in American foreign policy. The result has been the maintenance of the United States as an effective political faction for keeping conflict alive around the world.

"Lone assassins" continue to be significant today. Earlier in the book, we looked at the origin of the lone assassin phenomenon as a political tool. The substantial "conspiracy" evidence surrounding modern-day assassinations indicates that such killings continue to be crude political weapons. The primary difference today is that some "lone assassins" appear to be a cover for a second hidden assassin, and a pretense is made that the "lone assassin" really did act alone. In all other important respects, modern "lone assassins" are nearly identical to those programmed by the Brotherhood's Ismaili organization centuries ago in the Middle East. To illustrate, let us review some of the evidence behind recent assassinations.

A great deal has already been written about the November 22, 1963 assassination of U.S. President John F. Kennedy, so I will only summarize the events here. President Kennedy was killed by rifle fire while riding in a motorcade in Dallas, Texas. Almost immediately after the shooting, suspicions of a conspiracy arose. The alleged "lone assassin," Lee Harvey Oswald, publicly proclaimed that he was only a "patsy." The ballistics and physical evidence strongly suggested that Kennedy was hit by bullets fired from in front of him, not from behind where Oswald was positioned. Oswald never had a chance to elaborate on his claim that he was a patsy or go to trial because, two days after his arrest, he was murdered while in police custody by a night club owner, Jack Ruby—a man with known Mafia connections. Ruby went to prison and died there less than four years later.

An official government panel was convened to investigate the JFK assassination. Known as the "Warren Commission" after its chairman, U.S. Supreme Court Chief Justice Earl Warren, the panel concluded that Oswald had acted entirely alone. Years later, a U.S. House of Representatives panel spent 26 months re-investigating the murders of John F. Kennedy and black civil rights leader Martin Luther King, Jr. (who was slain in 1968 by an alleged "lone assassin"). The House panel concluded that the "lone assassins" did *not* act alone and that conspiracies lay behind the Kennedy and King killings. The panel felt that further police investigation was warranted. Despite rumors and evidence of CIA and Mafia involvements in the Kennedy shooting, no convictions of any co-conspirators have ever occurred.

John Kennedy's younger brother, Robert F. Kennedy, was assassinated almost five years later on June 5, 1968 inside the Ambassador Hotel in Los Angeles, California. RFK was running for president at the time he was shot and he was almost certain to win the Democratic nomination. He had just finished delivering a speech to enthused campaign workers and began to walk through the back pantry area surrounded by a throng of well-wishers and reporters. It was in the pantry area that the convicted assassin, Sirhan Sirhan, opened fire at close range with a .22 caliber pistol. A number of people were hit and Kennedy fell to the floor with head and body wounds. Sirhan was immediately apprehended. Kennedy died the next day and Sirhan went on to be convicted as the sole assassin. Despite the conviction, a great deal of controversy remained. In an extraordinary feat of investigative journalism, researcher Theodore Charach compiled a large body of evidence indicating that a second hidden gunman, not Sirhan Sirhan, had fired the shot which killed Kennedy. Mr. Charach used his evidence to create an astonishing feature-length documentary film entitled *The Second Gun*. The movie enjoyed a short theatrical release in the 1970's and has recently been made available on home videotape.* Mr. Charach's research was picked up by others and it eventually brought about the Los Angeles County Board of Supervisors hearings into the assassination.

The RFK "second gun" case rests on a great deal of fascinating ballistics evidence and eyewitness testimony. For example, the Los Angeles coroner performed an analysis of the gunpowder burns on Kennedy's head and clothing. The burns revealed that the muzzle of the gun was not more than one to three inches from Kennedy's head when it fired the fatal bullets; *i.e.,* the muzzle was at point blank range. All eyewitnesses, however, reported that Sirhan's weapon was

---

*_The Second Gun_ videotape was released by Video Cassette Sales, Inc. Please see Bibliography for address.

never closer than twelve inches; a significant difference as far as powder burns are concerned. *The Second Gun* suggests that the fatal bullet may have been fired from the gun of a uniformed security guard who was holding Kennedy by the right arm when the shooting started. The guard admitted pulling out his gun during the melee, but denied firing it. An eyewitness on the scene, however, did testify to seeing the guard fire. There is no record that the police ever examined the guard's pistol.

A bizarre diary reportedly written by Sirhan, and discovered in his apartment after the shooting, seems to lend weight to the conspiracy theory. In that diary, Sirhan wrote several times of the need for Robert Kennedy to die in connection with Sirhan receiving large sums of money. One entry mentioned $100,000. The most interesting diary entry is that one in which Sirhan, who seemed to relish the thought of receiving large checks made payable to him, appears to repeat an instruction that he has never heard a promise that he would receive money for Kennedy's death, which needed to happen by June 5, 1968—the date of the California primary. Sirhan's diary contained the following words:

> Robert F. Kennedy must be assassinated Robert F. Kennedy must be assassinated before 5 June '68 Robert F. Kennedy must be assassinated I have never heard please pay to the order of of of of of of.[1]

The LAPD considered the diary entries to be nothing more than the rantings of a mentally-deranged lone assassin. If that truly was Sirhan's writing, his references to money would certainly provide an additional motive for him to take shots at Kennedy, whom he greatly disliked anyway. The question is: who offered Sirhan the apparent money and does Sirhan believe that he will still receive it when he is finally released from prison? To this day, Sirhan maintains that he acted entirely alone, and the FBI and Los Angeles Police Department are content to agree with him.

If a security guard fired the shot which killed RFK, it is possible that he did it accidentally. The guard may have drawn his gun from his holster in an effort to defend Kennedy without even realizing it. The police, however, never even considered this possibility despite the powerful evidence that Sirhan's gun did not fire the fatal bullet. The LAPD was instead very one-minded in its "lone assassin" theory and, as pointed out by a Los Angeles Times article, badly mishandled some of the key physical evidence.*

Rumors again abounded of a possible Mafia and/or CIA involvement in the Robert Kennedy shooting, but no co-conspirators were ever arrested in the case.

In the early afternoon of March 30, 1981, President Ronald Reagan finished giving a speech at the Washington Hilton Hotel. Surrounded by his entourage and Secret Service agents, Reagan walked out to the driveway where a limousine awaited him. As in the Robert Kennedy shooting, an apparently crazed young man emerged from the crowd firing a pistol. Reagan was pushed into the limousine by a Secret Service agent, rushed to a hospital and underwent surgery to remove a single bullet which had struck him in the left rib cage and pierced his left lung. It is fortunate that the wound was not fatal. The "lone assassin," John Hinckley, Jr., went on to be convicted of the crime. According to a newspaper columnist, the FBI did all it could to prove that Hinckley had been the sole assassin

---

*The mishandled evidence included ceiling panels from the pantry area that may have contained bullet holes indicating the presence of a second gun. Incredibly, the panels were destroyed by the police. According to LAPD chief Daryl Gates, the destruction of the panels had been done routinely. Mr. Gates said that this did not constitute destruction of evidence because the panels had not been introduced as evidence at Sirhan's trial. He added, however:

... I just think that it [destroying the panels] was lack of judgment. It was a lack of common sense and inexcusable because the case had worldwide magnitude.

More importantly, Sirhan had been convicted and his appeal was not even in prospect yet. Potential evidence should never be destroyed until the entire case has run out.

What the hell were these things destroyed for? That borders on Catch 22 insanity. It was just like they were opening up the doors to total criticism and doubt. There's no way it can be explained.[2]

on the scene. Some people, however, have expressed doubts about the FBI's conclusion. In a press conference held a month after his recovery, Mr. Reagan answered questions indicating that he did not feel the impact of the bullet that struck him until he was all the way inside the limousine:

Q: What were your first thoughts when you realized you had been hit?
A: Actually, I can't recall too clearly. I knew I'd been hurt, but I thought that I'd been hurt by the Secret Service man landing on me in the car, and it was, I must say, it was the most paralyzing pain. I've described it as if someone had hit you with a hammer.

But that sensation, it seemed to me, came after I was in the car, and so I thought that maybe his gun or something, when he [the Secret Service agent] had come down on me, had broken a rib.

But when I sat up on the seat and the pain wouldn't go away, and suddenly I found that I was coughing up blood, we both decided that maybe I'd broken a rib and punctured a lung.[3]

In a later interview, Mr. Reagan's wife, Nancy, confirmed the President's impression.

Had Mr. Reagan simply suffered a delayed reaction to a bullet fired from Hinckley's gun, or had he actually been shot, perhaps accidentally, inside the car by a Secret Service agent, as the above testimony would suggest? According to the FBI, the bullet that wounded Mr. Reagan had ricocheted off the limousine door just as Mr. Reagan was being pushed into the vehicle. If the FBI explanation is true, why did the bullet not explode upon impact with the door since it was an exploding bullet? Perhaps the bullet was a "dud"? It is possible that two coincidences did occur at the Reagan shooting: a dud bullet followed by a delayed pain reaction. Another explanation which does not require a coincidence is that Reagan was shot, perhaps accidentally, by the Secret Service agent inside the car: this would explain both the failure of the exploding bullet to explode (it did not hit an intervening metal door) and Mr. Reagan's own recollection.

The FBI did not pursue the "second gun" angle in the Reagan shooting. This is troubling because the convicted assassin, John Hinckley, Jr., claimed that there was a conspiracy involved in the shooting. In its October 21, 1981 issue, the *New York Times* reported:

A Justice Department source late tonight confirmed a report that John W. Hinckley, Jr. had written in papers confiscated from his cell in July that he was part of a conspiracy when he shot President Reagan and three other men March 30.[4]

Hinckley's allegation should have set in motion an intensive conspiracy investigation. After all, John Hinckley, Jr., was not just a random individual out of the American melting pot. He was the son of a wealthy personal friend and political supporter of the then-Vice President who, of course, would have become President if Reagan had died. This is not to say that a conspiracy necessarily existed, only that such circumstances typically trigger a much more intensive investigation. The *New York Times* states that the FBI seized Hinckley's papers, followed up on the leads, and concluded that Hinckley's conspiracy claim was untrue. The judge hearing the case ordered attorneys and witnesses not to divulge the contents of Hinckley's papers to the public. The prison guards who had seized and read the papers gave their testimony in secret to the judge. At Hinckley's trial, neither defense nor prosecuting attorneys ever raised the issue of a "conspiracy," nor the second gun possibility. Instead, the entire trial centered around Mr. Hinckley's very visible mental problems.

Perhaps the three shootings just discussed really were committed by lone assassins, with two of the shootings involving the accidental discharge of a firearm by a security agent. An assassination in the Philippines proved, however, that such scenarios may sometimes be the cover for a murder committed by an intelligence organization.

The year was 1983. Benigno Aquino was a popular opposition leader in the Philippine Islands. The Philippines were then under the dictatorial rule of President Ferdinand Marcos. Marcos had declared martial law in the 1960's and never saw fit to lift it. After three years of voluntary exile from his homeland, Aquino made a decision to return to his country even though six years earlier he had been sentenced to death by firing squad for his political activities.

Aquino's airplane landed at Manila Airport on August 21, 1983. Surrounded by Filipino security officers, Aquino had just descended the stairs from the airplane when shots rang out. A bullet hit him in the back of the head and killed him. The "lone assassin," Rolando Galman y Dawang, was on the tarmac (runway area) and was instantly shot dead by a security man near him. The government immediately declared Galman the "lone assassin" and tried to close the case.

Suspicions arose immediately.

President Marcos had a motive for killing Aquino and Aquino had already been sentenced to death. To quash these suspicions, Marcos convened an official panel to investigate the killing, similar to the Warren Commission impanelled twenty years earlier in the United States to investigate the John Kennedy assassination. Critics charged that the Marcos panel was one-sided and pro-Marcos. Many doubted that the panel would come to any conclusion other than the official one. Something unexpected occurred, however. The panel pursued the investigation objectively. It heard evidence about the powder burn on Aquino's head indicating that the fatal bullet was fired from 12 to 18 inches away. The government claimed Galman had come that close, but eyewitnesses did not confirm this. A journalist on the plane testified that two security men standing right next to Aquino had pulled out their revolvers and had pointed them at the back of Aquino's head just before the shots rang out. Overwhelming forensic evidence and eyewitness testimony indicated that Aquino was shot by one of the security men assigned to "protect" him. The "lone assassin" was nothing more than a crude cover. The Marcos commission issued a finding to that effect.

The panel findings resulted in the criminal indictments of several high-ranking military officers. At trial, however, all were acquitted. The vagaries of the Filipino justice system did not permit a great deal of crucial testimony acquired by the commission to be introduced at trial. A number of important witnesses for the prosecution did not appear. Several witnesses had reported being intimidated. After Marcos was ousted from office and sent into a plush Hawaiian exile by Benigno Aquino's wife, Corazon Aquino, witnesses came forward testifying that the trial had been rigged by Marcos. Other eyewitnesses to the shooting also came forward with further evidence corroborating that Benigno Aquino had been shot by a security man.

The significance of the Aquino killing is that the scenario of the shooting is virtually identical to other "lone assassin" episodes. If, for example, there existed a conspiracy behind either the RFK or Ronald Reagan shooting, then the modus operandi would appear to be identical to the modus operandi in the Aquino shooting: a mentally-disturbed or politically-fanatical "lone assassin" is used as a cover for the true assassin who is on the scene as a security escort for the victim. This is important because the Filipino officers indicted for masterminding the Aquino shooting included General Fabian Ver and men under his command. Ver not only led the nation's military forces, but also its intelligence network. In other words, the "lone assassin" shooting of Benigno Aquino was a military/*intelligence* operation. This is significant because the Philippine Republic was a major U.S. ally at the time of the shooting, and the U.S. still has large naval and air bases there. The Philippines receive a great deal of aid from the United States, along with U.S. military and intelligence advisors. The Filipino intelligence apparatus therefore owes much to the American CIA and U.S. military intelligence. This is not to say that American sources were necessarily involved in the Aquino shooting. It simply shows how an important Western intelligence service recently utilized the "lone assassin" technique, but used it so crudely that people saw through it immediately. Even U.S. newspapers which have been quick to accept "lone assassin" verdicts in American assassinations ran editorials condemning the acquittal of the Filipino military men. Our hats should go off to those brave panel members who had the courage to look behind the "lone assassin" myth, and to those eyewitnesses who were brave enough to testify. Such integrity is a precious commodity.

Modern "lone assassins" are not just American-related

phenomena; they remain international in scope. On May 13, 1981 during his public appearance in St. Peter's Square, Pope John Paul II was shot. He survived and still holds the Papacy today. The convicted "lone assassin," Mehmet Ali Acga, had fired from a crowd that surrounded the Papal automobile. Interestingly, the Italian police also arrested a second gunman in connection with the shooting and accused Bulgarian intelligence agents of being involved in a plot to kill the Pope. Bulgaria was still a communist nation at the time. Russia accused the American CIA of manufacturing this so-called "Bulgarian Connection" for propaganda purposes; however, Western newspapers reported that the CIA had actually stepped in and put pressure on the Italian police to drop the "Bulgarian Connection" and the "second gun" case. The Italians succumbed to CIA demands after the accused assassin, Mehmet Acga, destroyed his own credibility by flip-flopping on his story and by engaging in bizarre behavior.

In Sweden, a significant "lone assassin" episode involved the killing of the very popular Swedish Prime Minister, Olaf Palme, on February 28, 1986. Mr. Palme was strolling home with his wife from a movie when a gunman ran up to the Prime Minister, fired twice, and fled into the night. Suspicions of a conspiracy arose immediately, but the word was quickly put out that the killing was the work of a "lunatic." A suspect was eventually arrested, but he denied responsibility and was acquitted. In 1990, the Swedish government even paid him restitution for the time he spent in jail. As of this writing, no other suspect is due to go to trial.

The final episode worth looking at occurred in West Germany on April 25, 1990 against Oskar Lafontaine. Mr. Lafontaine was premier of the Saarland state and running as the Social Democratic candidate for the office of Chancellor of Germany. He was on stage with another leading Social Democrat, Johannes Rau, during a political rally. A person who appeared to be a security guard led a woman up on stage; the woman was carrying a bouquet of flowers. When she reached Mr. Lafontaine, she calmly whipped out a butcher knife and slashed his throat. Fortunately, Mr. Lafontaine survived despite a significant loss of blood and he went on to finish his unsuccessful campaign. The assailant, Adelheid Streidel, was immediately apprehended and labeled a mentally-deranged "lone assassin." The attack, however, has the hallmarks of several previous "lone assassin" episodes we just looked at: involvement of apparent security personnel, the so-called "lone assassin" showing signs of severe mental tampering, and the act committed openly. The use of the butcher knife instead of a gun makes Ms. Streidel even more like the Assassins of medieval Persia, who used bladed weapons. This assassination attempt occurred at a politically crucial time: Mr. Lafontaine was running against Chancellor Helmut Kohl. Mr. Kohl was a prime advocate for rapid German reunification and European unity, which would involve major shifts in world economics, politics, and military matters. Mr. Lafontaine and the Social Democrats were running on a platform of slowing down the German reunification process.

As in the case of Adelheid Streidel, a significant element of nearly all recent "lone assassin" cases is the mental state of the "lone assassins" at the time of the assassinations. The apparent "mental illness" exhibited by so many of them may very well be evidence of mental tampering. Sirhan Sirhan was known to have been repeatedly hypnotized by "friends" whom the police inadequately investigated. Eyewitnesses reported that Sirhan seemed to be almost in a trance on the night he fired at Robert Kennedy. John Hinckley, Jr., had had a great deal of psychiatric intervention during his pre-assassination days, and we still do not know what all of it consisted of. Did Hinckley receive any visionary implants similar to the ones that Adolf Hitler had received as a psychiatric patient at Pasewalk? Like the ancient assassins of Persia, Hinckley was motivated by a crazed notion that he would attain to heaven by killing Reagan, except that Hinckley's heaven was the unattainable love of a certain female movie star. Hinckley thought that he would win that love by killing the President. The peculiar mental states of Mehmet Ali Acga and other modern assassins (such as "Squeaky" Fromme who tried to murder President Gerald Ford in 1975) are further indications that mental tampering may be a significant factor in most modern "lone assassin" episodes, just as it had been in medieval Persia.

In light of the above, it is perhaps not surprising to discover evidence of the Brotherhood network directly or indirectly linked to some modern assassinations. John Hinckley, Jr., for example, belonged for a while to an American Nazi organization. Modern American Naziism, through such organizations as the Aryan Nations, is as deeply influenced by Brotherhood-style mysticism as was original German Naziism. "Squeaky" Fromme was a follower of Charles Manson, who preached a bizarre apocalyptic mysticism in a small California commune. Manson and his "Family" were the ones who committed the horrific Tate-LaBianca murders in Los Angeles in 1969. Interestingly, Manson was once a police informer.

As long as the "lone assassin" technique continues to go unopposed, those nations victimized by it will never rise above the level of a banana republic. That includes the United States and nations in Europe. One need only look at the way in which such assassinations have influenced the succession of American Presidents to appreciate just how damaging the technique is to a democracy. The problem with American leadership today is not so much a difficulty caused by the electoral process or by shortcomings in the Constitution. The problem is that the electoral process and Constitution have been severely undermined by the assassination of leaders and candidates. When police organizations contribute to this by ignoring and suppressing evidence, and by otherwise hindering proper investigations, those police organizations become accessories to the crimes in a very real and legal sense. That is when democracy dies.

Throughout this book, we have noted the role of the Brotherhood network in perpetuating revolution. Revolutions and armed resistance movements are expensive to run, and so we find that most of them are financed today by intelligence organizations. One unfortunate by-product of this activity is terrorism.

Terrorist groups are an effective way to keep conflict alive. An interesting book entitled, *The Terror Network* by Claire Sterling, reveals the strong interconnections that have existed between seemingly unrelated terrorist groups. Terrorist organizations from around the world and of conflicting ideologies have been supported by mutual "safe houses" and suppliers. *The Terror Network* reveals that many of those mutual supply sources had connections to the Russian KGB, although the book fails to mention the role of Western intelligence services in supporting various forms of terrorism.

The goal of some terrorist groups is to maintain a so-called "Permanent Revolution," *i.e.*, a violent revolution that never ends. This goal is rooted in the Marxist concept that class struggle is inevitable and must continuously occur for a utopia to emerge. As we recall, this idea has its ultimate roots in the Calvinist teaching that a world at war is a world closer to God. The "Permanent Revolution" is therefore designed to keep people fighting constantly so that we will all be able to enjoy a future utopia. This sounds crazy, you say? Of course it is. The "Permanent Revolution," which has been financed by various intelligence services and is inspired by concepts that came out of the Brotherhood network, is yet one more way to keep mankind in a constant state of war and disunity.

Efforts to generate nonstop strife on Earth have apparently been so successful that they threatened to wipe out most of humanity. Powerful atomic weapons were built in preparation for yet another "Final Battle" between the forces of "good" and "evil." To those who believe that nuclear war is unthinkable: think again. In the climate of endless confrontation we share on Earth, rarely have weapons gone unused. Two atomic bombs were already dropped during World War II and, if we are to believe some evidence, they may have been used to wipe out human civilizations in the ancient past. There is a great irony in this. If manipulations by a Custodial society do indeed ultimately lie behind human turmoil, the Custodial society could soon find itself owning a very damaged piece of real estate. It is true that nuclear weapons are notoriously unstable so that many atomic warheads will not explode if launched, but there has been enough of an "overkill" built to ensure that considerable damage would result from a nuclear exchange. Happily, the end of the Cold War brought about pledges for significant reductions in U.S. and Russian nuclear arsenals. There is irony in this, too, in light of the factions and hostilities that have replaced those of the Cold War. Once nuclear arsenals are reduced far enough, large-scale warfare will be possible again without the threat that such warfare would render Earth useless to apparent Custodial owners.

The lingering danger from remaining nuclear weaponry and proliferation would not come from unstable flying missiles, but from stationary bombs hidden at their target locations. The Pentagon expressed concern about such a possibility in a top secret military report produced in 1945. This concern was expressed again in more recent years when efforts were under way to develop a so-called "Star Wars" anti-missile defense system which utilizes laser beams to shoot down enemy missiles.* Some strategists were afraid that a successful "Star Wars" system would encourage a hostile foreign power to smuggle and plant atomic bombs in the United States if it felt that its missiles would be ineffective. Such bombs can be easily stored and kept mobile in trucks or vans. The media-publicized "nuclear terrorism" scare of the 1970's indicates that some stationary bombs may already be in place in the United States. It is also important to keep in mind that the source of such bombs may not always be an enemy government or hostile terrorist group. There always exists the danger that a nation's own government may secretly plant nuclear bombs within its own cities as part of a "scorched earth" contingency war plan, in the same way that Switzerland has placed mines on all of its own bridges in the event an enemy invades and tries to use the bridges. In xenophobic nations, an internal nuclear threat of this kind can become very real. It is something that the people of every country with atomic weapons should remain wary of.

The Cold War between the United States and former Soviet Union affected us in many ways still felt today. Higher taxes, intrusive military and intelligence agencies, and a host of other ills were imposed upon human populations in the name of protecting against the enemy. We have

---

*Star Wars can also be converted to an offensive weapon for rapidly destroying enemy cities with laser beams. Such laser weapons would be far deadlier than a nuclear arsenal and could, if developed, replace our atomic stockpiles. In 1992, the president of the new Russian Republic suggested a joint venture with the United States to create such a weapons system.

been affected in other ways which are less well-known, but equally significant.

During the second half of the 1970's, revelations of American military and CIA germ warfare experiments emerged in the public press. Surprisingly, many of those experiments were conducted in U.S. cities and were directed against U.S. citizens. In the 1950's, for example, a "germ fog" had been sprayed by a Navy ship at San Francisco. According to the *Los Angeles Times:*

> In an experiment designed to determine both attack and defense capabilities of biological weapons, a Navy ship blanketed San Francisco and its neighboring communities with a bacteria-laden fog for six days in 1950, according to U.S. military records.
>
> The records contain the conclusion that nearly every one of San Francisco's 800,000 residents was exposed to the cloud released by a Navy ship steaming up and down just outside the Golden Gate.
>
> The aerosol substance released by the ship contained a bacteria known as serratia, which was believed harmless by the military at the time but which has been found since to cause a type of pneumonia that can be fatal.[5]

The *L.A. Times* added that at least twelve people were hospitalized around that time for serratia pneumonia. One of them died. That was just the beginning. The army disclosed that it had conducted 239 open-air tests between 1949 and 1969! Of those, 80 were admitted to have contained actual germs. The tests were directed against Washington, D.C., New York City, Key West, Panama City (Florida), and San Francisco. If we accept the army's figure of 80 live-disease experiments, we discover an average of four "germ attacks" against U.S. cities every year for twenty years! Other government documents have revealed additional CIA germ warfare experiments carried out in the same manner. This means that several major U.S. population areas were under fairly intensive germ bombardment for an admitted twenty-year period, all by the nation's own military and intelligence organizations!

These germ "experiments" reportedly ended in 1969. However, justified suspicions have arisen about sudden outbreaks of more recent diseases, especially those which do not seem to conform to our understanding of epidemiology. The most recent of such diseases is AIDS (Acquired Immune Deficiency Syndrome). After the AIDS epidemic broke, the Soviet Union published charges in its official newspapers that AIDS was a biological weapon developed by the United States military. The charges have been generally dismissed as false propaganda and the Soviet Union later publicly retracted the statements after pressure from the United States. Despite the retraction, a number of researchers in the United States contend that there is evidence to support the original claim.

U.S. citizens have not only been hit by germs, but also by another type of bombardment. An intriguing segment of the television program, *NBC Magazine with David Brinkley,* aired July 16, 1981, revealed that the northwestern United States was continuously bombarded by the Soviet Union with low frequency radio waves. The radio waves are set at the approximate level of biological electronic frequencies. Mr. Brinkley stated:

As I say I find it hard to believe, it is crazy and none of us here knows what to make of it: the Russian Government is known to be trying to change human behavior by external electronic influences. We do know that much. And we know that some kind of Russian transmitter is bombarding this country with extreme low frequency radiowaves.[6]

A U.S. government spokesperson stated that the radio beams were a kind of low-frequency radar system, but he was at a loss to explain how such a "radar system" worked. The fact is, low-frequency waves of that type will affect neurological and physiological functioning, usually by reducing mental functioning and by making people more suggestive. That is apparently the intent. A May 20, 1983 newspaper article from the Associated Press reported that a machine known as the Lida has been used by the Soviet Union since at least 1960 to influence human behavior with a 40 Megahertz radio wave. The Lida is used in

Russia as a tranquilizer and it produces a trancelike state. The Russian "owner's manual" calls the Lida a "distant pulse treatment apparatus" for dealing with psychological problems, hypertension, and neurosis. The machine has been offered as a possible substitute for psychotropic drugs. When the AP article appeared, a Lida machine was on loan to the Jerry L. Pettis Memorial Veterans Hospital in the United States through a medical exchange program. According to the chief of research at the hospital, the machine may eventually be used in American classrooms to control the behavior of disturbed or retarded children. The Lida is apparently a small-scale version of the very same type of machine described in the David Brinkley show, as the AP article reveals:

> [The chief of research] said some people theorize that the Soviets may be using an advanced version of the machine clandestinely to seek a change in behavior in the United States through signals beamed from the U.S.S.R.[7]

It appears that Americans were receiving electronic tranquilizing treatments courtesy of the Soviet government. It is incredible that the United States did not loudly demand an immediate stop to the intervention. Ironically, but not surprisingly, America appeared to have become more militant during the "treatments." Anti-Soviet sentiment increased and so did the military build-up. Certainly the increased militancy of the United States cannot all be attributed to the Russian machines, but, at best, the Soviet treatments were ineffective in making America calmer. In actual fact, electronic tranquilizers appear to be deep irritants which will ultimately contribute to heightened aggression. The Russians, and anyone else still operating such devices, would do well to shut them off and keep them off.

As the evidence has shown, major military and intelligence organizations have taken over doing to human populations precisely what UFOs and some "Ascended Masters" reportedly did earlier: they have spread dangerous germs and have bombarded human populations with behavior-altering electronic radiation. When we consider these facts, it might be significant that military and intelligence organizations, at least in the United States, were foremost in debunking UFOs for many years.

The first known official American government investigation into the UFO phenomenon was begun on January 22, 1948 by the U.S. Air Force. The investigation was known as "Project Sign." The startling conclusion of Project Sign, as announced in its "Estimate of the Situation," was that UFOs were craft from "another world." This conclusion was immediately rejected by the Chief of Staff, General Hoy S. Vandenberg, who dismissed the evidence as "insufficient." A new study group called Project Grudge was subsequently launched on February 11, 1949. The purpose of "Grudge" was to investigate the UFO phenomenon from the basic premise that extraterrestrial aircraft could not exist. Project Grudge pursued its work for several years and was eventually upgraded to the famous "Project Bluebook" in 1952—a year in which there was a dramatic increase in UFO reports. Project Bluebook concluded (not surprisingly, considering the basic premise upon which its predecessor, Project Grudge, was founded) that UFOs were all explainable natural phenomena.

In the year after "Project Bluebook" was established, the CIA entered the UFO controversy with an investigation of its own. In 1953, the CIA established a panel of eminent scientists known as the "Robertson Panel." The CIA Panel quickly rubber-stamped the official view that UFOs did not represent an extraterrestrial race. The Panel added that UFOs were not a direct physical threat to national security, and were therefore of no interest. The Panel did state, however, that reporting UFOs could be a threat to national security! The Panel wrote the following words to suggest that suppressing UFO reports was desirable in the national interest:

> . . . continued emphasis on the reporting of these phenomena, in these parlous [dangerous] times, result in a threat to the orderly functioning of the protective organs of the body politic.[8]

As a result, the CIA and FBI investigated many people who reported UFOs. The U.S. Air Force cooperated by issuing regulations in 1958 instructing Air Force investigators to give the FBI the names of people who claimed to have contacted UFOs in some way, on the grounds that such people were "illegally or deceptively bringing the subject to public attention."[9] Although these regulations have been eased and the FBI reportedly no longer investigates UFO cases, there existed back in the 1950's and early '60's a definite intention within the American government to inhibit public reporting and discussion of the UFO phenomenon.

Today, the U.S. government is publicly out of the UFO business. Most of the debunking torch has been passed to a private group called the Committee for the Scientific Investigation of Claims of the Paranormal ("CSICOP"). CSICOP boasts an impressive roster of scientific and technical consultants, many of whom hold professorships at prestigious universities. CSICOP has inspired the creation of local branches usually known as "skeptical societies." CSICOP publishes a quarterly journal called *The Skeptical Inquirer*.

A basic premise upon which CSICOP operates is that UFOs are not proven to be extraterrestrial craft. CSICOP also debunks all other phenomena that it considers phony or "pseudoscientific," such as clairvoyance, spiritualism, Bigfoot, the Abominable Snowman, the Loch Ness monster, and all spiritual phenomena. It brands any effort to seriously study UFOs or spiritual phenomena as "pseudoscience"—a term it bandies about freely. CSICOP naturally practices only "real" science. Many CSICOP and local skeptic members are quite energetic and some of them appear regularly on radio and television shows.

The influence of CSICOP today is quite strong. In addition to its presence in universities through CSICOP-affiliated faculty, CSICOP has exerted influence in the media. Celebrity astronomer Carl Sagan, for example, is listed as a Fellow of CSICOP. Other Fellows have included Bernard Dixon, European editor of *Omni* magazine; Paul Edwards, editor of the *Encyclopedia of Philosophy;* Leon Jaroff, managing editor of *Discover* magazine; Phillip Klass, senior avionics editor for *Aviation Week & Space*

*Technology* magazine; and the late B. F. Skinner, author and famous behaviorist who did so much to promote the stimulus-response model of human behavior in our own generation.

CSICOP has gained a following primarily because the organization successfully promotes an image of objectivity. In CSICOP's statement of purpose, for example, we read the following words:

> The Committee for the Scientific Investigation of Claims of the Paranormal attempts to encourage the critical investigation of paranormal and fringe-science claims from a responsible, scientific point of view and to disseminate factual information about the results of such inquiries to the scientific community and the public.
> . . .
> The Committee is a nonprofit scientific and educational organization.[10]

The Committee sounds like a wonderful organization. The world can greatly benefit from objective research into UFOs and paranormal claims. It is especially important for serious researchers to sort out the legitimate from the fraud, and that is not always easy to do. Sadly, CSICOP does not provide the objectivity needed to accomplish that task. The result of a CSICOP investigation has always been, to my knowledge, an utter debunking. This has puzzled those people who cannot understand how some evidence can possibly be rejected if it is looked at objectively. The solution to this puzzle comes by discovering who started CSICOP and why.

CSICOP was founded in 1976 under the sponsorship of the American Humanist Association. The American Humanist Association is, of course, dedicated to advancing the philosophy of "humanism." "Humanism" itself is difficult to define because it often means different things to different people. Essentially, humanism is a school of thought concerned with human interests and human values as opposed to religious interests and values. It deals with questions of ethics and existence from the perspective of human beings as physical entities on Earth. "Religious humanists" will have spiritual and theological concerns, but will approach them from a human-centered focus as opposed to the God-centered or spirit-centered orientation of most religions.

The best-known form of organized humanism in the United States today is called "secular [non-religious] humanism." Secular humanism admits only the reality of physical existence and rejects spiritual and theological reality. It is a philosophy of strict materialism. Many secular humanists adhere to the stimulus-response model of human behavior.

The founding and current chairman of CSICOP is Paul Kurtz, professor of philosophy at the State University of New York at Buffalo. For many years, Mr. Kurtz had served as the editor of *The Humanist* magazine. He was one of the drafters of the *Humanist Manifesto II* and authored a book entitled *In Defense of Secular Humanism*. His book is interesting because it expresses some of the doctrines and goals of the organized secular humanist movement. Those doctrines and goals are significant in light of the role that Professor Kurtz and other secular humanists have played in founding CSICOP. On the subject of spiritual existence, Professor Kurtz wrote:

Humanists reject the thesis that the soul is separable from the body or that life persists in some form after the death of the body.[11]

According to the *Humanist Manifesto II:*

Rather, science affirms that the human species is an emergence from natural evolutionary forces. As far as we know, the total personality is a function of the biological organism transacting in a social and cultural context.[12]

Such ideas are fine for those people who choose to believe them. The point I am making is this: individuals and organizations which actively promote such ideas will find it difficult to be genuinely objective when they investigate evidence which flatly contradicts their established view.

They have already declared what they believe and what they reject.

Objectivity is even more difficult when those same people actively seek to spread their way of thinking as a social goal. According to the *Humanist Manifesto II*:

> We affirm a set of common principles that can serve as a basis for united action—positive principles relevant to the present human condition. They are a design for a secular society on a planetary scale.[13]

We see in this quote that there exists a united intention among many secular humanists to create a worldwide secular society. The founding chairman of CSICOP, Professor Kurtz, helped draft the document which announces that intention. There is nothing wrong per se with having such a goal. It is common for activist religions and philosophies to try to shape the world in their own images. There is, however, a price to be paid for such activism: CSICOP and its affiliated skeptic groups lose their credibility. They have to be viewed as advocates for a certain point of view, not as disinterested investigators. They are prosecutors in the courts of inquiry, not the judges or juries.

We see in groups like CSICOP a problem that has existed for centuries. Most ideological battles are fought by extremists. Secular humanists, for example, represent a materialist extreme and they often do battle with modern "Christian fundamentalists" who represent the "religious" extreme. Both sides are extremist in that they hold views which can only be kept alive by ignoring large bodies of evidence. They make easy targets for one another because they both have so many flaws; yet people are encouraged to side with one or the other on the basis that because one side is so wrong, the other side pointing out those wrongs must be right. This can be dangerous logic to follow. It happens frequently that two people will passionately debate a fact, each certain that he or she is correct, but when they finally learn the truth, they discover that they were both wrong. Two lunatics can argue endlessly over which of them is the real Napoleon Bonaparte, but woe to the outsider who takes sides and swears allegiance to either one of them! As extremists fight, the truth often lies ignored in a completely different direction.

Despite the efforts of secular humanists and others of similar ideological inclination to negate religion and theology, religion continues to be a powerful force in human society. If all of the surviving truths from all of the long-established religions and mystical systems were to be brought together today, they would be insufficient to get a person over the formidable barriers which stand in the way of full spiritual recovery. At best, those accumulated truths would only offer clues to assist in wholly new research. This is not to disparage the genuine rewards that a great many individuals still receive as a result of following various religious paths. Most theologies do have something of value to enrich a person's life.

It is as true today as it has been throughout all of history that new religions come and go in great numbers. Very few of them survive very long, let alone become major religions. Despite this, new religions are attacked as frequently today as they were in the past. Modern attacks take the same form as they have for centuries: new religions are labeled mysterious evils that undermine everything good. The word "cult" is tossed around quite a bit today to label new religions, even though a great many of those religions are not "cults" in the true sense of the word. Properly used, "cult" refers to a subgroup of a larger religion, such as a Christian cult or a Moslem cult. Any completely new or autonomous religion is properly called a "sect," or better yet, simply a new religion. The word "cult" has apparently become popular because of its phonetic qualities. It also fits well into newspaper headlines.

The greatest danger from new religions is not that they represent anything especially new or different, it is that they can be effective tools for breaking people into factions, just as religions did in the past. This can be accomplished even through no fault of the religion itself. Just by existing and being attacked, a modern religion may become an embattled faction when it finds itself operating in a social climate of "cult hysteria." This type of social climate is easily generated today because most educated people fancy themselves knowledgeable about human psychology. By appealing to that vanity, it is easy to breed animosity against new religions in otherwise-tolerant people by couching religious intolerance in psychological terms. Ironically, most of the anti-cult activism today comes from the so-called Christian "right-wing" in its effort to stamp out the "works of Satan," which includes all religions not adhering to fundamentalist Christian beliefs. Christian bookstores are the primary outlets for anti-cult books in the United States today. These Christians have found strange allies in groups like CSICOP and in those other strict materialists (*e.g.*, some psychiatrists) who view all religion as unhealthy and find easy targets in the newer religions.

The key to analyzing new religions, therefore, is not to lump them all into an ill-defined category called "cults" and then spout out generalities about them. The proper approach is to look at each new religion individually, to recognize the unique features of each, and to analyze the good and the bad within them according to the specific characteristics of each. Some will be found to be but an unhappy continuation of all that we have looked at in this book, others will be sincere attempts at spiritual enlightenment. The reason it is important to try to remain objective about new religions is that genuine spiritual knowledge will probably only come about through a newer religion. The older theologies will not stray far from their established doctrines and most modern sciences will not even consider evidence of a spiritual reality.

There is one recent religious movement worth mentioning. It is the loosely-knit "New Age" movement. The New Age movement is called that because it seeks the dawn of a New Age on Earth in which spiritual freedom, physical health, and world peace will prevail. Some of the unique music associated with the New Age movement is quite nice and the New Age emphasis on eating natural, healthy foods is a very positive element of the movement. Some New Age doctrines contain maverick ideas about the nature of the spiritual being, but like Hinduisim, most New Age systems destroy the full benefits of those maverick ideas by mixing in large doses of mysticism, Custodial doctrine (*e.g.* some holistic doctrines that preach the desirability of a union of mind, body, and spirit instead of a separateness), and self-help methods that include hypnosis and subliminal programming (neither of which should be recommended).

Of primary interest to us are some New Age ideas about UFOs. A great many people throughout the world have been exposed to the "ancient astonauts" theory with its postulate that some ancient religious events were the doings of a space age extraterrestrial society. This has caused the veil of myth that once surrounded UFOs to partially fall. Perhaps as a result, an effort has been made through the New Age movement to re-establish the old religious beliefs that the extraterrestrial race seen flying about in our skies is composed of enlightened almost-godlike beings who should be accorded reverential awe and looked to as a source of salvation. This worshipful attitude has certainly been promoted through some New Age literature and in recent American motion pictures like *Close Encounters of the Third Kind* and *Cocoon*. Many other Custodial doctrines, including End-of-the-World messages, are now being promulgated with a modern twist in the New Age movement by people who claim to be getting messages from UFOs (and perhaps a few of them are). Instead of "angels," however, the New Age offers us "Space Brothers." If history is any indication, our nearby "Space Brothers" appear to have little to offer us but oppression and genocide unless they can be convinced to change their ways. It seems that it is the human race that must teach the extraterrestrial race compassion, and not vice versa. The reported Custodial humanitarians who may occasionally visit Earth and do nice things for human witnesses and abductees would seem to be a distinct minority which is powerless to do anything truly meaningful for the human race. Like the doctors, social workers, and priests who enter prisons to give comfort to inmates, Custodial humanitarians have never broken down the prison walls. It would appear that the only "angels" and "Space Brothers" available to you are you and your very down-to-Earth neighbors.

As this edition of the book goes to press, the world is witnessing many changes. Some are extremely welcome, such as the dismantling of communism in many nations, the current efforts of the South African government to ease apartheid, and the increase of democratic elections around the world. These events show that conditions can be improved, perhaps even enough to eventually bring an end to the human plight suggested by this book.

Unfortunately, ethnic strife and the continuation of the inflatable paper money system in changing Europe are signs that something is still amiss. As the world passes through the 1990's, we appear to be in an era much like the one that existed two hundred years ago (see pages 294 and 295) when republican-style governments were established around the world. As back then, factions with Brotherhood roots are still active in breeding war and social ills today:

Ballistic weapons are proliferating rapidly in Islamic and Third World nations, aided by China and Western countries; meanwhile, Islamic radicalism continues to cause upheaval in the Middle East and elsewhere. In 1990, a radical Islamic sect called the Muslim Brotherhood swept to victory in municipal elections in the Jordanian cities of Zarqa and Aqaba.

As of this writing, Marxist revolutionaries are still killing people in Peru and the Philippines. In Peru, the most feared Maoist guerrillas are members of a secret society called the Sendero Luminoso which, roughly translated, means, "Luminous (Shining) Path," or "Way of Illumination."

Drug cartels have become political powers unto themselves; as in Colombia where a cocaine cartel waged a violent war against the Colombian government. Evidence of Brotherhood involvement in the shadow of the world of drugs may be seen in the Sendero Luminoso of Peru, which has been involved in coca growing, and in the heroin trade where powerful Asian heroin-dealing triads are presently formed by secret societies with roots in the 17th century.

Rightist nationalist organizations, although generally unpopular in the world, still receive support from government entities, such as a current Russian alliance called the People's Russian Orthodox Movement which uses a cross symbol against a yellow background reminiscent of a swastika. In 1990, people affiliated with the movement were sponsored by the United States Information Agency to give talks in the United States, despite protests that the speakers were anti-Semitic.

In May 1990, the widely-publicized desecration of Jewish graves in Haifa, Israel was discovered to have been carried out by a secretive Jewish millennarian sect. A member of the sect admitted that his group perpetrated the desecration with the Machiavellian intent of heightening conflict between Jews and anti-Semitic forces.

New AIDS-like immune-destroying viral diseases are being predicted by the World Bank, and a group of doctors from the United States was sent on a five-year mission to Africa in March 1990 to find new viral diseases and conduct other activities. The grant money for this mission was provided by the U.S. government's principle AIDS research agency: the Institute for Allergy and Infectious Diseases. One of the doctors, Nicholas Lerche from the University of California at Davis, is quoted on page A8 of the March 15, 1990 issue of the *San Francisco Chronicle*: "This is the problem of what we're beginning to recognize as emerging viral diseases, and there may well be other animal viruses waiting in the wings to move into humans and ultimately to cause new diseases." In light of allegations and evidence that AIDS may have been induced deliberately into human populations, there are some legitimate concerns about how the new diseases discovered by the doctors may be used by some of those people sponsoring the research.

By the time you read this, many new events will have occurred. Leaders, political personalities, and institutions will come and go from the world scene; warring factions will continue to arise and disappear. I hope that the long-term historical patterns described in this book will provide an interesting, and perhaps useful, tool for investigating the causes of future conflicts as they occur. Better yet, we can hope that this book will one day become nothing more than a reminder of a bad dream from which we have all managed to awaken ourselves.

# 39

# Escape from Eden

IT IS NATURAL for people to wonder how they might be able to improve the world around them. A widespread misconception is that to be effective, a person must either be rich, a politician, or a saint. The truth is, one can successfully take responsibility for oneself and for one's fellow humans from exactly where one is without greatly disrupting one's life or livelihood. One may begin doing this gradually by first improving one's own life, then by giving help to family and friends where it is wanted, then by joining or starting groups with laudable social goals, and finally by pursuing a sense of direct personal responsibility for the human race. It is important that more people begin this process. As history has clearly shown, if you do not create your own surroundings, someone else is going to create them for you, and you may not like what you get.

Major constructive changes to our world actually do not require much to bring about. As a specific example, the inflatable paper money system, which continues to create indebtedness and instability at every level, can easily be replaced with a stable monetary system by merely ending bank-created money and setting up a system whereby money is issued by national governments in proportion to their gross national products and dispersed without engendering debt. Banks could continue to participate in the system by being the conduit for the release and circulation of the money; but banks could no longer create money on their own. Governments would no longer need to tax anyone or borrow; they could simply allocate to themselves the money they needed to operate, within limits imposed by their gross national products. Under this plan, all debts owed to banks could be instantly forgiven: banks could be paid by the governments for their services in dispersing and circulating the money, and by consumers for consumer services.

The Custodial society itself, if it exists, presents us with an extraordinary challenge, as we have seen. To reduce the human ability to meet that challenge by occluding the subject of UFOs and spiritual phenomena with false reports, dubious "evidence," obfuscating "explanations," and hoaxes is to do grave potential damage to the future prospects of the human race. At this time, scrupulous honesty from all sides is needed.

If Earth is indeed owned by an oppressive extraterrestrial society, then there must somewhere exist communication lines between human beings and the Custodial society. I am not talking about alleged telepathic communication, I am speaking of face-to-face contact between humans and Custodians. Part of the solution would be to find those communication channels and use them to begin negotiating an end to the pain and suffering on Earth. This proposal may sound utterly wild as it would mean trying to start a process of diplomacy with an extraterrestrial society which most governments do not even admit the existence of in order to win the freedom of the human race—a race which most people would deny is even imprisoned. On the other hand, some people might argue that such negotiations would be as futile as San Quentin prisoners trying to negotiate their freedom with the warden, or Nazi concentration camp inmates trying to bargain with their SS guards. The Custodial society would need to be assured that the human race desires no revenge or political upheaval. Mankind seeks only an opportunity to work out its promised salvation, and the human race would share its successes with the Custodial society. The goal would be to let bygones be bygones and to get on with the future.

In the meantime, the problem of human warfare can be addressed directly. It should be clear that there is no true "security" during any state of war, "hot" or "cold." People speak of nuclear disarmament, but why bother making a small reduction in nuclear arsenals when chemical and biological weapons are produced in greater number? Fortunately, many people understand that *true* national security is achieved through friendship and peace. Ask any American if they feel threatened militarily by Canada, or any but the most paranoid Canadian the same question about America. Both nations feel a sense of security not because they are pointing hair-trigger weaponry at one another, but because they enjoy a basic state of friendship. In Europe, one does not find the nation of Belgium bankrupting its treasury to arm itself against the "Dutch Peril," or the Dutch arming itself to the teeth against the "French Threat." Reliance on weapons, espionage, propaganda, and other tools of war to achieve national security will inevitably fail. Sooner or later someone is going to build a better bomb or find a way to get around yours. They will recruit a better spy or will tell a more convincing lie. No one's security should have to rely on such shenanigans.

There are many people today throughout the world who are striving to create security through friendship. Those people have not been able to overcome several major hurdles. World leaders have their ears bent by intelligence agencies which promote a chronic climate of fear and danger through secret briefings, alarming reports and grim scenarios. As long as artificial philosophical differences exist between national leaders, those leaders will not be able to think and communicate rationally with one another. If national leaders are convinced that a great utopia will arise if they maintain their side of the struggle, there will never be peace. Peace will only arrive if our leaders are willing to drop their great apocalyptic struggles and join the rest of humanity in a simple pact of friendship.

The first thing that people can do to bring about human freedom is to become aware of all of the small freedoms they have and expand upon them. In our world, there is a great deal of emphasis on broad and gigantic social, political and spiritual freedoms, but many people find it difficult to exercise even the smallest freedoms, such as simply expressing a fact or opinion in a social circle. The irony is that broad sweeping freedoms really exist so that people may enjoy all of the small freedoms that make existence worthwhile. One can begin enjoying those small freedoms simply by exercising them. As more and more people begin to do this, freedoms for all will expand. It therefore follows that sacrificing "smaller" freedoms in the name of achieving "broader" freedoms will actually cause all freedoms to be lost.

Perhaps the greatest hope lies in the fact that all spiritual beings, whether they animate human bodies, Custodial bodies, or none at all, appear very similar in basic emotional make-up. There seems to be a core of good and decency within every individual, including within the most malevolent despots, that can ultimately be reached, although reaching it in some people can admittedly be a difficult undertaking! With persistence, intelligence, and compassion, it may yet be possible to bring a resolution to all that we have looked at in this book in a manner that will leave everyone happy.

There are plenty of additional problems to be solved in our world. Now it is your turn to dream up solutions. Once you have thought them up, communicate them and act on them. What you think, what you perceive, and how you view the world around you is extremely important because you have an inherently unique perspective not shared by anyone else. Say what you have to say, discover what you want to discover, and pursue those humanitarian goals within you. It could help us all.

# 40

# The Nature of a Supreme Being

BEFORE BIDDING YOU adieu, there is one last subject for me to touch on. It is a topic which has been lurking in the background of this entire book, but one which I have successfully avoided thus far. It is the subject of a Supreme Being. Does a Supreme Being of some kind exist? If it does, what is its relationship to life on Earth and to the things we have discussed in this book? I will try to tackle these questions, but be forewarned that this chapter is the most speculative and philosophical in the book. My discussion will be a simplified one and it is not intended to be definitive; I advise the reader to consult other sources for more information. If this is not to your liking, then please feel free to proceed to the next, and final, chapter.

It is unfortunate that the term "scientific method" has become almost synonymous with materialism. The two should not be equated. The scientific method is simply an attempt to understand and explore an area of knowledge in an intelligent and pragmatic fashion. It strives to find cause-and-effect relationships and to develop consistent axioms and techniques that will lead to predictable results. This is the type of methodology which needs to be, and can be, applied to the realm of the spirit, but it has not been done to any large degree. The great universities and foundations are too busy with their "man is brain" studies to do more than superficial studies into the mounting evidence of spiritual existence. The major religions already have their "word of God" writings and so they rarely undertake scientific studies into this area either.

Some people deny the existence of a Supreme Being altogether. It is difficult to blame them considering the level to which spiritual knowledge has deteriorated. However, the overwhelming evidence of individual spiritual existence and the many characteristics which all spiritual beings seem to share in common would suggest that a "Supreme Being" of some kind probably exists as a common source of all spiritual existence.

If a Supreme Being exists, it is likely that most people would not recognize it if they encountered it. Many individuals expect a Supreme Being to be a giant man in a flowing beard who rants, raves, and kills people. Others think that a Supreme Being is a bright light that exudes love and warmth. Still others perceive it as some completely unfathomable mystery that no one can ever hope to comprehend except through strained mystical contortions.

A Supreme Being is probably none of those things.

While researching this book, I encountered many ideas of what a Supreme Being might be. Perhaps the best way to tackle the issue is to first try to determine what an individual spiritual being is.

A spiritual being appears to be something that is not a part of the physical universe, and yet it possesses both external awareness and self-awareness. The Samkhya definitions on pages 103 and 104 of this book appear to be fairly accurate, and I refer the reader to those pages. The mounting scientific evidence of spiritual immortality in near-death episodes and in documented past-life memories indicates that spiritual beings are best defined as timeless and indestructible units of awareness.[1]

Every spiritual being, or unit of awareness, seems to be completely unique and independent. Each appears to possess its own distinct viewpoint which cannot be entirely duplicated by any other unit of awareness. This uniqueness and individuality of viewpoint appear to be the very essence and purpose of spiritual existence. We may see some evidence of this in the fact that when individuals are crushed into a sameness, they become unhappier and worse off; their perceptions deteriorate and they are less creative. When true uniqueness and individuality are restored to people, they regain their vitality and creativity.

It appears that every unit of awareness is capable of infinite creation because creation by a spiritual being is accomplished by the act of thought or imagination.* If you imagine that there is a white cat on top of this book, you have created a white cat, even if it only exists for you. Such creations, when shared and agreed to by others, eventually give rise to universes that can be shared and experienced by all others. This seems to be how spiritual beings create universes of their own and in cooperation with others, and why there exists evidence in modern physics that our universe appears to be ultimately based on thought.

For any universe or reality to exist, an infinity must first exist in which a universe or reality may be placed. All reality, including this material universe, arise out of infinity and not vice versa; this has been demonstrated by some remarkable mathematics being done at various universities. Every unit of awareness is the source of its own infinity because thought and imagination have no bounds; any amount of space, time or matter may be imagined by any spiritual being and ultimately agreed to and shared by other spiritual beings.

Where did all of these countless units of awareness come from? Did there exist at one time only a single unit of awareness from which all others originated? The many similarities between all spiritual beings make it appear so. That original unit of awareness would be what is normally called a Supreme Being, which we might also call the Primary Being.

---

* The words "thought" and "imagination" are probably not the best to describe the actual process, but they are adequate for our purposes.

*It appears that individual spiritual beings are actually the units of awareness of a Primary, or Supreme, Being, yet each unit is possessed of its own self-awareness, personality, free will, independent thought, and infinite creativity.*

This would mean that a Supreme Being had created, or had given "birth" to, an uncountable number of unique and individual units of awareness through which that Supreme Being could experience the uncountable infinities, universes, and realities which all of those spiritual beings could freely and independently create. A Supreme Being might therefore be very crudely likened to a person sitting in a television control booth who puts out trillions of video cameras. Each camera (spiritual being) feeds a picture into its own individual monitor screen in the control booth to be viewed by the operator (Supreme Being). Each camera is situated a little differently and so each has a different viewpoint and perspective. Each camera is also capable of creating its own "special effects" (universes).

If the above theory is accurate, we might ask: how could a Supreme Being have been so foolish? Why would it create awareness units that were *self*-aware? After all, it is the quality of self-awareness, or the awareness of being aware, that allows spiritual beings to be completely independent and to engage in the silliness which has caused them to suffer the sorry plight that they now appear to be enduring on Earth and probably elsewhere. Why did a Supreme Being not simply throw out an enormous number of awareness units that were only externally aware and had no consciousness of their own existences? Better yet, why did a Supreme Being not do the sensible thing and simply retain its own single undivided viewpoint?

*Self-awareness is apparently the quality which gives spiritual beings the capacity for thought and imagination, and hence to be a source of infinity and creation.*

Without self-awareness, a spiritual being could not create on its own. Self-awareness appears to act as the "mirror" against which a spiritual being can be the source of an infinity, and within that infinity can create realities and universes.

Theoretically, of course, a Supreme Being was already capable of creating an infinity and of creating anything within it, *but only from its own single viewpoint.* A Supreme Being could only be the source of one infinity: its own. If a Supreme Being wanted to experience another infinity, it had to first create another unique self-aware unit of awareness like itself. So it apparently did just that. But it did not satisfy itself with just one more unit of awareness: it appears to have put out an uncountable number of them so that it could enjoy an almost infinite number of infinities and realities. This suggests that the potential scope of a Supreme Being extends far beyond the boundaries of this one small universe—it encompasses trillions of potential infinities and universes.

"Aha!" you might interject. "By definition, only one infinity can exist. It is redundant for something already capable of infinite creation to expand itself. Infinity multiplied by uncountable trillions is still infinity."

As noted, infinity appears to be solely the product of viewpoint. Only units of awareness are capable of viewpoint. There therefore would exist as many infinities as there are units of awareness (spiritual beings). Infinity does not arise out of the mechanical universe or from any of its laws; rather, the mechanical universe and its laws all appear to arise out of infinity.

What went wrong? How did so many spiritual beings, each capable of infinite creation, wind up with a dull thud on Earth thinking that they are nothing more than meat and electricity?

There are apparently many factors that caused this, including those discussed in this book. I will leave it to someone else to describe other, perhaps even more significant long-range, causes. I will only add that spiritual entities can become hopelessly caught up in the labrynths of their own intricate creations. Although the universe appears to operate on very simple building blocks (please refer to the discussion on pages 104 and 105 of this book), once those blocks are put into place and other arbitraries are introduced, a universe can become extremely complex and solid-looking, like the universe we share now. When that happens, spiritual beings may become fixated in those universes like cameras anchored in a dense rain forest; the cameras are unable to perceive beyond the foliage immediately in front of them. After staring at the foliage for a long enough time, the cameras may begin to believe that they, too, are nothing but foliage and they forget that they are cameras. Salvation would come by restoring to those cameras their true self-identities and by giving them the ability to come and go from the rain forest at will.

If we look at individual spiritual beings on Earth, we see that they are very small in relation to the universe. This is the situation that apparently occurs when spiritual beings become enmeshed in bodies or other physical objects. In that state, spiritual beings have lost their power to change perspective in relation to the physical universe. Perspective is apparently what determines the "size" of a spiritual being. Have you ever stood on top of a skyscraper and looked down? Your first reaction might be to think, "Gee, those people sure are small. They're the size of ants!" Those people look so small, and really are so small, because of your change in perspective. A spiritual being in an untrapped state can apparently change perspective in the same way in relation to the entire physical universe. The universe can appear no larger than a coffee cup, or an atom the size of a mountain. This is apparently how a spiritual being becomes "bigger" or "smaller." Changing perspective in this fashion is not an act of mere thinking, however. It is a matter of actually shifting direct spiritual perception in as real and tangible a fashion as the person who hops an elevator to the top of a skyscraper. Spiritual beings on Earth are largely confined to the single perspective dictated by the physical bodies they animate. Mental perspectives can still change, but not the direct perspective of the spiritual entity in relation to the universe itself.

The foregoing discussion has some rather clear implications in regard to the rest of this book. The act of repressing a spiritual being, entrapping it in matter, or otherwise seeking to reduce its vision, creativity, or self-awareness as a spiritual being is the act of trying to reduce a Supreme Being. If one reduces a Supreme Being's unit of awareness (*i.e.*, a spiritual being)—even just one unit out of many trillions—one has still reduced a Supreme Being by that much. Since only other units of awareness can engage in such repression, it follows that a bizarre psychosis has arisen. It is as though extensions of the same ultimate body are trying to repress other extensions, *e.g.*, the left hand is trying to reduce and trap the right hand. That appears to be one type of psychosis that can arise when beings possessed of free will become entrapped.

Some mystical religions teach that one's ultimate spiritual aim should be to permanently "merge with" or "rejoin" a Supreme Being. This appears to be a false goal. If spiritual beings were created to act as unique and independent viewpoints, it would be contrary to the purpose of creation to permanently "merge" with other awareness units or with a Supreme Being. It may not even be possible to do so. The true goal of any salvation program should be to fully recover one's unique spiritual self-awareness and perspective.

The above discussion suggests that many popular ideas about "God" may be inaccurate. For example, some people with "near-death" experiences report going through a tunnel and meeting a "being of light" which instills in the near-death victim feelings of love and "all-knowing." I met a man who belonged to a Hindu sect which attempts to contact and merge with this "being of light" in its meditations. The man wrote a paper describing his personal experiences. His descriptions of spiritually traveling down a "tunnel" and meeting a "being of light" are very similar to the statements of near-death victims. While I acknowledge the importance and probable reality of many such experiences, I question some of the beliefs which have arisen from them. The feelings of "love" and "all-knowing" conveyed by that "being" can be instilled by drugs, electronic emanations, and by other artificial means. Interestingly, some UFO abductees have reported such emotions during their alleged examinations aboard UFOs. In some of those UFO cases, the surrounding evidence strongly suggests that the feelings were caused by an electronic device used as a sedative. Whatever the near-death "being of light" might be (and I will not even try to guess), it is most assuredly not a Supreme Being. It may even be an object that contributes to post-death spiritual amnesia. People should not be counseled to "merge with" or "go to" the "being of light" during meditation or at death. They should stay away from it if they can. In saying this, I do not mean to deny the otherwise positive and profound feelings experienced by some Hindus and near-death victims as a result of temporarily re-experiencing their spiritual immortality.

What are we then to think of the idea of a Supreme Being sitting in "judgment" on the beings of Earth?

It is hard to imagine that a Supreme Being would condemn its own units of awareness, no matter how small and entrapped they have become, and no matter how insanely and destructively some of them behave as a result.

Would a Supreme Being, seeing how bad everything has gotten, perhaps end its experiment and vanish all other awareness units except itself? If such a thing were possible, I daresay it would not be done. Creating an almost infinite number of spiritual beings would actually have been a brilliant move on the part of a Supreme Being to expand itself immeasurably. The solution to what went wrong would be to preserve the awareness units and encourage them to achieve their salvation.

Spiritual salvation would probably not happen through the waving of a magical Godly wand, however. Because spiritual beings possess free and independent will, salvation appears to be something that spiritual beings must take responsibility for themselves. It is up to every individual to seek out his or her salvation in an intelligent fashion. Salvation appears to be something that can be achieved as pragmatically as any other goal in life, provided that a rational understanding of how to attain it is developed.

Many theologies teach that a Supreme Being is opposed by an enemy. Perhaps there is an element of truth to this, even if the truth has been distorted. We do observe that at every level of existence there exists a condition or "game" in which survival is challenged. At the personal level, an individual's survival is constantly opposed by aging, disease, and other factors. The survival of a family unit is often tested by financial problems, hostile relatives and outside sexual temptations. Organizations and nations usually have competitors and enemies. In the animal kingdom, the survival drama is most vividly played out in hunter-prey relationships. All physical objects face inevitable deterioration. Spiritual beings themselves appear to face survival challenges by being trapped in matter.

Since this survival game seems to exist at every level of existence, it is possible that it also exists in regard to a Supreme Being—a game in which a Supreme Being's own survival is tested by the diminishment of its awareness units and perhaps by the ultimate diminishment of the Supreme Being itself. For such a game to exist, a Supreme Being would have had to either negotiate with one or more of its own awareness units to be the Supreme Being's opponent(s), or a Supreme Being would have had to create in one or more of its awareness units an apprehension that a Supreme Being posed a threat to the continued existence of all other spiritual beings. A Supreme Being's opponent would not be any different or inherently more evil than any other spiritual being, any more than one neighbor who sits down opposite another to play a game of Monopoly is innately more evil just because he or she plays a different side. An opponent would simply be one who became a different marker on a game board and played as well as possible. If such a game has indeed existed, then we can certainly hope that it may end soon by a Supreme Being conveying thanks to the opponent(s) for a game well-played, promising the indefinite survival of its awareness units, and asking that the game be stopped. It seems time to put many old games to rest so that everyone may start moving into a new phase of fundamentally-improved existence.

# 41

# To the Researcher

*It is the customary fate of new truths to begin as heresies.*
—Thomas Huxley

THANK YOU FOR staying with me. I realize that many of the ideas I expressed have probably been as challenging for you to deal with as they were for me. If nothing else, I hope that you found some of the information in support of my ideas interesting. I have always enjoyed new perspectives and I believe that it is important to be willing to express them. Every perspective has something to contribute, but no perspective can contribute anything unless it is communicated.

An important fact to keep in mind is that knowledge is, to a degree, an historical phenomenon in itself. Nearly every civilization, at any given moment in history, has possessed a broadly-accepted body of historical, social, and scientific teachings to explain nearly everything. The irony, of course, is that many of those teachings are different today than they were back in the 1300's. More than likely, scholars working five hundred years in the future will be as amused by some of our 20th-century teachings as we are by some of the established teachings of the 14th century. It is therefore helpful to step back from one's own time and to understand that knowledge has never been an "absolute," despite assertions to the contrary. Rather, knowledge has been an ever-changing commodity as it is enhanced and refined over time.

The completion of this book marks the completion of my research. Except for the possibility of one revision to correct any errors which I may discover or which are pointed out to me, I plan to do no more work in this area. This book demanded enormous financial, emotional and social sacrifices that were enough to last me a lifetime. I hope to pass the torch of research to others.

Despite its length, this book is but an outline. It only begins to present all of the information and evidence available on the subjects discussed. There exists an enormous body of data that I never had the time, money or inclination to pursue, yet it is all highly relevant. I was also limited to the English language, so I barely utilized any non-English books or sources. Every chapter in this book could easily become a book in itself. My biggest problem was not one of scant and insufficient evidence; it was of being deluged with too much. I discovered that I could easily spend another eight to ten years accumulating it all and build a multi-volume encyclopedia from it, but that was not my purpose. When I began to realize the enormity of the project, I deliberately wound it down so that I would have some hope of presenting a one-volume book on the subject. I am trusting that others will add to what I have done by publishing writings of their own.

I ran across many theories that I did not use. As radical as the ideas expressed in this book may seem, they are, in fact, somewhat conservative compared to other theories in current circulation. I tended to accept historical facts, dates, and personages as they are commonly accepted by historians. This may have been a mistake in some cases, but it is the approach I chose to take. A person researching the topics covered in this book will encounter many revisionist theories that attempt to overturn commonly accepted historical facts. For example, I ran into the "George Washington-Adam Weishaupt" theory which speculates that George Washington had been secretly removed from the U.S. Presidency and that Adam Weishaupt of Bavarian Illuminati fame, who actually looked a bit like George Washington, had taken Washington's place after Weishaupt's disappearance from Bavaria. Another theory doing the rounds is that the television transmissions of U.S. astronauts on the Moon were actually filmed in a studio. Yet another is that the Earth is hollow and that UFOs originate from a civilization in the world below. Perhaps one, two, or all three of these theories are correct, but because I did not find enough information to conclusively validate them in my own mind, I did not adopt them.

People researching the role of secret societies in world history will sooner or later encounter the writings of Nesta H. (Mrs. Arthur) Webster. Mrs. Webster's works were published during the first two decades of the 20th century and they bear such titles as *The French Revolution, World Revolution, The Socialist Network, Surrender of an Empire,* and *Secret Societies and Subversive Movements.* The main thrust of her books is that secret societies, especially the Knights Templar Freemasons, have been responsible for instigating most of the major revolutions of the past two hundred years. Her works have provided later researchers with a great deal of ammunition upon which to build "conspiracy" theories of history.

It is unquestioned that Mrs. Webster was very successful in bringing forth a great deal of valuable information that probably would not have otherwise reached us today. All of her books reveal exhaustive work. Mrs. Webster might have gone down as the top researcher in her field, and her contribution to mankind might have been enormous, had her own personal perspective not been clouded. Mrs. Webster made a fatal mistake by concluding that the world's apparent Machiavellian source was a so-called "Jewish conspiracy." In her book, *Secret Societies and Subversive Movements,* she devoted an entire chapter to "The Real Jewish Peril" in which she blames the Jews for the Christian world's subversion. This anti-Semitic slant is so strong, as is an anti-German slant, that the value of her research is lost because a researcher cannot readily trust all of the information she presents. This is a shame, but it is also a good lesson to any researcher. It reveals that an anchored bias can utterly ruin any benefits that might otherwise accrue from this type of research. It also indicates the need to remain flexible in the face of changing history and evidence. Had Mrs. Webster lived longer and seen what happened to the Jews during World War II, her outlook might have been different.

There were many avenues of investigation that I never had time to pursue, but which could bring forth some fruit (although I make no guarantees). I present them here in no particular order for those who might be interested in digging further:

1. Throughout the world there is a very strong political and economic force: the labor union. Labor unions have done a great deal to improve working conditions for many working people, but there is no question that some union tactics have generated continuous conflict. Unionization has also had the effect of creating a mild form of feudalism by magnifying the superficial distinction between managers and non-managers, and bringing the two groups into conflict. Interestingly, one of the key forces behind the early American labor union movement was an organization known as the "Knights of Labor." The Knights were a secret society with secret oaths, just like other Brotherhood organizations. Although the Knights later dropped their mystical practices and eventually declined in strength, they played a role in creating the American Federation of Labor (A.F.L.), which has since grown to become the major union in America. Questions to research might be: who started the Knights of Labor? Were any of its founders members of other Brotherhood organizations, as seems likely from the character of the Knights of Labor?

2. One argument against the idea that there has been a Machiavellian source behind human warfare is the fact that primitive tribal societies untouched by the Western world have also engaged in repeated warfare. This would seem to disprove the "Brotherhood connection" and suggest that perhaps warfare really is just a part of human nature.

Let me repeat that there are definite psychological factors behind human warfare that must be handled before the entire problem is solved. Machiavellian machinations merely increase the frequency and severity of war; conflicts can still erupt without such machinations. It is, however, a remarkable fact that Brotherhood-style secret societies are extremely pervasive throughout the entire world and exist even among very primitive peoples. In fact, such societies appear to be as common in the "primitive world" as they are in the "civilized" one. For example, Captain F. W. Butt-Thompson, writing in his book, *West African Secret Societies*, says of Africa:

> The Native Secret Societies found amongst the peoples and tribes of the West Coast of Africa are many. Nearly one hundred and fifty of them are referred to in the following chapters.[1]

Captain Butt-Thompson divided those societies into two basic groups: mystical and political. Of the mystical type, he wrote:

> These approximate in organization and purpose the Grecian Pythagoreans, the Roman Gnostics, the Jewish Kabbala and Essenes, the Bayern [Bavarian] Illuminata, the Prussian Rosicrucians, and the world-wide Freemasons. In the course of the years they have evolved an official class that may be likened to the priesthood founded by Ignatius Loyola [the Jesuits].[2]

Some of the African secret societies were obviously brought in from the outside, such as the Muhammedan societies. In many primitive areas, however, from Africa to New Guinea, such societies are native. Questions to be researched might include: just how pervasive is this form of mysticism in primitive society? How did the primitive secret societies begin and do they have legends of extraterrestrials? To what degree have they taught mystical beliefs that exalt and encourage war?

3. If a Custodial society exists, then Earth's history may simply be a tragic footnote in a much broader history beginning long before human civilization arose on Earth. What might that history be? What caused the apparent

ethical, social and spiritual decay of the Custodial society? Is there any way to find out?

4. On November 18, 1978, a tragedy occurred in the South American nation of Guyana. More than 900 men, women, and children were mysteriously murdered in an isolated religious commune known as the "People's Temple" ("Jonestown"). A large vat of drink containing poison was found at the scene, leading to an initial assumption that the deaths were caused by suicide. The victims' bodies were discovered lying side by side in neat rows as though the people had drunk the poison and had then lain down together and died. However, when autopsies were performed on the victims, it was discovered that 700 of the 900 people had died of gunshot and strangulation, not poison. They had not committed suicide at all; they were brutally mass murdered. It is very likely that those who drank the poison either did so involuntarily or did not know what they were drinking. The only people to escape the tragedy were not present when the 900 victims were murdered. There are no known witnesses to the entire event. The question is: who murdered the inhabitants of Jonestown?

On September 27, 1980, investigative journalist Jack Anderson ran a column about the Jonestown incident. One newspaper headlined the column, "CIA Involved in Jonestown Massacre?" Mr. Anderson cites a tape recording made of People's Temple leader, Jim Jones, in which Jones referred to a man named Dwyer. According to Mr. Anderson, investigators have concluded that this was Richard Dwyer, deputy chief of the U.S. mission to Guyana. Dwyer had accompanied U.S. Representative Leo Ryan to the Jonestown encampment on that ill-fated day. Leo Ryan became one of the murder victims, but Richard Dwyer somehow was not affected and even claimed later that the reference to him by Jim Jones was "mistaken." Richard Dwyer, as it turns out, has been listed in the East German publication, "Who's Who in the CIA," as a long-time CIA agent. Dwyer had reportedly begun his career with the spy agency in 1959. According to Mr. Anderson's column, Dwyer replied "no comment" when asked if he was a CIA agent.

After the massacre, investigators found at Jonestown large quantities of weapons and drugs. The drugs included powerful psychotropics: Quaaludes, Valium, Demerol and Thorazine. Another drug found at Jonestown was chloral hydrate, which had been used in the CIA's secret mind control program known as "MK ULTRA." Was Jonestown a CIA mind control experiment which recruited subjects, especially poorer black people, through the guise of religion? The Jonestown massacre was triggered when a U.S. Congressman, Leo Ryan, flew to Guyana to investigate Jonestown personally after he had failed to obtain information about it from the State Department. Leo Ryan never lived to tell what he discovered and nearly every last man, woman, and child was silenced. The massacre occurred during a time when many American newspapers were carrying stories about CIA mind-control experiments—experiments which the CIA claimed that it was no longer conducting. Did the CIA slaughter 900 people to cover up the fact that it was still conducting such experiments on a massive scale in a small jungle compound in Guyana?

Additional questions to be researched are: what is the true history of the People's Temple prior to Jonestown? What is Jim Jones' background? Who supported him and his early "church"?

5. Books, movies, and other art forms tend to give a romantic twist to UFOs, spies, assassination conspiracies, and so on. As we are perhaps beginning to realize, behind the "romance" there lie some cruel and brutal psychoses. A significant problem in any society geared for overt and covert warfare is that sociopathic personalities tend to find a home in government. Sociopaths are not affected by qualms of conscience and often delight in harming others. They are frequently promoted to high positions within agencies engaged in warfare because such personalities are able to attack and harm others repeatedly without it adversely affecting them emotionally. Sociopaths with high IQs can be quite clever in how they harm others; this deviousness is often valuable to intelligence agencies. As history has shown, the more that a nation is oriented towards war, the more it will become dominated by sociopathic personalities. This domination, in turn, leads to a rapid decay of a nation

and will eventually cause its ruin. This is one of the great dangers any nation faces when it becomes involved in long-term conflict, no matter how democratic and humane that nation might otherwise be.

Questions to be researched might include: to what extent are true sociopathic personalities dominating governments today? Why do people tolerate them? Have those Custodial religions which demand the worship of criminally insane beings as "angels" and "God" perhaps blinded many people to being able to see sociopathology for what it is?

6. This book barely touched on the influence of Brotherhood organizations in Asian history. I discussed Hinduism, but there is a great deal more to be found. For example, the bloody Boxer Rebellion of China in 1900 was instigated by members of an Asian branch of the Brotherhood network: the Boxers. The Boxers were fiercely anti-foreign, they massacred over 100,000 people (and often photographed the beheaded victims), and they stirred up a revolt which brought to China the armies of several major western powers to quash the uprising.

Questions to be researched might include: what other wars and uprisings in Asia were caused by Brotherhood organizations? What has the full impact of the Brotherhood network been on the history of Asia?

7. A topic I had wanted to research deeper was the subject of drugs. We discussed drugs several times, but not in any great historical depth. While drugs seem to have always been a part of human culture, was there a time when drugs were really first "pushed" on society? If there was, when was it and who did it?

8. One highly-publicized problem today is that of vanishing children. Many children are abducted every year by parents during custody disputes, by relatives, and by strangers. Many more children vanish by running away from home. Runaways and parental abductions are easy to account for and they constitute the majority of missing child cases. There has been, however, some confusion about the extent of child abduction by strangers. In the early 1980's, the nation's leading missing child agency, Child Find, Inc., stated that anywhere from 20,000 to 50,000 children were

vanishing every year as the result of abductions by strangers. In 1985, Child Find revised that figure down to 600. I called Child Find to learn what caused such a dramatic change in the number. I was told that the earlier figure was really a broad "catch all" and that 600 was the true number of stranger abduction cases per year. To further confuse the issue, I later learned from another source that out of all runaways, about 3,000 in the United States disappear yearly without a trace. Will that figure also be changed? As the reader can see, there seems to be some genuine confusion regarding how many children are really vanishing. Many children are eventually found, of course. Others vanish completely.

I became interested in this problem because of reported abductions of humans by UFOs. The UFO abductions we learn of today are those in which the human victims are returned. Are there many known cases in which UFO abduction victims are *not* returned? Might some of those instances involve children? I even found myself asking this unthinkable question: if the human race had been created as a slave race, might it still be providing manpower, perhaps in the form of human children, to the Custodial society?

A respected UFO researcher of this generation is Jacques Vallee, who has authored several influential books about the UFO phenomenon. Mr. Vallee was one of the first researchers to focus on the fact that the UFO phenomenon has been very closely linked to episodes of social change throughout history. Mr. Vallee also noted an apparent connection between ancient folklore and UFOs. Some of the "little people" in folklore have been described in much the same way as modern UFO pilots. UFO-like phenomena have also occasionally been described in old stories of the "little people."

One activity attributed to the "little people" in folklore was their frequent kidnapping of children. Many of those children would never be seen again. This was a major source of upset between humans and the "little people." This raises some rather startling questions: Are there any recent child-stealing episodes with a UFO connection? Is it conceivable that there could exist on Earth today a child-stealing network which feeds an ongoing Custodial demand for human labor?

These questions are admittedly "far-out" and the stuff of supermarket tabloids (and certainly the most speculative of any asked in this chapter), but they may actually be worthy of investigation by some brave soul in light of all that we have come to know about the UFO phenomenon.

I hope that some of the above questions will provide good starting points for additional research. In the final analysis, the important thing is to be flexible with ideas, and even to have fun with them. By sticking my neck out as I have done in this book, I hope that I will encourage other people to explore those topics about which they are curious, and to share what they find. You and I may not always be right; the important thing is that we are willing to explore and communicate. Be careful that you do not base all of your beliefs upon a mere handful of writers, teachers, ministers, or scientists. Learn from them, but also explore on your own, and have fun doing it. Do not always look to others for approval of what you have discovered. If your integrity says that something is a certain way, stick to it, regardless of any snubs or criticisms. On the other hand, be ready to change if you discover, in your own mind, that you are wrong. Learning that one has erred is often a hard pill to swallow, but it is a part of the learning process. The man who pretends that he has always been right is either an egoist or a liar, and he does not learn much of anything either.

Good luck . . . and happy sleuthing!

# Invitation

The author welcomes questions and comments about his book. Readers are invited to write to him at the following address:

Dahlin Family Press
5339 Prospect Road #300
San Jose, California 95129-5020
U.S.A.

# Notes

CHAPTER 3: *UFOs: Truth or Fiction?*

1. Reader's Digest, *Mysteries of the Unexplained* (Pleasantville, The Reader's Digest Association, Inc., 1982), p. 208.
2. Pauwels, Louis; Bergier, Jacques, *Morning of the Magicians* (New York, Avon Books, 1963), p. 181.
3. Fort, Charles, *The Books of Charles Fort* (New York, Henry Holt & Co., 1941), p. 163.
4. *Ibid.*
5. *Ibid.*
6. *Ibid.*, p. 163-4.
7. *Ibid.*, p. 163.
8. Klass, Philip J., *UFOs Explained* (New York, Random House, 1974), p. 14.
9. Gillmor, Daniel S. (ed.), Dr. Edward U. Condon (scientific director), *Scientific Study of Unidentified Flying Objects* (New York, E. P. Dutton & Co., Inc., 1969), p. 305.

10. Klass, Philip J., "Radar UFOs: Where Have They Gone?", *Skeptical Inquirer,* CSICOP, Buffalo, Vol. IX, No. 3, Spring 1985, pp. 258-259.


CHAPTER 4: *The Gods of Eden*

1. Lambert, W. G.; Millard, A. R.; *Atra-Hasis, The Babylonian Story of the Flood, with The Sumerian Flood Story by M. Civil* (Oxford at the Clarendon Press, 1969), p. (43).
2. The Americana Corp., *The Encyclopedia Americana,* International Ed. (Danbury, Grolier, Inc., 1984), vol. 14, p. 545m.
3. *Ibid.*
4. *The New Encyclopaedia Britannica* (Chicago, Encyclopaedia Britannica, Inc., 1986), p. 965.
5. Lambert, *op. cit.,* p. 59.
6. Sitchin, Zecharia, *The Twelfth Planet* (New York, Avon Books, 1976), p. 356.
7. Lambert, *op. cit.,* pp. 65, 67.
8. *Ibid.,* p. (73).
9. *Ibid.,* p. (107).


CHAPTER 5: *Brotherhood of the Snake*

1. Sitchin, *op. cit.,* p. 90.


CHAPTER 6: *The Pyramid Builders*

1. Wilson, Don, *Secrets of Our Spaceship Moon* (Dell Publishing Co., 1979), p. 20.
2. *Ibid.,* p. 21.
3. Breasted, James Henry, *A History of Egypt, From the Earliest Times to the Persian Conquest* (New York, Charles Scribner's Sons, 1937), p. 62.
4. *Ibid.,* p. 60.
5. Weigall, Arthur, *A History of the Pharoahs,* vol. I (New York, E. P. Dutton & Co., 1925), p. 148.

6. Fakhry, Ahmed, *The Pyramids* (Chicago, The University of Chicago Press, 1961), p. 99.
7. *Ibid.*, pp. 6-7.
8. *Ibid.*, p. 7.


## CHAPTER 7: *Jehovah*


1. Lewis, H. Spencer, *Rosicrucian Questions and Answers With Complete History of the Rosicrucian Order* (San Jose, Supreme Grand Lodge of AMORC, 1977), pp. 79-80.
2. *Ibid.*, p. 79.
3. Machiavelli, Niccolo (trans. W. K. Marriott), *The Prince* (New York, E. P. Dutton & Co., 1935), p. 167.
4. *Ibid.*, p. 169.
5. Stark, Dr. W. (trans. Leslie J. Walker), *The Discourses of Niccolo Machiavelli*, vol. 1 (London, Routledge & Kegan Paul, 1950), p. 436.


## CHAPTER 8: *Melchizedek's Apron*


1. MacKey, Albert G., *An Encyclopedia of Freemasonry and Its Kindred Sciences* (New York, The Masonic History Company, 1919), vol. 1, p. 114.
2. University Books, *The Book of the Dead* (New Hyde Park, 1960), pp. 343-344.
3. Lewis, H. Spencer, *op. cit.*, photo section.


## CHAPTER 9: *Gods and Aryans*


1. Bloomfield, Maurice, *The Religion of the Veda, The Ancient Religion of India* (From Rig-Veda to Upanishads), (New York, AMS Press, 1969), p. 155.
2. A. C. Bhaktivedanta Swami Prabhupada, *Srimad Bhagavatam, Seventh Canto*, (New York, The Bhaktivedanta Book Trust, 1976), p. 10.

CHAPTER 10: *The Maverick Religions*

1. Americana Corp., *op. cit.*, vol. 14, p. 212.
2. Eliot, Sir Charles, *Hinduism and Buddhism, An Historical Sketch* (New York, Barnes & Noble, Inc., 1957), p. 297.


CHAPTER 12: *The Jesus Ministry*

1. Bock, Janet, *The Jesus Mystery, Of Lost Years and Unknown Travels* (Los Angeles, Aura Books, 1980), p. 211.
2. *Ibid.*
3. *Ibid.*, p. 211-212.
4. *Ibid.*, p. 213.
5. Durant, Will, *The Story of Civilization,* Part III, *Caesar and Christ* (New York, Simon & Schuster, 1944), p. 569.
6. *Ibid.*


CHAPTER 14: *The Plagues of Justinian*

1. Smith, John Holland, *Constantine the Great* (London, Hamish Hamilton, 1971), p. 102.
2. Hubbard, L. Ron, *Have You Lived Before This Life?, A Scientific Survey* (Los Angeles, Church of Scientology Publications Organization, 1977), p. 284.


CHAPTER 15: *Mohammed*

1. Americana Corp., *op. cit.,* vol. 8, p. 267.
2. *Ibid.*


CHAPTER 17: *Flying Gods Over America*

1. Pauwels, *op. cit.*, pp. 174-5.
2. Goetz, Delia and Sylvanus G. Morley, *Popol Vuh, The Sacred Book of the Ancient Quiche Maya* (Norman, University of Oklahoma Press, 1950), p. 86.
3. *Ibid.*, p. 89.
4. *Ibid.*, p. 168.

5. *Ibid.*, p. 169.
6. *Ibid.*
7. *Ibid.*
8. *Ibid.*, p. 190.


CHAPTER 18: *The Black Death*

1. Nohl, Johannes, *The Black Death, A Chronicle of the Plague* (London, George Allen & Unwin Ltd., 1926), pp. 56-57.
2. Deaux, George, *The Black Death, 1347* (New York, Weybright & Talley, Inc., 1969), p. 1.
3. Nohl, *op. cit.* p. 56-57.
4. *Ibid.*, p. 68.
5. *Ibid.*, p. 59.
6. *Ibid.*, p. 53-54.
7. *Ibid.*, p. 63.
8. *Ibid.*, p. 205.
9. *Ibid.*, p. 2.
10. *Ibid.*, p. 63.
11. Deaux, *op. cit.*, p. 2.
12. *Ibid.*
13. *Ibid.*, p. 4.
14. *Ibid.*, p. 78.
15. *Ibid.*, p. 4.
16. Nohl, *op. cit.*, p. 63.
17. *Ibid.*, p. 68.
18. *Ibid.*, p. 66.
19. *Ibid.*, p. 67.
20. *Ibid.*, p. 62-63.
21. *Ibid.*, p. 61-62.
22. Corliss, William R., *Handbook of Unusual Natural Phenomena* (Garden City, Anchor Books, 1983), p. 206.
23. Deaux, *op. cit.*, p. 10.
24. Nohl, *op. cit.*, p. 65.
25. Bell, Walter George, *The Great Plague in London in 1665* (Dodd, Mead & Co., 1924), p. 1.
26. Halsey, William D. (ed. dir.), *Collier's Encyclopedia* (The Crowell-Collier Pub. Co., 1965), vol. 13, p. 579.

CHAPTER 19: *Luther and the Rose*

1. Lewis, H. Spenser, *op. cit.*, p. 103.
2. Jones, Rufus M., *Studies in Mystical Religion* (London, MacMillan & Co., Ltd., 1923), p. 269.


CHAPTER 22: *Marching Saints*

1. Walzer, Michael, *The Revolution of the Saints, A Study in the Origins of Radical Politics* (Cambridge, Harvard University Press, 1965), p. 279.
2. *Ibid.*
3. *Ibid.*, p. 287.


CHAPTER 23: *William and Mary Have a War*

1. Brown, William Adrian, *Facts, Fables and Fantasies of Freemasonry* (Boyce, Carr Publishing Co., Inc., 1968), p. 131.
2. Wantoch, Hans, *Magnificent Money-Makers* (London, Desmond Harmsworth, 1932), p. 94.


CHAPTER 24: *Knights' New Dawn*

1. MacKey, Albert Gallatin, *The History of Freemasonry* (New York, The Masonic History Company, 1898), vol. 1. p. 280.


CHAPTER 25: *The "King Rats"*

1. Roberts, J. M., *The Mythology of the Secret Societies* (New York, Charles Scribner's Sons, 1972), p. 111.
2. Snyder, Henry L. (ed.), *The Marlborough-Godolphin Correspondence* (Oxford at the Clarendon Press, 1975), pp. 57-58.
3. *Ibid.*, p. 159.

4. Lewis, W. S. (ed.), *Horace Walpole's Correspondence with Sir Horace Mann* (New Haven, Yale University Press, 1960), vol. 19, p. 123.
5. *Ibid.*
6. *Ibid.*, p. 180.
7. *Ibid.*, vol. 20, p. 570.
8. Petrie, Sir Charles, *The Four Georges* (Port Washington, Kennikat Press, 1971), p. 101.
9. Katz, Jacob, *Jews and Freemasons in Europe, 1723-1939* (Cambridge, Harvard University Press, 1970), p. 64.


CHAPTER 26: *The Count of St. Germain*

1. Lewis, W. S., *op. cit.,* vol. 20, p. 570.
2. Cooper-Oakley, Isabel, *The Count of St. Germain* (Blauvelt, Rudolph Steiner Publications, 1970), p. 94.
3. Franco, Johan, "The Count of St. Germain," *The Musical Quarterly* (New York, G. Schirmer, Inc.), October 1950, Vol. XXXVI, No. 4, p. 541.
4. Cooper-Oakley, *op. cit.*, p. 233.
5. *Ibid.*, p. 169.
6. *Ibid.*, p. 170.
7. *Ibid.*, pp. 100-101.
8. *Ibid.*, pp. 147-148.
9. *Ibid.*, p. 135.
10. *Ibid.*, p. 7.


CHAPTER 27: *Here a Knight, There a Knight . . .*

1. Gray, Tony, *The Orange Order* (London, The Bodley Head, Ltd., 1972), p. 209.


CHAPTER 28: *American Phoenix*

1. Linn, Col. LaVon P., "Freemasonry and the National Defense, 1754-1799," *The New Age* (Washington, Supreme Council, 33rd degree, Ancient & Accepted Scottish Rite of Freemasonry of the Southern Jurisdiction, U.S.A., March 1974), Vol. LXXXII, No. 3.

2. *Ibid.*, p. 13.
3. De La Fuye, Maurice; Babeau, Emile; *The Apostle of Liberty: A Life of LaFayette* (London, Thames & Hudson, 1956), p. 42.
4. Miller, John C., *Sam Adams, Pioneer in Propaganda* (Stanford, Stanford University Press, 1936), p. 40.
5. Linn, *op. cit.*, p. 16.
6. Lunden, Sven G., "Annihilation of Freemasonry," *The American Mercury* (New York, The American Mercury, Inc., Feb. 1941), vol. LII, No. 206, p. 189.
7. Miller, *op. cit.*, p. 70.
8. *Ibid.*, p. 37.
9. *Official Masonic Record of the Third Annual Fashion and Home Exposition for the Benefit of Masonic Free Hospitals* (New York, May 13 to 24, 1924).
10. MacKey, *op. cit.*, p. 292.
11. Ford, Paul Leicester (ed.), *The Works of Thomas Jefferson* (New York, G. P. Putnam's Sons, 1905), vol. X, p. 57.
12. *Ibid.*
13. Rutland, Robert A. (ed.), *The Papers of George Mason, 1725-1792* (Chapel Hill, University of North Carolina Press, 1970), vol. 1, p. 296.
14. *Ibid.*, p. cxxv.

CHAPTER 29: *The World Afire*

1. Fay, Bernard, *Revolution and Freemasonry, 1680-1800* (Boston, Little, Brown, & Co., 1935), p. 259.
2. Lunden, *op. cit.*, p. 189.
3. DeHaan, Richard, "Fraternal Organizations," *Colliers Encyclopedia,* Halsey, *op. cit.*, vol. 10, p. 338.
4. Lunden, *op. cit.*, p. 190.
5. *Ibid.*
6. Cowles, Virginia, *The Rothschilds, A Family of Fortune* (New York, Alfred A. Knopf, 1973), p. 22.

CHAPTER 30: *Master Smith and the Angel*

1. Fryer, A. T., "Psychological Aspects of the Welsh Revival," *Society of Psychical Research, Proceedings,* 19:80, 1905 (republished by the Sourcebook Project, Glen Arm), p. 158.
2. *Ibid.,* p. 159.
3. *Ibid.*
4. *Ibid.,* p. 149.
5. *Ibid.,* p. 148-149.
6. *Ibid.,* p. 134.
7. The Church of Jesus Christ of Latter Day Saints, "Granite Mountain—Where a Billion People 'Live' " (advertising pamphlet, undated), p. 7.
8. *Ibid.*
9. O'Dea, Thomas F., *The Mormons* (Chicago, The University of Chicago Press, 1957), p. 57.
10. The Church of Jesus Christ of Latter Day Saints, *op. cit.,* p. 5.


CHAPTER 31: *Apocalypse of Marx*

1. Braunthal, Julius (trans. H. Collins and K. Mitchell), *History of the International,* vol. I: 1864-1914 (New York, Frederick A. Praeger, 1967), p. 46.


CHAPTER 32: *Funny Money Goes International*

1. Quigley, Carroll, *Tragedy and Hope, a History of the World in Our Time* (MacMillan Co., New York, 1966), p. 50.
2. *Ibid.,* p. 324.
3. Plomer, William, *Cecil Rhodes* (Edinburgh, Peter Davis, Ltd., 1933), p. 25-26.
4. Quigley, *op. cit.,* p. 951.
5. Imperialist, *Cecil Rhodes, a Biography and Appreciation* (New York, The MacMillan Company, 1897), p. 401-402.

CHAPTER 33: *The Workers' Paradise*

1. Ravenscroft, Trevor, *The Spear of Destiny* (York Beach, Samuel Weiser, Inc., 1973), p. 116.
2. Wallace, Irving, David Wallechinsky and Amy Wallace, "Significa," *Parade* (New York, Parade Publications, Inc.), December 20, 1981, p. 12.
3. Pearson, Michael, *The Sealed Train* (New York, G. P. Putnam's Sons, 1975), p. 15.
4. *Ibid.,* p. 113.
5. *Ibid.*


CHAPTER 34: *Robo-Sapiens*

1. Schultz, Duane P., *A History of Modern Psychiatry* (New York, Academic Press, 1969), p. 45.
2. *The American Journal of Psychiatry* (Washington, American Psychiatric Assn), August 1981, advertising insert.
3. *Ibid.,* Dec. 1981, p. A56.
4. *Ibid.,* Sept. 1981, p. A28.
5. *Ibid.,* Dec. 1981, p. A35.
6. *Ibid.,* Oct. 1981, adv. insert.
7. *Ibid.,* Dec. 1981, adv. insert.


CHAPTER 35: *St. Germain Returns*

1. Frater Selvius, "Descendants of Lemuria, A Description of an Ancient Cult in California," *Rosicrucian Digest* (San Jose, AMORC, May 1931), p. 497.
2. *Ibid.*
3. King, Godfre Ray, *Unveiled Mysteries* (Chicago, St. Germain Press, 1934), p. 82.
4. *Ibid.,* p. 83.
5. *Ibid.*
6. *Ibid.*
7. "Royal Teton, Thou Mountain of Light," *The Voice of the I AM* (Sindelar Studios, date and publication data unavailable), p. 16.
8. King, *op. cit.,* p. 89.
9. *Ibid.*

10. *Ibid.*, p. 88.
11. *Ibid.*, p. 89.
12. King, Godfre Ray, *The Magic Presence* (Chicago, St. Germain Press, 1935), pp. 352-3.


CHAPTER 36: *Universe of Stone*

1. Ravenscroft, Trevor, *op. cit.*, p. xxi.
2. Riefenstahl, Leni (producer), *Triumph de Willens (Triumph of the Will)*, 1934, 1975.
3. Quigley, *op. cit.*, p. 325.
4. *Ibid.*, p. 514.
5. Katz, Howard S., *The Warmongers* (New York, Books In Focus, Inc., 1979), pp. 78-79.
6. Ravenscroft, *op. cit.*, p. 233.


CHAPTER 37: *Modern "Ezekiels"*

1. Henry, William; interviewed by *California UFO* magazine (Los Angeles, Vicki Cooper and Sherie Stark, editors and publishers), vol. 2, no. 3, 1987; p. 12.
2. Bullard, Thomas E., "Abductions: A Comparative Study," *MUFON UFO Journal* (Seguin, Mutual UFO Network, Inc.), number 238, February 1988, p. 4.
3. Fowler, Raymond E., *The Andreasson Affair* (Englewood Cliffs, Prentice-Hall, Inc., 1979), p. 95.
4. *Ibid.*, p. 99.
5. *Ibid.*, p. 202.
6. *Ibid.*, p. 99.
7. *Ibid.*, p. 201.


CHAPTER 38: *The New Eden*

1. Kaiser, Robert Blair, *R. F. K. Must Die!* (New York, E. P. Dutton & Co., 1970), p. 550.
2. *Los Angeles Times* (Los Angeles, Otis Chandler), March 1, 1976, part I, p. 14.
3. *The New York Times* (The New York Times Company, New York), April 12, 1981, p. B12.

4. *Ibid.*, October 21, 1981, p. A22.

5. *Los Angeles Times,* op. cit., September 17, 1979, part I, p. 11.

6. National Broadcasting Company, *N.B.C. Magazine with David Brinkley,* New York, July 16, 1981.

7. *San Jose Mercury* (Anthony P. Ridder, publisher, San Jose), May 20, 1983, p. 2A.

8. Sachs, Margaret, *The U.F.O. Encyclopedia* (G. P. Putnam's Sons, New York), p. 269.

9. *Ibid.*, p. 7.

10. *The Skeptical Inquirer* (Buffalo, Committee for the Scientific Investigation of Claims of the Paranormal, Vol. 9, No. 1, Fall 1984), back cover.

11. Kurtz, Paul, *In Defense of Secular Humanism* (Buffalo, Prometheus Books, 1983), p. 169.

12. *Ibid.*, p. 42.

13. *Ibid.*, p. 41.

CHAPTER 40: *The Nature of a Supreme Being*

1. Hubbard, L. Ron, *Dianetics and Scientology Technical Dictionary* (Publications Organization, Los Angeles, 1975), pp. 431-432.

CHAPTER 41: *To the Researcher*

1. Butt-Thompson, Captain F. W., *West African Secret Societies* (London, H. F. & G. Witherby, London, 1929), p. 13.

2. *Ibid.*

# Bibliography

A. C. Bhaktivedanta Swami Prabhupada, *Srimad Bhagavatam, Seventh Canto*, The Bhaktivedanta Book Trust, New York, 1976

Adamski, George, *Inside the Spaceships*, Abelard-Schuman, New York, 1955

Alden, John R., *A History of the American Revolution*, Alfred A. Knopf, New York, 1969

Alfold, Andrew (trans. Harold Mattingly), *The Conversion of Constantine and Ancient Rome*, Oxford at the Clarendon Press, London, 1948

Allegro, John Margo, *The People of the Dead Sea Scrolls*, Doubleday & Company, Inc., New York, 1958

Allen, Gary, *None Dare Call It Conspiracy*, Concord Press, Rossmoor, undated (ca. 1971)

American Broadcasting Company, *20/20*, New York

Americana Corporation, *The Encyclopedia Americana*, New York, various years 1971-1981

Anderson, Jack, "CIA Involved in Jonestown Massacre?", *Seattle Post-Intelligencer*, Seattle, September 27, 1980

—*Jack Anderson: Confidential*, syndicated television series, Washington, 1983

Andrae, Tor (trans. Theophil Menzel), *Mohammed: The*

*Man and His Faith,* Books for Libraries Press, Freeport, 1971

Andreades, Andreas Michael (trans. Christabel Meredith), *History of the Bank of England, 1640-1903,* 4th ed. (1st ed. 1909), A. M. Kelley, New York, 1966

Andrus, Hyrum L., *God, Man and the Universe,* Bookcraft, Salt Lake City, 1968

Apfel, Necia H. and J. Allen Hynek, *Architecture of the Universe,* The Benjamin/Cummings Publishing Company, Inc., Menlo Park, 1979

Asimov, Isaac, *Asimov's Guide to the Bible, The Old and New Testaments,* Avenel Books, New York, 1969, 1981

Ballard, Mrs. G. W., *Purpose of the Ascended Masters "I AM" Activity,* St. Germain Press, Inc., 1942

Barnhart, Clarence L. (editor-in-chief), *The World Book Dictionary,* Field Enterprises Educational Corporation, Chicago, 1974

Bell, Walter George, *The Great Plague in London in 1665,* John Lane the Bodly Head Ltd., London, 1st pub. 1924

Binion, Rudolph, "Hitler's Concept of Lebensraum: The Psychological Basis," *History of Childhood Quarterly: The Journal of Psychohistory,* Atcom, Inc., New York, Fall 1973, Vol. 1, no. 2

Birch, Una, "The Compte de Saint-Germain," *The Nineteenth Century and After,* vol. LXIII, January-June 1908, Leonard Scott Publication Co., New York

Blom, Eric (editor), *Grove's Dictionary of Music and Musicians,* 5th edition, St. Martin's Press, Inc., New York, 1954

Bloomfield, Maurice, *The Religion of the Veda, The Ancient Religion of India (From Rig-Veda to Upanishads),* AMS Press, New York, 1969

Bock, Janet, *The Jesus Mystery, Of Lost Years and Unknown Travels,* Aura Books, Los Angeles, 1980

Bock, Richard, *The Lost Years* (motion picture transcript), Aura Enterprises, Los Angeles, 1978

Borkin, Joseph, *The Crime and Punishment of I. G. Farben,* Pocket Books, New York, 1978

Bouquet, A. C., *Comparative Religion,* Penquin Books, Baltimore, 1962

Bowart, Walter H., *Operation Mind Control*, Dell Publishing Co., New York, 1978

Braunthal, Julius (trans. Henry Collins and Kenneth Mitchell), *History of the International*, Vol. 1: 1864-1914, Frederick A. Praeger, New York, 1967

Breasted, James Henry, *A History of Egypt, From the Earliest Times to the Persian Conquest*, Charles Scribner's Sons, New York, 1937

Brown, W. Norman, *The Swastika: A Study of the Nazi Claims of Its Aryan Origin*, Emerson Books, Inc., New York, 1933

Brown, William Adrian, *Facts, Fables and Fantasies of Freemasonry*, Vantage Press, Inc., New York, 1968

Buckley, Kevin (editor), *GEO*, GEO Publishing Company, Los Angeles, various issues 1984/1985

Bullard, Thomas E., "Abductions: A Comparative Study," *MUFON UFO Journal*, Seguin, Mutual UFO Network, Inc., Seguin, Number 238, February 1988

Burke, J. Bruce and James B. Wiggins, *Foundations of Christianity, From The Beginnings to 1650*, The Ronald Press Company, New York, 1970

Burns, James, "Further Illumination," *Liberty*, The Review and Herald Publishing Association, vol. 5, no. 2, March/April 1980

Butt-Thompson, Capt. F. W., *West African Secret Societies, Their Organisations, Officials and Teaching*, H. F. & G. Witherby, London, 1929

Calkins, Carroll C. (project editor), *Mysteries of the Unexplained*, The Reader's Digest Association, Inc., Pleasantville, 1982

Catholic Biblical Association of America, *The New American Bible*, P. J. Kenedy & Sons, New York, 1970

Charach, Theodore and Gerard Alcan, *The Second Gun* (motion picture), Video Treasures, Inc. (c/o Video Cassette Sales, Inc., 200 Robbins Lane, Jericho, New York 11753), 1973, 1976

Cheesman, Paul R., *The World of the Book of Mormon*, Horizon Publishers & Distributors, Inc., Bountiful, 1984

Chesneaux, Jean (editor), *Popular Movements and Secret Societies in China, 1840-1950*, Stanford University Press, Stanford, 1972

—(trans. Gillian Nettle), *Secret Societies in China,* The University of Michigan Press, Ann Arbor, 1971

Chionetti, Marta Luchino, *Corrado Licostene, E le Antiche Osservazioni sui Fenomeni Naturali D'Interesse Geografico,* G. Giappichelli, Torino, 1960

Church of Jesus Christ of Latter Day Saints (Mormons), *The Doctrines and Covenants of the Church of Jesus Christ of Latter Day Saints/The Pearl of Great Price,* Salt Lake City, 1949, 1948

—"Granite Mountain—Where a Billion People 'Live' " (advertising pamphlet), undated

—"Read The Book of Mormon, It Can Change Your Life," Salt Lake City, 1975

Clymer, Dr. R. Swinburne, *The Book of Rosicruciae,* The Philosophical Publishing Company, Quakertown, 1947

—*The Rosicrucian Fraternity in America,* The Rosicrucian Foundation, Quakertown, 1935

Coil, Henry Wilson, *Coil's Masonic Encyclopedia,* Macoy Publishing and Masonic Supply Company, Inc., New York, 1961

Committee for the Scientific Investigation of Claims of the Paranormal (CSICOP), "Paranormal Beliefs: Scientific Facts and Fictions" (conference), Stanford University, Palo Alto, November 9, 1984

Conquest, Robert, *The Great Terror: Stalin's Purge of the Thirties,* The MacMillan Company, New York, 1968

Cooper, Vicki and Sherie Stark, eds. & pubs., *UFO* (formerly *California UFO*) magazine, Los Angeles, vol. 2, no. 3, 1987

Cooper-Oakley, Isabel, *The Count of St. Germain,* Rudolph Steiner, Publications, Blauvelt, 1970

Corliss, William R., *Handbook of Unusual Natural Phenomena,* Anchor Books, Garden City, 1983

Cowles, Virginia, *The Rothschilds, A Family of Fortune,* Alfred A. Knopf, New York, 1973

Crowther, Duane S., *Reading Guide to the Book of Mormon,* Horizon Publishers & Distributors, Inc., Bountiful, 1975

Daniel, Clifton (editor-in-chief), *Chronicle of the 20th Century,* Chronicle Publications, Mount Kisco, 1987

Darmesteter, James (trans.), *The Zend-Avesta*, Greenwood Press, Westport, 1972

Dawood, N. J. (trans.), *The Koran*, Penquin Books, New York, 1977

Deaux, George, *The Black Death, 1347*, Weybright & Talley, Inc., New York; also Hamilton, London; 1969

DeHaan, Richard, "Fraternal Organizations," *Collier's Encyclopedia*, William D. Halsey (editor), The Crowell-Collier Publishing Company, 1965

De La Fuye, Maruice and Emile Babeau, *The Apostle of Liberty: A Life of Lafayette*, Thames & Hudson, London, 1956

Denslow, Ray V., *Freemasonry and the Presidency, U.S.A.*, Missouri Lodge of Research, Missouri, 1952

DiPietro, Vincent; Gregory Molenaar; John Brandenburg; *Unusual Mars Surface Features*, Mars Research, P.O. Box 284, Glenn Dale, Maryland 20769; 1988

Dupuy, Col. R. Ernest and Col. Trevor N. Dupuy, *The Compact History of the Revolutionary War*, Hawthorn Books, Inc., New York, 1963

Durant, Will, *The Story of Civilization*, Part III, *Caesar and Christ*, Simon & Schuster, New York, 1980

Eberhard, Wolfram, *History of China*, University of California Press, Berkeley, 1960

Edelson, Edward, *Who Goes There?*, Doubleday & Co., Inc., Garden City, 1979

Eliot, Sir Charles, *Hinduism and Buddhism, An Historical Sketch*, Barnes & Noble, Inc., New York, 1957

Erman, Adolf (trans. H. M. Tirard), *Life in Ancient Egypt*, MacMillan and Company, London, 1894

Evans, Medford, "The Prince and the Bilderbergers," *American Opinion*, Robert Welch (editor), Robert Welch, Inc., Belmont, October 1975

Fakhry, Ahmed, *The Pyramids*, The University of Chicago Press, Chicago, 1961

Fay, Bernard, *Revolution and Freemasonry, 1680-1800*, Little, Brown, & Co., Boston, 1935

Fife, Austin and Alta, *Saints of Sage and Saddle, Folklore Among the Mormons*, Indiana University Press, Gloucester, 1956

Fiske, John, *The American Revolution,* Houghton, Mifflin & Co., Boston, 1891

Ford, Brian J., *The Earth Watchers,* Leslie Frewin of London, 1973

Fort, Charles, *The Books of Charles Fort* (containing *The Book of the Damned, New Lands, Lo!,* and *Wild Talents*), Henry Holt and Company, New York, 1941

Ford, Paul Leicester (ed.), *The Works of Thomas Jefferson,* G. P. Putnam's Sons, New York, 1905

Fowler, Raymond E., *The Andreasson Affair,* Prentice-Hall, Inc., Englewood Cliffs, 1979

Franco, Johan, "The Count of St. Germain," *The Musical Quarterly,* G. Schirmer, Inc., New York, October 1950, Vol. XXXVI, No. 4

Frazier, Kendrick (editor), *The Skeptical Inquirer,* Committee for the Scientific Investigation of Claims of the Paranormal, Buffalo, vol. IX, no. 1, Fall 1984

Free, Joseph, *Archaeology and Bible History,* publication information unavailable

French, Allen, *Charles I and the Puritan Upheaval,* Houghton Mifflin Company, Boston, 1955

Fryer, Rev. A. T., "Psychological Aspects of the Welsh Revival," *Society of Psychical Research, Proceedings,* 19:50, 1905; reproduced by The Sourcebook Project, P.O. Box 107, Glen Arm, Maryland, 21057 U.S.A.

Gillmor, Daniel S. (editor), Dr. Edward U. Condon (scientific director), *Scientific Study of Unidentified Flying Objects,* E. P. Dutton & Co., Inc., New York, 1969

Goetz, Delia and Sylvanus G. Morley, *Popol Vuh, The Sacred Book of the Ancient Quiche Maya,* University of Oklahoma Press, Norman, 1950

Goldsmith, Donald and Tobias Owen, *The Search for Life in the Universe,* The Benjamin/Cummings Publishing Co., Inc., Menlo Park, 1980

Gould, Robert Freke, *The History of Freemasonry,* Thomas C. Jack, London, 1887

Gowens, Lawrence, *Paintings in the Louvre,* Stewart, Tabori & Chang, New York, 1987

Graham, William Franklin (Billy), *Angels; God's Secret Agents,* Doubleday, Garden City, 1975

Gray, Tony, *The Orange Order*, The Bodley Head, Ltd., London, 1972

Grey, Ian, *Stalin, Man of History*, Doubleday & Co., Inc., Garden City, 1979

Grunwald, Henry Anatole (editor-in-chief), *Time*, Time Inc., Los Angeles, vol. 117, no. 23, June 8, 1981

Hale, Van, "How Could a Prophet Believe in Moonmen?" (pamphlet), Mormon Miscellaneous, Sandy, April 1983

Hall, Manly Palmer, *An encyclopedic outline of Masonic, Hermetic, qabbalistic and Rosicrucian symbolical philosophy; being an interpretation of the secret teachings concealed within the rituals, allegories and mysteries of all ages*, H. S. Crocker Co., San Francisco, 1928

—"The Masters at Work in the World Today," Philosophical Research Society, Los Angeles, October 25, 1944

—*Secret Destiny of America*, Philosophical Research Society, Los Angeles, 1944

Halsey, William D. (editorial director), *Collier's Encyclopedia*, The Crowell-Collier Publishing Co., The MacMillan Educational Corp., New York, various dates

Hamilton, Tolbert, *The Great Pyramid, Its Importance and Significance in Today's World*, Tobert Hamilton, Ukiah, 1979

Hanfstaengl, Ernst, *Hitler, The Missing Years*, Eyre & Spottiswoode, London, 1957

Hansen, Klaus J., *Quest for Empire, The Political Kingdom of God and the Council of Fifty in Mormon History*, Michigan State University Press, East Lansing, 1967

Haywood, H. L., *Freemasonry and Roman Catholicism*, The Masonic History Company, Chicago, 1943

Head, Ralph H. (editor), "Freemasonry—A Way of Life," Grand Lodge, Free and Accepted Masons of California, San Francisco, 1981

Hervet, Francoise (pseud.), "Knights of Darkness: The Sovereign Military Order of Malta," *Covert Action Information Bulletin*, Covert Action Publications, Inc., Washington, no. 25, Winter 1986

Hexner, Ervin, *International Cartels*, Sir Isaac Pitman & Sons, New York, 1973

Hitler, Adolf (trans. Ralph Manheim), *Mein Kampf (My*

*Struggle),* Houghton Mifflin Co., Boston, 1927, 1971

Hohne, Heinz (trans. Richard Barry), *The Order of the Death's Head,* Coward-McCann, Inc., New York, 1969

Hubbard, L. Ron, *Dianetics and Scientology Technical Dictionary,* Publications Organization, Los Angeles, 1975

—*Have You Lived Before This Life?, A Scientific Survey,* The Church of Scientology of California Publications Organization, Los Angeles, 1977

—*Hymn of Asia, An Eastern Poem,* The Church of Scientology of California Publications Organization, Los Angeles, 1974

—*The Volunteer Minister's Handbook,* The Church of Scientology of California Publication Organization, Los Angeles, 1976

Huber, Heinz and Artur Muller, *Das Dritte Reich, Seine Geschichte in Texten Bildern und Dokumenten,* Verlag Kurt Desch GmbH., Munich, 1964

Hughes, Richard and Robert Brewin, *The Tranquilizing of America, Pill Popping and the American Way of Life,* Harcourt Brace Jovanovich, New York, 1979

Hunt, Gaillard, *The History of the Seal of the United States,* U.S. Department of State, Washington, 1909

Imperialist, *Cecil Rhodes, A Biography and Appreciation,* The MacMillan Company, New York, 1897

Jacobs, David Michael, *The U.F.O. Controversy in America,* Indiana University Press, Bloomington, 1975

Jessee, Dean C., *The Early Accounts of Joseph Smith's First Vision,* Mormon Miscellaneous, Sandy, December 1984

Jones, Rufus M., *Studies in Mystical Religion,* MacMillan and Co., Ltd., London, 1923

Kaiser, Robert Blair, *R. F. K. Must Die!, A History of the Robert Kennedy Assassination and Its Aftermath,* E. P. Dutton & Co., Inc., New York, 1970

Katz, Howard S., *The Warmongers,* Books In Focus, Inc., New York, 1979

Ketchum, Richard M. (editor), *The American Heritage Book of the Revolution,* American Heritage Publishing Company, Inc., New York, 1958

King, Godfre Ray (pen name of Guy Warren Ballard), *The Magic Presence,* St. Germain Press, Chicago, 1935

—*Unveiled Mysteries*, St. Germain Press, Chicago, 1934

Klass, Lance J., *The Leipzig Connection, A Report on the Origins and Growth of Educational Psychology*, The Delphian Press, 1978

Klass, Philip J., *UFOs Explained*, Random House, New York, 1971

—"Radar UFOs: Where Have They Gone?", *Skeptical Inquirer*, CSICOP, Buffalo, Vol. IX, No. 3, Spring 1985

Knight, David C., *UFOs: A Pictorial History from Antiquity to the Present*, McGraw-Hill Book Company, New York, 1979

Kurtz, Paul, *In Defense of Secular Humanism*, Prometheus Books, Buffalo, 1983

Lafore, Laurence, "Lord Mountbattan: A Man for the Century," *TV Guide*, Triangle Publications, Inc., Radnor, November 24, 1979

Lambert, W. G. and A. R. Millard, *Atra-Hasis, The Babylonian Story of the Flood, with The Sumerian Flood Story by M. Civil*, Oxford at the Clarendon Press, Oxford, 1969

Lane, Hana Umlauf (editor), *The World Almanac and Book of Facts 1981*, Newspaper Enterprise Association, Inc., New York, 1980

Leggett, George, *The Checka: Lenin's Political Police*, Clarendon Press, Oxford, 1981

Lennhoff, Eugen, *The Freemasons: The History, Nature, Development and Secret of the Royal Art*, A Lewis (Masonic Publishers) Ltd., London, 1978

Leone, Mark P., *Roots of Modern Mormonism*, Harvard University Press, Cambridge, 1979

Leslie, Desmond and George Adamski, *Flying Saucers Have Landed*, The British Book Centre, New York, 1953

Lewis, H. Spencer, *The Mystical Life of Jesus*, Supreme Grand Lodge of AMORC Printing and Publishing Department, San Jose, 1957

—*Rosicrucian Questions and Answers, With Complete History of the Rosicrucian Order*, Supreme Grand Lodge of AMORC Printing and Publishing Department, San Jose, 13th edition, 1977

—*The Secret Doctrines of Jesus*, Supreme Grand Lodge

of AMROC Printing and Publishing Department, San Jose, 19th edition, 1981

Lewis, Ralph M., *Along Civilization's Trail,* Supreme Grand Lodge of AMORC Printing and Publishing Department, San Jose, 1940

Lewis, W. S. (ed.) et al., *Horace Walpole's Correspondence with Sir Horace Mann,* Yale University Press, New Haven, vol. 18, 1954, vol. 20: 1960

—*Horace Walpole's Correspondence with Sir Horace Mann and Sir Horace Mann the Younger,* Yale University Press, New Haven, vol. 26: 1971

Lien-Teh, Wu, J. W. H. Chun, R. Pollitzer, and C. Y. Wu, *Plague, A Manual for Medical and Public Health Workers,* Weishengshu National Quarantine Service, Shanghai Station, 1936

Linn, Col. LaVon P., "Freemasonry and the National Defense, 1754-1799," *The New Age;* Supreme Council, 33rd Degree, Ancient & Accepted Scottish Rite of Freemasonry of the Southern Jurisdiction, United States of America Washington, March 1974, Volume LXXXII, No. 3

Linn, William Alexander, *The Story of the Mormons, From the Date of Their Origin to the Year 1901,* Russell & Russell, Inc., New York, 1963

*Los Angeles Times,* Otis Chandler (publisher), Los Angeles, various dates

Lunden, Sven G., "Annihilation of Freemasonry," *The American Mercury,* Eugene Lyons (editor), The American Mercury, Inc., New York, February 1941, vol. LII, no. 206

Machiavelli, Niccolo (trans. W. K. Marriott), *The Prince,* E. P. Dutton & Company, New York, 1935

Mackay, Charles, *Extraordinary Popular Delusions and the Madness of Crowds,* Harmony Books, New York, 1980 (1st pub. London, 1852)

Mackenzie, Norman, *Secret Societies,* Holt, Rinehart and Winston, New York, 1967

MacKey, Albert Gallatin, *An Encyclopedia of Freemasonry and Its Kindred Sciences,* The Masonic History Company, New York, 1919

—*The History of Freemasonry,* The Masonic History Company, New York, 1898

—*Lexicon of Freemasonry,* Moss, Brother & Company, Philadelphia, 1860

Marx, Karl, *The Class Struggles in France, 1848 to 1850,* International Publishers, New York, 1964

Mazour, Anatole G., *The First Russian Revolution, 1825, The Decembrist Movement, Its Origins, Development, and Significance,* University of California Press, Berkeley, 1937

McGavin, E. Cecil, *Mormonism and Masonry,* Bookcraft Publishers, Salt Lake City, 1956

McWhirter, Norris (editor), *Guinness Book of World Records,* Bantam Books, Inc., New York, 1982

Menzel, Donald H., *Flying Saucers,* Harvard University Press, Cambridge, 1953

—and Ernest H. Taves, *The UFO Enigma, The Definitive Explanation of the UFO Phenomenon,* Doubleday & Company, Inc., New York, 1977

Michael, Douglas, *The Cartoon Guide to Economics,* Harper & Row Publishers, New York, 1985

Michell, John and Robert J. M. Rickard, *Phenomena, A Book of Wonders,* Pantheon Books, New York, 1977

Middlehurst, Barbara, et al., "Chronological Catalog of Reported Lunar Events," NASA Technical Report (NASA TR R-277), Washington, 1968. Available from The Sourcebook Project, P.O. Box 107, Glen Arm, Maryland 21057 U.S.A.

Miller, John C., *Sam Adams, Pioneer in Propaganda,* Stanford University Press, Stanford, 1960 (1st pub. 1936)

Miller, Ken, *What the Mormons Believe, An Introduction to the Teachings of the Church of Jesus Christ of Latter-day Saints,* Horizon Publishers & Distributors, Inc, Bountiful, 1983

Muller, F. Max (editor), *The Sacred Books of The East,* Oxford at the Clarendon Press, London, 1879-1894

National Archives of the United States, exhibits and displays, Washington, May 1981

National Archives Trust Fund Board, "Documents from America's Past, Reproductions from the National Archives," National Archives and Records Service, Washington, 1978

National Broadcasting Company, *N.B.C. Magazine with David Brinkley,* New York, July 16, 1981

Nemiah, John C. (editor), *The American Journal of Psychiatry,* American Psychiatric Association, Washington, various issues, 1981

*The New Age,* Supreme Council, 33rd Degree, Ancient & Accepted Scottish Rite of Freemasonry of the Southern Jurisdiction, United States of America, Washington, various issues

New York State Grand Lodge, *Official Masonic Record of the Third Annual Fashion and Home Exposition for the Benefit of Masonic Free Hospitals,* New York, 1924

*The New York Times,* The New York Times Company, New York, various dates

Nohl, Johannes, *The Black Death, A Chronicle of the Plague,* George Allen and Unwin Ltd., London, 1926

Noorbergen, Rene, *Secrets of the Lost Races, New Discoveries of Advanced Technology in Ancient Civilizations,* The Bobbs-Merrill Co., Inc., Indianapolis, 1977

Nugoshi, Thomas T., *Coroner,* Pocket Books, New York, 1983

Nutall, Zelia, "The Fundamental Principles of Old and New World Civilizations," *Archaeological and Ethnological Papers of the Peabody Museum*—Harvard University—Vol. II, Peabody Museum of American Archaeology and Ethnology, Cambridge, 1901

O'Dea, Thomas F., *The Mormons,* The University of Chicago Press, Chicago, 1957

Office of Educational Programs, *The Written Word Endures, Milestone Documents of American History,* National Archives and Records Service, Washington, 1976

Pauwels, Louis & Jacques Bergier, *Morning of the Magicians,* Avon Books, New York, 1963

Payne, Robert, *The Rise and Fall of Stalin,* Simon & Schuster, New York, 1965

Pearson, Michael, *The Sealed Train,* G. P. Putnam's Sons, New York, 1975

Philatelic Bureau, Malta, "The Malta Stamp," No. 52, April 1982

Plomer, William, *Cecil Rhodes,* Peter Davies, Ltd., Edinburgh, 1933

Quigley, Carroll, *Tragedy and Hope, A History of the*

*World in Our Time,* The MacMillan Company, New York, 1966

Ravenscroft, Trevor, *The Spear of Destiny,* G. P. Putnam's Sons, New York, 1973

Richards, LeGrand, *A Marvelous Work and Wonder,* Deseret Book Company, Salt Lake City, 1978

Ridpath, Ian, *Messages from the Stars; Communication and Contact with Extraterrestrial Life,* Harper & Row Publishers, New York, 1978

Riefenstahl, Leni (producer), *Triumph de Willens (Triumph of the Will),* motion picture, 1934, 1975

Roberts, J. M., *The Mythology of the Secret Societies,* Charles Scribner's Sons, New York, 1972

Robison, John, *Proofs of a Conspiracy,* Western Islands, Boston, 1967 (1st pub. 1798)

Rosicrucian Egyptian Museum, San Jose, displays and exhibits, 1981, 1988

Rosicrucian Order (AMORC), San Jose, telephone interview with instructor, 1981

Rutland, Robert A. (editor), *The Papers of George Mason,* The University of North Carolina Press, Chapel Hill, 1970

Sachs, Margaret, *The UFO Encyclopedia,* Perigee Books (G. P. Putnam's Sons), New York, 1980

Sadie, Stanley, (editor), *The New Grove Dictionary of Music and Musicians,* MacMillan Publishers, Ltd., London, 1980

Sagan, Carl, "The Man in the Moon," *Parade* magazine, Walter Anderson (editor), Parade Publications, Inc., New York, June 2, 1985

Sanders, N. K., *The Epic of Gilgamesh,* Cox & Wyman, Ltd., London, 1964

*San Jose Mercury,* P. Anthony Ridder (publisher), San Jose, various dates

*San Jose News,* P. Anthony Ridder (publisher), San Jose, various dates

Savelle, Max (editor), *A History of World Civilization,* Vol. 1, Henry Holt and Company, New York, 1957

Schalk, Louis Gott, *Lafayette Comes to America,* The University of Chicago Press, Chicago, 1935

Schiller, Ronald, "Decoding the Mysteries of the Ancient

Calendars," *Reader's Digest,* The Reader's Digest Assocation, Inc., Pleasanton, November 1980

Schultz, Duane P., *A History of Modern Psychiatry,* Academic Press, New York, 1969

Shklovskii, I. S. and Carl Sagan, *Intelligent Life in the Universe,* Dell Publishing Co., New York, 1966

Singer, Michael and David Weir, "Nuclear Nightmare," *New West,* New York Magazine Company, Inc., Beverly Hills, December 3, 1979

Sitchin, Zecharia, *The Twelfth Planet,* Avon Books, New York, 1976

—*The Stairway to Heaven,* Avon Books, New York, 1980

—*The Wars of Gods and Men,* Avon Books, New York, 1985

Skousen, W. Cleon, *The Naked Capitalist,* W. Cleon Skousen, Salt Lake City, 1970

Smith, Edward Ellis, *The Young Stalin,* Farrar, Straus & Giroux, New York, 1967

Smith, John Holland, *Constantine the Great,* Hamish Hamilton, London, 1971

Smith, Joseph (trans.), *The Book of Mormon, An Account Written by The Hand of Mormon Upon Plates Taken from the Plates of Nephi,* The Church of Jesus Christ of Latter Day Saints, Salt Lake City, 1980

Snyder, Henry L. (ed.), *The Marlborough-Godolphin Correspondence,* Oxford at the Clarendon Press, 1975

Sommer, A. Dupont, *The Essene Writings from Qumran,* Basil Blackwell, Oxford, 1961

Stark, Dr. W. (editor), *The Discourses of Niccolo Machiavelli,* vol. 1 (trans. Leslie J. Walker), Routledge & Kegan Paul, London, 1950

Sterling, Claire, *The Terror Network, The Secret War of International Terrorism,* Berkley Books, New York, 1981

Supreme Grand Lodge AMORC, "History of the Rosicrucian Order" (pamphlet), Department of Publications (AMORC), 1963

—"Mastery of Life" (pamphlet), The Department of Publications (AMORC), 25th edition, undated

—*Rosicrucian Documents,* Rosicrucian Press, Ltd., San Jose, 1978

Sutton, Antony C., *Wall Street and the Rise of Hitler,* '76 Press, Seal Beach, 1976

Selvius (Frater), "Descendants of Lemuria, A Description of an Ancient Cult in California," *Rosicrucian Digest*, AMORC, San Jose, May 1931

Taylor, Connie R., *Before Birth, Beyond Death*, Horizon Publishers & Distributors, Inc., Bountiful, 1987

Thieriot, Richard T. (editor), *San Francisco Chronicle*, Chronicle Publishing Company, San Francisco, November 30, 1981

Thomas Nelson, Inc., *The Holy Bible, Old And New Testaments in the King James Version*, Nashville, 1970

Tompkins, Peter, *Mysteries of the Mexican Pyramids*, Harper and Row, New York, 1976

—*Secrets of the Great Pyramid*, Harper Colophon Books, New York, 1971

Tryon, James Owen, "Count St. Germain," *The Catholic World*, The Office of the Catholic World, Paulist Fathers, New York, Vol. CXLIX, April 1939

Tucker, Robert C., *Stalin as Revolutionary*, W. W. Norton & Company, Inc., New York, 1973

Tyndale House Publishers, *The Way*, Wheaton, 1971

United States War Office, *Why We Fight* series (motion pictures), 1942-1945

University Books, *The Book of the Dead*, New Hyde Park, 1960

Vallee, Jacques, *The Invisible College*, E. P. Dutton & Co., Inc., New York, 1975

—*Passport to Magonia, From Folklore to Flying Saucers*, Henry Regnery Company, Chicago, 1969

Van Tyen, Claud H., *Founding of the American Republic*, Houghton Mifflin Company, Boston, 1929

Viola, Herman J., *The National Archives of the United States*, Harry N. Abrams, Inc., New York, 1984

*The Voice*, St. Germain Press, Chicago, various dates

Von Daniken, Erich (trans. Michael Heron), *Chariots of the Gods?*, Bantam Books, Inc., New York, 1969

—(trans. Michael Heron), *Gods From Outer Space* (a.k.a. *Return to the Stars* and *Evidence for the Impossible*), Bantam Books, Inc., New York, 1971

—(trans. Michael Heron), *In Search of Ancient Gods, My Pictorial Evidence for the Impossible*, Bantam Books, Inc., New York, 1973

Wallace, Irving, David Wallechinsky and Amy Wallace,

*The Book of Lists II,* Bantam Books, Inc., New York, 1980

—"Significa," *Parade,* Parade Publications, Inc., New York, various dates

Wallechinsky, David, Irving Wallace and Amy Wallace, *The Book of Lists,* Bantam Books, Inc., New York, 1977

Walzer, Micahel, *Revolution of the Saints,* Harvard University Press, Cambridge, 1965

Wantoch, Hans, *Magnificent Money-Makers,* Desmond Harmsworth, London, 1932

Weber, Max, *The Protestant Ethic and the Spirit of Capitalism,* Scribner's Sons, New York, 1976

—"The Protestant Sects and the Spirit of Capitalism," *From Max Weber: Essays in Sociology,* (trans. & ed.) H. H. Gerth and C. Wright Mills, Oxford University Press, Inc., New York, 1958

Webster, Nesta H. (Mrs. Arthur), *The French Revolution, A Study in Democracy,* The Christian Book Club of America, 1969 (1st pub. 1919)

—*Secret Societies and Subversive Movements,* The Christian Book Club of America, undated (1st pub. 1924)

—*World Revolution: The Plot Against Civilization,* Constable & Company, London, 1921

Weigall, Arthur, *A History of the Pharoahs,* Volume I, *The First Eleven Dynasties,* E. P. Dutton & Company, New York, 1925

West, Ray B., Jr., *Kingdom of the Saints, The Story of Brigham Young and the Mormons,* The Viking Press, New York, 1957

William Collins Publishers, Inc., *The Lost Books of the Bible and The Forgotten Books of Eden,* 1926, 1927

Williams, Gurney III (editor), "Metropolis on Mars," *Omni,* Omni Publications International Ltd., New York, vol. 7, no. 6, March 1985

Wilson, Colin, *The Occult,* Vintage Books, New York, 1973

Wilson, Don, *Secrets of Our Spaceship Moon,* Dell Publishing Company, Inc., New York, 1979

Ziegler, Philip, *The Black Death,* The John Day Company, New York, 1969

# Index